The Scribe's Promise

Jennifer Pollard

Bahá'í
PUBLISHING

Wilmette, Illinois

Bahá'í Publishing
401 Greenleaf Avenue, Wilmette, IL 60091-2844
Copyright © 2014 by the National Spiritual Assembly of the Bahá'ís of the
United States

17   16   15   14   4   3   2   1

Library of Congress Cataloging-in-Publication Data

Pollard, Jennifer.
  The scribe's promise / Jennifer Pollard.
      pages cm
  Includes bibliographical references.
  ISBN 978-1-61851-070-9 (acid-free paper) 1. Bahai Faith—Fiction. 2.
Iran—History—Qajar dynasty, 1794–1925—Fiction. 3. Religious fiction.
4. Love stories. I. Title.
  PS3616.O56826S37 2014
  813'.6—dc23
                              2014020773

Cover design by Misha Maynerick
Book design by Patrick Falso

Acknowledgments

Deepest thanks go, first and foremost, to God and His Manifestations for sending down His words and bearing the manifold burdens of telling the world.

Gratitude is also due to:

T. Mike Curry, husband and best friend, who gave support and cheers throughout the writing of this book. Leon Stevens, dear friend, advisor, first to read the novel and give an opinion ("Go, lady, go!"). Those patient, wonderful people who did the preliminary editing, catching many mistakes and pointing out improvements: Leon (again), Jeanne Engle, Paul Lang, and Farah Nieuwenhuizen. The several others who read or were willing to read the novel and urged continuing the work, including Megan Orr, Gretchen Seifert, Rosemary Stevens, and Brittany Williamson. And, naturally, to the family who are amazed and excited to be related to an actual author (really!): sister Carol, parents Sharon and Robert, and our adult kids James and Faith.

Thanks must be given to Kaiser Barnes who, when we were on pilgrimage, was a member of the Universal House of Justice and advised us to "learn to tell stories." (The old adage "be careful what you ask for" may apply.)

Bahá'í Publishing, naturally, is deeply appreciated for taking on the publishing and distribution of the book, and especially for coming up with a much better title than the author did. Specific thanks go to Chris Martin, who was of great help in the editing.

Finally, but quite importantly, thanks are due to all who read the novel and ponder its contents.

Your servant,

Jennifer Pollard

Table of Contents

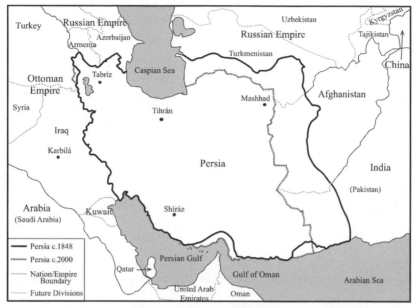

Regional Map of Persia

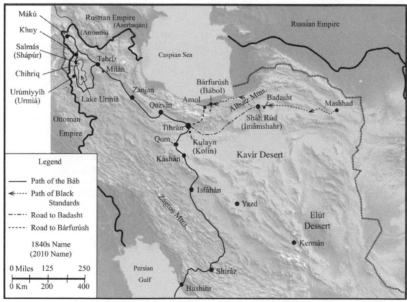

Map of Main Cities and Routes Used in Novel

Introduction

Pronunciation

The pronunciation of words from a different alphabet can be confusing. Vowels are pronounced differently in Persian but are represented in English by letters from the Latin alphabet. There are only three main vowels in Persian: A, U, and I. Without an accent, they are pronounced 'a' as in *mat* and 'i' as in *sit*. The 'u' does not perfectly equate to English—it's like the 'o' in *go* or *note*, but without the following 'w' sound we generally add. Just cut the long 'o' off partway to make the Persian 'u.'

With accents, these same vowels are pronounced 'á' as in the short 'o' of *logger* or *pot*, 'ú' as in the long 'oo' of *moose* or *roof*, and 'í' as in the long 'ee' in *deep*.

The single quote sitting in the middle of a word (Sa'dí) is a direction to do a glottal stop. "What the heck is that?" one may ask. We actually use glottal stops quite freely in English, only not in the middle of words. A glottal stop is a way of stopping air in the throat and letting it out suddenly. If we wish to clearly say, "It's an apple" to someone with hearing difficulties, we use a glottal stop at the beginning of each word that starts with a vowel to sharply enunciate the words. We don't run it together; otherwise, the person might only hear "tsanapple." Thus the celebrated poet, Sa'dí, has an air stoppage to separate the 'a' from the 'd' in the middle of his name. Any name that begins with a single quote, such as "'Alí," will always be set off from the previous word by this glottal stop.

Note on names

The form and pronunciation of Islamic names can be quite difficult for Westerners to grasp at first. It may be easier to understand the names, and the various ways to use them, if they are equated with Western names.

Family names (surnames) had not yet been instituted in Persia at the time the novel is set. Consider the vast number of men with the names John, Michael, or Chris, and how difficult it would be to know who is who on paper without the surnames.

An example of titles: One great mind of the early 1800s in Karbilá, Iraq, was Shaykh Ahmad-i-Áhsaí. This name would be similar to the English name *Dr. Chris of Smithton. Shaykh* is a title, *Ahmad* is the actual name, *i-Áhsaí* is *of the city/town Áhsa*. The full name would be the complete form of formal address. While Dr. Chris of Smithton might be introduced with the full form, later conversation would refer to him as *Doctor* or Dr. Chris, leaving his town of origin out. Similarly, wherever possible, the author has endeavored to use the formal address on first introduction of a character's name and afterward to use a shorter, and more easily remembered, form. It might be fun to add surnames, but that would not be historically accurate (an evil giggle echoes in the author's home).

Violence in the story

This historical novel is set in a time of great violence and cruelty. The culture of 1800s Persia was very similar to Europe during the Dark Ages. The author has attempted to find a balance between the reality of the time and the sensitivity of modern readers. Far from needing to exaggerate the events to keep readers' interest, it has been necessary to mitigate descriptions of the most distasteful parts of the culture to avoid alienating readers. As a result, the worst of the violence has been moved to a few footnotes and endnotes to allow the sensitive reader to skip it. Notes with violent content are marked as such.

History of Islam

The following is a very short and necessarily incomplete account of the early history of Islam. It gives more of the Shi'a (see below) view since the story takes place in Persia where the majority of the population are Shi'a Muslims. The full history of Iran is full of wonderful details and can be found in many places, such as http://iranicaonline.org. It cannot be worked into the story without greatly breaking the storyline, but it is vital to an understanding of several aspects of the story, and indeed of Islamic and world history. Names can be spelled in several ways due to vagaries in transliteration, so on the Web site, Husayn might be spelled *Hossein*, Muhammad could be *Mohamad*, Hassan might be *Hasan*, and so on.

Muhammad, peace be upon Him, met with great opposition to His teachings, as all Messengers or Manifestations of God do. As He continued to proclaim the new Faith, the opposition to Him grew as the Faith grew, attracting the attention of those who saw this new religion gaining power over the warring, nomadic tribes of what would later be called Arabia.

Muhammad was born around AD 570 on the Arabian Peninsula. He received His Revelation during a retreat to the mountains when He was forty years of age (AD 610). From then on, He preached a message of unification and peace to the warring tribes and settled peoples of the area. His message, a direct Revelation from God, sought to annihilate paganism and Godlessness while supporting the Revelations and Messengers of the past as a continuing Book of God. Jews and Christians were specifically included in the Qur'an as "People of the Book" to be respected.

Muhammad and His followers moved from Mecca, His home city, to Medina to further the spread of the new Faith and to avoid certain factions fighting against Him. This move, called the Hejira, took place in AD 622, which is the start of the Islamic calendar. By the time of His passing in AD 633, He had united the tribes of Arabia and formed a new nation and government.

The leadership of the believers was naturally held by Muhammad. Muhammad's daughter, Fátimih, married 'Alí, a dedicated and beloved disciple of Muhammad. He was the first Imám, or spiritual leader, of the faithful. 'Alí designated his sons by Fátimih as his successors, with Hasan being the elder and Husayn being the younger. However, upon the Prophet's passing, many believers were unsure about whether the succession should be by election or by Muhammad's designation of 'Alí. The most prominent believers elected the first four leaders in rapid succession, with the fourth being 'Alí.

One man, Muawiyah, of the Umayyad family, believed he should be the next leader instead of 'Alí due to having a large following of his own, and indeed contended with 'Alí during His reign. 'Alí died near Najaf, slashed by a poisoned sword while praying, purportedly by a follower of Muawiyah.

Imám Hasan took the reins of leadership upon his Father's passing, enduring repeated skirmishes with Muawiyah and his people. The battles were inconclusive, and Hasan, wishing to prevent the great bloodshed of a civil war, made a treaty with his opponent. The elderly Muawiyah could hold the caliphate for the few remaining years of his life, with the only condition being that he would not name a successor, and the followers of Muhammad would choose their next leader.

Muawiyah is assumed to have caused the poisoning of Hasan (the year was 50 AH, or AD 669), increased persecutions of Muhammad's family, and attempted to eliminate this potential threat to his reign.

Under these oppressive conditions, Husayn became the third Imam. He was inclined by nature to be much more the soldier in God's army than his brother, and he could not abide the example set by Muawiyah in flaunting the use of alcohol and other vices specifically prohibited by Muhammad. For ten years, Husayn reproved the lack of morals of the Umayyads but remained faithful to the treaty allowing Muawiyah to lead the caliphate.

Then in 60 AH, or AD 680, Muawiyah decided he had consolidated enough power to fight off any and all possible contenders. He named his son Yazid as successor, thereby breaking the treaty and causing a permanent rift in the believers. Husayn did not take the usurpation of power well, believing himself to be the rightful leader and a far better example of proper Muslim behavior. Many of the faithful turned to him for guidance and leadership. There followed an uprising with great violence on both sides, the accounts of which are quite different between the Sunni, who followed the caliphate and the Umayyads; and the Shi'a, who followed the Imáms. All agree it ended in terrible suffering, with the killing of seventy-some members of Muhammad's family including several women and children, and Husayn's martyrdom by beheading near Karbala.

The caliphate, upheld by the Sunnis, continued in the hands of the Umayyad dynasty for several generations, far outnumbering their Shi'a opponents. The Shi'as continued to faithfully follow the Imams while being persecuted by the Umayyads. Each successive Imám was murdered (all by poison except Husayn and the twelfth Imám) until finally, the twelfth and last Imám disappeared, leaving Shi'a adherents awaiting his return.

The line of Imáms with lineal names (their name follow by 'of' father's name) and titles is as follows:

1 - 'Alí ibn Abu Talib, Commander of the Faithful

2 - Hasan ibn 'Alí, the Chosen

3 - Husayn ibn 'Alí, Master of the Martyrs

4 - 'Alí ibn Husayn, Ornament of the Worshippers

5 - Muhammad ibn 'Alí, the Revealer of Knowledge

6 - Ja'far ibn Muhammad, the Honest

7 - Musa ibn Ja'far, the Calm One

8 - 'Alí ibn Musa, the Pleasing One

9 - Muhammad ibn 'Alí, the God-Fearing, the Generous

10 - 'Alí ibn Muhammad, the Guide, the Pure One

11 - Hasan ibn 'Alí, al-Askari (of Askar, a town)

12 - Muhammad ibn al-Hasan, al-Mahdi, Hidden Imám, the Guided One, the Proof

There are still descendants of Muhammad alive in the world today, many wearing green or black turbans to designate themselves as such rather than the usual white turban worn by the masses.

The martyrdom of Imám Husayn and his final battle are lived out every year in the Shi'a world during their most holy month of Muharram in the *Tazieh* (the Muslim version of the passion play). The Tazieh commemorates the Shi'a's beliefs, their grief at the loss they suffered, and their anger at those whom they believe to have perpetrated the murder of Husayn. The animosity between sects engendered by the struggle for leadership of all Muslims continues to the present time, some thirteen centuries later, despite both sects' beliefs in the Qur'án and material laws they hold in common.

The Sufi adherents of Islam are somewhat stuck in an odd position in the struggles between sects. The majority of Sufi schools trace their lineage back through the first Imám, 'Alí ibn Abu-Talib. They leave jurisprudence, doctrine, and philosophy to others and seek only the mystical path, striving to approach and connect to God through self-abnegation and service to others. Sufis usually do not see themselves as a separate sect but rather as a way to approach the Divine from within Islám as a whole. They are viewed by Sunnis and Shi'as with alternating admiration and persecution.

The information put forth in this summary is a conglomeration from several sources, including the internet (articles on Muhammad, Husayn, and Shi'ism at http://en.wikipedia.org/wiki/Husayn-ibn-Ali, /Islam, /Muhammad, /Imam#Twelver; article on Husayn at http://iranicaonline.org/articles/Hosayn-b-ali), the film *Islam: Empire of Faith* (PBS DVD, distributed by Warner Home Video, 2001), and books (Benjamin, *Persia and the Persians*, various chapters; *World Book Encyclopedia*, World Book Inc., 1985, Islam, Volume 10, p. 374).

Prologue

Citrus scents wafted through the streets of Karbilá.[1] Lemon and orange, lime and grapefruit, nearing the end of their fruiting season, gave hints to what lay behind the high walls surrounding each back yard. The windowless house fronts were right on the street in the normal custom. The homes and backyard walls, melding together in a united barrier along every thoroughfare and alley, gave no hint of any yard at all. Only doors and the occasional street broke the continuous, plaster-covered barricades.

The shrine of Imam Husayn, with its three minarets and great dome, could be seen from all the great thoroughfares. This shrine was the center of spiritual life for the city, attracting pilgrims from the entire Muslim world.

Through these streets walked a mullá, or Muslim priest, of thirty or so years, with his black robe, matching black locks, full beard, and once-white turban covered in the dust and dross of long travel. That travel had been long indeed, covering hundreds of miles to spread the news of reformation and expectation, explaining the teachings of his famous master to the greatest minds of the day, dispelling misunderstandings and quelling unjust rumors, riding from town to oasis to caravanserai. Mullá Husayn-i-Bushrú'í was glad to do so. His master, Siyyid Kázim-i-Rashtí, who had sent him on this mission, was recognized throughout the region for his sagacity, depth of knowledge, and astonishing perceptions. This siyyid had learned from another great master, Shaykh Ahmad-i-Áhsaí, who had started the Shaykhí reformation of Islám, working to prepare the faithful for the coming of the Promised One.

Shaykh Ahmad and Siyyid Kázim had sifted through the sacred writings, connecting clues and prophecies for many years together before the learned shaykh's ascension. Siyyid Kázim had carried on leading the Shaykhí movement, disseminating this gathered knowledge to masters and seekers, rich and poor alike. He knew the Promised One's advent would be soon, knew He was near, and knew that he, Siyyid Kázim, would continue to educate whoever would listen to him until his own ascension.

Mullá Husayn, having achieved his assigned objective, beat the dust from his robe as well as he could while nearing his destination, having returned to the home of Siyyid Kázim on 22 January 1844 (the first day of Muharram, 1260 A.H.). The welcome for the triumphant traveler, however, was not what he might have expected.

Several of his fellow disciples accosted him upon his entrance. Siyyid Kázim, guide and protector of them all, leader of modern Muslim thought, had passed on just a few weeks earlier. Now, guideless, unprotected, and in chaos, they asked Mullá Husayn what they should do. Protection was truly something they needed, for in the past, the jealous and the wayward among the clergy had uttered calumny, had pointed the finger of accusation, and had branded the promoters of reformation as heretics. Despite the accuracy of the reforms based on the Qur'án—the sacred words of God revealed through Muhammad—these same oppressors had claimed that the reformists had strayed from the Qur'án and worked to undermine the great traditions of Islám.

Such words could bring a quick death to the accused, but they would more often bring about the destruction of a cleric's career, the confiscation of his property, the physical punishment of the lash or bastinado, and a slow death in misery and poverty for the hapless victim and his family. The refutation of such accusations was the very reason for the mission Mullá Husayn had just finished. He had visited the two most outstanding clerics of that day, explained the teachings of Siyyid Kázim and refuted clearly the charges against them, and was given written statements of support from those two clerics to show the Muslim world that lies and innuendo would come to naught against the Shaykhí movement.

The death of Siyyid Kázim, however, left a vacuum of great proportions in the hierarchy of clergy-heavy Karbilá—a vacuum which many of the powerful were already positioning themselves to fill. Heaven help any mere disciple who got in the way.

First, Mullá Husayn calmed his fellows' fears and reminded them of Siyyid Kázim's countless statements of the nearness of the Promised One. Then, as the leading disciple, he went to a nearby house to receive visits from the bereaved of the city on behalf of his chief, consoling the mourners for three days. Finally, he called together the best and most trustworthy of his fellows and asked what their teacher's final exhortations had been.

They replied, "He told us that the Object of our quest was now revealed. [He had said] The veils that intervened between you and Him are such as only you can remove by your devoted search. Nothing short of prayerful endeavor, of purity of motive, of singleness of mind, will enable you to tear them asunder. Has not God revealed in His Book: 'Whoso maketh efforts for Us, in Our ways will We guide them'?"

Siyyid Kázim had done all he could to move his disciples on their way. He had informed and entreated them all, in groups and singly, in private and in public, "Persevere till the time when He, who is your true Guide and Master, will graciously aid you and enable you to recognise Him. Be firm till the day when He will choose you as the companions and the heroic supporters of the promised Qá'im. Well is it with every one of you who will quaff the cup of martyrdom in His path. Those of you whom God, in His wisdom, will preserve and keep to witness the setting of the Star of Divine guidance, that Harbinger of the Sun of Divine Revelation, must needs be patient, must remain assured and steadfast. Such ones amongst you must neither falter nor feel dismayed. For soon after the first trumpet-blast which is to smite the earth with extermination and death, there shall be sounded again yet another call, at which all things will be quickened and revived. Then will the meaning of these sacred verses be revealed: 'And there was a blast on the trumpet, and all who are in the heavens and all who are in the earth expired, save those whom God permitted to live. Then was there sounded another blast, and, lo! arising, they gazed around them. And the earth shone with the light of her Lord, and the Book was set, and the Prophets were brought up, and the witnesses; and judgment was given between them with equity; and none was wronged.'* Verily I say, after the Qá'im** the Qayyúm† will be made manifest."

Mullá Husayn, astonished that they remained after such exhortations, responded, "Why, then, have you chosen to tarry in Karbilá? Why is it that you have not dispersed, and arisen to carry out his earnest plea?"

His fellows admitted their failure, but then attempted to declare Mullá Husayn the Promised One.

"God forbid!" he answered them. "Far be it from His glory that I, who am but dust, should be compared to Him who is the Lord of Lords!" He continued to berate them, then exhorted them to do as they had been told, to disperse and seek out their Lord.

Excuses were given, evasions were made. Mullá Husayn spoke to each of the well-known disciples, but none would budge.

Realizing the futility of further efforts in this path, he turned away from them, setting out for Najaf with his brother and nephew. Once there, he settled himself and his companions in the Masjid-i-Kúfih (Mosque or religious school of Kúfih) where he prayed, fasted, and held vigils for forty days to prepare himself for the great quest that lay ahead—the search for the Promised One.

---

* Qur'án 39:68.
** Forerunner of the Promised One of all religions.
† The Promised One.

The Scribe's Promise

1

22 May 1844

Shíráz basked in its vast glory as the capital of art, poetry, civilization, and literature for the entire Middle East. Inhabited for over four thousand years, this city—situated within a fertile valley between beautiful, bare mountains—had been famed from China to Great Britain for its many gardens of roses and fruit in the midst of dry highland steppes.[1] Shíráz had been home to the great poets Sa'dí and Hafiz. It was the land of Cyrus and Darius, their ancient cities of Persepolis and Pasargadae just a few farsakhs* away.

Shíráz was gently baking in the morning sun of this late-spring day. In this great beauty and splendor walked a young man, carefully avoiding dung heaps and muttering deprecations at the ostentatious rich who rode the animals that made such obstacles. Kapriel Boghos Akopian was not a typical Persian, though his appearance was only slightly paler than those among whom he walked. He was, in fact, Armenian. Part of his family had moved to Shíráz one generation back, bringing their culture and language with them, tired of the Turks and their Ottoman Empire claiming ownership of Kapriel's homeland. The other part of his family had arrived

---

* Each farsakh (or farsang) is roughly four miles, changing with the regional understanding of the term. The author is using the four-mile equivalent, but the rest of the story will use miles. Five farsakhs would be twenty miles.

centuries earlier, perhaps by choice after wars against the Ottoman Turks, perhaps not by choice during the removal of populations and burning of cities by King Abbás I, famed and beloved by Persians, cursed and despised by his victims. This latter side of his family had long ago lost most of their cultural roots and adapted to the ways of their new country.

So here Kapriel was—medium height, medium weight, black hair, and generally average in appearance—having recently completed his twentieth year, making his way in the world as a young man should. His specific "way" was as a scribe. His father was a vintner in a long line of Armenian winemakers. Kapriel preferred something more portable and less likely to cause pain if dropped on one's foot (whether bottled or in kegs, wine could hurt!).

He wore the usual costume of a novice merchant in a light-weight brocade jacket of modest quality. The jacket hung to his knees, mostly covering the loose pants and long shirt worn by most of the population. His head was topped by a simple felt hat rather than the small turban worn by most merchants. The turban in any form was forbidden by law and tradition to non-Muslims. All of his clothing looked moderately prosperous. His father felt there was no need to provoke the populace by "strutting about in fine and easily damaged silks." That was OK with Kapriel, who preferred to blend in as much as possible to avoid casual violence against himself.

Scribing was a career that came naturally to Kapriel, with his education being far more extensive than most. It wasn't going to make him rich quickly, but it was respectable and something to do until a more exciting path came along. All young men were expected to spend time working up to a good income, a wife, and children of their own.

"A wife," Kapriel muttered, still agonizing over the last round of teasing from the women of his church at the most recent Feast. Yes, there was a Christian church in the midst of the sea of Islám. Though not as large as the new sister church in Ísfahán, the Armenian Apostolic Church in Shíráz was nearly two hundred years old. And, as in any community, the young were teased about their assumed future courtships. Fortunately, his well-trimmed beard hid most of the current blush. A wife would be nice, especially the girl who lived two doors down—beautiful, gentle, and kind. At least, she had been all these things in their childhood. She, however, was in a Muslim family and therefore completely, entirely, and permanently off-limits to Kapriel. He and she were both still quite young when she was put away behind veils, walls, and customs, and the church fathers would never allow him to marry an outsider.

Kapriel shifted his thoughts to more appropriate and less dangerous things as he shifted his load, avoiding a laden camel heading the other way and bumping shoulders with the crowds of morning pedestrians, ignoring the ensuing threats and curses. He carried a small, hinged-lid lap desk in one hand, his box of quills and ink in the other, and a tall folding stool under one arm. Nothing easily portable could be left out at the market or it would simply not be there in the morning, and no one would have seen anything. Everyone took great care with their belongings, lest things move out of sight of their own accord.

As scribes go, Kapriel was quite good but not artistic in basic correspondence. He plied his trade in three languages—Armenian, Persian, and Arabic. The copying of books was his main source of income. He also wrote the usual letters between families or businesses. His favorites, however, were the more poetic letters to distant friends describing daily activities in grand and greatly exaggerated terms. These all had to be quite clear in meaning, thus preventing the use of fancy calligraphy. He saved his artistic urges for work at home, where he would create drawings in ink, usually about Bible verses, for gifts. Some of the Old Testament scenes would be purchased by the Jews who visited from their quarter next to the Armenians'.

There was art all around Shíráz in sculptures, mosaics, glass, and tiling—beauty that he appreciated with awe. He walked past small parks in full bloom, monuments covered in mosaics, and mosques bejeweled in decorative and scriptural tile scattered among the homes and businesses on his way to work in the Vakíl Bazaar. His preferred spot to set up was close to the north end of the covered bazaar, near the Ísfahán Gate. There he could see newcomers entering to shop, though it was the farthest end from his home.

Kapriel looked up from his musing to notice a small gathering of mullás preparing to bastinado another hapless victim. The man was flat on his back on the ground, legs straight up in the air, with his ankles held in place by stocks. He was pleading to the black robes around him to no avail. One mullá had the bastinado stick in his hand and was about to begin beating the soles of the man's feet. Kapriel wondered what minor infraction had caused this punishment—insulting a mullá? Inquiring into another faith out of curiosity? Whatever the cause, the man would have to crawl home like an animal and would be unable to walk or work for at least a week, possibly months depending on how much punishment they deemed necessary. It was quite possible that he and his family would suffer greatly from the loss of income, and if infection set in, the loss of a husband and father.

The young scribe turned to pass on the far side of the street. No sense in inviting trouble. He couldn't easily go around the scene by other streets and preferred not to backtrack very far to circumvent the commotion. Besides, the mullás really had no cause to mistreat Christians, and he ought to be safe. He had secretly read the Qur'án and knew that the revelations of Christ and Moses were extolled in detail by Muhammad. This was why Muslims tolerated Christians and Jews as "people of the Book," although *tolerance* was a generous word. There was always an undercurrent of dislike that Kapriel felt around most commoners and many of the religious elite. Something about him simply screamed *Christian* despite his efforts to blend. Whenever some random event caused agitation of the faithful, the extremists would make threats, throw rocks and such. And in the month of Muharram near the anniversary of Imám Husayn's martyrdom, God save us!

Kapriel waved or gave the chin-lift greeting to a few acquaintances on the way through the bazaar. Rahmat'u'lláh, with whom
he had grown up and had a complex friend / enemy relationship,
sold vegetables in the bazaar when he wasn't delivering fruit to
Kapriel's father.

As Kapriel approached, Rahma asked, "Kapriel! Did you see the
crows, busy at their work again?"

Crows referred to the mullás' black robes. Rahma liked to see
violence and to occasionally inflict it on others. Sometimes he
would say, "Muhammad, peace be upon Him, forcefully subdued
the tribes of Arabia, bringing peace and unity through violence and
the Word of God, so violence can't be bad."

Kapriel stopped to answer, "Yes, I saw them. Do you know what
the man did?"

Rahma responded with a large smile, "No idea. I'm just glad it
wasn't me."

Kapriel nodded agreement and waved as he passed through the
shops of farm produce, entering the odiferous paradise outside a
spice shop run by Rustam Muhammad.

Husayn Reza sold intricately worked copper platters, Muhammad Darius had all kinds of blades and sharpened them at his
booth, and some people called out "Salám," "Salám malekum!"
Most ignored Kapriel, busy with their own customers and work.

Such names! he mused. Many Persian men were named for God
in some way, such as Rahmatu'lláh (might of God), 'Aziz'u'lláh
(sweetness of God), 'Abdu'lláh (servant of God), or Muhammad
and His Imám descendants. Some men were named for one of
the historical greats of Persia, such as Cyrus and his son Darius.
Armenian names were very similar, like his own: Kapriel (Gabriel)
Boghos (Paul), an angel and an apostle. Perhaps his parents had
had high hopes at his birth.

His countrymen were usually named after Christ, His twelve
apostles, and all the over two hundred saints of the Armenian
Apostolic Church, plus a few historical figures and names from

nature. Obviously Armenians had far more choices in naming children after religious figures than Shi'a Muslims had. The twelve Imáms had only six distinct names, which explained the extremely repetitive use of the names Muhammad, 'Alí, and Husayn. Muslims also used historical names and a few from nature, but mostly focused on religious names.

Passing the crossway where the east-west hall of carpet merchants met the north-south main street of the bazaar, Kapriel heard one merchant call out to a friend,

"Abbas, did you hear about the execution yesterday?"

His friend answered, "How could I not hear? The cannon blast was a big one!"

"One bang and a man learns to fly!"[4]

Several men laughed in appreciation of this clever remark, but Kapriel walked on a little faster.

Finally arriving at his preferred spot, he continued to muse and mull as he set his small folding stool in front of a column between shops. The height of the stool was about the same as the raised floor of the shops, putting Kapriel's head almost level with men standing in the ground-level aisle, and with the shopkeepers sitting to either side as they waited for customers. A wood carver who sold his own work and that of others had the shop to one side, and a seller of quality trinkets large and small was on the other side, both seated on the raised floor's ledge like most traders and craftsmen when they weren't standing over their displays. He ignored both of them at first, as they ignored him.

The Vakíl Bazaar was built over fifty years earlier by Karim Khan Zand, a remarkable leader who rebuilt Shíráz after a sacking by Afghans that was quickly followed by a sacking by their own shah, angry at the rebellious governor of Fars. Karim Khan had made Shíráz beautiful again, renewing its fortifications, building the Citadel, the Vakíl Mosque, Vakíl Bazaar, and several other great works of architectural art.

Kapriel was often inspired by the intricate brick work of the new bazaar, set in lateral rows, herringbone and feather patterns, and vertical columns that together created and decorated the arches and high vaults. Each vault spanned about ten feet, was open to the sun at the very top, and at the bottom opened to the east and west on enclosed chambers. Each chamber housed one of the many shops. The lower-arched sections in the carpet hall had lamps everywhere to supplement the light from the open peak of the vaults, while the taller main street had windows placed high in the arches to let in more sunlight. The selection was enormous, the quality moderate. The lower quality goods were sold in the old bazaar, the best were kept aside for personal sales calls on rich residents and well-to-do visitors.

Lap desk balanced nicely on his thighs, Kapriel unlatched the top to take out a sheet of paper. There was also expensive vellum in there, should a man of greater means choose to bring his patronage to a nonbeliever. This usually occurred when such an esteemed gentleman did not want his own secretary to know of the letter. Next Kapriel opened his box of quills and ink. This box was narrow and long enough to hold the feather quills, and the slender internal drawer could be pulled from one small end of the outer box. He withdrew a quill, a glass bottle of ink stoppered with cork, and a small knife for sharpening the quill points. With the quill sharpened, the knife in the drawer, and drawer in the box, Kapriel put the box on the edge of his desk where he could defend it if necessary.

This box was not only the holder of his tools but also his advertisement. He had decorated the top surface by drawing a long plume and a small inkwell signalizing to all passers what his trade was. Seeing no immediate customers, he pulled out a small book in Arabic that he was copying for a busy civil servant. He didn't like the civil servant. Civil servants tended to be greedy, demanding, and incredibly stingy. No matter, he had received half of his payment up front—along with various threats of his demise if he or the original book should disappear.

Musing further (musing and mulling were two of his best talents) about agitated Persians, Kapriel's mind rolled around to a young man who was neither stingy nor greedy. *Then there is Siyyid 'Alí-Muhammad,* he thought to himself, *named for both the Prophet and His first successor, and he is a descendent of the Prophet from both sides. His parents must expect great things from him. Even so, this siyyid is not like the big-head bully types. No ego problems, no lording his titles over others. Always humble and calm. How very different!*

Glancing surreptitiously to his right, he saw the woodworker marking an outline on a piece of maple, the wood probably coming from the forests near Bushihr on the ocean. The neighbor pulled out a carving knife for removing largish bits of wood and began, leaving high spots for the tops of the shoulders and rump of an animal, lowering the back, rounding the rump, gently cutting between the neck and legs. This was a master carver, who—with his fellows—produced the finest carvings in Persia. What an odd paradox to have master carvers in an area with so little wood. The city had many trees in parks and hidden in yards, and the surrounding mountains had grasses and some orchards, but not verdant forests.

Kapriel continued his copying, diligently ensuring clean lettering without blobs or drips. While re-inking his plume, he glanced again at the animal emerging from the block of wood next door. Eventually it took the shape of a chinkara, a very small type of gazelle native to the region. Those tiny, delicate points for antlers were left chunky, and the legs were far thicker than an artful rendering would allow. A toy, then. Nothing delicate could be safe in a child's hands. He was somewhat sad that the graceful gazelle would end up looking more like an elephant with antlers and no trunk, but it would be close enough for the imagination of youngsters and tough enough to survive most of their activities.

The wood carver collected chips in a leather lap guard. Every bit would be salvaged for sale to various people, whether as kindling, to flavor grilled or roasted food, or any of dozens of domestic and industrial uses. He then started on a flat piece, drawing an intricate floral design on the broad top surface.

Kapriel made himself focus on his boring copying. The book was a small treatise on why Muhammad must have ascended bodily to heaven, refuting the claims of some shaykh named Ahmad-i-Áhsa'í claiming the body was just dust, a vehicle for us during our time on Earth, and that only His soul ascended. It was a familiar argument to Kapriel, a topic Christians occasionally discussed about the ascension of Christ.

Thinking of Holy Christ, his mind turned once again to the mullás administering punishment and the contrast with that local young man, Siyyid 'Alí-Muhammad, whose family was practically famous in this city for their kindness. Kapriel mused that he had never seen him at fights or whippings to cheer on the bloodshed.

He never throws stones or hurls insults at anyone. He doesn't discriminate if one is rich or poor, Muslim or Christian or Jew, greeting each as a dearly loved friend. He and his uncle must be the most trusted merchants in the city, selling merchandise from all around, from Karbilá to Kerman, Tabríz, and Tehrán, he smiled at sounding like a street vendor hawking his wares, then thought on. *Never cheated anyone; if anything, his family gives too much away. What a contradiction—honest Shírázi businessmen. Seems as if they have no greed to drive them to success, yet they are so successful. Too bad Siyyid 'Alí-Muhammad had lost his father so young. Hmm. Well, thanks be to God, his mother had a brother who could take them in. Wonderful people.*

Now cheered by the remembrance of virtue in a difficult world, he finished the penultimate page of the treatise as Rahmatu'lláh approached to visit on his way home. He was wearing simple farmers' garb: loose trousers, long shirt, long vest, and small turban all of undyed cotton. Built like a mosque with a heavy body and smallish head, quite tall with large, well-muscled and calloused hands from his farming work, Rahma was not someone to offend lightly.

"Kapriel!" he greeted with a small, tired smile.

"Rahma! Done so soon?"

"You know how it is. Up late harvesting, up early to get here before things wilt. A khanum* bought the last onions, then someone else finished off the carrots. Greens were gone before you arrived. But then you don't buy greens."

"They don't take ink well." Both he and Rahma gave a small snort of laughter. "How is your family?"

Rahma's expression darkened. "You mean how is Mina, don't you?"

Kapriel tried not to let his pale face blanch and quickly resorted to offended dignity. "No, I mean your family. The whole family, not just your sister. Is it not the custom to ask after the family of a friend? Do you think I don't know better than to ask about the women in another man's family?" He knew it was the custom, but he also knew Rahma's temper and overprotectiveness of his younger sister. Sweat was beginning to break out under the layers of clothing. He could be dead in minutes, torn apart by an offended mob, or banned from the bazaar.

Rahma eyed him dangerously for a bit while Kapriel did his best to look injured and innocent at the same time, raising his chin and one eyebrow to look down his nose at Rahma with righteous anger. It was difficult, not only because Kapriel was seated and Rahma standing over him, but also because Mina was the girl two doors down—the one who came to mind when the church mothers uttered the word *wife*.

Finally Rahma decided his friend was probably sincere. "They are fine. All are well. I am well, father is well, mother is well, Navíd, Hasan, Mahnáz, and Mina are all well." He gave Kapriel a suspicious look at the mention of Mina.

---

* Respected woman.

"Good. God be praised! . . ." He waited for reciprocity as Rahma stared at him, still troubled by doubt. No response came, so Kapriel chose a gentle reminder. "My family is well also. Father has a small cough, but summer will fix that."

Somewhat abashed at the obvious social gaffe he had just committed, Rahma nodded his head twice before finally replying, "Wonderful! I am glad they are well. May God keep your family."

"And yours, Rahma," he replied as he returned his attention to the small book.

"Salaam," Rahma waved as he turned back the way he had come to continue homeward.

"Salaam." Kapriel put down his work, took a deep breath to slow his heart and clear his mind of the sense of imminent danger, and took another one. It took several deep breaths to get himself under control enough to continue writing without quivering. There were times when honesty and volatile friends were a dangerous combination.

The mid-afternoon quiet had settled in, with Kapriel finishing a letter from a young mullá to a schoolmate in Qum, the center of Muslim education in Persia. Kapriel glanced around at the many men buying and selling. Few women came here, usually widows with a woman neighbor or friend, occasionally a woman with a male relative. Commerce belonged to men.

Next door, he noticed a rather sturdy toy horse of mulberry standing next to the chunky chinkara, now smoothed and ready for play. Several other newly-carved items were at the display end of his neighbor's stall. He must have set aside the floral plaque for some easier carving. On Kapriel's other side, the trinket seller had sold some items and traded others, thus turning over his stock while making just enough profit. Kapriel saw this in a quick glance, since the trinket seller was one of those who didn't like Christians.

Packing up for the day as afternoon moved toward evening, Kapriel felt a familiar shadow descending. He looked around but saw nothing strange. Yet the shadow lingered, a reminder that yet another busy, interesting day was done. It was past time to get going to help his father and older brother clean and close the winery.

He stood up, stretching his back, and smiled as he noticed that nice Siyyid 'Alí-Muhammad passing the north entrance of the bazaar with a young and dusty mullá who looked to have recently arrived from some distance.* Kapriel would have waved, but they neither entered the bazaar nor looked his way. Ah, well, it wasn't as if he and the siyyid were friends. They moved in vastly different circles.

Kapriel admired the siyyid, who was five years his elder, and had done so since childhood for the tolerance and kindness he showed to all. Kapriel also revered the saints and martyrs of Christianity, but they were long dead and far away, and not very appealing to him as a child. It had been hard to emulate such distant icons when he lived here, in Shíráz, as one of only a few Christians in an overwhelming mass of Muslims.

Once he and Rahma had become teenagers, many doors had closed to Kapriel. He did not admire those Muslims whose doctrine did not match the sacred words it was supposed to be based upon, who separated friends because they followed different Messengers of God. Did those Messengers not bring Words of the one and only God? Did Jesus the Christ not prophesy Muhammad? Did

---

* Siyyid 'Alí-Muhammad and Mullá Husayn-i-Bushrú'í met outside the city gate on the evening of 23 May 1844. Since the largest caravanserai, and the one in which a traveler and his horse would most likely rest, was just outside the city to the north, the author has assumed they met near the north gate (Nabíl, *The Dawn-Breakers*, p. 52).

Muhammad not praise and glorify Jesus? The Holy Messengers could get along, so why not their followers? Lest anyone think his dissatisfaction rested only with Islám, he also found grounds to doubt his own church's traditions, and those of the Jews. What use were the rituals and traditions created by believers? Could mankind be so dissatisfied with the holy texts that it must make up such things?

Kapriel let these thoughts and their resulting frustration go. He had gone to school at his church, and Rahma had gone to his mosque. Kapriel had learned reading, writing, and math, plus the extra two languages drilled into him by his father. Rahma had been taught the Qur'án through oral lessons, no more.

More lanterns were being lit for evening commerce as the daylight faded. Heading south through the bazaar, he passed a lioness for sale, safely chained near her owner. She had probably been captured around Persepolis, the ruins where Darius I had built his great city a couple of millennia ago. Perhaps it was there that ancient Persian rulers had somehow trained lions for war, like in the drawings of the ruined city's art that Kapriel had seen in a book.

A few shops further down, outside the closest exit, he heard grumbling and shouting, with an occasional cheer. Warily he slowed, looking carefully ahead in the dimness under the deeply slanted sunlight that came through windows in the high, arched ceiling. Ah, of course, he chided himself. This was not a mob seeking someone to shred with their bare hands, but a large audience watching an organized fight. What an odd term—*organized fight*. He gave a quiet chuckle. There were frequent fights arranged for crowds to bet on. Kapriel had watched just such a spectacle a few years ago. The muscular combatants, who apparently each thought himself invulnerable, would strip to the waist and bring out a large club, the use of which they were well versed in. On the signal, if not before, they would begin to bludgeon each other. This usually resulted in terrible injuries, and often in death for one or both.

The fight Kapriel had witnessed had ended with both dead, but one slightly after the other to give the momentary survivor and his supporters the win.

The whole thing had made Kapriel quite ill. Rahma, who had convinced Kapriel to go with him, had been baffled at Kapriel's squeamishness. "It's part of life. Men fight, men choose a winner and bet on him. We all do it. What's wrong with you?" Kapriel had never again been interested in violence.

The crowd had grown and completely blocked the avenue of the bazaar. He would have to go back to the nearest cross street and take another way home, and hurry. He had let himself become distracted again, not packing up until the sunlight through the high windows had dimmed considerably. That was why the crowd had been growing around the fight—it had to be over before the evening Call to Prayer. Such things had to be planned to begin after a round of prayers and end well before the next. It wouldn't do to have the combatants and audience suddenly stop, face Mecca and kneel for prayers, then stand and continue. It would disrupt the flow of the fight.

He quickly walked back to the north, passed his rented scribing spot, and went out through the archway, dodging people, camels, and horses in the broad avenues, and slowed as he passed a carefully planted park, breathing in the perfume of roses in bloom. There wasn't time to stop, but he did take a long look as he walked, admiring the perfectly trimmed bushes, trees coming into fruit, flowering vines covering walls, and flowers of great variety bobbing their bright colors on the mild breeze. A deep sigh of near-contentment came over him as he continued past. In the cool of evening people would come out of their homes and walk in the gardens, married couples often walking together, sometimes reciting poems of Hafiz or Sa'dí. What an irony: Attempting to take in the beauty of thousand-year-old gardens while rushing past.

Would he ever walk there with a wife? Or become a traveling scribe, or even a traveling merchant, venturing to see sights strange and distant? Would he settle down with an Armenian woman (as his parents wanted) to have a wonderful life in this beautiful, deadly city? Could he, perchance, escape?

He was reminded of a short passage from Hafiz:

"Let neither pride nor rich delicacies delude you.
This world's episodes extend not to eternity."[3]

2

Mid-June, 1844

Business continued as usual over the next few weeks. Kapriel kept busy copying books, writing letters for the general public, and drawing beautiful art for more appreciative customers. His parents, with whom he still lived, shook their heads over his more fanciful drawings and his refusal to discuss marriage.

This evening he carried his accoutrements home in the slowly dimming swelter of early summer. He was done for the day after spending an hour or two helping clean up in the family winery. Those in the winery were busy preparing cherries for cordial and would soon be in peach brandy season. Mixing batches of grain alcohol filled in between batches of summer and fall fruits. While they were busy now, it wouldn't get crazy until early fall, when the grapes and other fall fruits would ripen.

People were coming out to enjoy the cool of twilight on the larger streets, the men walking with friendly hands on companions' shoulders or arm-in-arm, the women holding hands or also arm-in-arm behind the men. Married couples walked side by side, not touching. No woman walked alone, and not even married couples showed physical affection in public.

His thoughts revolved around and around a conversation he had heard earlier that evening, but the thoughts dimmed as he neared his own street and began waving a laden hand or chin-lifting to greet neighbors. The streets decreased from the wide avenues of the city center to narrow streets of small businesses and large homes, to the warrens of slim alleys having only small doorways and occasional branching alleys to break the monotony of the blank walls.

He and his parents lived in a mixed Muslim-Christian neighborhood at the edge of the Armenian quarter. The houses here had been around for a long time—at least two hundred years, maybe two thousand. Only the ostentatiously wealthy and those made homeless by an earthquake would build new homes. His older sister, Repega, had moved out when she married a fellow Armenian last year, and his older brother, Hagop, had married, moved into his own house down the street, and spent all his days working in the winery, preparing to take over the business as a good eldest son should. The house was a relatively small, two-story building with a larger yard, like all the homes on this alley. The success of the winery meant the Akopian family could have had a home in a more wealthy area with an actual garden and servants, but Kapriel's father felt it was not necessary. They had all they needed. Flaunting their wealth would be un-Christian and would invite jealous anger from the Muslims, making themselves a target during unrest.

Kapriel opened the front door, greeted his mother, and assured her his father was just a minute behind. After climbing the stairs to his room he set desk, stool, and quill box next to his bed mat, then used a small rag and very small amount of water to clean himself from the dust and sweat of the day. Being Christian, he was not allowed in the city baths where the masses of Shíráz cleaned themselves in the rarely-changed, fetid waters that had already cleaned thousands.

Water was very precious. It came to the city from three sources: First, rain in the winter was captured from every rooftop, draining into family cisterns. Second, a small river ran through the city for a part of the year, drying up in summer. Third, the ancient qanat, or underground canal built hundreds or even thousands of years ago, brought meltwater from the mountains. These sources provided water for the people of the city to bathe, clean homes, wash clothes, fill fountains and pools, water gardens, and raise livestock.[1] Little was wasted in this place where only a foot of rain came down over an entire year.

Finished with his ablutions, Kapriel managed a dignified trudge down to the living room to properly greet his parents and walk out the back doorway into the courtyard. Just one yard was between him and Mina. He took a seat on the bench next to a pomegranate tree to relax and take in the soothing greenery as twilight moved toward night.

The mulberry was dropping its white fruit, which would be quickly gathered by his mother, dried in the summer heat, and saved for holiday treats. The grapevine on a side wall was covered in small, loose, green clusters. The peach and plum trees had promising young fruitlets, still green but swelling rapidly. The pomegranates wouldn't be ready until fall, several months away. Every plant packed into their yard, except two yellow rosebushes and a sprawling purple clematis growing on the back wall, produced food.

Kapriel breathed deeply, listening to birds rustle the leaves, maybe a nightingale or two preparing for evening song. He heard nothing from the second yard over. After only a few minutes he went back in.

"You're not a child anymore, Kapriel," his mother cajoled.

His father, who had arrived while Kapriel was in the yard, gently admonished, "What's the matter, son? Are our good Christian girls not good enough for you?"

They knew he was still distracted by the unreachable, off-limits Mina. How they knew baffled Kapriel. He never spoke of her, could not stare at her through windowless walls, but there it was. They knew.

His mother sometimes commented, "You think she's beautiful, but who knows what's under all that black material. She could have nice hands and still be ugly as a bat."

"She was a beautiful child," his father distractedly commented sometimes.

"Children grow and change."

"Momma, she's Muslim. What she looks like is irrelevant."

"But you still look."

It was true. When he happened to be at an upstairs window and heard her voice, he looked, and looked more from his shadowed room to see if he could find her in the tiny visible part of her yard, for only his family might see him looking, and they would tell no one.

Actually, just a week ago, she had passed by his sales stand. At a moment when her parental escort was distracted, she looked at him, and he was sure she had smiled. At least she turned her head toward him and nodded. Why must women wear all that stupid material? It must be hot, and heavy. And frustrating. How could they breathe under the white veil that completely covered their faces and hung halfway down their robes?

Kapriel had carefully looked away, but nodded toward her all the same. Had she noticed the delay in moving his eyes from hers? He had longed to smile and wave, but he was not stupid and had no desire to be beaten by a mass of men enraged at his foreign Christian eyes upon a faithful woman. Even a Muslim man could be beaten for such an outrage. It would be much worse for someone else.

His father occasionally commented, "This must be why Muslim families choose their children's spouses, because the prospective husband can't look at her and must be told what the potential bride looks like until they are nearly married. Stupid custom. Women in Armenia don't wear such silliness."

Of course, they actually did, being recently under Persian rule until the Ottomans took over. Women in Armenia were nearly as well-covered in public, but they wore many colors and styles, and the restrictions were not as stringently adhered to as in Persia. Kapriel had never been to his home country to see such freedom of dress. On the streets of Persia, Armenian women had to follow the local customs and don the required fields of material, in primarily black and white, to prevent threats and accusations of prostitution and moral failure. Inside their homes and church, at least, they could relax, leaving the sea of excess linen at the door.

Maybe it was her remoteness that was so attractive. Maybe, he thought, it was safe, for if he mooned over any of the women in church that way, they'd be married the next day. Maybe he wasn't ready for marriage. Most men married later, in their early to mid-twenties or even thirties, when there had been time to get established in a career.

He understood why his parents wanted to rush him a bit. He had heard the rumors, whispered behind suspicious hands in church. He wondered if Rahma had to endure the same rumors in his mosque. Why, people wondered, did a Muslim and a Christian spend so much time together? Why did they not choose their friends from their own people? What were those boys doing when they ran around together? Why was neither married yet?

Mina would now be considered eighteen. Her family had to be getting desperate to find her a husband. Why hadn't she married two or three years ago? Rahma had once told Kapriel that he and Mina had been traditionally promised in marriage before birth, but Rahma's future wife had died of cholera as a child, and Mina's future husband had died of an infection after a farming accident. His other siblings had also encountered difficulties—though they had married—encouraging gossip among Muslims that Rahma's family had been cursed with the evil eye, or had crossed paths with a djinn.* Maybe that kept potential matches away from the two youngest.

Realizing the irrelevance of his thoughts, he sat with his father discussing the latest batch of mead (wine from honey) and the approaching start of grain deliveries while his mother prepared the dinner mats. She set out a platter of warm lavash bread and a large dish piled with rice, chicken, and vegetables on the center of the mat.

------

* Djinn were evil spirits that looked normal except for their feet being on backwards, so that they seemed to walk backward while looking forward.

The three of them sat around the platters tearing off chunks of bread they used to scoop up the rice dish. The Egoyan family, also Armenian, was coming over for tea after dinner, causing the meal to go a little more quickly than usual.

The Egoyans had no daughters of marriageable age (actually, no daughter at all), so everyone would be able to relax. If the family *had* had a daughter, he and she would have been constantly, and overtly, supervised. This had happened several times since Kapriel had reached eighteen. Young men and women were able to become friends, talk about anything, learn about each other without a veil to mask the woman, but never be alone together before marriage.

This caused Kapriel to frequently find something else to do if a family with a single daughter was invited. It saved him annoyance, let his father enjoy the evening, and kept his mother from envisioning future scenarios with a wedding and children. Unfortunately, it also fed the community rumors.

Kapriel shook his inner head. Useless preoccupations. He turned his mind a few hours back to the day's work, profits, and other events, avoiding thought on a conversation that had perplexed him earlier in the afternoon. He had finished several pages of a long letter to someone's relative, completed a complaint of a man against a government official, and copied a few pages of poetry when the conversation caught his ears. Persians and poetry, an eternally close marriage. Ach, no! No more thoughts of . . . marriage. He set aside these thoughts to focus on their guests.

Tea with the Egoyans was very nice, his mother and Khanum Egoyan being good friends. Kapriel played with their two boys, about ages eight and ten, for a while after tea, and he twice caught his mother looking at him wistfully. Both times he managed, with tremendous effort, to keep his expression from changing and his eyes from rolling. *She's thinking grandchildren again,* he thought. He went to bed as soon as the guests left. He needed time alone to think, to ponder that distracting conversation he had heard that afternoon.

He had recently met the young mullá who was hanging around Siyyid 'Alí-Muhammad and had been for nearly a month. Mullá Husayn, he was called. Wonderful gentleman, extremely knowledgeable on religious matters, and most remarkably, kind to Christians and Jews. Fiery, lit with some inner . . . something, always aglow. Kapriel had noticed several others, mostly also mullás, arriving alone or in groups as summer began, but always greeting Mullá Husayn with great nervous excitement, demanding to know if he had found something. He had also noticed them being escorted by Mullá Husayn, singly, each one with an expression of rapturous expectation, to the home of Siyyid 'Alí-Muhammad, and reappearing with that same fulfilled glow. Just this afternoon, close to Kapriel's booth* and just before he had packed up, a different encounter took place. A man in a white turban and black robe, about Kapriel's age, had met Mullá Husayn in great agitation as the latter followed Siyyid 'Alí-Muhammad toward his home.

The younger man, showing all the accumulated dust and stains of long travel, had walked right up to Mullá Husayn, given him an embrace, and asked if he had "attained his goal."[2]

Mullá Husayn had tried to put him off, sending him to get some rest, but he would not be delayed. The young man had protested while watching the receding figure of Siyyid 'Alí-Muhammad. He had returned his gaze to Mullá Husayn when Kapriel heard him say quite clearly, "Why seek you to hide Him from me? I can recognise Him by His gait. I confidently testify that none besides Him, whether in the East or in the West, can claim to be the Truth. None other can manifest the power and majesty that radiate from His holy person."[3]

Well, thought Kapriel, rather stunned. *I mean, well! What can one say to that? It answers several questions, and yet it begs so many*

---

* The location of this scene is placed in the bazaar for literary convenience since an exact location is not given in available texts.

more to be asked. Siyyid 'Alí-Muhammad a holy person? Well . . .
He watched Mullá Husayn walk in the direction of Siyyid 'Alí-Muhammad's home, leaving the agitated young man in the street to wait, then return some long minutes later to gather the new arrival and accompany him to that same home. After watching and thinking a while, Kapriel's only conclusion was, *Maybe?*

Now, alone in his room with the window wide open for air and safe from the many distractions of the day, he thought, reflected, and considered. Siyyid 'Alí-Muhammad had not studied in any of the great clerical schools—of this Kapriel was sure from discussions he had overheard from the townspeople. He thought about the rumors and the character of this gentle man, with such deep piety. He tried to take personal admiration out of the maelstrom of thought and examine the idea logically. The man's title, *siyyid,* meant that he was a direct descendant of Muhammad, and anyone so titled was allowed to wear the green turban. Said turban and title were strictly a mark of ancestry back to Muhammad and gave no other significance.

Siyyids were often accosted by the faithful, praising their ancestry, attempting to kiss their hands or feet, or otherwise publicly exhibiting their fealty to Muhammad. This, however, did not earn them the title of *holy.* Besides, Siyyid 'Alí-Muhammad seemed to avoid such displays.

The people most likely to be considered holy were steeped in the Qur'án and traditions of Islám, many having studied in the great schools in Qum or Karbilá, carrying titles beyond that of basic *mullá* (cleric), the titular equivalent of *priest* for Christians. There were titles for those who deeply studied the faith (shaykh); for those who issued the call to prayer; for those who led a large congregation; and for those who held sway over the faithful of whole cities (Imám-Jum'ih). The Ayato'lláhs, who held sway over entire regions or nations were surpassed only by the Grand Ayato'lláh.

This last group could be considered holy, Kapriel thought. The Islámic hierarchy was similar to the hierarchy in his own religion, which was directed, at the very top, by the Grand Católico. But Siyyid 'Alí-Muhammad was not a member of any of these groups and held no religious title.

It made no sense to Kapriel. Yes, the family of Siyyid 'Alí-Muhammad was deeply respected for their honesty and ancestry, they associated with the upper ranks of Shíráz society, they were admired and loved by the people, and there were even a couple of highly placed and influential clergy in his lineage. Plus, Siyyid 'Alí-Muhammad had some notoriety for his lengthy Friday devotions. Did that make one holy? Wouldn't the entire family be considered so? What about other devout worshippers?[4]

This conundrum was thoroughly beyond Kapriel. There was nothing that he knew of, in his limited understanding of Islám, that would cause such a title to be attributed to his deeply respected acquaintance.

Finally, having realized the futility of further thinking, he slept.

3

Early August, 1844

Kapriel was busy conducting his weekly gathering of supplies in the early morning heat of midsummer. He had risen early from his rooftop bed, awakened by the dawn call to prayer issuing from several mosques at once. Most of the city's inhabitants slept outside in summer to take advantage of any cooling breeze. Women, of course, had to be back inside by sunrise or risk being seen uncovered, despite the law prohibiting a person from looking at another's rooftop or into another's courtyard, on penalty of death.

The bearable hours between dawn and noon were taken advantage of to the greatest extent possible with work and commerce, allowing the city to shut down again for most of the afternoon.

It was necessary to take more precautions than usual in the streets now. The citizenry had become unstable in the past month, with rioting against the governor of the province and against edicts issued by the sháh.[1] The governor had been tossed out by mobs; any semblance of order was unravelling. Kapriel, being always aware of his precarious position, wore his oldest and most threadbare clothes, working toward appearing uninteresting to thieves and bullies. His main disadvantage was the headgear. If only he could wear a turban . . .

He negotiated with vendors in the Vakil Bazaar for new plumes, paper, and ink, and made the rounds of importers who may have brought in something special like a new book. He saved all of his scribe profits, setting a little extra aside each week in case an interesting volume came along.

Paper was far from inexpensive. Rock they had in plenty, keeping sculptors, masons, and other stone artisans up to their elbows in medium. Glassmakers had sand and ash in plenty; they only needed to find a bit of lime for the mix now and then, and metals to color the glass with. The metal artisans had to import their raw materials, mostly from the north in the Alburz Mountains near the Caspian Sea. But wood to pulp for paper? Kapriel understood there were places where a person could stand deep inside of a forest and not be able to see out. He listened to the stories of the merchants, tossing aside the impossible exaggerations to glean the truth of their far travels. What a thing, to have travel as part of one's life work, to be able to look upon a frozen lake, see an ocean, stand in a tall forest.

He also listened to the merchants' tales of harrowing escapes from marauders just to bring this paper to Shíráz through the burning deserts and mountain snows. Sure. Yes. And they had no other merchandise? No other destinations? Had they stupidly traveled alone instead of joining a caravan, or traveled at the wrong time? Shíráz was a crossroad city between Bushíhr on the coast to the southwest, Isfáhán to the north and on to Tihrán, or east to Kermán, and many other points of trade requiring access to the sea at Bushíhr. Whatever was available for trade in Persia would eventually go through Shíráz. The exaggerated tales were supposed to support the exorbitant prices being asked, but Kapriel had learned from his father how to bargain, and he negotiated the prices down to a reasonable level.

Books were somewhat rare and very expensive. He had a small but growing library at home. Even Rahma had no idea how much knowledge Kapriel had gleaned from paper and vellum pages. He had poetry, history, two Bibles—one in Armenian printed on the press in Julfa, one in Persian hand-copied—and a book with stick letters of a strange alphabet printed on a machine somewhere in

Europe.[2] The trader said the language was German, but he didn't know what it was about. Books printed on a press were very rare in Persia. The few to be found in Armenian were mostly from Julfa near Isfáhán. The Persians, most of whom cared little for the printed word, imported books in their language from printing companies in India.

The scribe even had an old scroll in Arabic that described some of the ancient Fire People, or Zoroastrian, beliefs from an early Muslim point of view. That faith had nearly been completely extinguished by the Arabs invading in the seventh and eighth centuries, burning every bit of Fire People's texts, killing every priest.

Kapriel thought there may still be a few followers about, in far places where they escaped the Arab fanatics carrying the new religion, Islám, all the way to the edges of China, but such followers would be unlikely to live in Persia. Kapriel had found that scroll to be both interesting and dangerous, keeping it hidden inside a cavity he had cut in a deeply worn volume on farming practices in Europe. He also had a Qur'án hidden inside a lesser-quality copy of the complete works of Hafiz (he had made a much better copy for himself over several months before hollowing out the other). This morning, however, he saw nothing to spend his income on.

There was a buzz about the marketplace today beyond the muttering about governors and the sháh's edicts, distracting both customers and vendors from their usually intense bargaining. Such a buzz had built up during the past few weeks with the news of Siyyid 'Alí-Muhammad's declaration as "the Báb" being preached to the city by his closest adherents. Those disciples were openly voicing the tenets of reform in mosques and on streets, discussing them with any who would come forth to listen or ask questions. He only heard snatches of conversations, hints at some great agitation beginning. He didn't want to hear it. Such things usually ended in a small group of people hiding in their homes until the populace calmed. Perhaps, however, it would be better to have an idea of what was to come. He listened purposefully in passing.

"Siyyid 'Alí Muhammad seems to be getting a bit of a following," said a vendor.

"How can he? Hasn't been to Qum, has he?" asked a customer.

Their voices faded as Kapriel walked along the street, with more voices becoming clear as he neared a small group of mullás.

"Yes, bunch of lunatics running around spouting reformation, glowing like noon-day sun, saying they want the people to turn back to God."

"Had we turned away?" This from a grey-bearded mullá.

"Seems he thinks so."

Again one group faded as another came clearer, this group mostly merchants.

"He changed his name to the Báb, the Gate of God." The words gave Kapriel a faint chill, though he could not think why at the moment.

"Gate of God? What does that mean?"

"Don't know. Maybe he thinks God speaks through him?"

"Through a merchant? Touched by illness, maybe?"

"His poor family. Such good people."

Then Kapriel came upon one of those mullás whom he had seen with Siyyid 'Alí Muhammad, reading aloud from a small book, and surrounded by many faces in the extremes of emotion. Some wept with joy, some seemed mesmerized, some had turned red in anger, while some seemed pale in shock.

He could feel another conundrum coming on. Should he stay and learn, trusting the angry faces not to become violent upon a convenient target, or leave and regret not hearing words that moved some to tears? He could not stop with his armful of supplies, so easily knocked about by traffic, so he slowed, annoying those walking behind him. He could catch only a few words as he walked, "O peoples of the earth! Verily the resplendent Light of God hath appeared in your midst, invested with this unerring Book, that ye may be guided aright to the ways of peace and, by the leave of God, step out of the darkness into the light and onto this far . . ."[3] The words slid by quickly, like water from a cool stream. He caught so little of the meaning, the rest spilling past in a rush.

A man behind him began cursing, "Move, you ugly pile of camel dung!" so he rolled his eyes, stepped up to a faster pace, and set out for his small patch in the bazaar.

———

Kapriel's weekly excursions were not only about supplies and searching for interesting books. He sought out and paid the manager of the Vakil Bazaar for the privilege of selling his service here. There was the small amount for rental of a space the size of his desk, plus whatever fees the manager felt like tacking on, depending on his mood and financial need. This was how the manager made his annual wage. Part of the rent naturally went to whoever was the manager's superior in the government to pay for having a job. That superior, being in charge of all the bazaars in Shíráz, would scrape whatever he could from his managers to pay himself and pay the city administrator for his job, and so on, right up to the top, with each man buying his job and doing his best to undermine his competition to gain more advantage, and thus more income, while the men at the bottom squeezed the vendors for every possible coin.

Kapriel had heard that the same system, called mudahúl, was used in wealthy households. The head caretaker of the house would not be paid by the owner, but would extract payment from other servants for his income. A man whose job was to answer the door would extract a fee from vendors to allow them to see the owner or caretaker in order to do their vending, and add a fee to any purchase made on behalf of the household. A messenger at the door meant extracting money from the owner or caretaker to pay the messenger, the required amount being somewhat exaggerated to pay the doorman for his trouble. A cook might put an expensive cut of meat on the menu for dinner, requiring enough money to buy it, then substitute old chicken and pocket the difference. Small valuables had to be closely watched, or they might become part of a servant's income. Meanwhile, each servant had to pay the top servant for the honor of fleecing the owner and all visitors.

Kapriel had recently been able to sit with a French trader for an afternoon, asking all kinds of questions about Europe. The trader had explained various economic systems, letting Kapriel know that the Persian system was based on, and encouraged, greed. He said, "Here men must be motivated by complete self-interest. If they are not, they will either starve from not pursuing all avenues of income or be out-maneuvered by someone else, lose their job, and then starve. This is problematic in building a cooperative society."[4]

The trader had given Kapriel much to consider. Once he was looking for it, he saw that men of Shíráz did nothing without some chance of personal gain. There were none of the charitable works or organizations the trader had described in Europe. People gave to their religious institutions because it was required in order to be a pious believer. The institutions paid clergy to help the poor, sick, and elderly. People who would help others just because they had time and help was needed were extremely rare.

Kapriel remembered this verse from the Qur'án: "And be steadfast in prayer and regular in charity: and whatever good ye send forth for your souls before you, ye shall find it with Allah; for Allah sees well all that ye do." He vaguely recalled a tradition that praised doing only what Muhammad said to do, no more, no less, and he saw many use that tradition to minimize virtue rather than for moderation of excess.[5]

Kapriel was raised in this society, was part of it. How much self-interest was proper, and what was too much? Had he also picked up this inherent greed? Had he been foolish for teaching Rahma math for free on open afternoons? Might there have been some selfish motivation behind the seeming charity? Perhaps it was a hook to keep Rahma behaving well and friendly. *Akh,* thought Kapriel, *That is an ugly possibility. Humbling, as well.*

He was again mulling over these thoughts in the quickly gathering heat. Entering the blessedly dim, cool, sheltering bazaar immediately gave relief. The high vaults let the heat stay above them while the ground cooled feet, and stonelike benches cooled whatever contacted them. Temperatures in enclosed gardens would pass 100 degrees Fahrenheit most summer days, and the tiled plazas would bake like a bread man's oven.

Unfortunately for Kapriel, Rahma found him before Kapriel could get himself seated. Rahma was agitated, again, which was easier to take sitting down.

"Kapriel, I found you! We must talk. Do you know what they are doing?"

"Who is 'they' and no, I don't know. Can we sit?"

"THEM! Those crazy heretics! How can we sit when holy Islám is under threat?!" People around them seemed to have heard it before, choosing to ignore this outburst.

"We can sit because it is too hot to stand. It will not change what," Kapriel gave an annoyed huff and rolled his eyes up, "the 'crazy heretics' do."

"Exactly, it would change nothing, which is why we should not sit! And do not roll your eyes at heresy."

"Are you sure it is heresy? Is that your conclusion based on paying close attention to the actual words of these reformers? Are you just spouting the vitriol of some disgruntled mullás who are unable or unwilling to reform?"

Rahma spit a few unintelligible sounds, and a bit of saliva, while throwing his hands in the air. "Why do I talk to you, you Christian dog?! You and your calm logic and endless questions!" A few passers-by smirked at the epithet.

"I have no idea. Why do you?" Kapriel still kept his voice calm, though his insides were churning.

"Because you make me think, you idiot!"

Kapriel could not, of course, insult Rahma back while in a crowded bazaar full of Muslim men. Instead, he tilted his head back, just a little, assuming a superior attitude over the taller and larger man, and said, "If you don't want to think, why do you come and bother me with your overexcited effusions, casting unjust aspersions upon my character and inferring religious inferiority?"

Rahma tilted his angry head to one side, breath slowing. "Wha?" He looked more perplexed then enraged now.

"Ah, now you are thinking. Good." The use of long, complicated sentences with big words usually slowed Rahma down. "So," Kapriel continued pleasantly, "have you checked out their claims, or just blindly taken offense and rushed off to raise an army to slaughter them all?"

Rahma shrank a bit, taking a more normal tone. "But, the mullás are saying we are under attack."

"All of the mullás?"

"No, some have fallen," Rahma looked a little embarrassed to say this in front of his logical friend, "under the Siyyid 'Alí-Muhammad's spell and are praising his teachings as God-sent."

"So, how will you know which to believe? Is there such a thing as a spell, evil or otherwise? Do you still believe in curses or the evil eye?"

Rahma looked uncomfortable. "Sometimes. How else can their actions be explained?"

"Well, could it possibly be that Siyyid 'Alí-Muhammad is right, and that some people, even some pious, devoted mullás, might see that?"

Rahma missed the careful sarcasm. "I don't know. Why are you asking me?"

Kapriel felt a "Rahma" headache coming on. Obviously his big friend had calmed, found his position uncertain, and had to save his dignity. "Of course. Silly of me. Are you on your way home?"

"No. I must go back to the farm, check the bee hives for signs of problems, keep them healthy for your spring mead making. We farmers must actually work for our wages."

Kapriel thought of several inflammatory responses, but settled for, "God be with you."

Once Rahma was out of sight, Kapriel turned around and took a walk out in the sun to burn off some old anger. The unfairness of the one-sided attacks had sent him running home in tears in his childhood. It was widely accepted to insult and harass foreigners, Christians, and Jews, but no foreigner, Christian, or Jew could return the slight without retaliation from all Muslims around, convinced that they, their faith, and their nation were under attack.

Perhaps it came from being invaded so many times. The great Persian Empire of Cyrus and Darius centuries before holy Christ's birth had been split up, bit by bit. Romans had attempted to invade; Greeks and Turks had taken their turns. Arabs had not only invaded and subjugated but virtually eliminated the state religion, Zoroastrianism. And, of course, the vast devastation wreaked by the Mongol hoards repeatedly killing off entire cities and leaving, quite literally, mountains of skulls had destroyed any Persian affection for foreign nations. The most recent invasion had been by Afghans in the 1700s. They not only did the usual sacking and murdering, but in Isfáhán, they specifically massacred artisans, destroying artistic knowledge along with homes and businesses. Several ancient secrets of beautiful dyes and ceramic glazes had been lost, and were not yet rediscovered.

Shíráz had escaped the devastation of the Mongols by simply paying a ransom. It was "liberated" from the Turkmen in 1503 by Sháh Esmá'il, a Shi'a who killed off the Sunni leaders to enforce Shi'ism. Later, the Sunni Afghans did not slow down for negotiations after destroying Isfáhán, ruining most of Shíráz. Then two decades later, the governor of Fars (the province over which Shíráz was the capitol) decided to rebel, causing their own sháh (Náder) to sack the city and destroy its fortifications. This litany of invasions over two thousand years explained to Kapriel the ingrained Persian distrust of foreigners.

It took another sháh, calling himself the Vakil (Regent), to rebuild the city to its former glory. Vakil Karím Khán Zand moved the capitol to Shíráz. During his reign, the fortifications were rebuilt to protect new mosques, mausoleums, shrines, the covered bazaar, and several more highly decorated edifices commissioned by this more benevolent ruler. The resulting jewel of a city was the one familiar to Kapriel, his mother telling him stories of their ancestors and how Karím Khán had greatly improved the situation for Christians and Jews.

The difficulties, however, had not ended with the arrival of Karím Khán. Shortly after his death, the Qájárs began their dynasty by force. Shíráz was again sacked by its own sháh, coming to impose his rule, destroying the fortifications, and violently rearranging the population by moving some out, killing others, and replacing the displaced with different tribal groups. The city housed over 200,000 people in the 1400s, but only about 19,000 in 1811.[6]

Kapriel's father and grandparents had arrived in Shíráz in 1820, moved into the Armenian quarter, and set up the winery in the midst of unrest between two of the resident tribal groups. Then came a pestilence in 1822, earthquakes in 1824, frequent cholera outbreaks, drought, famine, and a plague of locusts in 1830 and 1831.

Doubts had occasionally been voiced in the Akopian's home over his father's parents' choice to leave Armenia, though life may not have been any better back there with the Ottomans in charge and Russia showing signs of wanting to move in. Kapriel's mother lost her parents when she was young, and she had been raised by an older sister. His father lost one parent to cholera and one to famine. He had, however, found a beautiful wife, and they had three healthy, grown children. The winery, though less profitable in drought years, made up for it by far in other years. As for cholera,

Kapriel's mother always boiled all of their water, whether for drinking, cooking, or washing, because this seemed to keep them from getting sick.

Kapriel had continued walking off his temper, sweating profusely in the heat as he pondered history. Finding himself in the nearly empty Nazar Garden, he took a seat on a bench, rested his desk, stool, and quill box underneath, and gazed upon the pavilion created by Karim Khan Zand. He wished he could remove his hat, long jacket, and shoes to walk unadorned in the cool shade under the trees. He didn't even consider sipping from a murky pool or stinking fountain to ease his thirst for fear his mother might somehow know.

A group of men passed, mostly dark Africans in chains. A few lighter men, also in chains, were probably accused heretics or war prisoners sold into slavery. No doubt they were going to some wealthy man's home for an auction as household servants.

The sun had just passed noon, with the noontime call to prayer still echoing in the streets. Shopkeepers would soon be closing up to go home and rest during the worst of the afternoon heat. There would be no use in returning to the bazaar today. He turned his attention toward home and the cool, safe water there.

4

Late October, 1844

The summer heat had passed slowly. Fall brought an end to the sun's baking and to most of the harvest. The grapes were done; the date and pistachio harvests were in full swing. Pomegranates and citrus were still ripening as nights lengthened and days became pleasant. People were again milling in the early evening cool, enjoying each other's company, usually in large numbers to avoid the increasing boldness of gangs and thieves as the province continued without a governor.

A group of Qashqai herders passed Kapriel in the bazaar in their bright clothes decorated with intricate embroidery. The various tribes that made up the Qashqai came through Shíráz twice a year as they migrated to southern pastures in fall or northern pastures in spring, moving their wealth in livestock around the Fars province. Men and women both brought half a year's worth of handcrafts in for trade and sought out any entertainments available.

Kapriel had found several more books for his collection. One was a more complete collection of the poetry of Sa'dí than the version he already owned. The new version had been printed on a printing press in India. Other books that caught his eye were a compilation of stories of the Arabian nights, plus two old treatises on farming in semi-arid steppes.

His simple ink sketches depicting biblical scenes were starting to become popular outside the Armenian and Jewish quarters. This surprised him somewhat, for he knew Muslims avoided glorifying the body by including it in artwork. However, he had seen both the admiration of Muslims for biblical art and the cruel way Christians and Jews were treated. It was income, whatever the reasoning behind it. He was developing the habit of taking a sketch or two with him to the bazaar to sell.

Near noon, Rahma came by with a new expression on his face: rapture. Kapriel had never seen his friend in such a state and was beset by several emotions at once—amusement, joy, fear, and a chill of foreboding. Anything that moved Rahma so deeply could not be good for the Armenians.

"Kapriel, I must speak with you! It is wondrous, I tell you, wondrous!"

"What is, my friend? Come," he turned to one side on his stool and patted the nearest shop ledge. "Sit, rest yourself. You look to be having a fit!"

"No, you don't understand—"

"Rahma," Kapriel interrupted sternly, "sit or go."

He sat promptly. "I see it! It's right there for us all."

"What is?"

"Reality. It is like we were all living in an empty dream, without meaning. Now, now He has awakened us so we can live as we were meant to."

"Rahma, slow down. You're not making sense. Who has awakened you?"

Rahma answered, "The Báb. Over the last two months I listened to several of His followers reading from a book, just like you said to. Now, of course, they are mostly gone, off to teach in other cities when things got too dangerous here—too many death threats. This morning, I woke from a dream and it all made sense! The words, the beauty, everything, just like the Qur'án. You said to listen, and finally I did. It's true, He is the Gate of God, through Whom we Muslims can be as God and Muhammad, peace be upon Him, intended!"

The trinket vendor began rapidly packing the display of items outside his shop door, moving farther into his store while sending vicious glares at Rahma and Kapriel. The wood carver moved his carpet to the far side of his area, getting a safer distance from them without a single glance their way.

Suddenly Kapriel understood the chill he had felt at the first hearing of the title of the Báb back two months ago. Kapriel knew the Bible inside and out. He knew that Christ had said to His followers, "Verily, verily, I say unto you, He that entereth not by the door into the sheepfold, but climbeth up some other way, the same is a thief and a robber. But he that entereth in by the door is the shepherd of the sheep."[1] Christ had then explained that He referred to Himself as the Gate or Door to holiness. *Báb* means gate or door.

Rahma was still talking, so Kapriel set the connection aside for later.

"Today I listened to a man—not one of the disciples, they're not back yet—with one of the Báb's books, reading and chanting for hours outside the city, and then he answered some questions but didn't know more than what was in the book. But he said more writings from the Báb would come soon, when the Báb and His friend return from Hajj. That's our pilgrimage."

"What friend?" Kapriel was intensely curious about the stirring of this reform.

"That young siyyid, Muhammad-'Alí, the last Letter of the Living to arrive. Anyway, if I can get a copy of that book, would you read it to me?"

Ah, there was part of the reason for Rahma's sudden trust with this delicate matter. Surely there was more to it than that.

"What is a 'Letter of the Living'? Why do you ask me to read to you when these books are being read in the street?"

"The 'Letters of the Living' are the first vahid, or nineteen, believers in the Báb." Rahma stopped there.

"And why . . ."

Rahma suddenly lost his rapturous look. His face fell into shadows of embarrassment, and maybe shyness as he looked away, and around, and anywhere but at Kapriel.

"Rahma," Kapriel asked slowly in a deepened voice, like a parent speaking to a misbehaving child. "What is it?"

"They are not being read in the street anymore, and I was . . . it isn't . . . I mean," he gave up with a slump, then shrugged his shoulders in submission and said, "I am afraid."

That set Kapriel back a bit. "Afraid? Of what, Rahma? You, the man who last spring jumped in front of a running horse that had gotten loose, and frightened the horse to a stop? You who threatened to beat a man even bigger than you for insulting your mother, and made him apologize? What frightens you?"

"My friend, at least I hope you are my friend. Everyone knows Rahma is not the smartest man in the city. But a few things are plain even for me to see. This message, this new way to learn things in the Qur'án that we have all forgotten, did not come from the mullás. Most of them will not like it, not because it is bad or wrong, which it isn't, but because it takes power and attention away from them. From the mullás to the Ayato'lláhs, most of them will turn against whoever follows the Báb. And the people, they don't have you as a friend. They will believe what most of the mullás say. They will speak fire and vengeance in the mosques, and people will do what they say. You know how we are."

Yes, Kapriel knew he was right as soon as the words were said, knew more was coming, and waited patiently.

Rahma, now looking quite forlorn, fidgeted his hands a bit and continued, "You know how we can turn on anyone at the least cause. If I tell my other friends what I feel, what is changing in here," he thumped his chest, "they will denounce me, turn away, and I will be alone. They already think my family is cursed, and some say you and I are, ah, never mind."

He swallowed slowly, hanging his head, and spoke to the ground. "You know I never learned to read. You in your church learned to read and write! You could copy a book for me, and I will pay you! This thing that is coming, it will be between old ways and new, you don't have to be part of it. This country may be torn apart, but it will not be about Christians or Jews as I understand it."

Kapriel nodded his head, thought a bit, and asked, "So, you just want me to make a copy and read the book to you?" His heart was saddened at his friend's state. He thought himself too tenderhearted for this place, these people.

Rahma hesitated, looking to people passing on the street as if they could answer for him. Finally, he sat up, looked Kapriel in the eyes, and with great fervor said, "No. I would like you to go with me. I want to go—no, I must go wherever the Báb goes. It is strange, to be afraid to see my friends turn against me but to long for death if it furthers the Báb's Cause in any way. I must go! I would like to have a friend with me. You also want to go. I know this, too. Your feet itch to go to new places, your eyes long to see new things! What do you say, Kapriel!"

Kapriel said nothing, looking through the walls enclosing them, remembering past adventures with Rahma that he had later deeply regretted. Something in his expression must have shown his distrust.

"You're thinking about what happened years ago, aren't you?" asked Rahma.

Kapriel's gaze met Rahma's, showing no emotion at all.

Rahma was stung. "I apologized for that! I was only a child and stupid. When the mullás realized you were a Christian in the entrance to the mosque, I panicked."

"You claimed not to know me and said I was following you, after all your cajoling and reassuring me that they would not notice any difference between me and the Muslim boys."

"And I was wrong, very wrong, both in my words to you and in deserting you. But you know I tripped the nearest mullá so you could get away."

"And a couple of years later, when the mob went wild in Muharram during the commemoration of Imám Husayn's martyrdom."

"There was nowhere to hide you. What could I do? You did escape, after all."

"You could have defended me, told them I was not an 'infidel son of a whore.' And the escape came after the beating. Mother was in hysterics!"

"You are right," he said with humility. "I have not always been a good friend. But usually—"

Kapriel cut in, "And then, just last year, there was the incident in the tavern—"

Rahma cut him off, finally looking him in the eyes. "All right! Yes, Rahma is an untrustworthy son of a dog! But we also had good adventures. The times we snuck into Eram gardens at night, or slunk across rooftops to look into every courtyard on our street and see what they were growing, or wandered the gardens around the high judge's house. What about them?"

"We were lucky those times. You had no opportunity to betray me."

Rahma looked down again, words momentarily failing him. After a minute or two he said, "You are right. I am a coward. I have no right to ask you to come with me. Yet, I still hope." He looked at Kapriel with a shrug, and waited.

Kapriel looked around as he considered, thinking this was much too sudden, and answered, "I will have to think about this, talk to my family. You, too, must speak with your family, whether they would turn from you or not. Besides, until Siyyid 'Alí—I mean the Báb—returns from his Hajj, there is nothing for us to do. See if you can get your book, and I will read it to you."

Rahma sat still a moment, then gave a few large nods of his head. "Yes, you speak well. This we will do, though it tears my heart to wait even a moment." With grim determination in every muscle, he stood up. "I will get that book!" He marched off into the near-noon melee of men preparing for noon prayer.

Kapriel had all afternoon to meditate on that conversation, copying some poems of Hafiz for a young lady who had come by with her older brother. He kept trying to find ways to let Rahma down gently, but the truth was, the more he tried to deny it, the more anxious he was to go. Everything Rahma had said was true, including that Rahma was not the brightest lamp in the shop. His friend had always spoken from his heart, not from his head.

It was accurate to portray Persians as volatile, with swiftly changing sentiments. As Kapriel had seen in the small crowd around the disciples last summer, the Báb's teaching could cause a great rift if it continued for long. Surely, many would grasp at a renewal of their faith, while others would do everything in their earthly power to snuff out the call to change from an upstart merchant.

Yes, Kapriel decided, he would go. It would be hard to leave his parents alone in that house, but he knew he must. Maybe Hagop and his wife would move back in.

Walking home that evening, he noticed two women heading opposite him toward Rahma's house from further down the alley. His heart beat a little faster. Could this be Mina and her mother? One of them rubbed an itch on her temple and her veil came loose. She smiled at Kapriel as she quickly reattached the veil. Yes, it was Mina, grown up and more beautiful than ever. Heart pounding as he contemplated this possibly-accidental breach of chastity, he walked on as he had been, putting one foot in front of the other through habit only.

Arriving home in a daze, Kapriel prepared for dinner and checked the courtyard from the back door, as usual. His mother tsked twice and informed him, "We have been invited to the Saroyan's home for dinner tomorrow night. Will you come home a little early?"

Romantic notions suddenly quenched with icy apprehension, Kapriel blanched with no chance of stopping it. His mother continued in a sing-song voice, "Hasmig will be there. Such a nice girl—" She noticed his horrified expression.

He had good reason to feel trepidation over such a dinner. Hasmig had made dinner for them a few months ago. It took several days to get over the nausea. Whatever had been in that stew had been awful; not old or rotten, but similar to eating bitter poison.

Mother went on, "Oh, don't look so frightened! She's not a monster, is she, dear?" she ended to her husband.

He looked rather unhappy to be dragged into this, responding slowly, "No, she's not a monster. A very nice girl."

Mother nodded approval. "See? Don't you remember? Just last spring she made us dinner and—" Her complexion lightened a few shades as she remembered the results, one hand going unconsciously to her stomach. Back to the safe path, "She's such a nice girl."

She pasted a happy smile on and kept it there as Kapriel responded, "I'm so sorry, Mother. I have an engagement arranged"—well, he would have, shortly—"and will not be able to make it. Please give Hasmig and her family my apologies." He refused to turn red with the shame he felt for stretching the truth so far.

Pasted smile gone, replaced by an eyebrow up in an air of suspicion, his mother stated, "You didn't tell us about this earlier." She eyed him thoroughly.

A childhood full of incidents had taught him not to let her "mother eye" make him squirm. Surely "mother eye" was closely related to "the evil eye." "Well, yes. I've just come home and haven't really had the chance." He used his wide-eyed innocence expression. It usually worked.

"Fine. We will give them your regrets."

"Maybe we could invite them over next week. I'll bring home a lamb shank to make up for it," Kapriel offered.

His father perked up. "Yes, we should invite them. Let us ask tomorrow at," his excitement dimmed, "dinner."

Well after sunset, Kapriel snuck out to the courtyard and found a few small rocks under the mulberry tree. He slipped the stones into a pocket, carefully climbed over the wall into the neighbors' backyard, crossed the garden silently, and went over the next wall into Rahma's yard. He had not done such a thing since the recklessness of a ten-year-old. It was certainly more nerve-wracking this time as an adult, with the possibility of some horrible execution if caught.

Silently he listened and watched, hoping for a sign of Rahma. Eventually he picked out snores coming from one window. Did Rahma's father snore? God forbid that Mina could snore like that. Only one way to find out. He tossed a pebble in the window and hid under an orange tree.

Nothing. He tossed another one, a bit harder, and ducked under the tree again. This time the snores stopped. A sleepy head on large shoulders appeared. Kapriel whispered, "Rahma!" hoping to get only the intended person's attention.

Rahma looked out, looked at the rock in his hand, and said, "Hunh?"

Kapriel stood up slowly, again whispering for Rahma.

Finally, the sleepy man's gaze focused on the intruder. "Kapriel?"

"Yes, come out!"

Rahma seemed to dither a bit, his body swaying in the window as he shifted from foot to foot, finally turning around.

Kapriel waited below, wondering if Rahma had gone back to bed or would be appearing at the door soon. A thousand nights passed as he waited, his desperation growing with each moment.

Rahma appeared at long last, still dressed for sleep in a long shirt, waddling awkwardly over to Kapriel.

"Come, Rahma, to the back of the yard so we will not wake your family."

They were headed away from the house when, "You're not here for Mina, are you?" Rahma suddenly accused in a whisper, his expression hardening in anger. "Because if you are I will have to—Have you done this before? Have you been here to see Mina?"

"Oh, good God!" Kapriel replied in a harsh whisper, "You do have limited thoughts, don't you."

"Then what! Ooooh, is this about traveling? Are we leaving now?"

Having arrived at the far end of the yard Kapriel crossed his arms, leaned back against the wall, and lifted his chin enough to look down his nose at the taller Rahma.

"What? What did I say?" The large man was waking up.

"Rahma, I will go with you—no, no," he uncrossed his arms and held both hands up to stop an excited Rahma, bouncing from foot to foot, from speaking. "Please, let me say this. I will go with you if the Báb goes anywhere after his hajj, but I need a favor. We have to do something tomorrow evening at dinner time. Anything. I must be away from the family for the whole evening."

Rahma paused, "OK, we can have dinner at a bazaar and go to the Sa'dí café. They have someone performing part of the Shahnameh tomorrow."

Kapriel's knees nearly buckled in relief. "Thank you, you truly are my friend." He took Rahma in a great hug, thumping him on the back.

Rahma had no idea how to respond to such affection from a tainted Christian who may be his friend, patting Kapriel's back lightly until he let go. "But why? What is the great emergency that you take such a risk climbing walls in the night?"

"You see, my parents are going to dinner with a family that has this 'very nice girl' for a daughter—"

Rahma interrupted holding his hands up with palms out, nodding, "Say no more. Wait, say one thing. Is she mean, ugly, or unable to cook?"

"Cannot cook. Thought we'd all die last spring."

"My dear friend. Anything I can do to help you. My parents are trying to find me a wife, too."

"I'm so sorry." They had a moment of silence in mutual commiseration. After the moment Kapriel asked, "So, when is the Báb due back from His pilgrimage?"

Rahma explained, "Well, those who have gone on Hajj tell me they first travel to Búshihr. Then it takes a couple of months to sail all the way around the Arabian Peninsula to Jiddah, crossing most of four seas.* Then it is a short trip to Makkah, by camel, horse, or on foot. After the necessary preparations and circling the Kaaba for a certain amount of time, they go on to Medina, about a month's journey north. Let's say they leave Makkah around the first of Muharram."

Kapriel had cringed slightly at the mention of that month of martyrs and violence, remembering the beating he had suffered, but Rahma had not noticed in the dark of the yard.

"They get to Medina in late winter. They do what they must, then travel all the way back to Jiddah, get on another boat and sail back around Arabia, then land at Búshihr. That will get them back in late spring, maybe early summer. Then, of course, there are the storms, at sea and on land, and that can slow things down or speed them up. But, more than likely, they should land at Búshihr around the start of summer."

Kapriel thought that was a long time to be away from family and business, roughly two-thirds of a year.

—•—

The next evening, after shortening his evening ritual at home, Kapriel hurried along to meet Rahma. Once clear of the Armenian quarter in his flight to avoid Hasmig he slowed, merging with the thinning traffic of twilight. Falling temperatures and roving gangs of thieves sent many strollers indoors before sunset. If there were any decent men out, they would be in cafés or taverns for warmth and entertainment.

---

* By "four seas," Rahma is referring to the Persian Gulf, Gulf of Oman, Gulf of Aden, and Red Sea.

Not that it was so terribly cold. His father had told him of winters in Armenia, where snow could gather in large amounts and last all winter. Lakes could freeze; icicles could form in long tassels from roof edges. Kapriel had seen snow a few times, but it melted by the next morning. He purchased a quick dinner but did not see his large friend, so he went on to their final destination.

Arriving at the Sa'dí café, he looked toward the corner where he and Rahma sometimes sat. If Rahma was not there, Kapriel would wait for him outside rather than endure sitting alone in a room of mostly Muslims.

Fortunately Rahma was there and even waved him over, in public. Kapriel made his way through the full house of customers packed around small, low tables. Heads were close together to make conversation possible over the general babble. The men were from all classes, rich merchants to field workers. Each table stopped talking when Kapriel neared and leaned away from him as he carefully stepped through, avoiding physical contact.

The men—and there were only men—rested in various postures on the floor. Many knelt, sitting on their heels, and a few slouched sideways or sprawled against fellow customers. Some passed pipes around according to a longstanding custom where a water pipe would be prepared and started by the café owner. The pipe would then be passed around slowly, starting with the most eminent person at a table and making its way around to the least eminent. Non-Muslims were excluded, of course, in this centuries-old ceremony. The exclusion was fine with Kapriel who disliked even the smell of the pipes. The accumulating smoke always drove him out, eventually.

He seemed to have arrived before the performance began, giving them time to talk. There was a bottle of Kapriel's father's mead and a small glass in front of Rahma.

Kapriel commented, "I see you have the best out tonight."

"Nothing is too good for the Shahnameh. The tales of our ancient kings and heroes deserve the best."

"You say the same about Sa'dí, Hafiz, Rumí, and the tales of the Arabians."

"And it's true! Here, have some mead."

"No, thanks. Doesn't the Qur'án forbid the use of intoxicating drinks?"[2]

"I am told, by those who should know, that the original words mean 'Do not drink of the fermented fruit of the vine.' It says nothing about fermented honey."

"Yet your family grows grapes."

"There is nothing wrong with grapes, only with fermenting them. It's not our business what your family does with the grapes."

"Yet much of our wine is sold to Muslims."

"Rahma drinks only mead. Or brandy. Or whiskey. Even rum. Anything but fermented grapes."

"Isn't that rather evading the point?"

"Not at all. We stick to the letter of the law. Hafiz was the same. It's in most of his poems."

"I believe he spoke of intoxication with God, not so much with alcohol."

Rahma took a deep breath and quoted, "'They have closed the tavern doors—O God, do not condone; For they open the doors of lies and hypocrisy.'"

Kapriel replied, "And in the morning you will say, 'Kind cup-bearer, may your chalice always be full; And may wisdom heal all this pain of hangover.'"

Rahma swirled his glass of mead, looked deeply into the golden liquid, and responded, "'Do not grieve over the profane world, drink wine; Agitation is a waste for a wise heart.'"[3]

"You, refrain from agitation? I think not!"

"Ah, it is a waste for a wise heart, but never have I made such a claim of wisdom for myself."

Kapriel put up his hands in defeat. "You win, my friend." He chuckled quietly. "How ironic. The tea-drinking son of a vintner trying to talk a Muslim out of his cups."

Rahma smiled, ducking his head to hide the teeth his smile might show. "Why do you not partake? It is something I have never understood."

"I do, every Sunday at church as part of the holy Eucharist. Christ equated his blood with wine and said to drink of it. I believe he meant us to drink of His words and become intoxicated with God. Wine is too holy for me to ingest at non-sacred times. And before you ask, no, most of my brethren do not share my choice to abstain."

The large man nodded, becoming a little fuzzed with his mead. "So, you are a bit of a fanatic." He looked at Kapriel seriously, head tilted to one side. "And now, would you tell me something? It has been on my mind since yesterday."

"Depends. What is it you want to know?"

"Yesterday, we talked about some of the wrongs I have done to you. Why did you keep coming with me, giving me the chance to, as you said, betray you again?"

Kapriel reflected on his words, wondering how much he could safely tell Rahma. Quoting the Qur'án to him would probably not go over well. Rahma had no idea that Kapriel had read that particular Book of God. Admitting Rahma was his only friend would be too humiliating and honest. "You know the story of Jesus from the Qur'án, yes?"

Rahma nodded slowly, "Some of it."

"He taught his disciples to 'turn the other cheek,' that if someone strike you, fine, let him do it again. It is also in the Qur'án, is it not? Hafiz wrote about it."

"Hafiz was a genius! Tell me, what did he write?"

"'In book I seek guidance to better know ethics: Faithfulness and mercy, virtues of the divine. Enemy who oppresses you to immense pain—Give riches to him like a generous gold mine. Be no less giving than the sheltering shade tree; The one who throws stones at you, to feed him fruit fine. Learn from the oyster the subtle art of forbearance; She yields precious pearl to those who on her flesh dine.'"[4]

Rahma looked about somberly at the gathering of drinking, smoking men, Muslims, his brethren. Then he turned back to Kapriel, "I think, maybe, that this reform—"

"Sss, Rahma, not here. The whole crowd could turn on us."

Barely whispering, Rahma continued, "Maybe this . . . message thing will teach us what Muhammad could not. How could we, six hundred years after Hafíz, a thousand and two hundred and sixty years after Muhammad, still not understand how to have peace?"

Kapriel whispered back, "Every generation has to learn spiritual lessons from the beginning. After so many generations, is it any wonder things have gone a bit sideways?"

"But look at you, not drinking, not smoking, never harming others. You are perfect."

Rahma was definitely going toward drunk.

"Far from perfect, Rahma. No one knows what lurks in another's deepest thoughts. You understand little of my church, so you do not see how frequently the rules get broken." For instance, he rarely observed the twice-a-week fasting days, missed a lot of saints' Feasts, and generally did not behave well, hanging out with a Muslim instead of his fellow Christians.

Rahma grabbed Kapriel's shoulder with the beginning of a sob. "Thank you, thank you for such kind words to a stupid beggar of a man."

At that moment, much to Kapriel's relief, a man with a santúr* arrived from a back room, grabbing everyone's attention and silencing them all. Dressed in a simple tunic perfect for blending with the background, he set the many-stringed instrument on a table kept empty for him, knelt down to sit on his ankles in the Persian manner, and brought out the delicate hammers he would use on the strings.

A mournful trill from the santúr called forth a man in rich garb walking slowly from the rear exit. In deep, resonant tones, he started

---

* This instrument is very similar to a hammer dulcimer.

chanting part of the story of Rustam, hero of long ago, fighting the devils of old. Ferdowsi's chronicles of the centuries before the Arab conquest of Persia enfolded them all in ancient adventures.

"After his defeat of Arzang," the storyteller intoned, "Rustam freed his sháh, Kai Kaous. And Kai Kaous embraced Rustam and blessed him and questioned him of his journey and of Zal. Then he said, 'I must send thee forth yet again to battle. For when the White Deev shall learn that Arzang is defeated, he will come forth from out his mountain fastness, and bring with him the whole multitude of evil ones, and even thy might will not stand before them. Go therefore unto the Seven Mountains, and conquer the White Deev ere the tidings reach him of thy coming . . .'"

Kapriel, listening to the beauty of the story, wondered what devils he and Rahma would meet while following the path of the Báb.

5

Winter through June, 1845

The months passed in their usual manner, acknowledging nothing of the acts of men. There was no snow that winter, just cold rain falling on the dull grey of mountains and dormant fields. Murders had increased as fall ended, with thieves taking to stabbing anyone who resisted. Mobs had gathered in open areas for mass fights, throwing stones, using sticks, slings, and various arms. Nights were filled with the sound of matchlock firearms going off, greatly disturbing the sleep of the entire city.[1]

Kapriel's family and all members of the Armenian Apostolic Church celebrated Christmas in midwinter (early January) with a wary but hopeful awareness of the new governor's arrival.

The governor, Husayn Khan, set about imposing order with a vengeance. Mutilations and executions were carried out on perpetrators until the streets were again safe for good people. Without jails, sentences were carried out on the spot through the use of the bastinado, the removal of a limb, the blinding of an eye, or some other creative mutilation or form of execution. For a while, Kapriel avoided going near the governor's home where various punishments were meted out and the results, or remains, were displayed. Partly he wished to avoid the gore and screaming, but more than that, he wanted to avoid the deep pity he felt for those innocents wrongly arrested to whom "justice" was dealt without trial, often with no hearing at all. Any accusation could be made with little or no investigation.

The month of Muharram started just a few days after Christmas. The governor was busy imposing order for the first three weeks of that holy month of passion, and then most Christians and Jews withdrew to their homes for the final week—the dangerous one. Kapriel obediently stayed indoors, thereby subjecting himself to two fasting days. He felt no need to go watch the parade of mostly young men, partially dressed if at all, beating their chests raw and cutting their own heads with daggers or swords, commemorating the martyrdom of Imám Husayn by mutilating themselves.

Nor did Kapriel have any desire to sneak in to see the Tazieh, the dramatic reenactment of that martyrdom, one of the few public events women could attend. He simply stayed home for the week making his sketches, reading new books, and analyzing similarities of the holy books.

Naw-Rúz (21 March) came, marking the change of seasons from winter to spring at the vernal equinox. His family enjoyed setting out the traditional Persian table of seven things that begin with the letter 's' (Persian 'sín'*). Kapriel wondered how that tradition had started—if, for example, it had come from the Zoroastrians, who had started the tradition of jumping over bonfires during Naw-Rúz. That evening, everyone enjoyed watching boys, and a few brazen girls, jump over a fire to bring good luck for the next year.

Rahma and Kapriel met in the bazaar now and then to keep current on each other's news. The meetings were weeks apart to help reduce the rumors of inappropriate friendship between the two and to minimize the danger of anyone learning about Rahma's new obsession. Obtaining a copy of the book was more difficult than either of them had expected. Rahma appeared at Kapriel's spot in the bazaar just after Naw-Rúz with the not-so-small book.

---

* There are three versions of the letter 's' in Fársí: Se, sín, and sád.

"Finally, someone let me borrow a copy of the Qayyúm'l-Asmá.[2] It is a commentary on the Surih of Joseph." Rahma looked like a starving child begging for food. "Would you? . . . you said . . . I have money."

"No, keep your money. I will copy this for you, and in doing so learn what is in here that has caused so much gossip among our population."

Shíráz was still abuzz over the claims of the Báb. Most of His disciples, the Letters of the Living, had dispersed the previous summer, leaving only a few interested seekers, the Báb, and one disciple, Quddús, in Shíráz. The tumult had hardly dampened, even after the Báb and Quddús had departed on their Hajj (16 October, 1844). There were still many debates and arguments among all levels of society—often loud and threatening—over old dogma and new reforms. Some called for the elimination of this blasphemous reform and all of its followers. Some attempted to calm the agitation with well-thought arguments and gentle admonitions.

With spring came the return of natural beauty to the region. The numerous gardens of the city once again dressed themselves in green, with fruit trees gracing the view in pink and white flowers, and flowering bulbs sending up their colorful accents. The mountainsides bloomed, and the air smelled of life and growth.

The air was also increasingly full of expectation, for the pilgrims who left to perform their Hajj last fall were due back soon. Order had been reestablished—or at least as much order as was normal for the region.

Kapriel had begun reading to Rahma shortly after the acquisition of the book. Rahma explained that this epistle was what the Báb had partly revealed to Mullá Husayn nearly a year ago, marking the beginning of the reform movement.

They sat in the courtyard of Kapriel's home, since no one was comfortable with Rahma and Kapriel being alone in Kapriel's bedroom, and no other place was safe for either of them to have these discussions. It was just after sunset, allowing Rahma to come over under the cover of darkness. Blankets were piled on their shoulders to keep off the cool night air and mats cushioned them from the damp ground. Voices were kept low enough for neighbors to have difficulty hearing them clearly, yet loud enough for others to know nothing untoward was going on.

Kapriel's parents were nervous about having a Muslim man in their yard, as well as this book their son was transcribing. That first night, they listened from the bench in the yard while Rahma and Kapriel sat on mats under the trees with two oil lamps to read by.

Kapriel began, "All praise be to God Who hath, through the power of Truth, sent down this Book unto His servant, that it may serve as a shining light for all mankind. . . . Verily this is none other than the sovereign Truth; it is the Path which God hath laid out for all that are in heaven and on earth. Let him then who will, take for himself the right path unto his Lord. Verily this is the true Faith of God, and sufficient witness are God and such as are endowed with the knowledge of the Book."[3]

He paused, thinking, while Rahma squirmed at the edge of the lamplight. "Why have you stopped?"

"Because I see why many are thinking the Báb is claiming a direct revelation from God. You know this could get Him killed."

"Yes, my friend, I know," Rahma said sadly.

Kapriel continued from there, intoning the verses of the Báb, sometimes discussing a passage with Rahma to obtain a deeper understanding. He would read until his voice tired, usually an hour or so.

They met two or three times a week, depending on their varying schedules. More than a month was required to get through the entire book. The borrowed copy had long since been returned, Kapriel having put every spare hour into copying it.

Rahma was a man transformed. The glow that had emanated from the Letters of the Living was, week by week, suffusing the volatile Rahma with something akin to patience. They no longer went to the tavern to hear poetry or music, preferring the Qayyúmu'l-Asmá to less-weighty literature.

The senior Akopians were not reassured by the first reading they had heard. They did not forbid their son from teaching Rahma the contents of the book, but they admonished him by quoting the Lord's Prayer, "And lead us not into temptation, but deliver us from evil"[4] They feared the Báb's words of might and power as much as many Muslims did. Seeing the similarity of the Báb's writings to the words of the Bible, Kapriel's parents feared losing their wayward son to a charismatic cult. But he was not a child, so they left him to his reading.

Nature, seemingly unaware of the growing tensions between mere men, warmed with the flowing of spring toward summer. New flowers bloomed as the old withered to reveal young fruits. Various floral scents again wafted through the streets and alleys. The rain had ceased before Naw Rúz, allowing bright sunshine to rule over each day.

Kapriel was at his post in the bazaar on a fine morning just after summer had begun when Rahma arrived, sat down, and quietly said, "He is back."

Kapriel looked up sharply from his work. "The Báb?"

"Yes, of course. Well, He's in Bushihr, but his companion, that young Muhammad-'Alí, came in a few days ago and is staying at the home of the Báb."

"My home, tomorrow night?"

Rahma's face fell a bit. "Not tonight? Tomorrow is Sunday; you have church."

"No, I can't. Mother cornered me. We are going to a Feast as a family tonight. Church services are over in the late morning, so it should be OK."

"Tomorrow, then, after evening prayer."

The next morning went as usual for Sunday. All the Armenians of the city woke early, dressed in their best, and headed to the Church of the Holy Eucharist. From their homes at the end of the alley, the Akopians and several other families turned west to the ruined wall that had once protected Shíráz. At the wall they turned north and, joining more families, joyful greetings were exchanged. The growing congregation turned east into Nohahar Alley, then through the gates and into the church garden. The walkway led straight from the garden entrance to the church doors.

It was a wonderful church, square and solid, modestly decorated on the outside. Kapriel felt that the church was much like the Armenian people: They were solid, without ostentation outside, saving their beauty for those who chose to look inside. For inside, the church was quite different. The arch of the altar was painted red, with gold ornamentation. The ceiling over the wooden pews was flat, painted mainly in a blue pattern, much like a Persian carpet. Indeed, there were several matching carpets on the floor.

Kapriel deeply appreciated this place. He had been here every Sunday since his birth, minus a few days for illness. It was a foundation for him—an unchanging, permanent place from which to move forward.

After the services and social activities, the Akopians headed home for lunch, listening to the ringing voices of the noon Call to Prayer.

Mid-afternoon dinner had passed, and Kapriel was working on a more elaborate drawing from the book of Isaiah in his room, with the Bible open in front of him on the bed mat. He was enjoying the quiet of Sunday in the Christian district and had finished a couple of sketches, signing and adding his seal to the finished pictures. Everyone had a unique seal designed by or for the owner. This seal was in the form of a wooden stamp or ring. It was used in place of a signature for contracts, letters, and official documents, since most Persians were illiterate and did not know how to make a signature. It was also far more identifiable with a specific individual than a name. To steal a seal was to steal someone's identity.

There was sudden pounding on the door to the street. Kapriel ran downstairs to help his parents in case there was a problem. His round-eyed father was just opening the door to a highly agitated man—Rahma. In great anxiety and muttering half-words, Rahma nodded to Kapriel's father while pushing past him and looking quickly about to find Kapriel. Spotting his friend, he grabbed Kapriel by both shoulders and exclaimed, "They have arrested him!"

"The Báb?" Kapriel noticed his parents' expression of dislike.

"No! Of course not! He's still in Bushihr. Mullá Sádiq."[5]

Kapriel said nothing, since this name was not known to him.

"Mullá Sádiq—Mullá Ismu'lláhu'l-Asdaq Sádiq-i-Khurásání—is one of the mullás in the Masjid-i-Naw, my family's mosque. He is old, and they have arrested him!"

"Come, into the backyard, then tell me what happened." Kapriel led him out by the elbow, escaping the frightened faces of his parents.

Seated on the bench in the yard, Rahma related what he had seen and heard:

"It was at the end of the adhán, the Call to Prayer. You know—well maybe you don't—but the adhán follows traditional wording. It's the same, with almost no room for variation. Today Mullá Sádiq did the traditional call but then added words at the end of it. He said, 'I bear witness that He whose name is 'Alí Qabl-i-Muhammad is the servant of the Baqíyyatu'lláh.'[6] It is a recognition of the station of the Báb. I don't know what it all means, but people went crazy! Most of us were confused, but the mullás up front, the most educated and respected, shouted terrible things. They called him a traitor, a blasphemer, and said he had spoken heresy. They demanded his arrest, and everyone shouted along with them . . . Kapriel, what can we do?"

"Do?" Kapriel repeated, "What do you mean? We cannot go against the law if he has been arrested."

"But he is old and frail, and those demons are cruel! They will kill him if they can!"

"How can we find out what they plan?"

"We will go to the plaza by the mosque. News will reach there first."

"NO!" Kapriel's mother was in the doorway, her eyes wide in terror, with his father just behind her. "You will not go out to that mosque and come home a bloody mess, if you get home at all!"

His parents stepped into the yard and Kapriel could see that both faces were red—his mother's with fear and anger, his father's with suppressed rage.

"Your mother is right," his father said, his calm voice at odds with his expression. "Rahma, leave now. Do not come back today. Kapriel, you will stay. We will not get involved in this."

Rahma turned to go as Kapriel said, "I will catch up with you later."

"No," his father said, "you will not. We will go to church and pray for your soul."

Rahma quickly headed into the house and out the front door. They heard it shut behind him as Kapriel answered softly, "A friend is in turmoil and needs help. Would Jesus be afraid? Would He turn His back?"

His father's voice went higher with strain, "How dare you speak of holy Jesus to us! You, who do not attend Feasts, nor do any fasting unless you are stuck at home, who turn away from our traditions, our people, our Church! You, who avoid any contact with Armenian women as if they would contaminate you the way Muslims say we contaminate them. How dare you treat us this way! Your brother is already one of the deacons. Did you know that? Your sister organizes events for the church women. You do nothing!"

Kapriel let his father go on, unable to defend himself and sadly knowing this had been festering for a long time. There was no argument to make since it was all true, every word, though he certainly interpreted his own actions differently. His mother was now back in the house crying loudly.

Eventually his father ran out of anger and words, simply demanding, "What do you have to say for yourself?"

Kapriel waited a few seconds before asking, "Do you really want me to answer? Do you want to know what is in this wayward heart? Why I behave the way I do?"

His father hesitated. He had no doubt that his third child was far smarter than any of them, yet did such unwise things. Was it better to know just how wayward his son was and possibly not be able to tolerate it, or just let it go?

He sat on the bench with Kapriel, stretched out his legs, and said, "Yes, tell me."

"Whoosh. Where to start? First, I guess, with the Church. I have no quarrel with the Church. It has beautiful ways to keep God in our daily lives, to celebrate the great believers who have gone before us. But the words of Christ are what I try to follow. He says nothing about these trappings of belief. He fasted for forty days when He was called to His Mission, not twice a week all around the year, plus on certain holy days. These are traditions which have been created by men. I wish to live simply, like Christ."

"This is our culture, part of what makes us who we are. We are Armenian Christians, not Papists, or some new type of Christian, not Muslim or Jew. This is our history and has been for far more than a thousand years. They hate us for it, but it is good and beautiful."

"They hate us because of misunderstandings, on both sides."

"What misunderstandings?"

Kapriel searched his mind for a moment, scratching his scalp. "Let's start with what we misunderstand. Did you know that

Muhammad praised Christ and gave details of His life that are not in the Bible?"

"There is something about the people of the Book, but I don't know what it says."

"Well, he did praise Christ, lavishly. And Moses, and all the prophets named in the Bible. Did you know we have a lot in common with other faiths?"

"Not with Muslims. They are like animals, ripping and tearing each other and those around them."

"Even with Muslims. All the Messengers of God call everyone to recognize God as being single and alone, the Creator, the Source of all. They all call us to the same virtues, to lead a life of charity and simplicity."

"Then why do they hate us?"

"That's where the misunderstandings come in. The Qur'án states—"

"Wait," the senior Akopian interrupted, "you have not read that Book, have you?"

"Eh, yes." Kapriel waited, but his father just covered his own eyes with his hands in silence.

"So," Kapriel continued, quite uncomfortable with this openness and his father's disappointment, losing his original track, "the Qur'án states . . . wait, I'll be right back." He ran up to his room, grabbed the Qur'án from inside the book of poems, and dashed back out to the garden. Sitting down next to his father he quickly flipped pages to the place he wanted, trying not to notice his father looking at the holy Book with fear.

"Here it is, in the Surih of the Heifer: 'Verily, whether it be of those who believe, or those who are Jews or Christians or Sabaeans, whosoever believe in God and the last day and act aright, they have their reward at their Lord's hand, and there is no fear for them, nor shall they grieve.'[7] This says to me that God told Muhammad we are all brothers in belief in one God, the same God, no matter which sacred Messenger we follow."

Turning a page, he continued, "A little later He said, 'Say ye, "We believe in God, and what has been revealed to us, and what has been revealed to Abraham, and Ishmael, and Isaac, and Jacob, and the Tribes, and what was brought to Moses and Jesus, and what was brought unto the Prophets from their Lord; we will not distinguish between any one of them, and unto Him are we resigned." If they believe in that in which ye believe, then are they guided; but if they turn back, then are they only in a schism, and God will suffice thee against them, for He both hears and knows.'[8] Here He seems to convey that those who turn from acknowledging Muhammad and Islám are also deemed to have turned away from God and their own religion, and are hypocrites. This is where the contamination comes in. Those who turn away still call themselves believers, but they are not and so contaminate the Faith of God. It has nothing to do with personal hygiene and is not physically contagious, but Muslims misunderstand and treat us like we all have plague.

"Not only did the Christian clergy mostly turn away, they turned their flocks away by twisting Islám into something dangerous and demonic. They even blocked Muslims from building mosques. Here, a final quote: 'The Jews say, "The Christians rest on nought;" and the Christians say, "The Jews rest on nought; and yet they read the Book." So, too, say those who know not, like to what these say; but God shall judge between them on the resurrection day concerning that whereon they do dispute. But who is more unjust than he who prohibits God's mosques, that His name should not be mentioned there, and who strives to ruin them? 'Tis not for such to enter into them except in fear, for them is disgrace in this world, and in the future mighty woe. . . . The Jews will not be satisfied with thee, nor yet the Christians, until thou followest their creed. Say, "God's guidance is the guidance;" and if thou followest their lusts after the knowledge that has come to thee, thou hast not then from God a patron or a help. They to whom we have brought the Book and who read it as it should be read, believe therein; and whoso disbelieve therein, 'tis they who lose thereby.'"[9]

Kapriel paused a moment, then attempted to summarize his thoughts, "Muhammad came when 'Christianity' was at its worst, in the Dark Ages, when the followers were unable to read for themselves and depended completely on their priests, but the priests were in the throes of power, unwilling to give up even a drop of it. The priests could not acknowledge the truth of the Qur'án without potentially losing their flocks, their source of power, so they turned against it, taking their flocks with them. They set themselves against Islám saying the Muslims were barbaric infidels; therefore, Muslims believed the Christians to be dirty, contaminated. And here we are today, still thinking the same way."

"But why should Christians have listened to Muhammad, even back then?"

"Islám is in the Bible, or at least some hints of it. Look back in Genesis to Abraham. God promised Him that His children would number as the stars. He had three wives: Farah, Hagar, and Katura. Farah gave birth to Isaac, whose line eventually led to Moses and Jesus. Hagar gave birth to Ishmael, and Ishmael was promised by God in the desert that he, also, would found a nation. Muhammad is descended from Ishmael and is the first to fulfill the promise to Hagar. There is more, such as the prophecies of Ishmael's promised Descendant coming from the city of Muhammad's birth, that He would speak with a stutter—which Muhammad did when in the process of revelation—and that the Message would be revealed little by little, as the Qurán was. There is more, but it takes digging."

His father thought a while, finally saying, "So if these religions agree, why do Muslims promote violence?"

Kapriel opened his mouth to speak when his father waved his hands, "No, don't tell me. Och, my God. It is too much. And now this man, spouting new theology and making trouble." He put the heels of his hands to his forehead in a soothing motion, likely trying to mitigate a headache.

Kapriel gave his father a little time, then added, "I wonder if this is what it is like for every Messenger—coming into turmoil, with the threats, the voices raised against Him. Not that I'm saying this is a new religion. Maybe it is—or it could be a reformation, an update perhaps. We just don't know yet. However, I don't think the Báb is a raving lunatic, nor do His words seek power for Himself, rather for God and this . . . person he predicts."

"And women. Why do you avoid women?" It was an abrupt change of topic, quickly grasped.

"I'm only twenty-one. I have no steady employment, not enough savings to run a household, and I have no desire get stuck with a woman who cannot, or will not, hold her own in an intelligent conversation."

"You think Mina is so smart?"

"Yes. It is a problem." He looked sideways at his father. "She dropped her veil for me last fall. At least it looked intentional, and she looked right at mc and smiled."

His father nodded, speaking in a sepulchral tone, "Yes, it is a problem." He nodded some more, then said, "Go. Help your friend. But stay out of trouble, or your mother will burn dinner for a week!"

Kapriel left the confined, quiet alley for streets full of whispers and shouts, clusters of men gesticulating at each other and toward the Masjid-i-Naw. He headed west toward that mosque hoping to find Rahma in the plaza, but it held a large population of upset men, many of whom dressed like Rahma, which made finding him difficult. Warning bells were sounding in his head and getting louder, so he kept his head down and went toward the Vakíl Bazaar, hoping Rahma would look for him at his usual spot. Perhaps

Rahma would remember it was Sunday and not a day for Kapriel to be there, perhaps not.

He had to move carefully, avoiding the clustered people while consciously not appearing furtive. Toward mid-afternoon he finally entered the bazaar from the north. He found his place and leaned back against the column, ignoring the vendors to either side as he waited. And waited. The clusters of men formed even here, completely disrupting commerce. Not that many vendors cared, as they, too, joined the chaotic conversations.

Kapriel made himself as invisible as possible, but could not help hearing some of the comments. The name Mullá Sádiq came up frequently with the news that he had been whipped one thousand times. Someone had savagely objected to the inflated number of one thousand, but another had said that it was true. Several men had been needed to man the whip, with each one going until his arm grew tired beyond usefulness, and then passing the whip to the next man.[10]

He also learned that the Governor of Fars, Husayn Khan, had ordered the arrest of Muhammad-'Alí (the companion of the Báb during Hajj), with Mullá 'Alí Akbar-i-Ardistání, apparently another believer. Various hopes were stated for the vicious and bloody deaths of the three prisoners, the speakers using all their creativity to come up with the most violent torments and executions they could imagine. These conversations were repeated with no lessening of righteous anger as more people joined and others left the groups as the afternoon passed.

The sun was close to the horizon, coming low through the high west windows, and Kapriel close to going home when noise of a commotion approached from the north. He did his best to hold his ground and not panic, remembering his own words to his father, "Would Jesus be afraid?" Muhammad, peace be upon Him, Kapriel thought, was not only a gentle, patient man, but also a fierce warrior with a sword, so he was not likely to be afraid, either. However, they were both Messengers of God, and knew things far better than a simple scribe.

By the end of that thought it was too late to flee. A strange procession was entering the bazaar from the north, causing onlookers to block any potential escape down the central aisle toward the south. Three men were leading three prisoners by ropes strung through the victims' noses. All three had blistered faces where their beards and mustaches had been burned off, all three bled down their lips, chins and necks into their shirts from the puncture put through their noses. The outer garments of one of them, an old man, had been stripped off. He had blood seeping from his back where a thousand lash marks showed. They were bare-headed, though indentations of proper headgear showed in their hair. The frequent yank on a rope would cause an instinctive wince from the victim and appreciation from the audience. Yet, all three walked with as much dignity as conditions allowed, not a bit of humiliation showing.

Men crowded around in the suddenly confining bazaar to jeer and laugh at the prisoners, cursing the victims' fathers, mocking the burned faces. Everyone seemed to know what crimes these men had committed, and no one stepped up to help them. Indeed, many stepped forward to give coins to the executioners leading the hapless men, rewarding them for the great spectacle.

Kapriel was stunned. For a moment he thought to rush the horrible men holding the ropes and set the prisoners free when a whisper of his father's words made him hesitate. That was all it took for crowds to push in front of him and make assistance impossible. Why did it feel as though he had just lost the chance to give water to Christ on the way to crucifixion? He fell back against the column, overwhelmed by the scene and his own worthlessness. Surely, those three dignified men were no lawbreakers. Even murderers and marauders were not treated so inhumanely.

The procession had obviously started somewhere else and would move through most of the city before it stopped, allowing everyone to see what could happen to any who repeated the supposed crime of breaking tradition, even by a few words. The prolonged display also allowed the executioners holding the ropes to earn a month's pay.

He wondered if the old man, Mullá Sádiq, would survive the night with his ghastly wounds. Certainly all three would bear the scars of this day for the rest of his life. So, this was a further example of how the Governor of Fars administered his idea of justice.

Kapriel sat on the dirt floor for a while, contemplating, and suddenly remembered that his family would be terribly worried. He stood slowly, feeling years older than he had that morning, and headed for home in twilight.

6

Late June, 1845 to September, 1846

"Thank God, you are here!" Rahma was radiating emotions with little ability to restrain himself.

Kapriel had left home early for the bazaar on the morning after the inexcusable treatment of the Báb's companion and two mullás, in the hope of finding Rahma at his vegetable stand in the farm market section. And there he was, hands shaking as he attempted to do business with the rare customer willing to approach such an unbalanced man.

"Rahma!" Kapriel reproached in a harsh whisper, "control yourself! Show dignity. Was Mullá Sádiq frightened to tremors?"

"No," he replied without bothering to whisper, "he was laughing."

That caused Kapriel's eyebrows to shoot up in surprise. "Laughing?"

"Yes. Come back here so we can talk better." They took the two or three steps necessary to be at the back of the stall. "I was there, in the crowd, and was able to talk to him later. He said, 'The first seven strokes were severely painful; to the rest' he 'seemed to have grown indifferent.' He just didn't feel them. He was filled with joy of God, and had to cover his mouth to keep from laughing out loud."[1]

"And he is all right this morning?"

"It will take time to heal, but they are not going to give that to him. He and Mullá 'Alí Akbar and Muhammad 'Alí have been expelled from Shíráz forever, upon penalty of crucifixion if they ever return."

Kapriel was amazed at the depth of cruelty the governor was willing to wield to crush any form of disquiet among the populace.

"Kapriel?"

"Hmm? Sorry, lost in thought for a moment. Go ahead."

"Husayn Khan has ordered the arrest of the Báb. He sent some of his personal guard. They have orders to bring that holy Person back in chains."

Rahma looked a desperate plea at him. Understanding hit.

"No. We are not going to ride out to battle the governor's personal guard. If the Báb truly is the Gate of God—"

"Surely you know by now—"

"Rahma, just listen. If He is a Sacred Messenger then whatever happens is God's plan, and you have no right to interfere. In fact, you would be unable to interfere. If He is not a Sacred Messenger, then He must suffer the consequences of His actions, consequences He knew were likely to happen."

"Can we truly sit here in comfort when He is to suffer?"

Kapriel again had pains of remorse for not helping the persecuted yesterday. "We can carry some water and fruit out towards Bushihr a day or two before they should return. We can at least offer refreshment and compassion without becoming criminals. The round trip should take one week if they really hurry. In five days we will set out, yes?"

Rahma stood still in thought, except for the tremors in his hands. "I suppose," he finally agreed.

Kapriel addressed him again, "You must learn to contain your emotions. You will be of no further help to anyone if you lose your mind. Do you trust God?"

The round face of his friend looked at him, "What do you mean, do I trust God?! What kind of question is that?"

"If you trust God to have a plan, then there is no need to worry. If you do not trust God, then there is every need to worry. So, which is it?"

"Sometimes you really make me angry, you understand?!"

Kapriel smiled and slapped Rahma on one shoulder. "That's the Rahma I grew up with."

—•—

Just a few days later, the two friends found their plan of succor completely undermined. The Báb had returned with His escort, unfettered. The troop of governor's men acted toward Him with deference and respect. The news had rumbled through the city like thunder, and mere moments after His entrance like a nobleman with an entourage, Rahma was at Kapriel's stool.

"He is back!"

This time Kapriel did not bother to ask who. "So soon?"

"Farhád says the Báb met the guards forty miles from Búshhir at the village of Dalaki.[2] He came part of the way to meet them so that their journey might be shorter and less difficult. They did not put Him in chains. Now He is being taken before the governor and some of the city leaders."

"Wait, you are saying He initiated the journey toward a possibly horrific outcome, returning part of the way on His own, in order prevent inconveniencing the men sent to drag Him back in chains?"

"Yes."

"But they did not put him in chains . . ."

"No, Farhád was there when they came into Shíráz. He said they acted like an honor guard."

Kapriel threw his quill into its box while saying, "Let's go find out what we can."

The governor's home was surrounded by curious masses of men from all levels of society.* There were merchants in fine brocade abás (knee-length jackets), with small turbans; great religious leaders

---

* This part is fiction. The crowds were probably there, but no reference is made to them in the books available to the author.

with long, oversized robes and huge, floppy turbans; city adminis-
trators in black sheepskin hats and varying robes and abás; and poor
men in loose shirts and trousers with moderate turbans or felt caps.
The Báb and city leaders were inside and closed off, leaving the
onlookers to speculate until someone came out to tell them what
was going on. Kapriel and Rahma stayed at the back of the mass
of men to prevent anyone accidentally touching Kapriel and, thus
becoming contaminated, starting a riot.

Rumors were rampant and varied. One merchant gleefully stated
that the heretic was being tortured as they waited; could they hear
the screams? A course-looking ruffian insisted the leaders of the
city were being put under a spell and must be rescued. Arguments
over which of the many rumors was most likely to be true began
breaking out.

Finally the door opened, letting several people exit the large
house, including the Báb and his dear uncle, Hájí Mírzá Siyyid
'Alí. They calmly walked through the crowds and turned towards
their home. There was no blood, and no marks of torture marred
the Báb's serene face, though one cheek might have been slightly
reddened above His beard.

No one stopped to chat with the crowd or correct erroneous
assumptions. Kapriel saw it would take time for accurate information to be disseminated. He entrusted Rahma with the mission of
investigating and reporting to Kapriel as soon as he could. Most of
the work would have to be done in mosques and among Muslims,
making it impossible for Kapriel to gather information himself.

Just three days later, Rahma knocked on the Akopians' door
after dark had fallen. Kapriel's father, now used to Rahma's late
arrivals, ignored the knock, letting Kapriel get it himself.

Rahma waited politely to be invited in before apologizing to Kapriel's parents for his unmannered behavior some days earlier, and followed Kapriel to the yard. Mats resting on the bench were moved to the ground in the center of the garden. Kapriel had the nervous thought that this must be something like what spies and rebels do to keep secrecy. Perhaps soon they would be leaving the city by different gates to meet out in the countryside. The heat of summer was again moving people to sleep in yards and on roofs to catch the least cooling breeze, minimizing the friends' privacy. Able to see each other clearly by the stars and partial moon, the friends kept their voices even lower than they had in April and May.

Rahma began, "First, I will tell you where this came from, so you will have no doubt or question. We know it took place at the home of Husayn Khan, the governor. Shaykh Abú-Turáb, the Imám Jum'ih—he's the chief religious authority for the city—was also there, and a few others. There were, of course, several servants lurking. I finally was able to find one, a Kambíz 'Alí,* a most trust-worthy man who works in the governor's house. He heard all of it and saw parts of it, and swears on his beard this is God's own truth. Good so far?"

"Wonderful. Please continue." Kapriel trusted this source's words would be repeated accurately. Illiteracy may have been rampant, but everyone learned to memorize and could relate many things with perfect recall.

"So, Husayn Khan heard that the Báb had returned and sent for him right away.[3] Others arrived quickly, such as the Imám Jum'ih. As soon as the Báb arrived, the governor spoke unkindly to Him and told Him to be seated in the middle of the room facing the Khan. Then the Khan rebuked Him 'and in abusive language denounced His conduct.' He said, 'Do you realise what a great mischief you have kindled? Are you aware what a disgrace you have become to

---

* Fictional character.

the holy Faith of Islám and to the august person of our sovereign? Are you not the man who claims to be the author of a new revelation which annuls the sacred precepts of the Qur'án?'

"Kambíz says the Báb replied, 'If any bad man come unto you with news, clear up the matter at once, lest through ignorance ye harm others, and be speedily constrained to repent of what ye have done.'[4] It's a quote from the Qur'án, and Kambíz can read in Arabic, so he looked it up. Well, the governor took it wrong, thinking it meant he was the bad man instead of that bad men have spoken rumors to him that he should clear up, and he became even more angry. He said to the Báb, 'What! Dare you ascribe to us evil, ignorance, and folly?' Then he told his attendant to strike the Báb in the face, which he did, hard enough to knock the Báb's turban off.

"The Imám Jum'ih didn't like this. He 'ordered that the Báb's turban be replaced' on His head, then invited Him to come sit by his side. He explained the verse to the governor and how it came about. He said, 'This verse which this youth has quoted has made a profound impression upon me. The wise course, I feel, is to enquire into this matter with great care, and to judge him according to the precepts of the holy Book.' Husayn Khan agreed to that.

"The Imám Jum'ih then 'questioned the Báb regarding the nature and character of His Revelation. The Báb denied the claim of being either the representative of the promised Qá'im or the intermediary between Him and the faithful.' The Imám Jum'ih was 'completely satisfied' and requested the Báb to go to the Vakíl Mosque on Friday to say His denial in public.

"Kambíz thought it was over then, but the governor was not done. He demanded that someone give bail and surety for the Báb, and pledge in writing 'that if ever in future this youth should attempt by word or deed to prejudice the interests either of the Faith of Islám or of the government of this land, he would straightway deliver him into our hands, and regard himself under all circumstances responsible for his behaviour.' The Báb's uncle was there, so he did these things, and we saw them leave."[5]

A few minutes passed in thought. Eventually Kapriel took a deep breath, letting it out slowly before saying, "That explains the one red cheek."

"My friend, this distresses me greatly."

"Which part?"

"He denied everything."

"Oh, no no. He spoke very carefully. He denied being a representative of the Qá'im. That does not prevent Him from being the Qá'im. You see?"

There was quiet from the other man.

Kapriel continued, "A representative is external to the object or person being represented. A carved animal is a representation of the animal, not the actual being. He also said He is not an intermediary between the Qá'im and the faithful. This, again, does not deny the possibility that He is the Qá'im."

"Oh, yes, I see. But why not just say He is the Qá'im and be done with it?"

"Well, because then He would be done, completely done. He has taught a few disciples, written one book and a few treatises, and look at what has already happened. For this, His closest disciple and two followers were nearly killed in the streets, and He Himself has barely escaped execution. If He had not put up some smoke to confuse the issue, this new Revelation would have ended already. Yet He has neither denied nor announced that He is the Qá'im."

Kapriel paused. "Since, however," he pondered, "He is not a representative of the Qá'im, who is He the Gate of? Who is this 'Remnant of God' which is to come?"

They thought a few more moments and suddenly Rahma started to laugh quietly.

"What's this about?" Kapriel inquired.

Rahma laughed louder. "They are fools, the governor and his sort. Between what happened last week and this, people are asking all kinds of questions. They want to know what is so dangerous about a deluded son of a merchant that He must be confined to His home without chance of visitors. They have done exactly what was needed to spread the word."

Kapriel gave a small snort of humor, but his mind was following several paths at once. Would the Báb soon be banished like His secretary? Could Kapriel and Rahma follow Him? The promise of last fall still stood, but he had not shared that with his father. What would his family say or do if a time to leave came?

"Rahma," Kapriel quietly intoned in the starry night, "have you told your family yet?"

The silence was followed by a deep sigh. "No, not yet. They will all disown me, you know. They already suspect, though I do all the same things as before—all five prayers every day, in the mosque Fridays, all of it. But they have stopped trying to find me a wife and seem to avoid me sometimes. Maybe they think you have contaminated me. I don't know. They wonder why I came over here so much in spring. I told them you were teaching me to read."

"Mm. Then we shall have to make that true. Late, but true. Shall we start with Hafiz or Sa'dí?"

Several weeks passed, during which pressure increased daily on the Imám Jum'ih to call the Báb for a public statement. At last he invited the Báb to make clear His mission in a Friday service. This time the Governor had ordered all of Shíráz to gather and witness the event. Rahma was able to get there early to be near the front where he could hear each word, relating it moment by moment to Kapriel on their next lesson night.

Thousands had gathered at the Vakíl Mosque having heard that the nephew of Hájí Mírzá Siyyid 'Alí would at last come to speak. They had accumulated from early morning well into the late afternoon when the Báb would address them. The floor of the main room was crowded between the thick, spiraling columns that held up the roof of many arches. The courtyard was crowded, and even the roofs and minarets had men on them hoping to hear what the Báb would say. A simple construction of fourteen steps at the front of the room led up to a small pulpit recessed in the high wall. The

Imám Jum'ih had just taken his position in the pulpit to deliver his sermon when the Báb and His uncle arrived. The Imám Jum'ih welcomed his guest and invited Him to the pulpit for His address. The Báb moved forward, turning around on the first step to make His speech. The Imám Jum'ih bid Him go higher, causing the Báb to go up two more steps.[6]

The Guest began, "Praise be to God, who hath in truth created the heavens and the earth," when a siyyid in the front row interrupted, shouting, "Enough of this idle chatter! Declare now and immediately, the thing you intend to say."

The Imám Jum'ih rebuked him, saying, "Hold your peace and be ashamed of your impertinence." Then he asked the Báb to be brief.

So, He was. He said, "The condemnation of God be upon him who regards me either as a representative of the Imám or the gate thereof. The condemnation of God be also upon whosoever imputes to me the charge of having denied the unity of God, of having repudiated the prophethood of Muhammad, the Seal of the Prophets, of having rejected the truth of any of the messengers of old, or of having refused to recognise the guardianship of 'Alí, the Commander of the Faithful, or any of the imáms who have succeeded him."

Then He said, "O people! Know this well that I speak what My Grandfather, the Messenger of God, spoke twelve hundred and sixty years ago, and I do not speak what My Grandfather did not. 'What Muhammad made lawful remains lawful unto the Day of Resurrection and what He forbade remains forbidden unto the Day of Resurrection,' and according to the Tradition that has come down from the Imáms, 'Whenever the Qá'ím arises, that will be the Day of Resurrection.'"

Then He climbed to the top of the stairs, gave the Imám Jum'ih an embrace, and went down to join the congregation for the service. The Imám Jum'ih gently suggested the He and His uncle head home, where His family was surely anxiously waiting to hear from them.

"And they left. The sermon was given, and afterward we all left, and tonight I am here," Rahma concluded his long tale.

"No one chased after them, threw rocks or anything?"

"No, because they left early. There was mumbling, and some wanted to go get Him from His uncle's house, but by the end of the sermon, most people just wanted to go home."

⚊•⚊

The next few weeks proved that the speech of the Báb had deeply affected many.

The Báb was allowed guests in His home for only three days after His return from Búshihr before the ban on contact with others began.[6] From then on, He was not seen in public for many months, lessoning direct reminders of the upsetting events. More and more men sought Him out, arriving from all parts of Persia and going to the house of the Báb's uncle 'Alí as word spread of His gentle, confident manner under great duress, His effect on the men sent to harm Him, and the words, seemingly from God Himself, uttered and written by this humble merchant.

Mullá Husayn returned, cautiously and by night, to the home of the Báb's uncle. He stayed for a while, the Báb coming to that house in darkness, letting the first declarant once again spend long nights in direct communion with his Lord. The citizenry recognized this "mischief maker" from a year ago, quickly denouncing his arrival and the breaking of the rules of confinement of the Báb.

Soon Mullá Husayn's safety was again directly threatened. Rumors abounded that he and the Báb were plotting rebellion. Before the situation could explode, Mullá Husayn was sent on a mission to his native province, Khurásán, in the far northeast of Persia, to continue teaching the Cause.

The believers, now called Bábís, who had heard the Message from the dispersed Letters of the Living, found ways to get to the

Báb's home or His uncle's and meet with Him. The Báb Himself kept to His home during the days, writing tablets and giving instructions to His rapidly growing body of followers. They, too, however, were sent away, many to Isfáhán, to prevent further distress to the citizenry of Shíráz.

Great leaders of Islám came to challenge Him, including Siyyid Yahyá, who was sent by the sháh to verify the claims of the Báb. All left either subdued and bewildered or acclaiming His truth, overpowered by the words spoken to them. No argument was too obscure, no mystical question too abstruse for the gentle, undeniable replies He gave.

Rahma spoke with many of the guests, feeling himself too unworthy to seek an audience directly. In this way he learned of, and related to Kapriel, the interviews of Siyyid Yahyá. That highly learned and widely respected siyyid had brought up every minute point for the Báb's response, and every point had been answered. For the third interview, he had decided on a test, a miracle to be expected but not asked for. If the Báb revealed a certain commentary for him, he would believe. If not, there would be no need of further interviews. However, Siyyid Yahyá, who had stood unperturbed in front of kings, found himself shaking uncontrollably upon entering the Báb's chamber for that interview. The Báb had lovingly helped him, offering to reveal a commentary on the Súrih of Kawthar, the very miracle Siyyid Yahyá had decided upon.[7]

Soon Rahma was able to join other Bábís of Shíráz in their homes to hear the latest messages. His casual first attempts at learning to read had become a dedicated, aggressive need to know. He practiced at every opportunity and was learning so quickly it shocked Kapriel. Rahma's entire intent was on learning letters and words so well that he could read the Báb's tablets and commentaries for himself.

Kapriel worried that his friend would forget to be careful, that he would let the city know of his new allegiance to the Báb. Yes, others were exceedingly brave, or perhaps so filled with the spirit of God that they could not help themselves in speaking of their faith openly. They risked their lives, and those of their families, but so what? They were not Kapriel's friends, and he had just the one.

The seasons passed. Rahma could understand nearly any Persian writing he came across by Naw-Rúz. Meanings still had to be puzzled out with Kapriel, but he had a firm grasp of the letters and told Kapriel he was considering learning Arabic so that he might read the Qur'án. Rahma's father had threatened to throw his son out several times, but Rahma had learned patience, seeing the love of his father and fear for Rahma's well-being behind each threat. The young man had become a new person, as if the Rahma of a year ago were a child, and this Rahma the adult.

Kapriel, however, was becoming short-tempered in his discontent. He could neither deny the Cause of the Báb nor join it and lose his increasingly tenuous connection to his family. His father did not shout, but those sad eyes, watching his son slip away, were far worse to Kapriel. They knew he felt the need to leave, to go someplace where he could make a difference, and be himself, without being stifled by one group or another at each turn.

Nor had he seen Mina in a very long time. She seemed to have disappeared. Rahma would have mentioned a wedding, so she was probably still there, in the second house on the other side of the moon.

Rahma brought word in summer more than two years after the Báb's declaration that the Báb had moved into the house of His uncle, Mírzá Siyyid 'Alí, after bequeathing all of His property to His wife and mother. This was seen as quite portentous to both Rahma and Kapriel. The Báb was apparently preparing for something.

An order of execution prepared by several leading ulámás to rid themselves of the source of this religious plague was thrown out by the Imám Jum'ih, causing further rumors. Husayn Khan, Governor of Fars, was said to be going mad with rage at his inability to kill the Báb. The sháh, his concerns over this religious movement completely eased by the reports of Siyyid Yahyá, had apparently sent a message to the governor to stop behaving badly toward the Báb, rendering the Khan's rage impotent.[8] The insinuations Husayn Khan put forth, the calls to vengeance, the repeated verbal attacks from his seat of governance—all came to little more than occasional upsetting of the populace.

Crowds of seekers, believers, and the curious grew outside the uncle's home. Each night there were more, and toward September they numbered more than those who awaited a hearing each morning outside the governor's citadel.

Kapriel, meanwhile, felt he would burst with the need to be several very different people at once. He desperately wanted to be the good son his parents had envisioned at his birth, attending all church functions and staying within the bounds of their faith, but he also desperately wanted to be out at the home of the Báb's uncle, seeking more sacred verses, approaching the ideal example given by Christ and now seemingly embodied in the Báb. He had also recently turned twenty-three, an age he felt was adequate for moving into an adult life of marriage and children. His savings had accumulated to a point where he could afford to support a wife and modest home. Even if he should decide to become a Muslim, go through all the necessary ceremonies, and prove his new loyalty, it would be up to his and Mina's parents to arrange a marriage—an impossibility. His parents would disown him, destroying any chance of marriage in either religion.

Adding to his difficulty was the fact that nearly two years had passed since he had agreed to accompany Rahma on some great adventure. Were they ever going to go? Was the adventure never to happen? To no one, not even Rahma, could he turn for consolation or support.

His mother worried, fussing over him at every meal. "Eat, son. You need to eat. You're getting so thin!"

"Yes," his father agreed somewhat distantly, "you begin to look like someone who has been ill for a long time. No matter what you plan to do, you will need your energy. You must eat more."

However tempting the food was and encouraging his parents were, his stomach was simply not very interested. It twisted frequently at the innocent mention of many things.

Finally something happened to break Kapriel's slow disintegration. One night, near the end of summer, sometime after midnight, most of the city was awoken by screams and cries of despair, coming from homes all around Shíráz. Kapriel and his parents met in the front room and opened the door just a bit to hear what was happening.

A few men ran through the streets, and the family heard one word: cholera.

An extremely virulent strain had hit, one which killed in mere hours. The screams were from families whose loved ones had fallen ill and died in less than a night.

The Akopians dressed quickly, setting out to check on family before heading to church to pray. They carried bags of boiled water with them to avoid the infested, disgusting water available around the city.

They met Hagop, Kapriel's brother, and his family in the street on the way to his sister Repega's home. Hagop's family was fine, though frightened. They found Repega and her husband at home, weeping quietly over their youngest child, lying in bed covered in sweat and bright red. "He drank from one of the fountains before we could stop him," she sobbed. They spent the next several hours in prayer over him, but the cholera prevailed. By morning they had wrapped him in the white cloth on which he had been lying, built a small casket, and joined the many families slowly carrying deceased loved ones to the fields for burial. Many others were going in other directions, heading rapidly to the nearest road gate with their most precious belongings in hand, fleeing the plague. Some made it safely to other towns, some died on the way, while others carried the plague with them, spreading the devastation.

Shíráz was in chaos. After laying Repega's child to rest, Kapriel went to the Vakíl Bazaar—not for work but to gather news for his family. Word spread of the governor's exit the previous night at first hint of cholera's arrival. Mixed with that news were assertions that at midnight, just before the plague hit, the governor had sent the chief of police to arrest the Báb and anyone with Him. They were to invade the home secretly, entering by the roof. The orders had been carried out, catching the Báb with one disciple who was acting as an amanuensis, but before reaching the governor's citadel with their prisoners, the police chief came across a train of coffins being borne off for burial. The chief hurried to the citadel, finding the governor gone and the household empty. He then reached his own home with his captives, the confiscated papers and policemen in tow, to find his own family wailing in grief.

One policeman whom Kapriel met in the street claimed to have been there. He saw his chief beg the Báb to save his son, who was at the point of death. The chief then repented of his transgressions and resigned his post. The policemen said the Báb, who had started on ablutions to prepare for prayer, gave the water he had used to wash his face and hands to the chief and told him to give it to his son. As the chief watched his son recover, he wrote a letter to Husayn Khan in which he said, "Have pity on yourself as well as on those whom Providence has committed to your care. Should the fury of this plague continue its fatal course, no one in this city, I fear, will by the end of this day have survived the horror of its attack."

The policeman elaborated to Kapriel that the intent of the arrest had been to execute the Báb and anyone with Him to put an end to the Man and Cause so hated by the Governor.

The message was delivered to Husayn Khan at his isolated estate outside the city by this policeman, who immediately brought back the reply, "the Báb should be immediately released and given freedom to go wherever He might please."[9]

The policeman said that the Báb, still at the ex-chief's home, sent His disciple to His uncle's home, requesting said uncle to come to the chief's house. After the uncle's arrival, the Báb informed him of His intention to leave Shíráz, entrusted him with the welfare of His mother and wife, and asked him to give them a message. Part of that message the policeman recalled as, "Wherever they may be, God's all-encompassing love and protection will surround them." And to His uncle He said, "I will again meet you amid the mountains of Adhirbáyján, from whence I will send you forth to obtain the crown of martyrdom. I Myself will follow you, together with one of My loyal disciples, and will join you in the realm of eternity."[10]

The Báb was leaving, Kapriel realized. It was time to fulfill his promise to Rahma. It was time to go.

7

Late September, 1846

The information supplied by the policeman sent Kapriel straight to Rahma's home.

This would be a first for Kapriel. He stood at the door, hand poised to knock. He had never knocked on Rahma's door before, nor even stood in front of it. In twenty years of living two doors away, he had not once felt welcome to do such a thing. He had always met Rahma in the street or bazaar until his friend's recent visits to the Akopians' home. Kapriel fully felt the weight of this moment, the turning of events to something unknown.

He knocked. Prepared to be faced by Rahma's father, enraged and cursing this visitor for daring to stain his door by touching it, Kapriel was instead dumbstruck by the bare face of Mina. She smiled sadly.

"You are here for Rahma?"

"Eh . . . yes." He was having trouble adjusting to this shock.

"I will get him. We lost two nephews and a niece this morning. He is preparing for the funerals."

That brought Kapriel back to himself. "I'm so sorry. We, too, lost a nephew. My sister's youngest son. I would like to send my condolences, but they probably would not appreciate it."

"Probably not, but I do. Thank you, Kapriel. And if you can, please also give my condolences to your sister."

"Thank you . . . Eh, won't you get in trouble for talking to me?"

"Only Rahma and I are home. He cannot bully me, and he will not harm you. "

Kapriel was greatly relieved, though he now began feeling fleas running up and down his back as he imagined her family coming home while he stood there.

"Mina, I have not seen you in a long time. You are well?"

"Yes, thank you, at least for the moment. Only God knows who will live through this plague. And you? You look thin."

Kapriel smiled. "Yes, thank you, I am well. My parents want me to eat more, but, sometimes, it is difficult."

"The Báb is leaving, yes? And you have come to tell Rahma so you can both follow Him?"

"You have heard, then."

"No, we have been busy with the cholera. Rahma has told me of your promise, and nothing less has ever brought you to our door."

Kapriel smiled again, now feeling timid to show all the emotions threatening to overtake him.

Mina, too, sensed their approach to a line not to be crossed as they stood looking at each other. "I have to close the door while I get Rahma."

"All right. It was very good to see you."

"And you, Kapriel."

She shut the door, leaving him on the verge of fainting. He put a hand on the wall next to the door to steady himself. A few moments later his emotions were nearly sorted out when the door was opened with such sudden force it swung in and around to hit the inside of the house wall, adding a loud bang to the surprise.

"You spoke to Mina!"

"Of course I did. She answered the door."

"Did you at least cover your eyes and look away?!"

"No."

"You disgusting son of—"

"Shut up, Rahma! I will not tolerate your temper when I was simply speaking to the one who answered the door! Now, the Báb is leaving. We need to make arrangements and go if you still want to follow Him."

Rahma was going red in the face, attempting to speak but obviously torn between old Rahma and new Rahma. Old Rahma wanted to beat and berate this dog of a Christian for speaking to his saintly sister and looking at her naked face, while new Rahma wanted to practice patience, to be gentle, to listen to his friend before acting.

New Rahma won, finally, and let go of the whole Mina issue for the moment. "You said He is leaving? When?"

"Well, now, today or tomorrow. We will have to buy horses, a donkey, tack, supplies, and tell our families."

"This is not a good time. Three children died, there will be funerals, my family, . . ." Rahma's voice caught.

"We can wait. We know which way to go and we can catch up eventually. You said He sent all the Bábís to Isfáhán."

"I don't know, Kapriel. How can I leave now, but how can I not? Should we talk, tonight, your house?"

Kapriel hesitated, thinking of his own family's needs. "Let's meet out here in the street, an hour after evening Call to Prayer. I don't know how my parents will react to this."

—•—

That settled, Kapriel went home to relay news to his parents. He stood with them in the front room, his mother busy with cleaning to distract herself from the loss of the grandchild, and his father having risen from his seat when the door opened.

They received the news of the governor's flight with disgust. When they heard of the arrest of the Báb, with the intention to execute Him, and His subsequent decision to leave, the senior Akopian said, "You will go, yes?"

Kapriel was again rendered nearly speechless by his father's unex-
pected words. "Well, yes, but the funeral . . ."

His mother interjected, "Never mind the funeral. Repega knows
how much you love your nieces and nephews. This cholera is very
bad. You should go, find someplace safe."

His father added, "Shíráz is killing you, cholera or no. You must
go, find what you are looking for. Find your future."

Tears of gratitude and sadness began to flow down Kapriel's
cheeks, matched by those of both parents. They spent several minutes huddled together in grief and hope, sniffling and finally breaking apart to wipe their faces.

"My son," his father spoke first, "you will need to organize. Two
horses, yes? One for you and another for Rahma? Then a pack
mule. A donkey will not be big enough to carry everything you
need. We will make travel water for you, boiled and cooled with
a little wine added to keep it clean. We must hurry. The people
fleeing the plague may have already taken all the good horses. Go,
buy them now, and bring them back here. You know what to look
for. Do not let go of the ones you choose, or the horse-seller may
switch them for old nags. We will give you some money . . ."

"No, I have plenty to buy the animals and supplies. I'll get that
done now."

He rushed up the stairs to his room to locate the box holding
all he had saved over several years of scribing and drawing. His
father arrived with some small bags to put the money in and hide
it around Kapriel's body under his clothing. "There is no point in
saving all your money if some desperate man steals it on the way to
the caravanserai."

Kapriel was ushered down the stairs out into the alley as his
father spoke. "Now, remember: young horses, but well-trained.
And ride them before you buy. If they move badly and shake your
bones, there is no point in having them. Get saddles that fit the
shape of the horse and plenty of blankets to protect its back."

"Yes, Father. I'll be back as soon as I can."

"Go, quickly!"

There were two caravanserais for Shíráz. One was inside the city walls, east of the Armenian district. The other, larger one was north outside the Isfáhán gate and across the river. Kapriel trotted most of the way to the caravanserai inside the city since it was closer. He passed through the gap between buildings surrounding the livestock pens. As suspected, few animals were left, and those had bleeding sores from ill-fitting equipment and lack of care.

He changed course for the north gate, now walking quickly rather than trotting. It was a bit of a distance for someone on foot in a hurry, through the city center and Isfáhán Gate, across the bridge over the now-dry river, and up the road. That gave him time to think, and worry. He had ridden the family donkey as a child while it walked in circles turning the fruit press. He had also learned grooming and feeding with that small beast, his father having given Kapriel that chore when he was old enough. It had been years ago. He'd never been on a real horse, with a saddle and reins.

The central pen of the northern caravanserai was nearly surrounded by a round brick building holding many alcoves for vendors and rooms to rent. There he found a bit of luck. There were still animals in good shape left. He found the owner at the horse pen negotiating with another customer. Apparently that customer did not have the cash needed, so began cursing the horse's seller, his beard, and his ancestors for charging far too much in a time of crisis.

The herdsman turned his attention to Kapriel, as if the man berating him did not exist. "You have money?"

"How much are you asking? Two horses, good gaits, and one pack mule, all healthy and trained."

The dickering began. It took a while, the offers and counteroffers interspersed with comments for or against particular animals, claims of insult from the herdsman, claims of reassurance and his own unworthiness from Kapriel, condolences from both sides on the calamity taking their city. The negotiations took a hiatus when they were close enough to a deal that Kapriel suggested he ride the horses in question and handle the mule to assure their suitability.

This was quickly accomplished with the herdsman leading the mule over, a solid beast the same size as the horses with few white-haired scars from previous sores. She was reddish with the common buff face, chest, belly, and legs, her long ears lazily following Kapriel's least sound. While he checked her over the herdsman slapped an old saddle on a nice bay gelding, his red body and black ears, mane, tail, and socks showing off sound legs and a broad chest, probably of mostly Arabian heritage.

Satisfied with the mule, Kapriel tied her to a fence and rode the bay. He endeavored to look casually confident, as if he rode frequently and well. In actuality he was fighting back terror at being so high off the ground on an energetic mount. He mounted up and wiggled in the saddle to adjust it and himself, then nudged the bay forward, remembering to grip with his knees and nudge with his heels. It went well, and was even a bit exciting to trot fast enough for his hair to be blown back.

Happy with the gelding's performance, he tied that horse next to the mule while the vendor changed the saddle to the second horse. This one, solid black and beautiful, had a stiff-legged trot fit to smash the bones of any rider, and was immediately rejected. A third horse was saddled, an unusually large mare of a drab brown all over and a rather long, ugly head on a thin neck, typical of the Barb breed. Unbeautiful though she may have been, her gaits were heavenly—smooth and gentle.

All three animals being tied to the fence together, negotiations were quickly finished. Kapriel turned to face a horse for a little privacy when reaching into his inner shirt, removing two of the small money bags, emptying one and greatly reducing the amount in the other into the horseman's hands. The cash disappeared swiftly to some unknown pocket deep in the man's clothing. With a smile, the vendor then moved to take the animals, saying, "I'll put these in the back for you to take when you are ready."

Kapriel put out a hand to stop him gently, "I'm ready now. I'll keep them, thank you for your thoughtfulness."

"But you must buy saddles and things for your journey. Holding the horses will be a burden to you. I will take care of them."

"Thank you, but I will take them now."

"I must insist. How will you check through your purchases and bargain a good price if you are distracted by holding three animals? You are an intelligent young man, I can see it! Go, do your shopping. The beasts will be safe with me."

Ah, the custom of tarof. The offer had been made three times. Kapriel could now accept or reject and the answer would be final.

"You are most kind, but I like these animal very much. I have already become quite attached to their gentle faces and wish to take them with me now."

The herdsman's cajoling expression suddenly changed to rage. He stomped off into the horse pen soundly and loudly cursing Kapriel and all his customer's ancestors, frightening the few remaining animals.

Kapriel untied his new beasts and looked around for the saddle-maker's booth in the alcoves of the caravanserai's building. The nearly empty display of saddles brought him to a group of tradesmen jovially conversing.

"Good morning, young sir," a weathered and well-tanned man greeted him. "Good to see someone finally walk away with the prize."

Not quite sure how to reply, Kapriel simply said, "Thank you."

The weathered man continued, "Mm. Saw those beasts of yours sold at least eight times today. Each time the customer walked away in a panic to get his supplies, and each time he returned to old and peg-legged nags. Ibrahim, the herdsman, will be livid over this for weeks. Those were his best animals. I'm Ahmad, leatherworker and purveyor of fine tack for your fine purchase."

"Nice to meet you, Ahmad. I'm Kapriel. Do you have saddles of the right size and shape for these horses? And, of course, a good pack saddle for the mule that won't give her sores."

"We'll have to see. Been nearly bought out today, what with so many gone crazy to escape the plague. Oh, this is Jamshid, he'll have your basic travel food, dried meat, pots, and such," they nodded to each other, "and here is 'Alí Rezá, who carries the other supplies you'll need, like sleeping rolls, blankets, fire tins, and all that."

Kapriel spent the morning there with the jovial men, checking saddles, padding, and bridles for wear and proper fit, buying bags to go on the pack saddle and filling the bags with food and dry supplies, assuring Jamshid he did not need the bags of water, as he had a supply ready at home.

The vendors occasionally glanced at Kapriel's continued grip on the lead ropes, smiling and continuing their work. Once the horses and mule were tacked up, he tied the brown horse to the saddle of the bay, then tied the mule to the brown. This way he could keep a firm hold on just the lead horse's rope while loading packs and tying on gear. The vendors continued to offer him things, mostly unnecessary now that he had the basics. He took a good look at the animals and their loads, went over the trip in his head to check what he might be missing, and decided to ask his father. They could swing by here on the way out if necessary. At last, he could head back to the city, riding the bay gelding in the lead to get some practice.

Even with the beasts walking single file, it was a tight fit to get them up the alley to his home. Kapriel had to dismount in the previous wider street and lead them in. "How will they get turned around?" Kapriel wondered. They clip-clopped up to the door, which swung open as they arrived. His father stood back, motioning Kapriel to lead the animals through.

"We are going into the house?"

"Only on the way to the yard. Come."

Doorways into homes were barely tall enough for humans to walk through slightly stooped, and usually had a lintel to step over. Would the horses even fit?

Kapriel looked at the doorway, then at the bay. The saddle would have to come off.

"Father, would you hold the brown horse while I take off the saddles?"

"Yes, of course."

The bay balked at being pulled through the small, dark opening. With one man leading the way and encouragement from behind, the horse managed it, brushing both sides against the doorway. The second horse also managed, though actually rubbing the sides with her larger girth. The mule had to be unloaded before being unsaddled, but also managed the strange demand of the humans to follow her equine companions.

All three wandered curiously in the suddenly small yard, tasting of this tree and that bush. They ripped the grass growing between the trees, finding patches to feed on. A large brazier was placed on the patio and filled with water for them.

The next task was for Kapriel to go through all of his belongings, mostly books, and decide what to take. The copies of the Báb's writings, one Bible and one Qur'án, definitely. Something from Hafiz and Sa'dí, yes, but the Sháhnameh?

Somewhere in that decision it struck him that he may not return. Whatever was left behind may never be seen again, books, bed, parents . . . He had been born in this house, had never lived elsewhere, nor spent the night in any bed other than this. Was there an alternative to leaving?

He considered the current situation—his desire to travel, the plague, his promise to Rahma, his family, the winery, prospects for future happiness, the Báb—from many angles, and looked for some other solution, but could find none.

At some point his mother called him to lunch. It was such a simple thing his mother did every day, but this could be the last time he would hear it. He called up all of his determination, set aside this useless melancholy, and went to enjoy one more lunch with his parents.

They did enjoy the meal. Old times were laughed over, Kapriel's youthful escapades were drawn out to his agony and his parents' delight. When the food was gone, his father bought out another money pouch, placing it in Kapriel's hand and telling his son how much was in it, many rials.

"What? I can't take that! It's too much. Please . . ."

"Yes you can, and don't argue, and don't tarof me. We have money hidden all over. You know we could run a palace off the income from the winery. Where do you think the extra goes? You think you have enough, but things can happen. Take this, hide it well. You may be traveling a long time and will need more supplies, rental for rooms, feed for the horses. A horse may die; you may get sick. Do your scribing in every town you can. Try to earn your way without spending this or the rest of your saved money. Even if everything goes well, you may want to settle down sometime, buy a house of your own.

"You did well with the horses. Do as well with your finances. This is all the advice I can give you."

His mother handed him a letter. "This is for your Aunt Marem in Julfa. She will give you and Rahma a room for as long as you are near Isfáhán. And don't forget to eat! You are as thin as a twig! You will need your energy for traveling, so eat all you can."

Kapriel smiled warmly, crinkling his eyes at his mother. "Yes, Khanum," he said respectfully. "Thank you." Turning to his father, he said, "Thank you, Áqá. I don't know what else to say."

"Then go back to packing."

—•—

Kapriel not only packed, but slept for several hours when fatigue overcame him. The day had been so full of emotional swings that he had forgotten the cholera had struck just that morning, not several days ago as it seemed.

Kapriel and his family had dinner at the evening Call to Prayer, finishing in time for Kapriel to meet Rahma, already waiting in the alley.

"Mina said you took horses in your house." Rahma sounded a bit better, more at peace than that morning.

"Well, through the house to the yard. Are you still coming with me?"

Rahma gave a snort. "Now it is me accompanying you? Yes, I will come. My father has kicked me out, disowned me, as I knew he would. So, I have no other place to go anyway. I am to be shunned."

"Oh my God, I am so sorry Rahma! Were you able to pack anything?"

"Mmm. It is all right here." He must have gestured to a bag made invisible in the darkness of the alley.

"Would you mind sleeping in the kitchen? It's warm, and we can put blankets down to soften the floor. The front room is nearly full of saddles and supplies."

"Your family wouldn't mind?"

"Just a moment, I'll check."

Rahma could only see Kapriel's silhouette against the light through the doorway as his friend went inside, returning after just a moment.

"It's alright. Bring your pack in."

Kapriel settled Rahma next to the hearth. This was the same form of hearth used in every home—a ring of bricks a few inches to a foot high that held a fire of wood or coal with a channel for air underneath.[1] Pots were set on the brick edges to cook. There was no chimney or smokestack, just the backdoor and a window to let the smoke out, though sometimes this arrangement allowed a wind coming from the wrong direction to blow the smoke into the rest of the house. The kitchen smelled warmly of eternal fires and food. Cleaned pots and cooking tools hung on the walls. Bags of rice, wheat, spices, dried legumes, and other staples sat on shelves on one wall.

Rahma was content there, mumbling how it was just like his mother's kitchen.

The next morning had a fine, clear sunrise. They were still in the first few days past the autumnal equinox when Rahma and Kapriel began packing. The Akopians' farewells were short once the horses were headed the right way in the alley and all loaded up. Kapriel had promised, "I will write to you from Julfa, and each town where it is possible. Please, give my love to Repega and Hagop and their families. I will write to them, too."

His parents had responded with hugs and waved to them as the young men rode slowly out of the narrow alley. The wider avenues allowed them to ride side-by-side, with the mule in tow behind Kapriel.

The people of Shíráz were adjusting to the plague. A few were still leaving, and they went on foot, pushing a hand cart—if any had been available to buy, borrow, or steal—or carrying packs, trudging to different gates depending on their destination. A steady stream of families bearing aloft caskets large and small headed south and east to the fields. The rest were at home, caring for the ill or hiding from contagion. There was no more panic, but quiet desperation and grief permeated the city.

Rahma and Kapriel were joined by pedestrians carrying or pushing their belongings toward the north gate. They crossed the dry river, passed the Mir Hamza caravanserai where Kapriel had purchased their gear, and Kapriel recited poetry of Hafiz from memory as they passed the poet's shrine. The slope was changing from a slight incline to more steep climbing as they followed the track northeast across one arm of the Zagros mountains that cradled Shíráz. They were passing many on foot who stopped to rest. The horses and mule were working hard, the riders leaning slightly forward in the saddles.

The road ran nearly straight, from the Isfáhán Gate all the way up to the pass at the Qur'án Gate. There the friends rested their mounts as they looked back to Shíráz. Kapriel already felt some discomfort building in muscles unused to the odd leg position and rocking motion of riding.

Rahma, who had been silent since stepping out of the Akopians' home, suddenly quoted Hafiz, "'Sweet Shíráz—gorgeous city of worldly wonder rare, May your spirit never wander, this is my blessing prayer.'"[2]

Next he asked the very question Kapriel had been thinking. "Will we ever see Shíráz again, my friend?"

Kapriel responded quietly, "We will not know that until we return or die."

The city was beautiful, bright and shining in the mid-morning sun. The air was cleaner up here, away from the cooking fires and less palatable smells of any city, but it also smelled strangely empty to Kapriel.

Rahma asked, "When did you get the sword?"

"Sword? What sword?"

"The one with the hilt sticking out of a pack on the mule."

Kapriel looked at the pack mule, now noticing the hilt. "Never saw it before. Must be something father snuck in for emergencies. Is that your club?" He noticed the wooden handle protruding from Rahma's bag, also on the pack mule.

"Yes. I bought it years ago in case I had to fight someone for insulting Mina."

"Ah. Come along. We need to put on a few miles before stopping for the night." Kapriel turned to face forward, nudging his horse to a walk. "Let's go find our future."

8

Isfáhán, Fall 1846

The first difficulty came toward evening. Rahma and Kapriel had ridden down the northeast side of the mountain from the Qur'án Gate while discussing the gate itself. It was a gate with no wall, and it was essentially a very large marker above the road to frame the descent into Shíráz and plains to the southeast. Kapriel pondered aloud about the giant Qur'án held within its topmost room. Rahma assured him that yes, it really was there. An uncle of his mother had seen it himself.

The road meandered down the slope, cutting sharply at switchbacks where the terrain became too steep for gentle curves. The conversation changed as the gate disappeared behind them. Their hearts slowly lightened, looking forward to adventure rather than back to pain.

Sadly, by noon they began to see the bodies of those who had fled the plague not knowing they carried it. The scene silenced the riders. This was not the place for graves, as digging was impossible on the rocky mountainside. Those who did not have animals to carry the bodies had been forced to cover their companions with rocks, perhaps having wrapped them in a blanket first. A few bodies, maybe having fled the city alone, were left where they fell, belongings and all. Few would take anything touched by a plague victim.

By mid-afternoon, they had traveled further down the road and saw bodies only intermittently. Rahma's and Kapriel's moods again lightened, and for the first time, Rahma asked what news Kapriel had learned the day before, other than that the Báb was leaving.

Kapriel told him all the policeman had said. He was able to quote most of the final words of the Báb to His uncle, about Azerbaijan and meeting His uncle in heaven. Together they examined the possible meanings. Martyrdom was fairly obvious, but did the Báb intend to travel to the Azerbaijan of the northwestern-most province, or the Russian territory by the same name on the northwest border of Persia?

At the foot of the mountain, they stopped briefly to unpack some food—both of them moving with some difficulty after the hours of riding—then mounted and munched as they rode on.

Near mid-afternoon, they passed a small town made up of some mud-and-brick homes, with a tall wall surrounding the town and a single gate for access. There was a line of people, some with horses, many on foot, waiting to get into the obviously overwhelmed town. Both Rahma and Kapriel preferred to press on to a less-crowded village.

They snacked in their saddles, sipping from the thinly alcoholic water the Akopians had prepared and packed. Each had a small wineskin hung from the saddle to be refilled from the larger bags on the mule.

There was nothing out here—no towns, no homes, no pastures or tended fields. The very emptiness called them to fill the quiet with sound. They found themselves talking openly, without reservation, of many things they could never have discussed back home—religion, women, clergy, forms of trade, taboos. All the ingrained fears and limitations imposed by their society slowly fell away. Out here, where no one could hear them, they unburdened their hearts.

Except, of course, for the topic of Mina. Neither one brought her up for fear of ruining their excellent mood.

Rahma started to burst into song, one written for a tale of the Arabian Nights, when Kapriel shushed him.

"What, no one is out here. Only you get to appreciate my beautiful voice."

The beauty was dubious, but that was not Kapriel's point. "I don't see any village coming up. The sun is near setting. Up ahead, is that open plain?"

"Oh, God! It is! Did we pass the only village between Shíráz and Persepolis?"

"Why didn't you tell me there was only one?"

"Did I know? I'm a farmer, not a traveling merchant. You are the one always listening to merchants' tales."

"No one mentioned this. It's too far to get back to that town before sunset. What idiots we are! That's why it was so crowded! There is no other place."

Rahma's voice was slightly tremulous as he said, "Well, we will have to camp out here."

"Are you crazy? This is where they capture lions from. And there are wolves, and other scavengers."

"Do not forget the murdering thieves."

"Thank you so much! That is so helpful!"

"Kapriel, you seem a bit cranky. Maybe we should say some prayers, quiet ourselves, and ask for an answer."

Kapriel struggled with himself. He was supposed to be the calm one dealing with Rahma's tantrums. He was also supposed to be the smart one, to have planned the route, the one thing he forgot to do.

Drawing in a deep breath, he apologized. "Sorry. I should have planned this better. The traders must expect everyone to know such basic things as this. Well, you are the country man. Tell me, how do we set up camp?"

"Actually, I just work outside the walls. We never stay outside the city after dark. Things live out here. Everyone goes inside for the night, including farmers. I have heard even tiny villages have walls to protect their people and flocks. I don't know any more about camping than you do."

"Fine . . . .do you know what plants we should avoid camping on?"

"Oh, that I can do. I guess we will make this up as we go. Do we build a big fire to keep back the lions and wolves, but maybe attract the murdering thieves, or have no fire and hope they all leave us alone?"

Kapriel thought a minute before saying, "Maybe some prayers will give us inspiration."

———— ✦ ————

Full darkness was soon kept at bay by a fire just large enough to boil water. They found a place used previously as a campsite, with a ring of stones for a fire and dead wood under one of the few trees. The dismounts were painfully slow and clumsy, with Kapriel's legs collapsing on contact with the ground. Dried grass made good tinder, catching fire quickly from the sparks of the striker and flint that came in the fire tin Kapriel had bought the day before.

They had to unsaddle their horses and mule to let their mounts' skin breathe and prevent sores, though it worried Kapriel. If something happened, they would have no time to saddle up and pack.

The horses also had to eat. They had stopped just short of the dry, nearly-barren plains of Persepolis. There was enough grass to feed the animals tonight. They were tied on lines rather than hobbled, giving the mounts greater mobility to defend themselves if necessary while keeping them close. Whoever was on watch would move the deep stake with the lines progressively around the campsite.

They put water, dried meat, lentils, and a few spices into a small pot, setting it on the ring of rocks to boil. Soon they had a good, filling, hot dinner.

They agreed to sleep in turns, Rahma going first. Kapriel let Rahma sleep until well past midnight, reading from Qur'án and Bible, referring back and forth to understand their relationship better, while occasionally feeding the fire and moving the stake. Nothing happened, not even a distant roar.

Rahma took over for the rest of the night, waking Kapriel as the sky began to lighten. He was silently pointing at something farther out on the plain to the east. Sitting up, Kapriel nearly moaned out loud from the stiffness of his body, which had seized up while he slept. He held the moan in and looked where Rahma pointed. A pride of lions lounged well away in the ruins, paying no attention to them at all. Kapriel realized the fire was out, the gathered wood having been used up, so they had no protection should the lions choose to notice them.

Then the wind lightly ruffled his hair, coming from the north. It blew the scents of lions and horses to neither set of noses.

"That's good. We should eat breakfast and rest until more people come. When we see movement to the west, we can pack up and be ready by the time they arrive."

Rahma agreed, "Just what I was thinking. Except we should do prayers, not just rest."

"You are beginning to sound like my parents."

"Is that a problem?"

Kapriel considered. "Not yet."

"Good." Rahma unpacked a prayer rug, oriented himself to face Mecca, and began his devotions.

Kapriel felt suddenly pressured, just as his parents had constantly pushed him to be religious their way. A rebellion inside him sparked anew—against religion, prayer, and God in general. He wanted to be free of such controls and constraints. The more rational part of him realized this feeling was silly, and he forced himself to go along with Rahma's plan.

The sun had not yet passed the mid-morning mark when they were able to join a group of riders—those riders refreshed from a safe night in the crowded village—to pass through the ancient city of Persepolis. They all marveled at the history they were riding through—Persepolis itself, the home of Darius. The ruins of the ancient city protruded like bones from the sands. Kapriel wondered how close they were to Pasardagae, the home of Cyrus the Great, and thought they might be able to see his tomb in the distance. Shíráz held a lot of history and art, but this was ancient! This was the seat of the Persian Empire nearly two and a half thousand years ago, which ruled lands far more vast than the sháhs of Kapriel's lifetime.

The friends stayed with this group all the way to Isfáhán, stopping with the others at villages or prepared rest areas every night, wanting never again to risk camping outside protective walls. They crossed the plains and followed a river upstream to the northeast for a few days, then left the stream behind to turn more northerly across a mountain into a long, wide valley between dry, baked foothills. The hills were the eastern flank of the Zagros mountains, the distant hills to their right hiding the central deserts of Persia on the other side.

Occasionally, someone would point to or remark on bones protruding from the track. These were the remains of beasts of burden stuck in mire when winter and spring rains turned the track into deep mud. Once an animal was exhausted from struggling, the owners would either reapportion its load to other overburdened animals or simply dump the load and leave the stuck animal to die.[1]

Rahma commented gratefully that the fall rains had not begun, meaning the road was dry and solid. Both friends were slowly getting used to the saddles over the days, and their muscles were becoming accustomed to riding.

The weather cooled with the slightly higher altitude, and the progression northward brought a definite chill, especially when the wind came from the north. Warmer clothing and heavier cloaks were unpacked or traded for in the next town or walled rest area. Occasionally, they would pass a caravan going south—long lines of donkeys, mules, and camels loaded with goods from around the world, with the traders usually on horses and the drovers on foot. The leaders of the pack train would be informed of the plague in Shíráz and left to argue over continuing or turning back.

The walls of Isfáhán came into view late one day after more than three hundred miles and two weeks of riding. The day was fading fast. The friends bade farewell to their fellow travelers and agreed to find Aunt Marem's home in Julfa to rest for the night before seeking the Báb or exploring the Armenian town. They wound their way southeast from the southern entrance gate of Isfáhán down to Julfa. This was a town built by Sháh Abbás about two hundred years earlier to house the Armenians he was displacing from their native land.

They asked for directions from random men several times in the growing darkness, finally finding a door to knock on. They rapidly explained their presence to an affronted Armenian man who did not appreciate two unknown men, two horses, and a mule on his doorstep at nightfall. Kapriel internally slapped his own head and handed over the letter from his mother.

With that, the situation smoothed out nicely. They were invited to unload their animals and place their belongings into the small bedroom they would be using. Once inside Kapriel, met his extended family, introducing them to Rahma. He had a cousin, Alexan, perhaps a year younger than himself, who led the horses and mule off to arrange their care at the nearest caravanserai—one owned by a relative who would ensure that their animals would not be switched for nags. His uncle was named Hovnan. Other relatives were noted as living nearby, but Aunt Marem put her foot down on further exhausting the young men and forcing them to meet more family that night.

After a wonderful, hot dinner it was necessary for Kapriel to spend several hours with these three relatives he had only heard of through letters to his mother. He updated them on his nieces and nephews, what events were happening at the church in Shíráz, and then the general news of the upstart Bábí religion and sudden cholera attack.

His aunt and uncle reciprocated by updating him on the New Julfa family branch, and they told him not only did they know of the Báb but knew He had arrived the day before. He was staying at the home of Isfáhán's Imám-Jumih.

Kapriel imagined Rahma's joy at hearing that news in the morning. His friend had gone to their room to check on supplies to be replaced in the morning, but he had not returned. Kapriel was sure Rahma had fallen asleep shortly after entering their room, supplies unchecked.

—◦—

Morning came too soon for Kapriel. Rahma woke well-rested and ready to start searching for other Bábís. Their hosts warned him that if Rahma became known by the city people as a Bábí, they would have to ask him to find other accommodations. He would not be allowed to put their family and the Armenian community at risk.

Rahma understood, offering to find a room at a caravanserai until the Báb moved on, as they knew He would. Kapriel would stay with his family and keep the supplies ready until Rahma came for him.

They shared a delicious breakfast with the family, then Rahma went off on his way, and Kapriel's uncle gave his nephew a guided tour of New Julfa.

The air was more humid this morning, a light rain having fallen overnight signaling the start of the wet season. Kapriel was captivated by this small city. Everywhere he looked were Christians. They were not cursed or shunned by resident Muslims since there were no resident Muslims. The women were well-dressed from head to fingers to toes, but they rarely wore a veil. None was covered by acres of black or white cloth obscuring their shape.

He stared open-mouthed at the Vank Cathedral. It was huge and beautiful. It made the church at home look like a nicely decorated closet. The outside was graceful brickwork, and the inside was covered in murals depicting moments in the life of saints.

The people here—his people—were happy. He had not expected that. His uncle explained that they ran New Julfa themselves, under the dictates of the sháh but no others. As long as they did nothing stupid, such as foment rebellion, they were protected.

He also learned more history of the Armenians in Persia. His father had told him of the Dutch East Indies Company and the Armenian traders who caused great pain to the English trading companies. The young colonists in Julfa back in the 1600s had quickly learned what raw materials were available and, being natural craftsman, had begun turning those materials into works of art. They then took this art, and that of Isfáhán, to other cities, moving out over the decades to establish markets as far as England, Holland, and Moscow.

The family took him along that evening to a Saint's Feast. There were so many people! Several girls flirted lightly with him, causing him to blush deeply each time. His cousin doubled over in gales of laughter after the third incident. Kapriel felt like an ignorant bumpkin from a village so small it had no name. He supposed that was what the Armenian District of Shíráz was. His aunt and uncle ran interference for him the rest of the night, keeping the admiring and curious young ladies a small distance away.

There was much to consider that night as he prepared for sleep—the town, the history he had learned of Armenians in Persia, like the one who interpreted between the leader of the invading Afghans and Sháh Sultán Hossein in 1721. The sháh surrendered in a futile attempt to save Isfáhán, then the capitol of Persia, from slaughter, and the Armenian interpreter had reported later on the words of both the sháh and Afghan leader.[2] However, Kapriel's tired body made him lie down, and his mind suddenly went silent for the night.

—•—

The first letter to his parents was done soon after sunrise, including notes to his brother and sister. Uncle Hovnan had already left for work: One day off had been enough to orient his nephew. Kapriel asked his aunt where to go to find the couriers' office.

It would be frivolous and expensive to send a personal messenger all the way back to Shíráz with a letter, but for the right price, a letter could be added to a packet going out with the next south-bound courier. The couriers were primarily for government use, not private citizens, so such postings would also be expensive.[3] Aunt Marem suggested an Armenian merchant who would soon be leaving on his usual route through Shíráz to Bushíhr.

Kapriel found the traveling merchant at the caravanserai Aunt Marem had mentioned. The man was glad to take Kapriel's letter, with a small contribution to pay for a messenger once they reached the right city. He also warned that it could be a while before the plague quieted enough to allow the caravans safe passage.

Next the scribe wandered the street looking for a likely place to set up his occupation. His uncle had suggested a particular market street near the center of Julfa.

He found a likely spot and asked where to find the market manager to pay rental. The vendor he spoke to informed him that they had a different system here. The vendor owned his own shop, and Kapriel could pay him a few dinars (pennies) a week to sit outside it. The shop owner would even loan him a chair, since the streets would soon be too cold to sit on.

The townspeople were happy to employ Kapriel for their scribing needs. Many of them spoke some Persian, but very few could read or write in that language or in Arabic. He was soon known as the man to go to for complex translations.

His father's words of financial advice were put into practice when his savings had rebuilt enough to pay rent for his room. Aunt Marem would not consider it, but Uncle Hovnan understood Kapriel's need to pay his own way. He also spent a happy hour in a clothier buying two real Armenian outfits, just like the other town residents.

The traveling supplies were replenished, the horses and mule happy and well-fed in the caravanserai. Weeks passed with no word from Rahma. It was odd for Kapriel, living in such a calm place and without any way to contact his companion or the Bábís to get news.

Cousin Alexan worked for an Armenian trader in Isfáhán, and he appreciated opportunities to repeat information gleaned during the usual jocular transactions with customers. Sadly, the news was of growing turbulence in the city as once again Bábís and seekers crowded in from all corners of Persia, to the dismay and outrage of the majority of 'ulámá (clergymen).

Five weeks after Kapriel's arrival, Alexan reported, "People are coming from all provinces and even from Iráq to see this Báb. The 'ulámá are upset and openly plot against him. The crowds outside the home of the Imám-Jumih are making them deeply jealous. They call him unkind things, say he is unlettered and cannot be who he claims to be. However, many have seen tablets and epistles he has written in his own hand, so I don't see how he can be unlettered."

Kapriel explained, "They do not actually mean illiterate. The Báb has attended no religious schools, so they believe he can have no knowledge of the intricate meanings in the Qur'án."

"From what I heard, he can explain things the 'ulámá cannot even understand. One customer said he was there when the Báb wrote out and chanted over fifty pages of those intricate verses in only two hours, and in clear writing, without stopping to think or needing to make corrections."[4]

He stopped to inhale a few more bites as many young men do before adding, "The people flocking to Him are not just there for religious insight. They ask for advice and judgments, which are usually the territory of the 'ulámá."

Kapriel pondered a moment before responding. "The clergy must feel threatened. They have to see that their positions as leaders would disappear if this movement is successful. They have to undermine the Báb to save themselves. The easiest way to do that is to claim He is subverting Islám. This nation is Muslim, and to take people out of Islám is to upset the whole system. If the Muslim leaders have no Muslims to lead, what will they do?"

Uncle Hovnan quietly stated, "Praised be God we have our own town, and do not have to be part of this. May our Lord and Savior watch over Julfa, and protect the innocent from the machinations of the evil-doers."

Several "amens" sounded around the room.

— · —

Less than a week later (late October), Alexan brought more news. The Báb had been moved to the home of the Mu'tamid, governor of the Isfáhán province, to protect Him from the 'ulámá plotting against Him.

On Kapriel's next visit to the caravanserai to check on the horses and mule there was definite dampness to the ground away from cobbles and tiles. Several more light rains had passed through. He had a happy surprise awaiting him at the horse pen in the center of the caravanserai. Rahma was there, already looking their charges over.

"Kapriel!"

"Rahma!"

They gave each other a sound hug with a few back slaps. Rahma was full of news: "I have a room here, that one three from the end." He pointed to the third archway from the southeast corner. "Twice I have seen you and not been able to get here before you left. Tell me, how are you? You look as if you are eating well now."

Kapriel laughed. "Yes, I am eating well now. You have not been to visit. Why?"

"As your uncle said, it is dangerous. I do not want to be the cause of violence in your peaceful town. I took this room hoping to catch you. I found work at a farm just over there," he pointed to the southwest. "It is not much pay, just enough for renting this room, but they feed me well. You, I am sure, are earning plenty of money making squiggly lines on paper, yes?"

"Well, some."

"Enough to buy that fine suit, eh? You make it look good!"

Kapriel had never heard such a compliment and nearly blushed. "Thank you! And you look fit and happy."

"The farm life is good!"

"So, now that you can read, do you want to learn to write?"

"Writing! Well, what would I do with it? No, I am happy with reading. Very happy. Some of the Bábís are making copies of the Báb's new writings for everyone, so there is always more to read."

"That's wonderful, Rahma!" Kapriel truly meant it, but part of him was a tad jealous, or maybe disappointed that his friend was no longer dependent on him. "Could I get a copy to read myself?"

"Of course! I will get them and you can pick them up here. Now, have they found you a wife yet?"

Kapriel gasped and then choked on his own saliva. Rahma pounded on his back hard enough to leave bruises. Shortly he managed to croak out, "Hate it when that happens." He cleared his throat several times as Rahma smiled widely in an effort not to laugh.

"No, they have not," Kapriel eventually said. "It doesn't look as if we'll be here that long. What about you? Any Bábís introduced you to their daughters?"

Rahma had been at the edge of a sneeze and then inhaled to snort, confusing the sneeze into a series of half coughs. He finally opened his eyes to see Kapriel chuckling in great amusement.

"Fine. I deserve that. No, they do not know me well, and I have no family."

Kapriel's smile fell. "Sorry, I did not mean to remind you of that."

"No, do not be sad. This is not the time for romance. Maybe later. I have decided I want a woman who will stand up for her belief like the men do. So I will find her myself, if she exists, in the Bábí meetings."

"So you are at least keeping open the possibility."

"Yes, exactly. Maybe you should, too." Rahma said these last words while looking around the caravanserai, not meeting Kapriel's eyes for a few moments.

"Why, if we might leave soon?"

"Kapriel, you are my friend. I would see you happy, and there is a better chance for that here in Julfa than back in Shíráz. Many Armenian women, yes?"

Kapriel paused, experiencing an oddly protective moment, wishing Rahma complete ignorance of Armenian women. *How very Muslim,* he thought to himself. "You know, we divide ourselves up by religion far too much in this country."

Rahma answered sadly, "Maybe so, but that is the way it is."

"Maybe someday that will change."

Rahma gave Kapriel a measuring look, keeping his thoughts to himself. He asked, "Are you busy Friday? We can meet here again. Since I do not have to attend mosque, I do prayers in my room."

"I would like that."

They passed a few more minutes amiably before heading back to their individual destinations.

—•—

Kapriel pondered their conversation on the walk home. Maybe he should have an open mind. Mina was even more unavailable now. She seemed to like him, or she would have grabbed a veil at their last meeting. Did it matter? If they were able to admit deep, eternal love for each other they would be killed for it, executed before they could escape Shíráz.

Maybe it was time to bow to the inevitable—either find a new prospect or give up thoughts of marriage.

He consulted his Uncle Hovnan, a man of reason and wisdom Kapriel thought highly of. The question presented was whether or not to initiate such a search in light of the possibility of leaving. As hoped, his uncle had a simple, clear response: "If you find a wife, stay. If not, go, stay, whatever path God leads you to."

This gave him something to contemplate as he worked up his courage over the next few weeks. Meanwhile he kept up his Friday meetings with Rahma, catching up on news of the Bábís and farming.

One of these times, Kapriel looked out from Rahma's apartment at light snow swirling across the ground. "It is nearly winter. What is it you do out on that farm when nothing is growing?"

"Actually, we plant wheat, so that it will be ready for warmer weather and will absorb the winter and spring rains fully. There are other preparations to make, such as repairing walls, cutting back fruit and nut trees, all that. They have maybe another two weeks of work for me. And you, do you still sit out in the cold, hoping your ink will not freeze?"

With a soft laugh Kapriel told him, "No, fortunately. The owner of the shop I sat in front of has invited me inside, to the front corner. Customers who come looking for me often also buy something from him, so now he lets me work there for free."

"Ah, nice for you! Keeping that skinny frame out of the wind."

"I have put on weight, you know."

They joked with each other the way normal friends do, further erasing the lines drawn between them as children.

The snow did not accumulate, except a small amount in corners and on the leeward side of trees and buildings. Late in the afternoon, the clouds cleared off, and the tiny amount of snow melted.

The next day Kapriel was fairly warm in the shop where he worked. It was unheated, as were most shops and homes. He just bundled up for the day, getting up at least once an hour to generate heat with movement. Near noon, a very young man in Persian garb burst into the shop, babbling in the national language while looking frantically at Kapriel.

The shop owner began to throw the crazy boy out when Kapriel said in Armenian, "No, wait. He said my friend is hurt and needs a doctor."

He then turned to the intruder, saying in Persian, "Please, you say Rahma is hurt. How badly? Where? What happened?"

"Badly, at my father's farm. His leg, it is broken. We cannot move him! Do you have a doctor?"

Kapriel translated for the shop owner, who answered, "Yes. His name is Asdvadzadour. He is across the street and to the right, three doors down. I'll go get him. Don't let that boy touch anything!" He hurried through the door and sprinted to the doctor's place.

"What's your name?" Kapriel asked the Persian teen.

"Parvíz."

"Good. Parvíz, do you know where we can borrow a cart? It needs to be horse-drawn if it is a long way, or a hand cart if close."

"We have a hand cart at the farm. It's not too far."

The shop owner quickly returned with Dr. Asdvadzadour, introducing him to Kapriel. Kapriel asked the shop owner, "Please, would you tell my Uncle Hovnan what has happened and ask if we may use my room?"

"Yes, of course, right away."

The doctor and Kapriel headed out, following Parvíz at a light jog. The doctor was on the young side—maybe thirty—and Armenian. He carried a large bag that was slung over one shoulder and which bounced heavily against him as they hurried.

It took only a quarter of an hour to get there. Parvíz took them straight to Rahma, who was lying on the ground under a large, bare tree. He looked terribly pale and frightened. One leg was bent in the middle of the shin.

When he saw Kapriel, he screamed praises to God in a tense, broken voice. "Thanks to God, Muhammad, and all the Imáms! I'm dying! Kapriel, take my things to my family—"

The doctor cut him off in broken Persian, "Quiet you. Lay still you. No move you." He turned to Kapriel, "We will need that cart. He will have to stay indoors and warm for two months or more. Now, we need sticks, about five of them, this big," he gestured, "to hold his leg still while we move him. Does he use alcohol?"

"Yes!" Kapriel then translated and sent the two farm boys—the younger being an exact duplicate of Parvíz—to fetch the sticks. He watched the doctor dig in his bag, pull out a bottle of brandy, and tell Rahma to drink as much as he could.

Not knowing Rahma as Kapriel did, the doctor was surprised at the swiftness with which the brandy was going down Rahma's throat. The doctor grabbed the bottle, tipping it upright as he took it from Rahma's grip. "That's quite enough for now. Well done." He had forgotten to speak in his pidgin Persian, so Kapriel translated, adding a few words of humorous admonition.

Rahma retorted to Kapriel, "Go burn your own beard!"

The brandy went to work relaxing muscles and minimizing Rahma's awareness. In a few minutes, the doctor was able to cut open Rahma's pant leg to reveal the shin, a small tip of broken bone protruding from it. He immediately splashed some brandy on it, causing a small scream to come from Rahma. The doctor ignored him, placing folded cloth over the bone tip and pouring more brandy.

"Now that you are paying attention," he looked at Rahma but spoke Armenian, "tell me if any other place hurts."

Kapriel translated.

Rahma, panting with the effort to restrain further screaming, looked daggers at the doctor and, with a hearty voice, said, "Yes, you Armenian sadist. My left arm, around the wrist."

"Thank you, Kapriel, no need to translate. I understood every word." He smiled brightly, having been cursed far worse by most Muslims and even by Armenians. "I can see why you are friends. He's funny!"

Kapriel choked back a laugh, letting Rahma know what was said.

"Funny, am I? You!" he shouted to Kapriel. "Is this doctor any good?!"

Again, Kapriel only had to translate one way since the doctor understood Rahma. "He says yes, quite good. He studied in France for several years, and now he's home."*

Rahma's eyes widened with new respect and the hope that he might live. However, he renewed his dagger aspect when Dr. Asdvadzadour checked his arm.

"The radius is cracked, maybe broken."

"Radius?" Kapriel asked.

"The long bone on the thumb side of the forearm."

The farm boys returned with gathered sticks they had quickly scraped free of bark and smoothed.

"Nicely done!" the doctor complimented. "Now, how drunk is he?"

---

* It is interesting to note that around the year 1000 A.D., Muslim doctors were greatly preferred by soldiers in the Crusades, since European doctors were still attempting to cure with leeches, bleedings, and amputations compared to the Muslim's more educated and patient medicine emphasizing cleanliness. During the 1800s, the preference was switching, with European medicine having advanced greatly and surpassing that of the Middle East.

Rahma was pleasantly sloshed. He could still look angry, but his focus was off, with his eyes and head rolling randomly. The doctor checked his muscle tension, finding it loose and stretchy. He tied the sticks around the upper portion of the shin above the break and extending to the ankle, placed so as to leave the open wound reachable for further treatment. Next he placed two loops of rope around the ankle with the lengths coming off on opposite sides of the leg. He explained the procedure to Kapriel.

They would have to pull the ropes with equal pressure straight out from Rahma's hips to pull the bones back into place, then hold perfectly still while he tied the splint sticks around the break and the lower shin. He said if this did not work, or had to be done twice, Rahma could be crippled.

Thus informed and warned, they began.

9

Julfa and Isfáhán,
Winter 1846 to Spring 1847

There was a great deal of screaming as the doctor, farm boys, and Kapriel attempted to put Rahma's leg back together. Only some of the screams came from Rahma. He was a big man, while the rest were average. The two farm boys, maybe fifteen and seventeen, pulled with all their might while Kapriel held down Rahma's thigh and the doctor worked his magic with the splints.

Rahma screamed with pain, the boys screamed with effort, Kapriel screamed in sympathy, and the doctor calmly screamed at them all to "Shut up!"

They were all relieved when the last knot was tied, the ropes slowly relaxed, and the bones stayed in place. Rahma fainted, allowing his arm to be tended to with no fuss at all. The arm was splinted from hand to above the elbow to keep the bones still, then well-wrapped with cloth as further restraint.

The farmer had left before the bones were set, claiming he had to retrieve the cart. Once the screaming was done he reappeared, pushing the cart ahead of himself and stopping right next to Rahma.

When their patient came back to the present, they got him up on his good leg, and the three men worked hard to maneuver him onto the cart. They wrapped him in all the blankets and coats the farm family had available. Dr. Asdvadzadour told Kapriel he would walk back to Uncle Hovnan's with him and that, when the alcohol wore off a bit, he would give Rahma some opium for the pain.

"Why didn't you give it to him right off?"

"If he had had enough opium to dull the pain of the straightening, he would have been a lump of loose flesh, unable to hold himself up. Could you have put him in the cart?"

"Ah, good point." Kapriel reached to the cart handles to begin the walk home, but Parvíz, much more muscular than a city scribe, excused himself and pushed in front, taking the handles. Kapriel decided this was exactly the type of situation where a Persian would expect tarof and be insulted if Kapriel just said, "Fine," so he insisted on pushing the cart. They went back and forth three times for custom to be honored, and then the young man happily started them forward.

Back in New Julfa, the doctor stayed with the cart and let Kapriel run ahead to be sure his family would not mind having an injured patient for a while. Upon entering the home, he got as far as, "Is it all right—" when Aunt Marem cut him off with a dismissive wave.

"Of course it is. Go find some rocks, the size of both fists together. Hurry!"

Having no idea what the rocks were for, he ran back outside and to the nearest unpaved area at the edge of town. He gathered as many approximately two-fist-size rocks as he could carry and hurried back with his load. Taking a bag along would have been a good idea, Kapriel mused, but such is life.

The cart was empty in the street. Parvíz, the doctor, and Uncle Hovnan were helping Rahma hop to Kapriel's room as he arrived with the rocks. Aunt Marem immediately redirected Kapriel to the kitchen where she helped him put the rocks around the edge of the fire pit.

Now he understood. Warming rocks, enough to have half on Rahma while the other half warmed in the kitchen. Unburdened, Kapriel rushed back to his room to find Rahma lying down on several stacked mats, piles of blankets being tucked around him.

A large cup of steaming tea was carried in by Aunt Marem, and gratefully taken by Rahma who sat up with help and freed his arms from the blankets, momentarily confused as to how he would use the padded hand.

Parvíz said his goodbyes, gathered his family's blankets and cloaks, then left for home with the cart.

The doctor gave Rahma his first dose of opium, then gave Kapriel and Aunt Marem specific instructions for its administration. He casually remarked, "You know, Isfáhán grows the best opium in the world. Doctors in many places seek our poppy crops for the most pure opium, which makes the best morphine." He looked at Rahma, "You are quite lucky, you know." Then he promised to return the next afternoon to check on the patient.

Soon the rocks were warm enough to wrap in clean rags and place against Rahma's sleeping form inside the blankets. Aunt Marem remarked their patient would need all his energy for healing, so they would have to keep him from getting cold. The front door was busy with Uncle Hovnan accepting gifts of food and putting them in the backyard to keep in the cold weather.

Kapriel asked his aunt, "Where did all the mats come from, and the food and extra blankets?"

"When Ardag the shopkeeper told us what happened, we told the neighborhood women, and they told more, and we gathered most of what we would need from many homes."

"Did they know it was for a Muslim?"

"Yes, of course. We are Christians. Our compassion does not stop at the church door." She gazed at Kapriel a moment, watching him struggle for something to say.

She understood. "Life in Shíráz is difficult, yes? You are now perhaps seeing just how difficult."

Her nephew was overwhelmed by too many thoughts and emotions. They sat watch over Rahma for a while before he could say, "In Shíráz we do not help Muslims out of charity. Those who do would be accused of contaminating the one helped, of putting our dirty hands on him. Most Christians hate the Muslims as much as the Muslims hate them. And the Jews, well, they are shoved down even lower than Christians. My parents could barely stand to have Rahma in the house. They got used to him, but never would they have done all this. He would have been left for the Muslims to take care of, and without family he would have died in the street, like other crippled beggars. And farmers there would die before going into the Armenian district for a doctor."

Marem thought a few moments before responding. "When your mother, my sister, has been able to send letters, she has included news about you, and worries. Now I see why she has feared for you so much. God has given you the gift to see beyond what you are taught. In that place where each person is right and all others are wrong, where a silent war goes on between Muslims and everyone else, you chose Rahma as your friend. You saw past all the things you were told to see, and found the good heart hidden in that Muslim child.

"And here you are, in Julfa, able to live the things you believed long ago."

Kapriel smiled ruefully, "Almost, anyway."

"I know, you want to see all people mingling together in perfect contentment, but it seems the rest of us are not yet ready for that."

Kapriel left later to pack up Rahma's belongings in the caravanserai and, if needed, to pay for his room.

—◆—

The doctor arrived as promised the next afternoon. He checked the splints on leg and arm, noting the swelling of the leg. That worried him a bit. He checked for feeling in the toes and fingers before nodding.

"If the swelling gets too bad, the splints will cause the blood to stop flowing, and he will lose the leg. Keep the covers off of it and

see if cooler air will help." Rahma watched groggily, not understanding Armenian and having difficulty paying attention under
the effects of the opium.

Checking the wound, the doctor said, "No signs of infection,
yet, and no fever. Fever and swelling are the two things we have to
watch for in the next few days. If we can get him through that, and
he keeps still for long enough, he will be fine."

Rahma spoke up, "You are all smiling. Is it okay? Will I live?"

Kapriel passed along the doctor's words.

Rahma asked, "And how do I thank the good doctor . . . what
is his name?"

Kapriel slowly intoned, "Asdvadzadour."

"Oh my God. I can't say that. What is his first name?"

"That is his first name."

"What is his last name?"

"Worse."

"Oh my God!"

The doctor interrupted, laughing, to say in rough Persian, "You
call me Zadour. That good?"

"Thank you. Yes. Very much I thank you. Dr. Zadour." And he
faded back to sleep.

Several days later, the swelling had eased, and no infection had
appeared. All looked good, if they could keep Rahma still. He was
wanting to get up and move around, and especially to have a bit
of privacy during use of the chamber pot. Dr. Zadour, however,
absolutely forbade it, for at least three weeks.

Kapriel paid the doctor, not wanting to worry Rahma with
financial difficulties just then. He also went with Aunt Marem to
thank each family who had sent supplies or food.

That night at the family meal, Alexan brought news from
Isfáhán, as usual. This time, however, the news was different.

"The Báb is gone. Escorted to Tehrán by a hundred of the governor's men. Seemed more to keep the Báb safe than thinking he
would give them any trouble.

"The guy said all seventy-some mullás of the city, or all but two actually, signed this death warrant for the Báb.[1] Want him gone forever, and maybe the Bábís will give up and go back to being Muslims."

Uncle Hovnan asked, "Where did he hear this?"

"Claims he saw the document himself. Works in the house of the governor. Of course the Báb was living in the governor's home, so he—the governor—was supposed to hand him over for execution. Sent him away instead."

Uncle Hovnan became curious. "Isn't this . . . religion thing supposed to be a reform? Are the Bábís not still Muslims, just as Sufís or Shía are still Muslims?"

Alexan simply shrugged.

Kapriel answered, "There is debate. Some say it is a new religion, some say reform. Could be either. One history book I read had a section on a Martin Luther, who began a reform movement of Catholicism to eliminate corruption in the Church. The Lutherans were attacked on all sides by Catholics who couldn't stand what they saw as rebellion and an attack on the state religion."

Several heads nodded with comprehension.

"I think," Uncle Hovnan began, "I would not have liked to live at the time of Martin Luther."

"Too bloody?" Alexan wondered.

"Too hard to decide. Stay with mother Church, imperfections and all, or go with a reform. Heartbreak either way," Hovnan replied. He turned to Kapriel, "So, it is time for you to continue your journey, but your companion cannot move. What will you do?"

"Not tell him, I think. He tends to be a bit fanatical." Several pairs of eyes rolled as if to say, 'of course he is, he's Persian!', and Kapriel smothered a laugh at the family trait. "I might tell him in a month or two, when the doctor says it's OK to ride."

A week after the accident Kapriel was able to go back to scribing, though only for half days. He didn't wish to burden his aunt with care of his friend.

Dr. Zadour weaned Rahma off of the morphine slowly, explaining that sudden withdrawal could do him as much harm as the broken leg. Rahma healed impatiently, acting polite to excess with Kapriel's family, but raising his voice frequently with Kapriel in his frustration at captivity and withdrawal from the drug. He noted the beginning of the month of Ramadan, doing what he could of his prayers and a little fasting.

Kapriel, in turn, participated in the grand Christmas festivities. He even took Rahma's suggestion of open-mindedness toward the women of Julfa. He happily met quite a few young women over the next few weeks, whether at Church functions or in the market with their families. While they were all intelligent and beautiful in one way or another, none captured his interest for more than a moment. He sadly resolved to be single, celibate, and childless for life.

Two months after Rahma's fall, the splint on his arm came off. He was not allowed to use it but had to begin stretching and moving before the joints stiffened permanently. He was also allowed to move his toes and ankle, but the leg splint stayed on. Two large crutches brought by Dr. Zadour gave Rahma the ability to range further, to take care of his own hygiene, and to join the family for meals. The crutch on his injured side had to be held with his armpit and elbow to prevent overworking the freshly released arm.

He gained in strength day by day, pushing to regain the abilities he had lost. Tendons and muscles that had contracted under the splints did not return to suppleness quickly. Much of his great strength had dissipated in his confinement. He was forced by circumstances to exercise the patience so recently learned and reinforced by the words of the Báb.

Kapriel spent his time doing what scribing he could while helping Rahma and occasionally exercising the horses and mule (and his riding muscles). He was able to work most mornings and afternoons, making the short walk home to play nurse at noon.

The time finally came when Kapriel felt he could give Rahma all the news Alexan had been bringing home about the Báb and His followers. He had to hush Rahma several times when he interrupted with anxious questions.

"Yes, the Bábís are fine. They were terribly upset, near hysteria when it first happened. All sorts of rumors were tossed about the city: The Báb was going to be executed, they were torturing Him, He escaped, He was killed by bandits, anything creative minds could come up with. Since then, a few of the Bábís have calmed their fellows, claiming their leader is safe, somewhere. There has been no news of the Báb, at all, from anywhere, since He was escorted to Tihrán. If anything had happened—well, you know the Persian news system."

Kapriel continued, "As it stands, nothing at all is known. When you are completely healed, you can contact your fellows and see if they have heard any definite word of Him."

"I could go now! I have the crutches."

"Ah. Well, there is that issue of not involving Julfa in the struggle. You know what a precarious position we are in. There is too much good here to risk it."

Rahma was downcast. Every possible avenue of obtaining the information before he was healed involved at least some risk of bringing the wrath of the 'ulámá down on the Armenians. No Armenian could investigate, and Rahma had to sleep here until he could find work and take a room elsewhere. No, he saw the inevitability of it. He had to wait.

Taking a deep breath, he quoted Hafiz to Kapriel, "'I spin the wheel of life but if it turns not my way, I will not be weakened by the fates of Heaven and Earth.'"[2]

———

A couple of weeks before Naw-Rúz, Alexan brought home more important news from Isfáhán.* The mu'tamid, or governor, of the Isfáhán province, had passed away. His nephew, Gurgín Khán, would replace him as governor.[3]

The family lamented the loss of a governor who had done what he could to protect the Báb, and had often shown a good bit of justice amidst the usual cruelty.

Just a few days later they were shocked by more news traveling around streets and markets, not awaiting Alexan to bear the news to them. The Báb was still in Isfáhán! It took some sorting for Kapriel to get to the facts.

The departure of the Báb just before winter had been a ruse. The deceased governor had contrived with his guards to send his Guest out in full public view, then return Him in secrecy during the night to enter the governor's mansion by a private entrance.

There the Báb had stayed for several months, continuing to reveal sacred verses and write letters, uninterrupted by the accusations and calumnies of the angry clergy.

---

* References put the Báb's arrival in Káshán at Naw-Rúz, 1847, but do not give an exact date for the governor's death. Balyuzi's *The Báb* puts the death of the governor in the month of Rabí'u'Avval, 1263 A.H. This month started on 16 February 1847 AD. Thus, the author takes a guess at "A couple of weeks before Naw-Rúz."

He had been revealed—a few days after the mu'tamid's passing—to the new governor, Gurgín Khan, by a servant. Gurgín Khan had immediately sent word to the sháh in Tihrán.

Rahma waffled between bliss at still being near his Prophet and hysteria at both his limited movement and fear of what might soon happen. He could now limp on his injured leg, preferably while still using the crutches, so the friends set out together to prepare for another ride.

They replaced most of their foodstuffs, much of which had gone a bit off or become infested in the intervening months. Saddles and bridles were cleaned and checked for wear, and a few pieces needed repair or replacement. The water bags were also checked over and cleaned in case any form of vermin had taken up residence.

Both Kapriel and Rahma expressed hope for roads dry enough to keep them from riding into a bog. Occasionally, the memory of bones sticking up from the road to Isfáhán popped into Kapriel's mind. Most of the wet season had passed, but the land was not dry yet.

Kapriel consulted a local merchant about the road to Tihrán. He learned there were only simple, unoccupied rest stops between here and Káshán. No towns, no help of any kind would be available to them as they crossed a long mountain and rode on its outskirts at the edge of the central desert. From Káshán to Tihrán, towns were dotted along the road crossing the plains between the Zagros mountains of the south and the Alburz mountains to the north. This small branch of plains opened up to the east to become the vast eastern deserts of Persia. The small northwestern branch they would be crossing had far more water than the extensive eastern plains.

When they reached Tihrán, they would be on the southern edge of the Alburz, just a few dozen miles south of the Caspian Sea.

Rahma was finally able to walk, limping but without crutches, into Isfáhán to meet with his Bábí friends, exchange news, and get what copies he could of the Báb's writings from His months in the governor's home.

The final task of their preparations was to boil water and lace it lightly with wine to fill the water bags. They were ready to go just two days before the escort of government couriers arrived from Tihrán to take custody of the Báb.

They packed up on the morning of the Báb's departure with both sadness and anticipation. Kapriel had felt more at home here than at any other time in his life. He chose to ride out in his Armenian clothes rather than changing back to the more Persian-looking outfits he had worn before.

Rahma looked like Rahma, a traveling peasant.

They rode out of Julfa and into Isfáhán, giving Kapriel his final chance to have a glimpse of Sháh Abbás's capitol city. They passed the Blue Mosque, built by the order of that sháh, its intricate tiles blending subtly with the sky on this warm, near-spring day. The gigantic maydan, or square (which was rectangular, of course), at the center of the city could be glimpsed beyond some buildings. Kapriel wondered if this huge, green area was what the city had originally been named for by Cyrus the Great, since Isfáhán meant *Soldiers' Assembly Ground.* If so, then that square or parade ground had been there for over two thousand years.

Sháh Abbás had done for Isfáhán in the 1600s what the Vakíl Karím Khan had tried to do for Shíráz in the late 1700s. He imported artisans from Italy, India, and China to make his city beautiful. They taught the locals how to work marble into art, create dyes of deeper and more vibrant shades, and produce exceptional pottery.

Rahma pointed out the vast marketplace as they rode near. The market was grouped by wares and guilds, so the carpet area might take an entire block, as could the weavers and clothiers, metalsmiths, tanners, leatherworkers, and so on, making their own city within the city.

Isfáhán was far larger than Shíráz. Rahma said it had held over a million inhabitants before the Afghan onslaught 130 years ago. On their way out, they could see sections that were still not fully reoccupied, areas in ruins that were not rebuilt, and an underlying theme of aging decay.

Then they were outside the city walls, heading east around the long mountain toward the desert, then north along the desert border. They had hoped to catch up to the Báb and His escort enough to keep them in view, but it quickly became apparent that the escort of experienced riders was outpacing them. After some consultation, they decided it was better to arrive late than not at all. They would stick to the plan and sleep in the protected rest areas.

Rahma happily commented on the track being neither dry nor muddy, but nicely damp to cushion the horses' steps.

That first night on the road, they were the only residents of an empty rest stop. Thanks to the occasional ride over the winter, Kapriel was able to dismount without collapsing, though they would both be sore for a few days. They unloaded, watered and fed the horses and mule, closed the outer gate at sunset, and camped with their animals rather than occupying the small sleeping hut. They set up on a dry spot a little higher than the surrounding ground.

Once they had unrolled their sleeping mats, Rahma wondered aloud, "How do they move so fast? We should have caught up to them here."

"Well," Kapriel began, "with twelve in the escort, the group is large enough that no wild animals will bother them even when they camp. And the escort must be heavily armed, so there would be no fear of bandits. I guess they just go until they have to stop, and camp wherever that may be."

It was a bit frightening to be alone at the rest stop. Any sort of person could bang on the gate at any time demanding to be let in, then murder the two friends and abscond with all their belongings. Kapriel tried to comfort himself with the surrounding high wall and the contented munching of their mounts.

Farmer and scribe spent Naw-Rúz on the last leg of the ride to Káshán. They had no gifts to give each other but sang a few traditional songs loudly into the empty wastes to their right and to the mountain on their left. Neither could hold a tune worth listening to. Their horses' ears swiveled back and forth, unsure of whether to listen or point their ears away.

The singing stopped when one horse spotted a caravan in the distance heading their way. Both men decided it would be best not to frighten the oncoming animals, so the singing stopped.

They reached Káshán that evening, the end of the fifth day on the empty, desolate road. The city's caravanserai was bustling with muleteers, merchants, and camel drivers celebrating the holiday before putting together a caravan to go out in the morning. Kapriel was greatly relieved to be back among people, in the safety of a city.

Rahma stayed with their belongings as Kapriel rented a room for the night and made arrangements for the horses and mule. Rahma's limp was less noticeable, but his strength was not all back yet. Before the broken leg he could have carried all their belongings in two loads; now, however, he could only manage half as much. They took turns carrying the loads to the room and staying with the horses.

When the horses were settled in the large pen for the night, the two headed into the city for a meal and some fun. They hit the main road and were joining the throng of revelers when Kapriel froze and an expletive forced itself from his mouth: "Damn!"

Rahma stared at his friend, wide-eyed. He had never heard Kapriel curse, ever. Never. Not once.

Kapriel glanced up at Rahma furtively, then apologized. "Sorry. That came out before I knew it was coming."

"What's wrong? Here, let's get out of the main path before we get run over."

Rahma guided his friend to one side, then asked again, "What happened? Did we forget something at the caravanserai?"

Kapriel, feeling guilty for the outburst, answered, "No, it's nothing like that. I just . . . suddenly looked around, and realized we're back in the Muslim world, and I don't think I can stand being thrown out of a tavern for being Christian, or spit on, or cursed for existing. I might quote the Qur'án at them and get us both killed."

Rahma was shocked. "I'm so sorry! I, too . . ." he was at a loss for a moment, then finished, "forgot. It has been good to not worry, hasn't it?"

"Yes, very."

Rahma brightened with an idea. "Here's what we'll do. You go back to the caravanserai and I will get kabábs for both of us. We will still celebrate together. Good?"

Kapriel smiled. "Great! Here, I brought a bag in case we found things to buy."

"Wonderful. I will be there soon."

And he was. Kapriel had finished cleaning and arranging in their room when Rahma arrived with a bag of delicious smells. They had spiced rice with shísh kabáb and fresh nán,* washing it down with the wine-laced water in the packs.

Appetites sated, Rahma asked, "What did you mean when you said you would quote the Qur'án to them?"

"I meant just exactly that."

"How would you know what to quote? You have read the Qur'án?"

---

* English speakers commonly say "shish kabob" to mean anything cooked on a skewer, but that only applies to kabáb. Shísh (pronounced 'sheesh') mean six. Thus shísh kabáb consists of six ingredients—meats and vegetables—on a flat, sword-like skewer, cooked over open coals. Nán is a large, flattish bread.

Kapriel considered the question and decided he might as well say it now. "Yes. Read it several times, memorized it, and have a copy hidden in my pack."

"Oh my God! You want to be killed? You know . . . they think your . . . Christian hands would be defiling the Sacred Book!" Rahma was obviously editing his words as he went.

"Of course. That is why it is hidden. That is why I don't throw quotes in their . . . unkind faces." Kapriel was finding he had grown a bit of an attitude, perhaps some self-worth while in Julfa, and had to do his own editing. "Are the Báb's writings not also dangerous? Do you have them well-hidden?"

Rahma spluttered for a moment before saying, "Don't turn this back on me. You know the laws, and you know how crazy we can be. Ach, fine. It is true both ways." Rahma huffed and suddenly smiled. "That is funny, you know? Two religious men carrying dangerous religious materials in deeply religious country. Why the danger?"

"Good question!"

There followed a long evening of discussions, greatly enjoyed by both. When the topics were all finished and neither had more to add, they blew out the lamp and lay back on their mats, both tired and well-contented.

After a moment of reflection Kapriel spoke up. "Rahma, thank you."

"For what?"

"You understood the possible problems and brought dinner here instead of dragging me into an adventure. This is a big change. Thank you."

Rahma thought before replying, "You, my friend—and I do mean *friend*—are most welcome. It seems we have both grown up some. You never used to cuss."

Kapriel threw an empty water flask at him and they both broke into childlike giggles.

—•—

The next morning began the first day of spring. The air was fresh, other than the smells from the livestock pens. The chill in the air was brisk and energizing as Kapriel walked to the nearest bazaar, unworried now that the celebratory day had passed. Most shops would be closed for the next few days of family visits to start the new year, but some were open. He was doing a little quick shopping while Rahma contacted local Bábís to learn how far behind the friends might be.

They were both surprised to find the Báb was still there, at the home of one Hájí Mírzá Jání. He had arrived one day earlier than Kapriel and Rahma and would stay one more night. This gave them a leisurely afternoon to see the city.

Rahma stayed with Kapriel as they walked, ready to protect his friend from any insults. From outward appearance they seemed to be a well-to-do Armenian merchant with his retainer/bodyguard. This went over well with the vendors, who went out of their way to offer the best fabrics, the most expensive perfumes, the highest quality merchandise in all the world!

Kapriel ignored them. Granted, there was perhaps a little more variety than in Shíráz, but these were the same general offerings of exaggerated worth. He did, however, light up considerably when he came across a book vendor. He instantly regretted his lapse in demeanor as this told the salesman that a higher price could be demanded.

Rahma whispered to Kapriel to mind the weight limit for the mule as Kapriel commenced sifting through the volumes. There were large and small books, mostly handwritten but a few in mechanical print, in both Arabic and Persian. Nothing in Armenian here, and nothing very interesting.

Kapriel expressed his disappointment at the lack of texts in his native language to stop the vendor from chasing him down the street with some obscure Arabic text.

Before leaving the market Kapriel bought a gift for Rahma—a new set of clothes, of a slightly higher quality than the farmer was used to.

"No, I can't take this! You can't!"

"I can, I did, and don't you tarof me! If you continue in those rags with nothing to change into, you will soon be unable to enter any town without showing your backside to the world. You need a fresh set to wear while we patch the old."

Rahma gave in, blushing and running his hands over the seat of his robes to find the holes.

They splurged on another dinner out that evening, taking in calories for the next leg of the journey. Rahma then told Kapriel the rest of the morning's news on the Báb's travel.

"The escort has orders to ride from sunrise to sunset every day, no matter where they end up at sunset. The stop here was unplanned, at least by the escort. The Bábís say there was quite an argument between the two courier leaders before they agreed to stay three nights, with one of them—a Muhammad Big—wanting to help the Báb, and the other wanting to stick to their orders not to enter any city. The escort is camped outside of Káshán. If we leave before dawn, we might keep up this time."

"Good. So we'll know if we can keep up by tomorrow night."

10

Qum to Zanján, Spring 1847

"I'm not going in there," Kapriel stated with finality.

"We have to go! How will we find out where the Báb is if we do not go? The argument had already gone on for a while.

Kapriel glared at the city ahead of them—Qum, the sacred city, burial place of Imám Reza's sainted sister, full of schools dedicated to various branches of Islám and the study of the Qur'án, replete with clergy of all levels. "You go. I will happily stay here awaiting your improbable return." He folded his arms across his chest in a firm denial of any argument Rahma could make.

Rahma debated violently within himself, back and forth between dragging Kapriel along on one hand, and knowing his friend was right on the other, rubbing his chest with one hand in distress.

He suddenly shouted, "But, I need a bath!"

This was the third evening after leaving Káshán (26 March, 1847). Their hopes of keeping the Báb in sight had once again come to naught, with the escort outpacing them in the afternoon of the first day.

Kapriel added, "You cannot go in either. There will be no Bábís in that den of wolves, and even if there were, none could admit to it without getting instantly torn to shreds. Just to ask about them would get you killed. If you don't mind, I am not ready to give up my friend yet."

Rahma's frustrated features softened. He looked over at his companion, refusal etched in every unmoving bit of Kapriel's posture. The farmer may as well have argued with a stone.

"Fine. We will go around. If we don't find a village, we will have to camp outside somewhere. And find a stream to wash in!"

Kapriel gave one quick nod, still staring at Qum, marveling at the loathing that filled him at seeing this place he had never been to before. "Alright then. We go around."

He slowly unlocked his arms and urged his horse onto a path to one side of the road that looked as if it would circumvent the city. They had perhaps an hour of usable light left. Neither spoke, both lost in their thoughts.

Kapriel felt a great darkness coming from the city, a feeling of impending doom reaching out to him. He wondered why this was. There were certainly good mullás out there, those who taught love and forgiveness. Did the nice ones learn in different schools? Had they attended lessons in Karbílá, the approximate equal of Qum in Iráq? He knew that most of the Letters of the Living, the first nineteen believers in the Báb, had been part of the clergy. What made them different?

Deep in their own reflecting, the two did not notice the city receding to the south as they regained the main road to the north of Qum, nor the small village they passed in the fading twilight. They had long ago lost track of the escort, and had no idea how far behind they were. When it was far too dark to continue they stopped, unpacked, set the animals to grazing, ate a small, cold meal of dried meat, fruit, and biscuits, unrolled their mats, and slept.

—•—

Kapriel awoke in the dim light of near-dawn to an odd sound. Something was snuffling. He opened his eyes to see a large dog

142

pulling at the bindings of one of the packs. The dog was multicolored, wide-headed, and vaguely hairy in the tiny amount of available light. The dog also noticed him. Growling ensued as it turned its attention to possible danger from the now-awake man.

Kapriel considered, his heart pounding. Dogs were not pets in Persia. They were only used as guards, trained not to harm the flocks and herds they watched over but also trained to kill humans who threatened their charges. Feral dogs would kill anything. Domestic or feral, this dog meant Kapriel was in trouble. He kept perfectly still on his mat, hoping the dog would decide to ignore him. The man was incapable, however, of closing his eyes, or even looking away.

"Stop staring at it!" Rahma ordered in a loud whisper. "Look at the ground, now!"

Kapriel did so, staring at the tuft of grass between the dog's front feet. The dog changed its focus, looking from one man to the other, and its growling becoming more insistent and aggressive. Rahma was getting up slowly, keeping one side to the dog and using his peripheral vision to avoid looking it in the eyes. As he stood taller and taller the dog backed up, snarling with great volume and anger. The scribe watched his friend take a step toward packs and dog while still looking down. Another step, and Kapriel sat up, slowly moving to stand, glad to be less vulnerable than he was while lying down. The dog added vicious barking, warning them both off as it backed further, eventually turning tail and running.

Kapriel began to pace through the campsite with rapid steps, breathing hard. "Dear God . . . I thought I was dead! . . . It was huge! . . . Thank you, God, . . . for waking Rahma!"

"You are welcome," Rahma said. "We have dogs like that at home in the pen at night. We are . . . were . . . very careful with them. Never stare a dog in the eyes. That is how they challenge each other to fight. Oh, and you might thank God that there was only one. The feral ones can run in packs, and the farmers' dogs are often in pairs."

The scribe felt a bit faint for a moment, then thanked God some more. Finally he remembered the horses, looking over to see them blowing a few snorts of relief, then placidly returning to their browsing.

The bag the dog had pulled loose was not damaged beyond a few tooth marks. It was the one containing their dried meat. They had another cold, dry meal and packed up. Everything was ready to go at sunrise when a group of horsemen cantered gently past.

Joy filled both of them! It was the Báb and His escort. They must have stopped somewhere nearby.[1] The friends fairly leapt onto their mounts, hurrying in the wake of the escort. This time, riders and horses in good travel condition, the friends were able to keep the escort in sight for the whole day. Their condition, however, was not as good as the escorts', which could comfortably put on more miles through the long day than Kapriel and Rahma would prefer. They all stopped at sunset, with scribe and farmer a small distance from the escort.

The next day was the same—Rahma and Kapriel doing their best to get on the road by sunrise and keep the escort in sight all day.

They stopped late in the second day near the ruins of the fortress of Kinár-Gird. The friends slowed, not wanting to approach too closely and be beset by the armed men. Just as it seemed they had all stopped for the night and the exhausted friends could rest, a rider appeared from the direction of Tihrán. He rode right up to the escort and conferred with them, leaning over to hand something to one man.

A moment later, they were on the move again. Neither Rahma nor Kapriel had any idea where they might be off to nor how much longer they would be in their saddles. The escort and their charge headed east-southeast, going another four miles to the village of Kulayn before stopping once more.

Scribe and farmer were too tired to do more than dismount, almost without falling, and watch from a distance.

The men of the escort spoke to someone in the village and were working on something in an orchard just outside of that hamlet. It took only a few minutes for their purpose to be known: They were putting up a large tent and arranging an encampment around it.

This was enough of a signal for Kapriel and Rahma to waddle wearily to the edge of an adjacent meadow and set up their own camp. Kapriel barely registered the greater humidity and verdure of their current location. They ate little, too tired to chew the hard rations much. The horses were thrilled with the nearby stream and abundance of juicy grass, ripping great gobs off the roots and barely chewing before biting off more.

Morning found Kapriel in an unfamiliar circumstance. He was wet. Lying on one side, the parts of him in contact with the mat were wet, and the side toward the sky in contact with the blanket was wet. There had not been rain overnight—surely that would have woken him. He looked up to see clear skies and the sun just above the horizon. Lowering his gaze, he saw that the grass, and everything else, was covered in a heavy dew. Yes, they had dew in Shíráz occasionally, but not like this.

He sat up and looked about at the view. The grass was definitely thicker, more abundant, than at home, and native trees were grouped here and there on the edges of meadows and orchards. It was green, all around. Shíráz was also green in spring, but this was more green, with more grass, more trees, more.

Kapriel thought of the tales of traveling merchants who spoke of great forests. He realized he was closer to the forests but not there yet.

Eventually, it occurred to him to wake Rahma. Rahma, however, was not on his mat. Not seeing his companion anywhere, Kapriel set to making a good, soft, filling and warming breakfast. He had no worries of the Báb and His escort leaving this morning. One did not go to the trouble of putting up a large tent for just one night.

The moment he started into the bordering trees to find firewood, Rahma returned, looking clean and pleased with himself, wet cloth held in one hand.

"You lazy son of a God-fearing Christian. It's about time you got up!"

"And where have you been, you curse-mouthed son of a decent Muslim?"

Rahma laughed, "It just isn't the same, you know?"

Kapriel shrugged, his first foray into cursing apparently not successful. "So where have you been?"

"To take a bath and wash some clothes." He had put on an old set of long shirt and trousers, well-washed but with patches and some stains. Laying out the freshly washed old and new outfits, he continued talking, "Then to the village, talking to the head man. It is the village of Kulayn, owned by Hájí Mírzá Áqásí, the Grand Vizier of the Sháh." That caused Kapriel's eyebrows to jump up. Rahma continued, "We are only twenty-four miles from Tihrán, one day's easy ride. The headman said we could stay here but that we needed to set up a tent of some kind to keep off the morning dew, or we would wake up wet." He considered his friend, wet to the left and right but dry down the middle, and smiled. "That's what you get for lying around past dawn."

Kapriel smiled back. "So, where do we get a tent, and how will that make the ground dry?"

They rented a small tent from the headman and set about making a nice camp. The dew dried quickly in the midmorning sunlight, encouraging them to hang their mats and blankets over bushes at the meadow's edge. By late afternoon, their bedding was dry and inside the tent. They had also borrowed some old rugs to act as flooring, keeping the mats from soaking up too much ground moisture.

Kapriel, too, enjoyed feeling clean after a good scrubbing in the cold stream. He also scrubbed most of his clothes, laying them out on yet more bushes until near evening.

The horses and mule were moved to stock pens inside the village's protective walls at night, and back to the meadow by day where all three beasts were hobbled to keep them from getting too far.

Scribe and farmer enjoyed not being in saddles, spending their day going over leather straps and buckles of their tack for wear and other problems.

⚫⚫⚫

Four Bábís arrived on the second day at Kulayn (31 March 1847). Farmer and scribe watched as the escort respectfully let them pass to the tent of the Báb. The visitors spoke with Him, and the escort arranged campsites for them nearby.

Kapriel asked Rahma, "Why not go yourself? You followed Him this far: Go a few steps more."

Rahma, eyes wide at such audacity, replied, "I cannot! You know I cannot. What if he sees what a fool I am and sends me away? I cannot!"

"Are we not all fools to some degree? You are far less foolish than many. You have talked about His love for all of humankind. That includes you."

Hand to his heart, Rahma repeated, "I cannot." Then he turned and walked to the trees for bits of wood to start the evening fire.

Busy with their preparations for dinner, they did not notice the visitor until he was just a few feet away. One of the escort had come to ask them why they had followed all the way from Isfáhán, though he said "follow" with a bit of a smirk.

Kapriel answered, "We were following the Báb. Could not keep up for most of the trip, and we thought we lost you near Qum."

The escort rider was a young man in a courier's uniform. "Yes, obviously you follow the Báb. But why? You do not ask to speak to Him, or send messages. You have puny weapons that neither of you touch, so you are hardly assassins. Nor do you wear religious garb or show any signs of being 'ulámá intent on tracking His whereabouts. So, why?"

Kapriel just looked at Rahma, waiting for him to speak.

Rahma, on the other hand, looked lost. With both scribe and courier staring at him, he finally capitulated, once again repeating, "Because I cannot."

The courier inquired, "Cannot what?"

Frustrated with his lack of words, Rahma started gesturing with his hands and face. "Cannot talk to Him! It is . . . He is . . . and I am just a . . ."

"Oh," the courier said, as he understood. "You are one of those. 'I am not worthy, dirt at His feet,' all that, right?"

Rahma nodded.

"That is rubbish. None of us is worthy. What makes you less worthy than anyone else? Nothing. He cares not at all for what we have done, but for what we choose to do now. The Báb is graciousness itself, infinitely forgiving of all. Get yourself together and come along." He turned to Kapriel. "And you?"

"Sorry, I'm here to keep him company. This is his journey. I'll keep the campsite while you go."

The courier put an arm around Rahma's shoulders and gently nudged him in the right direction. Rahma looked frightened and tried to slap, brush, and scrape every bit of dirt or stain from his old farm clothes as they walked.

Kapriel stayed up late in the night, copying by firelight one of Rahma's copies of a document written by the Báb, contemplating his reasons for not going along with his friend this evening. He found at least some of the answers.

The farmer finally stumbled back into their camp after midnight, flopping himself down on the semi-dry ground. He simply sat there staring blankly into the flames.

The scribe gave him a few minutes, barely able to contain his curiosity. When concern overtook curiosity he gently called, "Rahma?"

Suddenly the blank face twisted into fury, "I will kill him! With my own bare hands, his neck will break, and he will die!"

Shocked completely, Kapriel could only watch as Rahma got up, went to the nearest tree and began to assault it, pounding it with fists and elbows, ramming each shoulder into the trunk, and hugging it in a massive effort to uproot the tree and throw it to the ground. The tree was nearly as big around as Rahma and would have nothing to do with these paltry efforts, other than slight shaking of the leaves.

Rahma kept it up, guttural sounds pouring forth in his struggle, "RRRrr, ach, heee, nnnnggg, aaach," etcetera. When enough of the anger had burned out for the man to accede total defeat he fell to the ground weeping and sobbing.

Kapriel felt the appropriate moment had come to help. He sat next to his friend among the leaves and debris of the tree line, then reached out a hand to put on Rahma's shoulder. Slowly the sobs eased, his breathing evening out until he was ready to sit up.

Kapriel exclaimed, "Rahma! You are a mess! Come back to camp. We'll clean off your face and take care of those scrapes on your hands, and you can tell me exactly what has caused you to behave in such a manner. Come on." He stood and offered a hand to his friend, then staggered as Rahma took the hand to pull himself up, nearly pulling Kapriel over instead.

Back in the firelight the scribe brought out a clean cloth soaked in wine-water, starting on Rahma's hands and checking other points of contact with the tree for damage.

Rahma began, "I don't understand, why would anyone do this?"

"Whom are you speaking of, and what has he done?"

"Hájí Mírzá Áqásí, the grand vizier. The sháh invited the Báb to have an audience, to tell him about the reform. Everyone could have known. The whole country could have been told, and all the hatred and misunderstandings would have stopped. But Áqásí influenced the sháh, changed his mind. The vizier sent the message to come here and wait for the sháh to return from some journey. Is he really on a journey? Or has he turned against us? Or are we here because the vizier wants more time to influence him? Whatever the cause, Áqásí is behind it and is acting to prevent the sháh from meeting the Báb."

"The Báb told you this?"

"No, the courier who came to talk to us, Zíá Husayn. He also told me about Qum and why we lost the escort. They had orders not to enter any town to avoid problems, but they were going to let the Báb go to the shrine of Imám Reza's sister there. He called it an 'unholy city,' its people wicked, and said that, 'Outwardly they serve and reverence her shrine, inwardly they disgrace her dignity.'[2]

"You were right to go around. And now I need another bath."

Kapriel chuckled, "At least your clean clothes are dry now. They are in the tent. So why did we lose them?"

"There is a small village of the captain's relatives just outside Qum called Qumrúd. They stopped there. We must have passed it without noticing."

They were quiet for a few minutes before Kapriel noted, "You have not yet mentioned your meeting with the Báb."

Rahma's expression changed to reverence, even awe. "He is . . . there are no words. He is God, yet He is not God. How can I say it? I look at Him, and He is a man, but so much more, as if He does not really fit in His body or belong here with us. He is the essence of gentleness, kindness, everything good. He carries much sadness, but gives joy to everyone." The farmer's eyes were tearing up again.

"He is so much more than us. It is as if He could see into my heart, know everything I have ever done wrong. But He smiled with such love and . . ." That was all he could say, for he was again weeping and sobbing.

Kapriel sat next to him, putting an arm across his shoulders—a gesture that was common between men of the same religion but that would have been so dangerous in any Persian city between the Christian and the Moslem.

When Rahma had moved past that emotional hurdle, he asked Kapriel, "Why do you not go talk to Him? You should go."

"Just a few hours ago you had to be dragged over to His tent, and now you want me to go?"

"Yes, but Rahma is stubborn and not so smart. You are smart; you know this would be good for you."

"Truthfully, yes, I know that. I also know that I am not ready to give up my faith, history, and all I have recently learned."

"Why would you have to?"

Kapriel thought out his words first. "If this is a reform, then to join it means becoming a Muslim, becoming that which persecutes my family and so many others. If this is a new religion, then it still means giving up the Church, and no one can be a true Armenian without the Church. No, the Báb writes often of Another, One Whom God shall make manifest, Whom He has come to prepare the way for. Perhaps by then I will be ready."

Rahma nodded sadly at this, but the length of the day was quickly wearing on them both. There would be time enough for talk in the morning.

—•—

The next day two more Bábís arrived, and one of them was carrying a package for the Báb. Kapriel was later told by Rahma that inside the package were a letter and several gifts, sent by a Mírzá

Husayn 'Alí, a wealthy nobleman who had immediately accepted the cause of the Báb when he received a message sent by Mullá Husayn about two years ago. This nobleman had quickly left homes and extended family to set about spreading the message of the Báb throughout the district of Núr (Light) in the province of Mázindarán, and he had gained many adherents in his travels.

The Báb had received the gifts and message with exclamations of joy and had "overwhelmed the bearer with marks of His gratitude and favour."[3]

The days passed happily for the Báb, couriers, and visitors. Orchards and meadows were beautiful with bloom. Birds enhanced the quiet with sweet melodies; nothing disturbed their tranquility.

There was one odd event, deep in one night, when people near the Báb's tent, including the scribe and farmer, were awakened by the sound of hooves galloping on the terrain. Upon investigating, Kapriel and Rahma were told that the Báb's tent was empty and that those couriers who had ridden off to search for Him had come back unsuccessful. Muhammad Big, who they learned was the captain of the guards, had admonished his men, "Why feel disturbed? Are not His magnanimity and nobleness of soul sufficiently established in your eyes to convince you that He will never, for the sake of His own safety, consent to involve others in embarrassment? He, no doubt, must have retired, in the silence of this moonlit night, to a place where He can seek undisturbed communion with God. He will unquestionably return to His tent. He will never desert us."[4]

Muhammad Big had then set off along the path toward Tihrán to "reassure his colleagues." The Bábís followed him, and the guards, still on horseback, slowly followed them.

Kapriel waited in the campsite, wondering how far they would walk, and whether they had even gone in the right direction.

Not too long after their departure, they returned, with the Báb, radiant, in their midst. Rahma later imparted to Kapriel that the Báb was found alone on the trail returning to the camp, and the seekers were "awed by the serene majesty which that radiant face revealed . . ." causing them to withhold questions and remarks.

Rahma reported that the sadness which had weighed upon the Báb had lifted, had been replaced with absolute confidence, and as one Bábí said, "His words were invested with such transcendent power, that a feeling of profound reverence wrapped our very souls."

The travelers were there one day short of three weeks when their blissful interlude was ended by the arrival of a letter which the sháh himself had sent. Rahma memorized it as the words were spoken to the Bábís. It read, "Much as we desire to meet you, we find ourself unable, in view of our immediate departure from our capital, to receive you befittingly in Tihrán. We have signified our desire that you be conducted to Máкú, and have issued the necessary instructions to 'Alí Khán, the warden of the castle, to treat you with respect and consideration. It is our hope and intention to summon you to this place upon our return to the seat of our government, at which time we shall definitely pronounce our judgment. We trust that we have caused you no disappointment, and that you will at no time hesitate to inform us in case any grievances befall you. We fain would hope that you will continue to pray for our well-being and for the prosperity of our realm."[5]

Yet again preparations were made to travel. The Báb was only allowed one companion and one attendant. He chose two of the Bábís, Siyyid Hasan and Siyyid Husayn of Yazd, brothers who had arrived during the second full day at Kulayn, to accompany Him. The others sadly made ready to head out on their own tasks or go home.

Rahma had not been specifically told to go home, so he chose to continue. They returned the tent and carpets, paying the headman and thanking him for the spot in the meadow. The friends collected their horses and mule, packed up, and were on their way.

They were once again to avoid cities, causing Kapriel some disappointment. Rahma, however, chided the scribe, "So what if Tihrán is the capital. It is just the capital now. Shíráz was the capital before that, and Isfáhán before that. The next city on the way to Mákú is Qazvín, capital of Sháh Tahmasp I, just before Sháh Abbas switched it to Isfáhán. And Tabríz was the first capital of the Safavids.* Capital this, capital that—over thousands of years we have had too many capitals."

Kapriel looked at his companion, eyebrows raised. "Since when did you become Shaykh Rahmatu'lláh-i-Shírází, historian?"

Rahma looked back at him, unsure whether to be insulted or amused. "I'm not completely stupid, you know."

"Yes, but you didn't read until recently."

"I have ears. They've been there since I was born."

"Ah, someone taught you out on your farm."

"Of course not. Besides the history in the Shahnameh, they do tell more recent stories in the taverns."

"Mmm, yes. How silly of me. So, we know where the Báb is going. Why don't we just nip into Tihrán on the way? It is the capital now, and the largest city. I have heard the main bazaar is even bigger than in Isfáhán!"

"Are you going to buy something you can only get there? It's all the same as the other bazaars, you know, just more of it." Rahma started rubbing his chest with worry again.

"How would you know? You've never been there either. And no, I do not want to buy something—I want to send another letter home."

---

* Qazvín was capital from approximately1548 to 1597 AD. (Encyclopedia Iranica, "Cehel Sotun, Qazvín"). Tabríz was capital from approximately 1501 to 1555 AD. (Encyclopedia Iranica, "Tabriz x. Monuments x(1). The Blue Mosque.")

"Ah, that I understand. Maybe we will meet someone on the road who is going to Shíráz."

Kapriel thought that rather unlikely unless they met another caravan. Even then, finding a trustworthy letter carrier was unlikely. Most of them would pocket the fee and lose the letter, possibly washing the ink off to save the pages for himself. The scribe gave a great, heaving sigh, resigning himself to the inevitable.

One aspect of this leg of the journey was the vastly increased number of villages between cities. Should there be any emergency, at least shelter could be found every twenty miles or so, giving the friends great comfort.

The escort was to consist of mostly the same men until Tabríz, where the guard would change. They stayed well out of Tihrán, skirting Karaj. Then they turned west-northwest and followed the edge of the Alburz mountains, keeping the tall and dominant mountains to their right with foothills and open plains to the left.

Rahma and Kapriel stayed well behind for two reasons. First, they knew for sure what the eventual destination was. Second, the two attendants had been chosen, and Rahma was not one of them. He did not wish to intrude on the great spiritual conversations that must surely have been taking place, nor did he want to appear to defy the Báb's choice by riding too close.

The first leg of the journey was uneventful, culminating after a few days in a nightly stop at the town of Síyáh-Dihán, just to the south of Qazvín. The scribe and farmer were surprised to learn that Qazvín already had a large population of Bábís, taught by several Letters of the Living and other adherents of great knowledge residing in the area. Though the escort avoided that city, somehow the news of the Báb's approach reached the Bábís who lived there in time for some to make their way to Síyáh-Dihán and meet their heart's Desire.

The friends were able to camp close enough to hear much of what was spoken by the seekers and the Báb that night. A few received letters, whether for them or to be delivered to others. Each left with greater confidence and a more defined purpose, inspired and enlightened by their encounters.

Two Bábís chose to visit with Rahma and Kapriel on their way home—Mullá Táhir and Hájí Aziz'u'lláh.* Rahma was able to draw out some information on the city and how its inhabitants had heard of the Báb.

The topic most often referred to was a woman renowned throughout the city for her religious scholarship, piety, chastity, and poetry. Born to the name *Fatimih* in a family with many clergymen of high rank, she had a depth of knowledge unsurpassed by any man in her native city. She learned of the Shaykhí movement from her brother-in-law, Javvád, and in her correspondence with Siyyid Kázím of Kárbilá, she was given the name *Qurratu'l-'Ayn*, which meant *Solace of the Eyes.*

She and her relative Javvád became Letters of the Living, devoting their lives to the promotion of the Báb's cause. The two Qazvín Bábís spoke of her with an awe far more potent than simple admiration. They related their experiences in her father's and uncle's classes as she sat behind a screen as she listened and corrected not just the students, who numbered over two hundred, but even the instructors. She did so with powerful arguments which left them no rebuttal.

Kapriel asked with urgency, "Is it possible that we could meet her?"

Rahma began to berate his friend for such an infringement on propriety, but one of the visitors interrupted, "Many of us would like to hear from her again, but, alas, she is not here at this time. She has been teaching with great success in Iráq, upsetting much of the clergy. She was banished from the Ottoman Empire and is returning. However, it may be a while yet before her arrival."**

* Mullá Táhir is historical; Hájí Aziz'u'lláh is fictional.
** This is an assumption as no dates are given for her expulsion from Hamadán (for agitating the citizenry by calling them to the Cause of the Báb), which forced her return. She was definitely in Qazvín by midsummer.

The Qazvínís soon took their leave to head home. This gave Rahma the opening to finish his earlier berating. "You can't ask such things! You know it is dangerous to ask about any woman not related to you."

"She is obviously in the public quite a lot, and as a public figure it is obvious she is being discussed by large numbers of people not directly related to her. I did not ask for a private meeting. Besides, she has three nearly-grown children and may be old enough to be my mother,* not someone I would be romantically attracted to."

"And now you insult her!"

"Stating facts is not an insult. With age comes wisdom and respect, even veneration."

Despite their differences, the two had similar reactions to the story of Qurratu'l-'Ayn—wanting to hear her. It was their differing reasons that caused the current argument. Kapriel wanted to meet the woman who had been able to break the shackles of servitude and anonymity enjoined by the Persian culture, and Rahma wanted to hear the voice of a brilliant poetess who, despite speaking in public, did so from behind curtains and screens, making her the epitome of chastity.

The travelers continued on in the morning, climbing higher as the land rose in altitude, with the sharp rise of the snow-capped mountains continuing to their right. Spring was further along in some areas, having protected pockets of vegetation blooming in profusion while colder, more exposed areas of the plains were only beginning to flower. They had been on the road from Tihrán for nearly two weeks before the city of Zanján appeared on the western horizon.

---

* Qurratu'l-'Ayn was 33 in 1847 and therefore not old enough to be Kapriel's mother. Her oldest child would have been about 17 at that time.

Kapriel was surprised when they approached Zanján directly, rather than skirting it. The escort was taking the Báb through, not around. Both young men were dumbfounded at the reception the escort was moving through as they rode on the city streets. House-tops and alleys were crowded with a multitude hoping to glimpse the now-famous Prisoner. These crowds were not riotous or angry, but composed of curious and devoted people cheering the arrival of the One about Whom they had heard so much. Kapriel noted the fewness of ulámá in the adoring crowds and wondered what that might signify. He suspected the worst.

The caravanserai that had been prepared for the Báb lay on the far side of the city. The friends were once again able to camp close enough to see much of the activity around the illustrious Man they followed. Rahma was able to wave over a local Bábí to appease their overwhelming curiosity regarding the populace of Zanján. The man, a trinket-seller going grey in his beard, was happy to fill them in.

"There is a man who lives here, Mullá Muhammad-'Alí of Zan-ján, who is greatly loved by most of the people. He sent a mes-senger to the Báb two years ago seeking clarification of His mission and message. The response the mullá received so delighted him that he immediately took up the cause of the Báb. He was the given a surname by the Báb of Hujjat-i-Zanjání (Proof of Zanján), and most of us now refer to him simply as Hujjat. The messages and writings he received from his Savior he has taught from the pulpit in his mosque, converting many of us to Bábís.

"The ulámá, however, are jealous of Hujjat's growing followers and the indulgence shown to him by the city leaders. The more who convert to the Báb's cause, the less followers there are for the other ulámá. They plot against him, doing what they can through lies and subversion to take away his prestige, sending their lies in complaints to the authorities in the capitol. Hujjat is currently a prisoner in Tihrán, awaiting trial before the sháh and grand vizier."

Kapriel mulled this over a moment before commenting, "So the ulámá of Zanján are like those of Shíráz and Isfáhán, working to destroy anything that may bring change."

The man shrugged with his hand out to each side. "They cannot see beyond yesterday, so they try to stop tomorrow. They will be as successful as someone trying to stop the sun from coming up."

Rahma, who had been quietly taking in the information, asked, "Sir, you are well spoken for a simple trinket-seller. Have you had some schooling?"

The man smiled widely, his eyes lighting up. "Ah, yes, by the school of life. One's profession is largely a matter of circumstance, no? And a salesman could hardly sell trinkets if he could not convince his customers to buy them." He winked, excused himself, and left for the night, still smiling brightly.

Late in the night when the friends finally settled themselves to sleep, the Báb was still deep in conversation with the caravanserai owner, passing along warnings of a dire future in store for Zanján.

11

Tabríz, Late April, 1847

The next afternoon, outside of Zanján, a rider in obvious haste rode up behind Rahma and Kapriel. When he was near enough to see the escort they were following in the distance, he slowed and came up even with the friends, his horse blowing to catch its breath and sidling away.[1]

"Salám. Excuse me, do you know who is in that group of riders ahead?"

Rahma answered, "Yes, of course. It is the Báb, two disciples, and the escort of couriers."

"You are sure?"

"Of course," Rahma countered, "and why are you asking?"

The man looked askance at the friends and up to the escort. "You will not inform the guards?"

Rahma suddenly puffed up his chest. "That depends! Do you intend harm to the Báb or His fellow travelers?"

The man was suddenly shocked. "Dear God, no! We mean to rescue Him!"

Kapriel butted in, "'We' meaning who?"

"Several of us. Some have ridden from Tihrán under the instructions of Hujjat, and others joined us at Qazvín and Zanján. We have ridden hard to catch up that we may set Hujjat's plan into action."

Kapriel was not in favor. "The Báb has had innumerable opportunities to leave. He has taken none of them. His escort trusts Him implicitly, but He has never taken advantage of that, nor of their relaxed attitude toward security. The Báb will not go with you."

The man was unimpressed. "If you wish to join us, camp near the road. Otherwise, stay out of the way."

He wheeled his horse around, racing back the way he had come.

Rahma took a great sniff through his nose, then let it out with a huff.

"What does that mean?" Kapriel inquired.

"You can be so . . . insensitive! And you talk like you are so superior."

Nonplussed, Kapriel thought a moment. "Still not getting it. Please explain."

"He is a Bábí, and he wants to do something besides sit on his backside at home while his Lord is taken off to some terrible fate!"

"But they cannot change the Báb's path. He spoke of Azerbaijan before leaving Shíráz, long before the message came from the sháh directing Him here."

"Right! They will try to rescue Him, and if He refuses to go, then they will have at least tried. It is something, whether it ends as they want or as you say."

Now Kapriel understood. He was accidentally undermining the spiritual path of the rescuers. "I had not seen it that way. I was hoping to save them from embarrassment."

———

That night was one of the few where no town or rest station was available when the sun set. As a result, Kapriel and Rahma decided to camp in the open.

Scribe and farmer camped near the trail, just close enough to the escort to see the couriers' evening fire. Well after dark they heard hoofbeats on the back trail, slowing and then stopping a distance away. Soon a rather large group of men walked into the friends' firelight, among them the rider they had met on the trail. Kapriel watched as the men settled on the ground, chatting with Rahma and apparently waiting for something.

Near midnight the men, minus Kapriel, gathered themselves for the assault on the couriers' camp. They had learned of the escort's devotion to their prisoner and expected little resistance. They crept along in near silence, Kapriel following on a whim to see what came of it.

The couriers were asleep when the rescuers quietly rushed in. They found the Báb and prepared to whisk Him off to some safe destination. The Prisoner, however, refused to go. He told them, "The mountains of Azerbaijan too have their claims."

After further conversation the disappointed rescuers left the camp, yet Kapriel noticed not one courier had awakened during the entire raid. Or at least, none had given visible signs of waking up. Could some have been feigning sleep the whole time?

Kapriel and Rahma met up back at their camp. Rahma tossed out, "Go ahead, tell me how you were right and told them so."

"I wasn't going to."

"But you were right."

"Maybe in fact, but as you pointed out, it was none of my business, and I have been properly chastised."

Rahma did not know how to answer that, so he nodded once and went to bed.

Only a couple of days later, the Báb and His escort arrived at Mílán, a town one day short of Tabríz. Many of the town's people ventured close to see the Báb "and were filled with wonder at the majesty and dignity" of Him.[2]

Kapriel and Rahma were rather close behind the escort as they left the next morning, close enough to see an extraordinary episode.

An old woman was begging the Báb to heal a child she held. The child's head had been scalded and was covered with scabs down to the neck, giving the head a white appearance. The guards would have blocked her approach, but the Báb forestalled them.

He called the child to Him, put a handkerchief over the child's head, and recited some words that the friends could not make out. He removed the cloth to the gasps of the crowd. The child was healed.

There must have been two hundred or more people, Kapriel estimated, who saw the miracle and believed.

The scribe himself was stunned. The party moved out as Rahma looked at him with one eyebrow up and inquired, "What did you expect from a Messenger of God? . . . Infidel."

Kapriel took umbrage at that. "You know quite well I am not an infidel."

"Fine then. Unbeliever."

"That also is not applicable."

"It applies if you do not believe, and the shock on your face says you did not believe." Rahma was smiling as he continued his jibes.

Kapriel responded, "Believing and seeing an actual miracle are not the same thing! Why are you laughing?! Oh, I see, poking fun at the guy caught with his mouth open. Well, I wasn't the only one, you know."

Rahma laughed harder still, with further attempts by Kapriel to quench his friend's humor only giving him further cause.

And then they both stopped, staring ahead at the rapidly disappearing figure of the Báb.[3] The couriers were also surprised, needing a moment to comprehend before they rode hard after Him. Rahma once again was prompted to gales of laughter, nearly falling from his horse. Kapriel could see the joke. The lightly-built horse ridden by the Báb did not seem capable of outrunning the trail-hardened mounts of the couriers, but the friends could see that the escort had no chance of catching up.

Rahma, wiping his eyes, mused, "Maybe one of them made a joke about the Báb's horse."

Kapriel smiled and added, "Maybe one, or several, were thinking they could stop Him. Either way, I suppose we should move a
little faster to catch up while they rest, once the Báb stops."

Neither had any doubt that He would, indeed, stop and wait for
His guards when His point was made.

The friends once again had the escort in sight just a couple of
miles outside of Tabríz when another incident occurred. A man,
or perhaps a youth from his limber gait, appeared running toward
the couriers from the direction of Tabríz. He continued right up to
one of them, grabbed a stirrup that he then kissed, and spoke some
words they only later learned.

He had said, "Ye are the companions of my Well-Beloved, I
cherish you as the apple of my eye."[4]

Farmer and scribe continued to approach, though the escort had
stopped for the young man. They saw him next throw himself on
the ground by the Báb's horse, and they could hear his weeping.
The Báb dismounted, helped the youth to his feet, gave him a loving embrace, and cleared the tears from his face. The young man
was aglow with devotion.

The escort reorganized and was beginning to move forward
when Kapriel was close enough to see the youth had no shoes, that
his run from Tabríz had been accomplished barefoot.

The reception at Tabríz was even more wondrous than at Zanján.
Guards were at the entrance, holding back crowds of the curious and
the devout, preventing Bábís and seekers from approaching the Báb.

Kapriel realized this was why the young man had run so far
to meet his Beloved. He also wondered how, since no riders had
passed them to inform the city, did the residents know of the Báb's
imminent arrival? Had the escort sent a rider ahead, unnoticed by
the friends?

The populace crowded the narrow streets and chanted, "Alláh-u-Akbar" (God is Greatest), the voices of the multitude echoing through the city. Some invoked blessings and cheered Him, a few attempted to kiss the dust touched by His footsteps. As the chanting slowly quieted, the friends could hear town criers calling through the streets, warning the populace not to attempt any approach to the Báb. "Whosoever shall make any attempt to approach the Siyyid-i-Báb, or seek to meet Him, all his possessions shall forthwith be seized and he himself condemned to perpetual imprisonment."[5]

Rahma voiced what both friends thought, "So, that is how they act here to stop change. If the Báb wants to see someone, nothing will stop them."

They found a decent caravanserai, rented a room, and took care of their beasts of burden, paying a little extra for their horses to remain theirs. Dinner was excellent as they spent some of their savings on lamb kabábs, a ground mixture of meat, onions, and spices shaped onto flat skewers and grilled over coals. They added spring vegetables (a delicacy during travel), bread and rice, and sat in their room stuffing themselves.

The Bábís were easy to find later in the evening, and this time Kapriel went along with Rahma. They told their tales of travel from living in Shíráz to the arrival in Tabríz. When the residents' curiosity was sated, it was their turn to speak. The friends learned several important things that night. A man with contacts in the city government said the Báb was spending the night in the home of Muhammad Big, the courier captain, and the next day would be moved to the citadel, seat of the city government, for a while. The two brothers, Siyyids Hasan and Husayn of Yazd, would stay with Him in the citadel.

Kapriel and Rahma quickly asked what farms may need an extra hand and what location would be good for a scribe, as they needed to replace their slowly diminishing savings. They were conducted individually to prospective employment—Rahma went to a farmer whose son was injured and unable to work (with whom Rahma deeply sympathized), and Kapriel was led to a shopkeeper who conducted business in Persian, Arabic, and Armenian. It was there the scribe learned how close they were to the western border with the Ottoman Empire (about eighty miles to the closest point) and the northern border with the Russian province of Armenia (about forty miles). There were several towns in the area settled primarily by Armenians, causing Kapriel a bit of angst desiring to go visit every one. He also, finally, found a man soon to leave for Isfáhán, who agreed to deliver a parcel to Aunt Marem.

Scribe and farmer went their separate ways early the next morning. Both were exceedingly glad for the interlude off of horseback. Rahma lumbered out to a farm with orchards, the young fruit in need of thinning.

Kapriel, relieved to be again using his mind and clinging to his lap desk rather than wandering desolate roads while clinging to a horse, began work writing up orders and answering letters in three languages for the shopkeeper. The shopkeeper had a large backlog of correspondence, inventory, and other paperwork ignored due to a lack of time in the busy spring season.

Tabríz was much colder than Shíráz. Even now, at the end of April, nights were as chilly as Shíráz in February. Kapriel shivered briefly at the thought of being this far north in winter.

That evening, he rubbed the cramps from his hands—no longer used to hours of writing—and washed them to lighten the black ink stains. He finished letters to his relatives in Shíráz and Isfáhán, made them into a parcel, and addressed the parcel for his aunt's home. She, he hoped, would take out the letter for her and Uncle Hovnan and forward the rest of the parcel to his parents. He had just finished when Rahma entered, his hands also cramped and stained, but brown with dried sap from separating excess infant fruit from their trees.

Several days were necessary for the pair to adjust back to the working life. They picked up bits of information from street talk and visiting with Bábís in evenings. Wild conjecture was being noised about regarding the future of the Báb and what might be done to Him next. The friends did not understand why such confusion would reign. It was commonly known that the order of the sháh had been to escort the Prisoner to Máкú. Kapriel deduced they were waiting for a new escort of courier soldiers to arrive and finish the journey.

Two Tabríz disciples had mysteriously been allowed in to visit the Báb. All others could only see Him from a distance, if at all. The guards kept the populace far back, not only refusing entry but also refusing to allow loitering in the area around the citadel, preventing even a glimpse of the Báb by His anguished followers. The two privileged disciples carried out various tasks and proceeded back and forth to His cell unhindered, despite the guards' strict orders to the contrary.

Weeks passed. Rahma flourished in farming and associating with Bábís. His leg was completely healed, with no trace of limp marring his lumbering gait. When the fruitlets were properly thinned he was hired by another farm to assist in plowing and planting.

Kapriel had gotten the shopkeeper all caught up, and then he had moved out onto a busy market corner to ply his old trade. He had found some resident Armenians and chose to spend some of his spare time with them. He was missing his family and the sense of belonging he'd had in Julfa, and with these Armenians, he was able to speak the language of his ancestors and feel part of a community again, if only for a while. The Muslim residents of Tabríz, who lived so close to his homeland with many Armenians around, were less likely to mistreat him. They did, however, have the same habit of leaning away and keeping a safe distance from his contamination.

Farmer and scribe had been in Tabríz for five and a half weeks before the people heard of the renewed orders. The next escort had arrived with papers requiring the immediate removal of the Báb from Tabríz, bound for Mákú.

12

Máků, Summer 1847 – Spring 1848

It was bleak and grey, even in the near-summer heat. The castle-prison had been built long ago in a huge natural cleft or hollow in a mountainside. The cleft faced west to Ottoman territory, just over four miles distant. Twenty-five miles to the north lay the border of the Russian Empire and its province of Armenia.

The trek from Tabríz had been arduous. The trail west-northwest left the mountains of Tabríz for wide, open ranges. Most of the journey gave only distant views of bare mountains to the south and taller, occasionally snow-capped mountains to the north. The approach to Máků was increasingly narrow and winding as they neared the western mountains, rocks having to be more frequently navigated to save the horses' feet as they climbed an increasingly steep trail. Finally they rounded the last bend in a high pass to see their desolate destination.

Three mountains created the valley of Máků. Two of them ran east-west, forming the eastern section of the town in the narrow valley. This valley opened to the west on a wide, flattish area, where the third mountain blocked the view to the southwest and formed a short north-south valley. The dry, bald mountains themselves gave no life to the region. Only sparse grasses could anchor themselves in the thin soil of the steep and rocky slopes. A creek ran down the center of the east-west valley, and cottonwoods and other hardy trees dotted the path of the creek. The small village nestled in the valley's opening, seated directly below the cleft where the castle sat. From the village, the path to the castle wound up the scree of boulders large and small to the base of a vertical wall, as if part of the mountain had been sliced off. Steps were carved where the path through the scree led up to the mountain wall. This wall rose to the cliff edge of the hollow. The natural cleft was so large the entire castle fit inside it, and the four protruding towers were not even close to touching the weighty stone roof.

This formidable castle looked west out across the valley to the Ottoman lands beyond. Only late afternoon light could touch the castle, leaving it cold and dark the rest of the day. A manmade wall and gate cut off access from the town to the scree path, and another locked gate refused access to the castle itself. Up in that unreachable fortress, the Báb and His two disciples were ensconced.

The nearly four hundred miles from Tihrán to Tabríz had almost doubled to reach Mákú. The tiny town saw little sunlight with the height of the mountains blocking much of the sky. Predators and thieves were scarce in such high, cold, and sparsely inhabited areas, but so was prey for either. It was more probable for a traveler to run into Persian scouts patrolling borders, or Ottoman scouts checking for military movement.

The Bábís of Tabríz had encouraged the farmer and scribe to buy simple gifts with which to curry favor at their destination, especially Rahma. Mákú was mostly inhabited by Sunní Kurds, vehemently opposed to Shi'a Muslims, especially siyyids, whom they saw as the chief promulgators of the hated Shi'a doctrine. Neither scribe nor farmer spoke Kurdish, and their Persian accent would immediately lead them to believe Rahma was a Shi'a. Kapriel, in his Armenian clothing, would be ignored as insignificant.

Small packages of dates, dried fruit, and sugar, given with lavish respect and politeness, paved the way for Rahma and Kapriel to rent one room in a house and to be able to leave their mounts with a shepherd and his flock. There were few horses in the area, and they were mostly for the small garrison of scouts who patrolled the eastern border. There was no caravanserai—only a masjid, or Muslim school, next to the mosque outside the town wall, where most travelers would stay.

The air was thin and dry, burning Kapriel's lungs when he exerted himself and causing him to feel tired even after sleeping.[1]

"Maybe we should have left the horses in Tabríz," Kapriel mused the second evening.

"What? And walk all that way? My feet hurt just thinking about it. Besides, how would we have kept up with the escort?"

"We knew where they were going. There was no option for them to detour and go off on a fling somewhere else."

Rahma rubbed his chest with one hand. He had developed this habit in Shíráz, now demonstrating it whenever he felt he might be separated from the Báb.

"They rode here, we rode here."

"Yes, but the escort left the Báb here and rode right back to Tabríz. Our horses and mule are stuck here. How will we acquire hay and grain for them if we are still here in winter?"

Rahma trembled with imagined cold. "God! Winter must be awful in this dead, airless place."

"We could go back to Tabríz and wait there. Surely any place the Báb is moved to will take Him back through Tabríz."

"Summer has just started. Why think of winter now?" Inconsistent though he was, Rahma was not to be dissuaded in his desire to remain near his Master. Whatever was to happen, Rahma needed bear witness.

—◦—

The Báb was completely inaccessible at first. The officer in charge of the castle and border security was 'Alí Khán, also a Kurd of the Sunní Muslims. A rough man in rough terrain, he let it be known that he had strict orders from the Grand Vizier himself to isolate the Báb and prevent disorder such as had arisen elsewhere. Only one man, Siyyid Hasan, companion of the Báb since their encampment outside Tihrán, was allowed in and out of the castle to the town. He was accompanied by a guard to buy food and other supplies for the Prisoner Himself and Siyyid Hasan's brother Husayn, who was acting as a scribe for the Báb.

Rahma was, by nature, too self-effacing to approach Siyyid Hasan, but he and Kapriel were nearby when a well-known Bábí, Shaykh Hasan-i-Zunúzí arrived. The newcomer had taken a room at a religious school just outside the town and sought to connect with the Báb. Unlike the cities farther east, in Mákú there were no native Bábís with whom to share information. This Shaykh, however, was able to meet with Siyyid Hasan and secretly exchange letters. In this manner, the rare Bábís who visited were able to send questions and requests to His Holiness and receive answers.

During their first few days, Kapriel found himself to be completely useless. No one needed a scribe who could not translate to or from Kurdish. Therefore he sought out children who might teach him basic words and phrases, playing games with them and later checking with a friendly Persian-speaking adult to be sure they had not taught him anything inappropriate or childish.

Rahma, too, had to seek out things to do. There was little farming except grains and legumes in the wide area to the west of town. Fruit trees could not produce fruit with late frosts after blooming, so only a few small fruits were grown. He managed to find occasional work as a "muscle man"—helping carry, load, or unload when needed.

Both of them needed time to acclimate. The intermittent activity let them rest a lot, slowly gaining strength as their bodies found ways to use the thin air better. Two weeks after their arrival, they were close to feeling normal.

Something else happened at that same time. Suddenly the restrictions on visits to the Báb were completely relaxed. Mystified as to the change, Rahma investigated. He came back to their room with an extraordinary tale.[2]

Early one morning ʿAlí Khán, head of the scouts and the prison, was riding outside of town. At the hour of dawn, he found the Báb at the creek in the valley, rapt in His devotions, singing His praises to God. The rider did not wish to disturb such devotion, despite his dismay at the Prisoner being out on His own, breaking every restriction set upon Him. He attempted to get closer, but his fear increased as he approached the Báb to such an extent that he decided to investigate the lapse in security before confronting the loose Prisoner.

He arrived at the gate to the castle path and found it closed and locked, as it should be. He called for the guards to let him through, then charged up the mountain to bang on the castle gate, also locked as required, and demanded to be let in. His dismay was complete when, upon arriving breathless at the Báb's cell, he found his Prisoner and companions just where they should be.

Throwing himself at the Báb's feet, he begged forgiveness and pledged to correct his mistakes, asking to escort the Shaykh at the masjid into the Báb's presence. The Báb allowed him to go outside the town walls to Shaykh Hasan-i-Zunúzí and guide that visitor to the One he so desired to see.

This change in ʿAlí Khán's attitude brought a loosening of the restrictions and allowed those whom the Báb wished to see free access to Him in the daytime, although the gates were still locked at night. Messages were sent back and forth freely. And one morning, to the delight of many, a melodious, wonderful voice was heard coming from the castle heights. Rahma nearly fainted with the beauty of it. The Báb was chanting His prayers and tablets openly.

Each morning as the sun struggled through the winding eastern valley, the Báb was already deeply into His devotions, intoning words of holiness and love that flowed across the town and echoed between mountains. Each evening, as the sun set above the Ottoman horizon, it shone directly into the mountain cavity where the Báb and Siyyid Husayn were at work, the Báb dictating through chanting, and His assistant writing with great rapidity as letters, tablets, and books were revealed.

———————

The summer passed with little change. The friends awoke each morning at first hint of light to the voice from above, pulled themselves together and got to work. Kapriel had agreed to help with the hay harvest, taking half pay until he had the whole scythe swing figured out. He was thrilled to get to the point of modest efficiency without taking off one of his own feet. Rahma, of course, needed no practice to slice through great swaths of grass stems.

Bábís arrived in increasing numbers from all directions, seeking an audience with their Lord. Those whom He agreed to see were given just three days to fill their spiritual cups before being sent on to further the Cause in some way.[3] The townspeople's original and deep dislike of the siyyid Prisoner and His siyyid companions was transformed to respect for the Holy Man, causing many to seek His blessing.

The summer heat was nothing compared to Shíráz. When the Kurds would complain of the soaring temperatures, the two southerners would laugh. The Kurds, however, would remark about winter and see who would laugh then, causing the friends to shiver despite the sweaty work.

Meanwhile, word filtered to them of the work the Báb had undertaken, to reveal the laws and ordinances of His Cause.[4] This actually bothered Rahma somewhat.

"Reformers," he commented, "do not write books of laws. They leave stories of their lives and the miracles they saw, but not books.

Only the big Messengers—Moses, Jesus, Muhammad—only They leave books. If this is a reform, why is He writing a Book?"

"What is the difference to you if this is a reform or a new religion?" Kapriel asked.

Rahma blustered a bit, "Well, you know . . . Islám is my life. I can't just leave it."

"But you already have. At least, you left the old form of Islám behind. Since you have come that far, why not finish the leap?"

Rahma paused, then relented. "It seems my heart has decided for me, and my mind is just now catching up."

Kapriel gazed at his friend, pondering the similarities and ramifications of several religions.

Rahma noticed the silent gaze. "What?"

"A couple of things. I am sympathizing with people over thousands of years who had to realize the same thing and make the same choice: Stay with the old religion or move forward with a new revelation."

Rahma saw that his friend was heading off into unknown territory again, taking their current circumstance and applying it to the entire world back through all of history. What other incomprehensible concept was his friend contemplating? He had to ask, "And?"

"Remember the references in the Báb's early tablets and in the things He chants now to this 'He Whom God shall make Manifest'"?

Rahma nodded, bracing for an answer beyond his ken.

"He defers to this future Person in every way, and implies, or even outright states, that this Person will be here soon. His laws are subject to approval of the next Messenger, He yearns only to serve that One."

"So?"

"So considering the depth and volume of His writings, the greatness and miracles surrounding the Báb, how much more will this next and even greater One bring?"[5]

"Oh my God! It's too much to think about!"
"Exactly."

⸻

The harvest continued with threshing grain, digging roots, pressing and boiling sweet sorghum canes for molasses, and so on. Summer cooled, and fall began with a light snow marking the autumnal equinox. The friends were shocked.

"Snow, now?!" Rahma exclaimed as they rose to chanting at dawn in a freezing room.

Kapriel began shivering as soon as he emerged from the blankets. "The Kurds were right; they can laugh all they want. We won't be able to take much of this."

"Much of this? With snow now there may be snow until well into Spring! Think how cold it will be in January! We're going to die!"

"No, we're not. Let's go back to Tabríz for the winter. They have more hay and several caravanserais for the horses and us. Also, we can find more work there instead of starving here."

Their savings were getting low despite taking every job they could find. Food was expensive due to scarcity, pay was low due to the poverty of the community, and care for the horses was at least half their budget. It was unlikely they could pay their way through to spring.

"I can't leave, you know that! Just hearing His voice every morning is worth any hardship."

"Rahma, I'm sorry. I've been thinking about this all summer. I have to go. The horses will suffer here. Neither they nor we are accustomed to cold or hunger."

Rahma looked at the floor before slowly and painfully saying, "Fine, you go. Take the horses. Go to Tabríz. I will find you there if the Báb goes back that way."

Kapriel thought a moment. "How about this plan? I take the horses back to Tabríz and stay there for winter. You keep all of our summer money. No, wait," Kapriel stopped Rahma's objection. "You can still get some work with heavy loads and such. I can get work in Tabríz that pays well. You don't get as cold as I do, probably because there's so much more of you to hold in the heat. You can survive here: I cannot. Move to the masjid with the other Bábís. Living there, without the expense of me and the horses, you should have plenty of coin for food and other necessities. Agreed so far?"

The farmer grudgingly nodded.

"So, we plan to get together in spring. I will come back with the horses to be here by Naw-Rúz unless the Báb heads back east before then. If you need to find me, I'll be in the same caravanserai we stayed in last spring. When we meet, we will decide what to do next. What do you say?"

Rahma looked up. "I will miss you, my dear friend."

"And I you."

They parted the next morning with horse care and room paid off. There were a few tears as Kapriel left, both of them already feeling an old emptiness that had been filled during the last two years.

Kapriel took under three weeks to get to Tabríz. The climate improved as they descended from the mountains. He had pushed the horses a bit under threat of more storms and increasingly muddy ground. There were no other travelers that he could see. Twice he had to urge the mounts to a gallop in the face of an oncoming thunderstorm to reach a rest area or caravanserai before they were soaked. It was cold enough without getting wet.

There were no thieves or murderers jumping out from the scant cover. Perhaps they stayed in hiding when they saw the nearly empty packs on the mule and Kapriel's rather worn appearance. He mused on this, realizing the animals alone would be well worth stealing. Perhaps it was the change in weather that sent desperate people to homes or caves somewhere. Maybe the desolation was enough, with not a single tree to hide behind. However in some areas there were rocks—large ones, enough to hide a small army.

"Fine," he decided, "for whatever reason, thieves are just not on the trail at the moment. And thank You, God!"

He and the horses were jubilant to see Tabríz in the distance. The pace picked up to a gentle canter without Kapriel's conscious urging. Perhaps the beasts smelled hay and whatever scents meant rest ahead.

He pulled his last stash of savings from under several layers before entering the caravanserai. Only the funds his father had given him were still untouched. Once keep for the beasts was paid for and they were munching with relish on recently harvested hay, Kapriel went to the shop he had worked for six months earlier. The owner was glad to rehire Kapriel for inventory work. Shipments of everything to get through the winter were arriving from the east. Every crate had to be checked for content and quality before being taken into the storage room. This left the shop empty for hours at a time. With Kapriel's help in the store, the owner could take more time inspecting his purchases before letting the delivery man and his unburdened camels go.

The scribe helped keep ledgers of sales, purchases, and income, and he was able to do a little translation work when he was not otherwise busy. He tried to find a traveler going east to deliver another package in Julfa; however, most were hurrying west as fast as possible to pick up fabric, carpets, and other luxuries in warmer parts of Turkey before winter set in and closed mountain passes with snow as high as a camel's tail.

Some travelers were heading to Tihrán—well, more like evacuating as fast as possible—to escape the early onset of winter. The shopkeeper explained that the cold had come a month early, portending an unusually harsh season.

Kapriel thanked God and every saint he could think of for his quick departure from Mákú, and he prayed also for Rahma's safety and health, as well as for the Báb, for the Bábís, and for everyone else caught in cold weather. He decided he most definitely did not like cold.

The room at the caravanserai kept out the worst of the wind, for which he was grateful. But no one could call it warm. He inquired of several people how they planned to stay warm through the coldest days. Every one of them replied the same way.

"Put blankets or rugs on the floor. Put something that does not burn in the middle like rocks or tile. Then put your cooking brazier on that and keep a fire burning in it. A tall table goes above the brazier. You will cover that with every blanket and rug you have. Put your bed in there under the table and you will be warm enough."

Kapriel's main thought, growing in strength with each repeated answer was, *This is SO wrong!* He wondered what would kill him first: The fire as he was incinerated under layers of burning wool blankets, the smoke as he choked to death, or the cold seeping into every crevice of room and clothing, draining the heat from his skin, bones, and organs. By the end of fall, no amount of clothing could make him feel warm. He spent an unfortunately large part of his pay on those things listed for his indoor tent and on thick, woolen clothes. He went outside the city to find rocks like they had used for Rahma when he broke his leg, put the rocks against the brazier, and when the smoke threatened to overwhelm him, pushed the brazier out and hugged the rocks.

The winter was, indeed, harsh. The cold was bitter, threatening frostbite during the walk from his room to the shop. While in the shop, his ink froze in its jar and had to be replaced. He kept the fresh ink in his pockets to prevent it from icing up. Patronage had been light through the first half of the season while people used up all they had in their homes and waited for a break in the cold to go shopping. The breaks did not come, or were not warm enough to call "breaks." By mid-season, families were running out of things—first spices, then more necessary foods. The bazaars were too open and frigid for the vendors to survive, and as a result, they were forced to sell out of their homes, if at all.

Kapriel was frequently amazed to go to work or back to his room and find himself still alive when he arrived. The pot of water in his room would freeze overnight and often stay that way until he warmed it the next evening. Snow came and did not melt, slowly building up and choking streets and alleys. Sometimes the weight of the accumulating snow and slow melting on roofs would cause a roof to collapse, killing all or part of a family.

The Persian custom for roof building was to embed lateral posts in walls at ceiling height, cover them with grass, then add a thick layer of mud—two or three feet thick—on top. In dry, hot weather it was the perfect insulation. Kapriel had sometimes helped his family roll rainwater off the roof to prevent the roof from returning to mud. All this snow, however, added insulation and allowed seepage of water into the roof, undermining its stability as it added weight. A collapse could mean total destruction of the home, crushing those within.

Others died of the cold, whether directly as they foraged for burnables outside the city or begged in the streets, or as a consequence of constant energy use to stay alive, with their bodies slowly weakening until they failed in illness or from cold stopping the heart. Whole weeks passed without the outside temperature warming above the freezing point. Families began burning whatever was available—furniture, carpets, anything to get warm. Regular customers at the shop were appearing more blue, some from smoke damage to their lungs, some from the unbearable cold.

Kapriel sometimes crossed paths with an English physician, Dr. Cormick, who lived in Tabríz. The doctor occasionally came into the store, but more often Kapriel saw him in the frozen streets, bundled up with his medical bag going to or from some unfortunate home.

Once in a while a caravan would arrive with the overburdened animals lame and shivering and the caravanserai owner sending an assistant to fetch a doctor for the drovers. Some of the mules, donkeys, and camels had obvious late additions tied on top of their

more neatly arranged loads, probably saved from fallen companions left in the deep snows of the mountains. The drovers would
unload the cargo into a storage room, then feed the animals. Kapriel
wondered if it would be better to leave the empty pack saddles on
as blankets rather than exposing the animals' damp, flattened hair
to the extreme chill. The drovers must have left the loads on the
animals during the entire journey, which would have saved them
time but would be deeply damaging to the animals. The mules,
donkeys, camels, and horses did not get rubbed down or have their
open sores treated. Drovers were, for that time, more interested in
their own survival than in that of their beasts of burden.

The first day of real snowmelt caused great celebration. Virtually the entire stinking, dirty, unwashed population went outside,
breathed great amounts of fresh unfrozen air, then went back in. It
was glorious!

When the snow was melting in earnest, Kapriel's thoughts
turned to Mákú. Naw-Rúz was only four weeks away. The melt
meant the roads would be difficult, if passable at all. He would
have to start soon in returning to that bastion of cold to the west if
he was going to make it before the appointed day.

Feeling deep misgivings and a selfish desire to stay in Tabríz, where
it was undoubtedly warmer, he set about his preparations. The shopkeeper was happy to have his spring letters already done, and he
gave Kapriel a bonus package of dates for the trip. The scribe tidied
his room, selling the carpets, brazier, and other winter warmth
needs but keeping all the blankets.

With three weeks to go, the snow had mostly melted, and traffic
to and from the city had resumed. Caravans arrived to pick up the
famous Tabríz carpets while delivering tools, trinkets, and delicacies to the city. Destinations to the south and east had experienced

a snowmelt earlier, which allowed traffic from those areas to head north and west before many caravans coming from colder regions. The few caravans that had struggled through during the winter to get the better prices when supplies were scarce moved out early, but the risks had been gigantic, and many of those animals and men were either lost or injured in the snow, ice, and storms.

Kapriel began saddling up one fine morning and found others doing the same. There were a few Bábís also heading to Máku who were willing to ride with him. This relieved him greatly and diminished his fear that his luck in avoiding bandits had run out.

The return trip was somewhat happier than the first one, as Kapriel shared the trail with joyful men on their way to meet their sacred goal. Some did not have rides, so they all took turns on the horses. Kapriel was glad to be able to get down and stretch his legs for a while each day. Rahma's horse had a different rider every hour.

Other than turning to mud, the landscape around them had not yet shown any sign of spring, and the slopes had remained brown with snow-crushed dormant grass and bare trees.

The melted snow naturally caused the greatest threat to this journey: mud. It took an hour to extricate the first horse to plunge knee-deep into a mud hole. After that, the men walked in front, giving riders time to stop if someone suddenly fell into muck. They would help him out, clean him up, and, if necessary, help get him changed into dry clothes before he got a bad chill. Then the party would maneuver around the mud trap.

It was a little slower traveling with pedestrians, but they traveled the same distance each day as Kapriel had with Rahma—about twenty miles. The main differences between riding and walking were the level of exhaustion and the later hour of arrival. The scribe found himself to be definitely more tired than when he only rode, but also less sore in the riding muscles after a winter spent indoors.

The group climbed the final pass to Máku—not before Naw-Rúz, as hoped—but the day of that vernal equinox. They found themselves welcomed at the Masjid by a few Bábís who had stayed the winter or arrived before them.

Kapriel saw Rahma among the hardy believers, welcoming the travelers and holding Kapriel's reins as he dismounted. They gave each other enthusiastic hugs (Kapriel suddenly remembered how strong Rahma was) and began talking. Well, Rahma began talking, but Kapriel had to wait until Rahma let go so he could breathe.

The farmer was already happily relating recent news. Mullá Husayn had arrived the day before and was staying with the Báb. "And Kapriel, he walked here."

"No!"

"From Mashhad."

"You are lying!"

"No, it is true!"

"But that is . . . I don't know, how far is it?"

"At least eight hundred miles, probably more."*

"And he walked!?"

"All the way, out of reverence for the Báb, with just one companion. Like a pilgrimage. You know he was the first one the Báb revealed Himself to, back in Shíráz. I remember seeing him around."

"Me, too. That seems like half a lifetime ago, yet it was only three and a half years." Kapriel was still thinking of the walk from Mashhad. "You know, that means he was walking for at least half the winter—the worse half."

Rahma changed the topic as they carried the tack and Kapriel's belongings to Rahma's tiny room in the masjid. "Remember that book the Báb was chanting as He revealed it? It is called the Bayán. Actually He wrote two of them, one in Persian and a different one in Arabic. Of course, I don't understand much of what the Arabic one says, but thanks to you I can read the Persian one."

---

* It is about 1,097 miles from Mákú to Mashhad.

When they had set down their loads, Rahma picked a book up from a mat next to his bed. "This is your copy." He handed it to Kapriel with reverence.

Kapriel, however, noticed the hands that passed him the book were not the same as they had been last fall. "Rahma, your fingers! What happened?" Several digits were shorter than normal. "Was it an accident, or frostbite?"

"It is unimportant. Please, take the book. Look in the back cover."*

Kapriel's mind was buzzing with questions, but he saw a little shyness in his friend's expression. He opened the back cover to a barely legible scrawl: "Kapriel, thank you for teaching me to read. Your friend, Rahmat'u'lláh Husayn-i-Shírází."

He was stunned! "Rahma, you can write!" He thumped his beaming friend on the back a few times with great pride.

Rahma demurred, "I did not do the rest of the book, so don't worry. Someone who writes well did that."

"This is wonderful! Is this how you spent your winter?"

"Yes, partly. It has been an unbelievable few months. We have learned so much! The Bayán is not just about laws, but about God, and explaining things. You will see. And how did you spend your winter in warmer places?"

"If Tabríz was warmer, then it must have been awful here."

"But what did you do?" Rahma again dodged the question of coldness.

"Well, remember the shop I worked in our first time through the city?"

They talked for hours about Kapriel's adventure and the Báb's activities. Somehow Rahma avoided speaking of himself.

---

* Persian is written from right to left, the opposite of English. Because of this, the right cover is the front, and the left cover is the back.

The next two weeks showed Kapriel just how much his friend had changed over the winter. Rahma was constantly in search of ways to help others—not for compensation, but out of a desire to be of service to his fellow humans. He had become part of the community, as if he had been born there. He helped the poor and elderly, carried heavy loads for women, and assisted men with their labors. He also worked for wages on the farms, and he was trusted by the farmers.

One day Kapriel was sitting with a Bábí who had also stayed through the winter. He wondered aloud at these changes.

The Bábí responded, "How could anyone not change, listening to the Báb chanting His beautiful melodies week after week, no matter the weather, or the temperature? This winter there were weeks of unendurable cold, when the water in a bowl would not melt unless put on a fire. We had to heat the water to do our morning ablutions before prayer, but it would refreeze so quickly we had to hurry. Droplets would freeze on our hands before we could dry them. Even the local people had great difficulty, telling us they had never seen a winter so frigid. But no matter the cold, the Báb was up, prepared, and chanting in the dawn half-light every day.

"Awakening to His music warmed our hearts and minds, overcoming the cold of our bodies. Every morning we learned more of God; every day we cared less for ourselves. This is the change you see."

It explained much to Kapriel, who wondered why he had not been so affected by the Báb's chanting over the summer. Perhaps great suffering through the winter helped in letting go of self. Maybe it was the continual contact with holiness. *Or,* Kapriel thought, *maybe I am so closed off from God that I chose not to change.*

During these days of learning for the Armenian scribe, the Báb's chief disciple, Mullá Husayn, left—on foot still—to continue his teaching work. He headed south toward Khuy and the western edge of Lake Urmía, speaking to the believers in villages, towns, and cities as he continued around the southern tip of the lake, up the eastern side to Tabríz, and then headed east toward Mashhad, as directed by the Báb. He cheered and encouraged the Bábís in each place, passing along the message of love sent by their cherished One.

Shortly after Mullá Husayn's departure from Mákú, most of the other believers left as well, sent on their way to promote their faith as their capacities allowed. Rahma was, for once, willing to be obedient and leave for a while, and the two friends agreed to return east.

Then word came of yet another move. The grand vizier had sent new orders: the Báb was to be taken from Mákú and sent further from the Russian border to the castle at Chihriq.[6]

Neither Rahma nor Kapriel had ever heard of such a place. The farmer, wishing only to see where the Báb would be staying, decided to follow the new escort and see what this next prison would be like before heading back toward Tabríz. Once again, they gathered supplies, packed up, and headed out, this time riding to the south.

13

Chihriq to Qazvín, Spring 1848

Kapriel thought it impossible for such beauteous fields of flowers to bloom after the harshness of the past winter, yet there they were, on the approach to Chihriq, riding the lows between long, rolling hills. Spans of red poppies bobbed in the breeze on tall stems and mingled with clusters of yellow and orange flowers. Small, white clovers showed closer to the ground. The further south the riders traveled, the more relaxed Kapriel felt.

It took a week to get to Khuy, a large town / small city twenty miles north of Lake Urmía. The trails were not direct, requiring a somewhat circuitous path around mountains where paths joined and split and valleys connected, forming crossroads. The friends did not mind. This time, they chose not to hurry or try to keep up. Their only goal was to take a look when they reached their destination.

From Khuy, the road—now the only road—turned a bit more west than due south, leaving behind the high mountains and taking the travelers to the town of Salmás* in a few days. From there, the road turned to a narrow track going mostly west and paralleling a winding creek bed. Roughly twenty miles after Salmás, they arrived (in late April) at a tiny village, not even large enough for a real market. It was simply a wall with a few primitive huts inside.

---

* Now called Shápúr.

Beyond that hamlet, up the side of an isolated, rocky outcrop of a mountain, sat a castle. This was the prison of Chihriq. They could make out one round tower amid the walls. The whole fortress was old and in need of repair, with parts of it crumbling, like much of Persia.

The upthrust rock formation just behind the castle towered above the structure at its foot, and the darkness of the weathered stone added gloom to the large hill it rested upon.

The friends sat on their horses, staring at the bleak outlines of the edifice. After some minutes Rahma spoke first, "You know what this means, yes?"

"Yes. They have finally succeeded in sending Him away."

Rahma humphed low in his throat, "Away from everyone, away from any thought of comfort, away from even us. There will be no work for you, maybe none for me."

"And any who are able to visit after the Báb wins over His guards will have to stay in Salmás, a day's walk each way. Siyyid Hasan will have to walk there every time something is needed."

"Well, He will win over His guards. We can be sure of that." Rahma spoke with great assurance, causing Kapriel to smile once again at his friend's maturation. Rahma's hand was rubbing his chest again, as if to soothe away pain. In unspoken agreement, they turned their mounts toward the town to ask respite for the night.

Later, finishing a meal of trail rations rather than procuring food from the hamlet's meager supplies, they considered what to do next.

Kapriel voted for Tabríz. "We can both get work there, and we already have contacts."

"Yes. Or we could go a little farther. They did not send the Báb to this desolate place for just a little while. I think He will be here a long time. And it would be nice to spend next winter some place warmer. Maybe Qazvín?"

"And if we are lucky the poetess, Quratu'l-'Ayn, will speak in public?" Kapriel smiled at his now soft-spoken friend.

Rahma stayed serious, "That would be lucky."

—◆—

The next morning they left for Salmás, purchasing basic travel needs upon arrival in the afternoon. Next was Khuy, where they could resupply more completely, then up and around Lake Urmía. The seasonal cessation of rain around Naw-Rúz meant the roads were firm and nearly dry. The verdant fields looked as they had a year ago when the friends had left Tabríz for Mákú.

Between Khuy and Tabríz, the two unpacked their copies of the Bayán and began reading it to each other, studying as they let their horses ramble along the road. Kapriel soon had a favorite verse: "There is no paradise, in the estimation of the believers in the Divine Unity, more exalted than to obey God's commandments, and there is no fire in the eyes of those who have known God and His signs, fiercer than to transgress His laws and to oppress another soul, even to the extent of a mustard seed. On the Day of Resurrection God will, in truth, judge all men, and we all verily plead for His grace."[1]

Kapriel wondered aloud, "Did we not already have a Resurrection Day when the Báb made His first declaration to Mullá Husayn?"

"You are asking me? You have the brains. But I think we are still on a theme of the next Messenger, the One Whom God shall make Manifest."

"Oh, yes, that makes sense."

A few more chapters brought them to Rahma's favorite:

The reason why privacy hath been enjoined in moments of devotion is this, that thou mayest give thy best attention to the remembrance of God, that thy heart may at all times be animated with His Spirit, and not be shut out as by a veil from thy Best-Beloved. Let not thy tongue pay lip service in praise of God while thy heart be not attuned to the exalted

Summit of Glory, and the Focal Point of communion. Thus if haply thou dost live in the Day of Resurrection, the mirror of thy heart will be set towards Him Who is the Daystar of Truth; and no sooner will His light shine forth than the splendor thereof shall forthwith be reflected in thy heart. For He is the Source of all goodness, and unto Him revert all things.[2]

Kapriel noted, "Again He is referring to the next One. So far that seems to be a large part of this Book—preparing the Bábís for the Promised One."

"Yes, but it is also a guide on how to behave. Look again at this . . ."

—•—

A week after leaving Khuy they arrived in Tabríz with a much better understanding of the new faith. Approaching the city, the countryside was dressed in spring glory, with grass abounding and fruit trees bearing the tiny promises of future harvests. The city itself was clean from snowmelt and rain, though no amount of washing could reduce the cracks and patching of walls. Down alleys, treetops were visible above yard ramparts, lush with young leaves.

They stayed at the same caravanserai they had used before, and its Bábí owner was happy to converse for the evening. They passed along the description of Chihriq and its environs. Their host talked of the recent trembles, minor earthquakes under a city too often devastated by large shifts of the earth.

The friends were glad to leave in the morning. They understood earthquakes. Shíráz had been thrown to the ground several times in its history, but not as frequently as Tabríz.

The next large city was Zanján, which meant another week of riding. There they also made contact with Bábís to get local news. Hujjat, beloved leader of the believers at Zanján, was still imprisoned in Tihrán. Despite his absence, there was even more friction between 'ulámá and Bábís, with the clergy relentlessly agitating for the extermination of the beleaguered believers. The Bábís had been greatly encouraged by Mullá Husayn's recent visit.

One more week found the friends at the western gate of Qazvín, about a month before the summer solstice. They had not seen the city previously due to the Báb's escort stopping at the village to the south, avoiding Qazvín itself.

This city, much like Tabríz and Isfáhán, showed its age in crumbling fortifications, cracked walls and pavement, and in generally appearing run-down. They found a clean-looking caravanserai in which to park their horses, and then asked by name for the two Bábís—Mullá Táhir and Hájí Aziz'u'lláh—they had met during the stop in Síyáh-Dihán, the small town to the south, over a year ago. The man was suddenly quite suspicious and openly hostile.

"What do you want with them?!" he thundered.

Kapriel put a hand on Rahma's arm to forestall his friend's probable response—admitting to being a Bábí. The gesture, however, further infuriated the caravanserai owner who glared at them suspiciously.

Kapriel then answered, "We are travelers who came across them last spring and found them quite helpful. We happened to be back this way and are looking for further assistance." He hoped he struck the right tone for a merchant and servant, not haughty enough to provoke the man, not servile enough to seem the lowly peasant he was.

The man only slightly moderated his attitude. "You should be more careful who you ask for. They were heretics, Bábís," he spat after saying the name. "One is dead, the other is working in the market. You should stay away from those sons of burnt fathers if

you do not want to be burned with them." He then made the gesture to ward off the evil eye and went back to work.

Kapriel thanked him for the advice and imperiously signaled
Rahma to follow him out to the street. Then he turned to his large
friend, finding the farmer not enraged or offended but resigned,
saddened by the encounter.

Rahma preempted the imminent question from Kapriel as to his
emotional state. "I am fine. We knew this was coming. We saw it
start in Shíráz. Let us see if we can recognize anyone in the market
without asking."

They walked to the bazaar without speaking. Kapriel was trying
his utmost not to think about an execution he had accidentally
seen, happening by at the wrong moment when an accused heretic
was burned to death as a warning to all not to go against accepted
doctrine.

The main bazaar in Tabríz was similar to every other bazaar they
had seen. Vendors were grouped according to the type of item sold,
with the metalsmiths in one group, the woodworkers over there,
and a long line of carpet sellers down this way.

Doing his best to look like a prosperous merchant with his large
(yet humble) servant, Kapriel found a few booths selling scribe supplies, and he purchased some replacements.

Coming upon a bookseller, the friends found a familiar face,
Hájí Aziz'u'lláh. That face suddenly paled, the eyes going wide as
he recognized the visitors. He was fairly young, at most twenty-five,
with thin features and a wiry frame. His height was just slightly
more than Kapriel, his brown hair thick and a bit bushy where it stuck
out from the small turban of a merchant. He wore a moderate-quality
aba over the usual long linen shirt and trousers.

Kapriel asked, "Do you have any volumes in Armenian?"

The man looked at his books for a moment, several volumes
coming quickly to hand. Kapriel looked them over with great interest, giving the vendor time to scribble a note that he slipped into
another book. When his customer had checked through the first

offering, the man handed him the book with the note, saying, "Every Armenian should have a copy of this. You will find the quality high, though it is not a recent printing."

Kapriel examined the printing-press copy of "Saints in the Armenian Apostolic Church." He browsed several pages before and after reading the note. The note simply stated, "If you want to talk, ask for more to look at." Going along with it the scribe inquired, "Do you have any more? This is an acceptable volume, suggesting there may be more in, perhaps, storage somewhere?"

"You like this, then?"

Actually, Kapriel really did. "It seems to be in adequate condition. How much are you asking?"

They negotiated a price, and Kapriel handed the purchase to his bemused retainer. "Now, do you have any other volumes with a similar theme?"

"A few, but I am sorry, they are not here. There is not room for everything in this small closet of a booth. My humble apologies, the rest is in my meager home."

"Enough that a man may not bring them all at once to the bazaar in the morning?"

The book seller tipped his head to one side, then the other in an ambiguous gesture. "Surely even a large man such as your servant would be challenged to do so, but you see before you an unworthy weakling, barely able to carry himself to and from his abode."

Hardly. Kapriel put on his "mother is staring at me" face to keep laughter at bay as the merchant continued, "It would be most gracious of you, sir, if you could lower yourself to visiting the humble abode of this simple vendor, the more easily to peruse all available volumes."

Kapriel rocked back on his heels, gazing in consideration around the bazaar. "This is most inconvenient." He hesitated again. "But, perhaps, it will lessen the number of visits to the bazaar."

"Yes, indeed." The vendor did further scribbling on another scrap of paper, less hurried this time, while saying, "if you would grace my home with your presence you will find the directions here. Perhaps this evening would be acceptable to you?"

After another delay for considering Kapriel replied, "Yes. Good day, then." He nodded to Rahma to take the proffered directions and walked away, looking with interest at booths on the way out.

When they had finally left the market area, Rahma looked at Kapriel with one eyebrow up. He looked forward with a puzzled expression, then the eyebrow again lifted as his focus returned to Kapriel. At last he asked, "You enjoyed that, didn't you?"

A large smile spread across the scribe's face, "Yes, absolutely! Didn't you?"

"I just stood there looking unimportant. Maybe you are in the wrong profession. You could be an actor, or a spy."

—•—

Back in their room at the caravanserai Kapriel took out the first note and dunked it in a small bowl of water, washing off the ink. He dried his hands while Rahma read the second note. It gave directions to the merchant's home and requested they come for dinner just after sunset.

The note led them to a somewhat better home than the book seller had implied. It was at least as large as Kapriel's family home, well-kept for its age. Hájí Aziz'u'lláh welcomed them, still in his role as humble purveyor of books. As soon as the door closed he smiled gently to his guests, requesting they address him as Aziz. The friends relaxed, reintroducing themselves since their first meeting had been so long ago. Wonderful smells drifted to them from the kitchen.

Aziz noted their interest and called toward the source of the aromas, "Farah, please, can you come to meet our guests?"

"In a minute," came the feminine response.

The home was clean and tidy to every corner—until they entered the storage room for the extra books. Volumes of every size were piled waist-high along walls and stacked to head-height at corners. Kapriel was in heaven, looking from title to title.

Aziz chuckled at the avid interest. "So, you like books?"

Rahma interjected, "Ha! He loves them. He has a Qur'án, and the Bayan, and a Bible."

Just then Farah entered, wearing a pretty, well-fitted dress, with no veil or head covering. She was about a hand-span shorter than her husband, slightly built, with very long hair in a braid down her back. Her features, with intelligent eyes, were more rounded than her angular spouse. They were introduced, and Rahma was unable to completely cover his distress at yet another barefaced woman.

Aziz noted his discomfort. "Rahma, you know the Báb has declared men and women equal, yes? If we don't have to wear all that suffocating material, why should my wife have to here in our own home?"

Rahma nodded, struggling valiantly against deeply ingrained customs.

Aziz found a few volumes that Kapriel really might like, then invited them back to the front room to sit on floor cushions and discuss events. He was saddened by the descriptions of Máku and Chihriq, but had also been able to meet with Mullá Husayn when that disciple recently held gatherings to encourage the believers. He related one meeting to the friends, both humbling and cheering them with his description of Mullá Husayn's unmatched character.

Dinner arrived then, with Farah settling herself next to her husband and shifting the conversation to less weighty topics. Scribe and farmer were fascinated to hear where various parts of their dinner came from—dates from the Fars region, greens from local farms, rice from the swamps of Mázindarán.

"Swamps?" Kapriel inquired.

"Yes, swamps, or bogs," Aziz restated.

"I have read of these, but I have never seen one." He thought back to the agricultural book he had hollowed out for the Qur'án. "It's a low-lying place with slow-moving water, yes?"

"Ah, yes, you are from Fars. Yes, that is a good description of a swamp. They are usually stinking, often stagnant, and full of disease." Aziz had a little glimmer of mischief in his smile as he added, "You can see them on the other side of the Alburz. One of the main roads goes north from here, over the ridge and up to Rasht where vast amounts of rice are grown."

Kapriel had lit up, "Rahma, shall we go?" He returned his focus to Aziz, "Are there forests? Real ones, where a man can get lost and not see out?"

Aziz, Farah and Rahma were all grinning. Kapriel looked at them uncomprehendingly. "What?"

Aziz bowed with one hand on his heart. "Please do not take offense. You have the joyful curiosity of a child; something most of us lose far too soon. Yes, there are forests, and the sea. The Caspian is not some large lake, but a vast body of water you cannot see across. The weather there is very wet . . ."

They talked about such things until the end of the meal.

Finally, the last of the rice was scooped into Rahma's never-full digestive system, the platters had all been taken to the kitchen, and Farah was busy with cleaning. They resumed their seats in the front room, soon joined by their hostess.

Rahma began, "So, please, can you tell us what happened to your friend, Mullá Táhir? And why you and Kapriel were playing games in the market?"

"It is a sad tale, and a long one. It is dangerous for you to stay here any longer. Our house is watched. Are you sure you don't wish to leave with some books? If you stay, you will be in danger."

Kapriel and Rahma glanced at each other, then Kapriel responded, "Please tell us what has happened."

"All right. It started last summer. You have heard of Shaykh Ahmad and Siyyid Kázim?"

Scribe and farmer nodded yes.

"The lead judge of Qazvín, Hájí Mullá Taqí, hated them. He vilified them at every opportunity from his pulpit. So you can guess how he felt about Bábís. "Our poetess, Qurratu'l-'Ayn—"

His wife interrupted, "A woman of knowledge unsurpassed by any."

Aziz smiled and continued, "And strong, unyielding in her assertions, undefeatable in debate. She returned from her travels where she had taught and confirmed thousands of Bábís on her return from Karbilá. She returned here to her home, summoned by her family. She set to work teaching God's Cause here. Her husband was the son of Hájí Mullá Taqí, and he has done his best to be just like his hate-filled father. So, the rift between them was impossible to mend, and she divorced him."

Rahma was astounded, "She divorced him?"

Farah answered, "In clear, and ringing tones. The last thing she said to him was that she had cast him out of her life forever."[3]

Kapriel, who would have congratulated the poetess on her feat of independence, eagerly awaited more of the story.

Aziz moved on, "A young Mullá 'Abdu'lláh walked into this mess. He was an ardent admirer of Shaykh Ahmad and Siyyid Kázim but not a Bábí. He arrived on a day when Taqí had declared a man a heretic for speaking the ideas of those two great divines, decreed his expulsion from the town, and let the masses loose on him. The man's turban was wound around his neck, his shoes stolen, and he was dragged through the streets by the end of the turban cloth.[4]

"Mullá 'Abdu'lláh was enraged by this torment of someone who had spoken highly of Shaykh Ahmad and Siyyid Kázim. He awaited his chance, but during that wait Taqí had switched back to vilifying the Bábís. One night the young man found his opportunity and stabbed Taqí in the throat."

Nobody winced, though they had the manners not to cheer.

Farah jumped in, "It was chaos! When they finished accusing each other, the 'ulámás turned on the Bábís."

Aziz elaborated, "There was a great frenzy. Bábís were grabbed off of the street and imprisoned. Mullá 'Abdu'lláh saw this terrible treatment of innocents and went to the authorities, admitting his guilt so that the rest would be released. They arrested him, too, but they did not release the others, sending them all to prison in Tihrán. Seeing no possibility of justice, the murderer escaped with inside help some time later."

Farah said, "A nobleman staying in Tihrán, one Mírzá Husayn 'Alí, went to visit the prisoners and negotiate their freedom. Several of the authorities were after exorbitant compensation for care of the prisoners. He was able to get some out of chains and provide at least proper food and comfort for the others."

The conversation switched back to Aziz, who said, "Meanwhile, Taqí's family explored every possibility for exacting revenge on the Báb and His followers. Qurratu'l-'Ayn was imprisoned in the cellar of her father's home, purportedly for her safety. Her ex-husband forcibly took their three children. They sought execution for all of us but were denied permission by the sháh. When the murderer escaped, they accused Mírzá Husayn 'Alí of being involved in the scheme. He was in captivity for several days before powerful friends and his wealthy family intimidated or embarrassed the ward chief to set Him free."

Farah said, "Further angered, the local mullás named one Bábí still in Qazvín, Shaykh Sálih, as the murderer and executed him. By this time it was early fall, and people of Qazvín had been rallied, exhorted, and lied to so much that they thirsted for the blood of Bábís. When the remaining prisoners were finally released—into the hands of Taqí's family, no less—Hájí Asadu'lláh was immediately executed while still in Tihrán, and they tried to cover it up as an illness."

Aziz added, "As soon as they reached Qazvín, the released prisoners were set upon by the prepared crowds, who carried any and every weapon they could find and obliterated the bodies of the Bábís. There was nothing left." He paused a moment, overcome by emotion.

Farah put a gentle hand on his arm, finishing the story. "One of those murdered men was Mullá Táhir-i-Shírází, our friend. Another was Mullá Ibráhím-i-Mahallátí. They were both well-admired for their character, and very knowledgeable of religious matters."

Kapriel sympathized, "I am so sad for your loss." He waited a moment, and then asked, "Is Qurratu'l-'Ayn still imprisoned in her father's home?"

Aziz and Farah both smiled and glanced at each other. Aziz told them, "No. She disappeared."

"She what?" Rahma was afraid she may have been secretly murdered.

"We think she is all right," answered Aziz. "After the murder of our friends, there was great pressure on her and threats on her life. Her ex-husband had become chief ecclesiastical judge in his father's place. She sent a message to him, which, of course, was read by everyone who could and repeated to others. It said, ""Fain would they put out God's light with their mouths: but God only desireth to perfect His light, albeit the infidels abhor it." If my Cause be the Cause of Truth, if the Lord whom I worship be none other than the one true God, He will, ere nine days have elapsed, deliver me from the yoke of your tyranny. Should He fail to achieve my deliverance, you are free to act as you desire. You will have irrevocably established the falsity of my belief.'"

"My God!" Rahma exclaimed.

Kapriel waved hushing motions at Rahma, breathless for the finale.

Aziz continued, "Of course, by the end of the ninth day, we were terribly worried. Oh, how we prayed! During the night there were shouts about the city, with runners going from gate to gate. Then soldiers went searching from house to house. She was gone."

Kapriel asked, "You don't think she was kidnapped and murdered?"

Aziz answered, "It would be completely against their hopes to undermine her if they helped her fulfill the prediction. It would make no sense."

Rahma pleaded, "But she has been heard from in some safe place?"

Farah shook her head, "No, not a word. Nor have the local authorities calmed in their agitation over her escape."

Aziz added, "Though we did win several new converts from her supernatural disappearance."

Farmer and scribe left late in the night, noting the sudden steps of one person turning to run up the alley ahead of them. Kapriel had another book under his arm, thinking that he might be able to use it as a weapon if necessary. Back in their room, they considered their options.

Kapriel began, "So, we were watched."

"Yes. Which means it may be hard to find work, if they pass the news of the two southern Bábí visitors."

"Which they will, making assumptions and all."

"Things are very tense in Zanján, too."

"No work in Chihriq or Salmás. Khuy may be large enough to keep a scribe alive, but is still largely Kurdish." Kapriel looked out the window for a moment, then turned to Rahma. "We could go home."

The farmer began rubbing his sternum, his face in a scowl of concentration. He eventually shook some thought from his head and asked Kapriel, "Would backtracking to Tabríz be okay? We know people, we could work. They are not trying to kill Bábís, yet."

The two years since Kapriel had seen his family, plus the frequent travel were beginning to wear on him. Nonetheless, he had made a promise.

"Tabríz it is."

14

Tabríz, June through July, 1848

Summer in Tabríz was pleasantly warm: Certainly warmer than Mákú, but not aridly hot like Shíráz. The friends had quickly found work. Rahma was back in the fields planting, weeding, herding, and otherwise enjoying himself.

The shop Kapriel had worked in did not need him, so he set up in the bazaar according to his long-learned habit. He was surprised at how quickly he built a customer base. The nation was astir, and people wanted to write about it.

The customers found Kapriel to be neutral on all issues. He was neither openly shocked at the vitriol spewed by those opposed to the Báb, nor upset by the unstinting support of Him in letters from fans. He was asked both to write outgoing letters and to read correspondence to the illiterate. At some point, the few Kurdish of the city learned he could understand them, if not read or write in their language. They chatted with him on recent news and asked him to translate letters into Persian or Arabic for distant relatives and business purposes.

He was often able to glean news even before Rahma. The strictures of the Báb's confinement had once again been relaxed. Letters to and from Urmía spoke of long lines of pilgrims seeking an audience in Chihriq. A good portion of leading divines, government officials, and others had given themselves over completely to the Báb's Cause, teaching their city and creating great excitement. Letters reported a constant stream of seekers between Khuy and Chihriq.

A couple of customers who had come to Tabríz from witnessing these events claimed to have seen a dervish, one who came on foot all the way from India, who was teaching the Cause to the Kurds with great vigor and success. Such news had spread quickly to Tihrán, with rumors of the grand vizier's displeasure arriving with return couriers.

Rahma's evening forays to visit Bábís brought news of a young man imprisoned in his stepfather's home in Tabríz. This youngster, Muhammad-'Alíy-i-Zunúzí, was a stepson of the Bábí the friends had met in Mákú, the one 'Alí Khan had gone to invite to see the Báb. This youth had wholeheartedly accepted the message of the Báb and wished to sacrifice his own life for the new religion. The stepfather, truly well-meaning, thought the young man to be unbalanced and in need of care. The Bábís had discussed what to do about it, but relatives had conversed with the anguished, weeping lad several times, unable to calm him.

Yet another round of excitement swept through the already-tense city a week after summer began. A new escort was to be dispatched with orders to bring the Báb to Tabríz for trial. The news swept through the town like an earthquake, shifting opinions and swaying views, creating a maelstrom of rumor and supposition.

Several weeks passed with growing expectation. People were arriving from neighboring towns and outlying villages to see the spectacle, whether ardent adherents, vicious opponents, or neutrally curious.

When the escort arrived (around 20 July), they did not enter the city, which was ready to explode. They instead took the Báb to the governor's mansion on the outskirts.

Kapriel and Rahma, unable to restrain their curiosity, hunted down members of the escort and, finding one alone, politely accosted him with questions. He, however, was not in the mood for questions, suggesting the friends find someone else to interrogate.

And they did, in the bazaar. The second member of the escort the friends could track down was far more jocular, a storyteller by nature. The three found a spot away from the agitated masses where they could sit and chat.

Kapriel started the conversation by stating, "There are rumors all around about the journey here from Chihriq. Can you truthfully tell us what happened?" He slipped a few coins onto a nearby barrel.

Farhád* looked shocked at the word *truthfully* and replied, "I am an honest man and will only tell you what I saw with these eyes. May the mullás burn my beard if I stray from the truth for even an instant!"

Not that he had much of a beard to burn. He was one of those who preferred a short beard trimmed to a sharp point below the chin—probably doing the trimming with one of the various very-sharp-looking knives and swords he wore about himself. The coins had already vanished from the barrel.

Rahma was impressed. "Wonderful! Can you start with telling us about Urmíá?** What was it like? What happened there?"

"Well," Farhád rocked back a little, "Most of what happened did happen in Urmíá, but any story must begin at the beginning. And this story begins in Khuy.

"We had orders to retrieve the Báb and bring Him here with the least possible excitement but also the least possible delay. On the way through Khuy we saw the frenzy of the people, all of them talking

_____

* Fictional character.

** At the time of the story Urmíá was called Urúmíyyih, later short-ened to the form used in the story, and currently called Riḍáiyyih.

about the Báb, whether for or against Him and His Cause. There was no other topic of conversation. To bring His Holiness back through Khuy would have caused the greatest of excitement, agitating the people to the last man. It was therefore decided to go south, through Urmíá and around the south of the lake of that name.

"In Chihriq, when we took custody of the Báb, we were impressed by several things. First, the guards and warden of the prison were completely deferential to their august Guest. Despite the instructions of the authorities in Tihrán, despite the isolated location and crudeness of the local people, and although He stayed within the prison fortress, it seemed He was the governor of the province, not the least a prisoner.

"Second, the holy Man Himself in no way behaved as a prisoner. He graciously greeted us, we who had come to take Him to trial and possible execution, as though we were long-lost family, beloved brethren who had finally arrived. His bearing was worthy of the Sháh-han-Sháh (King of Kings) of prophecy, with nobility, majesty, and yet humility beyond anything we had come across, ever.

"Third, His height had nothing to do with His immense reputation. Is it not odd that we picture great men as also being large men? But He is just a bit shorter than average, and a little pale, perhaps from the lack of sunlight, perhaps from the rigors of confinement. Or maybe He was born on the light side.[1] Yet these physical descriptions are completely irrelevant in His presence.

"So, without delay, we collected our charge and headed south to Urmíá, a town in a mountain valley. If the agitation there is any indication of what would have awaited us in Khuy, it is good that we went through the much smaller town. The prince graciously received—"

"Excuse me," Kapriel interrupted gently, "could you tell us which prince?"

Rahma and Farhád laughed, the storyteller saying, "Yes, as the saying goes, 'camels, fleas and princes are everywhere.'"

Rahma asked, "How many are there? Hundreds, surely."

Farhád answered, "Thousands, actually. You know the early Qájárs liked large harems and many progeny. All the governors are princes, and most of their assistants, the mayors, military leaders . . . so, where was I?"

Kapriel said, "Arriving at Urmíá."

"Ah, yes. The prince," he glanced at Kapriel, "Malik Qásim Mírzá, received Him with ceremony and wonderful hospitality. Every effort was extended to show respect and deference to the Báb, and none were allowed to speak ill of Him.

"The city itself is much in ruin. There was a terrible earthquake eight years ago that devastated the buildings and the population. They are rebuilding and have far to go, repairing what they can, knocking down what is not safe, and building anew what is needed.

"We took a rest there, and on that Friday, the prince decided to 'test the courage and power of his Guest.'[2] As the Báb prepared to leave for the public bath the prince ordered his groom to bring one of the wildest horses the prince owned. The particular horse brought forth had never been successfully ridden, having thrown the most experienced and skilled of horsemen. The entire town knew of the upcoming test and crowded the main square, with excitement and expectation all around.

"When the moment came the horse was lead up to the Holy Man. He took the bridle, stroked the horse, mounted with no difficulty and rode to the bath. The horse did nothing to upset its rider: not a single sidestep, no misbehavior at all. We were all astonished, the entire town having seen this miracle. People rushed to kiss His stirrups and had to be held back by the guards to prevent endangering His person. He went on to His bath with just one attendant. When the Báb had finished and left the bathhouse, the people grabbed every pot, urn, and pitcher they could find to take the bathwater blessed by His presence, leaving not a single drop in the bath house."

Kapriel jumped into the space left for a dramatic pause, "What did they do with it?"

This slightly disoriented Farhád. "Do with what?"

"The water from the bath, what did they do with it?"

"God knows! What, did I follow them to find out? No! That is not the concern of visitors. So, the entire populace arose to proclaim their allegiance to Him, but when He was informed of this He said—and I carefully memorized this—'Think men that when they say, "We believe," they shall be let alone and not put to the proof?'"

He paused there, looking at the two friends emphatically, as if to say, "here is where you can discuss . . ."

Rahma sadly noted, "So they will be tested, and many will fail."

Kapriel agreed, "It sounds that way. . . . Does anyone need a drink or meal?"

Farhád was inclined, "Yes, that would be very kind of you, but let us finish the tale first. We are almost done."

"Very good," the scribe agreed, having thought it already ended.

The escort man continued, "We traveled from Urmíá around the great lake, as I said before. From there, only small towns were on the way, so no fantastic circumstances arose. When we neared Tabríz, we learned the city somehow already knew of our imminent arrival and of events in Urmíá, throwing itself into turmoil. Throngs, of which you were probably part, crowded our path and had to be kept back. We were ordered to take the Báb to the governor's mansion outside the city to escape the multitude. We turned Him over to the local authorities, and here we are.

Farhád paused. Then he said, "Now, I believe someone mentioned dinner . . ."

——◆——

The next morning Kapriel was at his spot in the bazaar. There had been a flurry of letter-writing activity early, followed by the usual lull. He was working on drawing a scene in the bazaar while

listening to the increasing buzz and hum of speculation, supposition, and superstition. Suddenly one voice was raised above the general babble. A man came running through shouting, "The trial is
starting!" He kept running, shouting every few steps to tell everyone.

The change was instant. Conversations ended, customers hurried out, and vendors pulled inventory into their alcoves and locked
their doors. Kapriel threw his sketch into the lap desk, grabbed his
stool as he stood, and headed out after the customers. He considered stopping at the caravanserai to drop off his desk and stool,
then thought of the unfettered customers pulling ahead. This was
not like one of the spectacles roaming the city that a person could
wait for; he would have to get there quickly to have any chance of
seeing the proceedings. He bypassed the caravanserai and headed
straight for the governor's mansion.

He wondered, as he nearly trotted, whether Rahma had heard
the commotion yet, out in some field, digging or weeding or
whatever he was up to. Approaching the mansion Kapriel saw, to
his amazement, that he had somehow gotten to the front of the
throngs rushing to find a spot.

He found himself propelled forward even faster by the combined
masses and their excitement, into the mansion, to the entrance hall
just outside the chamber where the trial was to begin. He could see
into the chamber that the highest clergy in the realm, including the
Nizámmu'l-'Ulamá or lead ecclesiastical judge over all clergy in Persia, were seated and muttering to each other, occupying every chair
around the room except one at the point of honor. That seat had
been left empty for the crown prince, heir to the throne, Násiri'd-
Dín Mírzá.

The clergy were all wrapped in their loose robes over several dull
colors of clothing, with large turbans adorning each head. Their
beards were the main difference between them, varying in length
from somewhat trimmed to long, tamed, or bushy, and white with
age or black with dye.

The crowds behind Kapriel were in such agitation that the scribe was momentarily shoved into the chamber, then quickly pushed back by guards. The entrance hall was completely filled, with further masses crowding the approach to the building. Such was the chaos and mindlessness of the men that none noticed they were all smashed together, in full physical contact with an Armenian Christian.

At last, the noisy agitation was transformed into impatient murmuring as they awaited the final two arrivals: the prince and the Báb. The hearing was opened by the lead judge, and a guard was immediately sent to bring the Báb in from his nearby cell in that same mansion. That guard had to push through the stuffed hall on the way out, then force a path for himself and the Báb on the way back, shoving the men in the overcrowded hall to the walls.

The Báb walked not as a prisoner to a trial, but as a king, with majesty and grace so overpowering that the entire assemblage was silenced.[3] All were dumbstruck with awe from the power radiating from the Man they would try to condemn. Kapriel had to fight the urge to kneel, or better to prostrate himself right there in the crowd. To do so in that human press would, of course, require others to trample him. Thus he stood and watched as the prisoner, with more dignity than any had ever seen, greeted the assembled clergy and placed himself upon the only chair available, the prince's. This placed Him next to the lead judge rather than in the expected place standing before them in a position of submission.

It was some moments before even the lead judge felt able to speak, asking the first question, "Whom do you claim to be, and what is the message which you have brought?"

Somewhere a chair appeared for the prince, who then sat upon it joining the proceedings.

Calmly, and with the utmost confidence, the Báb replied, "I am, I am, I am the promised One! I am the One whose name you have for a thousand years invoked, at whose mention you have risen, whose advent you have longed to witness, and the hour of whose

Revelation you have prayed God to hasten. Verily I say, it is incumbent upon the peoples of both the East and the West to obey My word and to pledge allegiance to My person."

The words vibrated through the chamber, down the hall, and out to the masses beyond. Most were stunned, but one, a mullá seated next to the Báb opposite the high judge, was not impressed. This mullá had a white beard and one good eye, and had rejected the Báb's claims years before. He spoke in tones dripping with arrogance, "You wretched and immature lad of Shíráz! You have already convulsed and subverted 'Iráq; do you now wish to arouse a like turmoil in Ádhirbáyján?"

The Prisoner replied, "Your Honour, I have not come hither of My own accord. I have been summoned to this place."

The one-eyed mullá interrupted, "Hold your peace, you perverse and contemptible follower of Satan!"

Again the reply, "Your Honour, I maintain what I have already declared."

The lead judge felt it was time to intervene, "The claim which you have advanced is a stupendous one; it must needs be supported by the most incontrovertible evidence."

The Báb responded, "The mightiest, the most convincing evidence of the truth of the Mission of the Prophet of God is admittedly His own Word. He Himself testified to this truth: 'Is it not enough for them that We have sent down to Thee the Book?' The power to produce such evidence has been given to Me by God. Within the space of two days and two nights, I declare Myself able to reveal verses of such number as will equal the whole of the Qur'án."

The lead judge requested, "Describe orally, if you speak the truth, the proceedings of this gathering in language that will resemble the phraseology of the verses of the Qur'án so that the [crown prince] and the assembled divines may bear witness to the truth of your claim."

The Báb immediately responded, "In the name of God, the Merciful, the Compassionate, praise be to Him who has created the heaven and the earth—"

The one-eyed mullá interrupted, "This self-appointed Qá'im of ours has at the very start of his address betrayed his ignorance of the most rudimentary rules of grammar!"

Unperturbed, the Báb answered, "The Qur'án itself does in no wise accord with the rules and conventions current amongst men. The Word of God can never be subject to the limitations of His creatures. Nay, the rules and canons which men have adopted have been deduced from the text of the Word of God and are based upon it. These men have, in the very texts of that holy Book, discovered no less than three hundred instances of grammatical error, such as the one you now criticize. Inasmuch as it was the Word of God, they had no other alternative except to resign themselves to His will."

He then reiterated His introduction to a Qur'án-like description of the proceedings and was, again, interrupted by the same mullá with the same complaint. At that point another of the inquisitors interjected another question, "To what tense does the word Ishtartanna belong?"

The reply was a quote from the Qur'án, "'Far be the glory of thy Lord, the Lord of all greatness, from what they impute to Him, and peace be upon His Apostles! And praise be to God, the Lord of the worlds.'"[4]

At this point Kapriel was disturbed by a scuffle against his back, distracting him from the scene inside. Suddenly he was pushed face-first into the crowd against the wall. Glancing back down the hall, he saw the Báb leaving, maintaining the dignity and majesty He had carried in with Him. The scribe looked again to the chamber and found the ulámá sorely upset.

The lead judge stated to them all, "How shameful is the discourtesy of the people of Tabríz! What could possibly be the connection between these idle remarks and the consideration of such weighty, such momentous issues?"

Several others agreed with him; however, the one-eyed mullá insisted over the other voices, "I warn you, if you allow this youth to pursue unhampered the course of his activities, the day will come when the entire population of Tabríz will have flocked to his standard. Should he, when that day arrives, signify his wish that the [crown prince] himself, should be expelled from the city and that he should alone assume the reins of civil and ecclesiastical authority, no one of you, who now view with apathy his cause, will feel able to oppose him effectually. The entire city, nay the whole province of Ádhirbáyján, will on that day unanimously support him."

Arguments went back and forth, with some demanding the end of the Báb, His Cause, and His adherents, and others siding with justice and reason, and still more requiring some "humiliating punishment" for the Báb sitting in the prince's seat and leaving without permission. They were ready to order yet another trial to make such a punishment happen. The crown prince, however, refused to allow the latter proposal, but otherwise let the debate continue.

The crowds had not lessened by much, with everyone still waiting to hear the final verdict. Kapriel wished to leave but could not do so without an armed guard to make a path for him. If only Rahma could have made it! Stuck there, his mind wandered to another trial—that of Jesus the Christ, put before the leading clergy of Pharisees and secular leadership of Pontius Pilate. The place of His crucifixion had, like Tabríz, welcomed Him with great accolades upon His first entrance.

Finally, the gathered clergy and crown prince decided to take the Báb to the home of the chief clergyman of Tabríz, Mírzá 'Alí-Asghar, where he would receive physical punishment at the hands of the chief clergyman's head guard. The guard, however, objected, not wishing to get involved in the doings of the 'ulamás. This Mírzá 'Alí-Asghar therefore agreed to apply the bastinado himself.

The crowd dispersed slowly, masses in the back having to leave before earlier arrivals could make their way out. It was some time before Kapriel, still gripping his lap desk and stool, found himself out in open air. Overwhelmed with relief at exiting the now-empty building, he felt the great strain of anxiety he had hidden, even from himself, while confined by bodies in that hall.

Rahma was, naturally, waiting for him in their room in the caravanserai. He had heard the news out in the fields; however, it had taken him so long to get there that he could hear nothing at the back of the crowd. Not seeing his smaller friend, he had trusted Kapriel would be up there at the front and would bring the news to their room.

The entire "trial" was retold in utmost detail, with Rahma hoping for even more than Kapriel could tell. Then Rahma gave Kapriel a bit of news; something he had heard at the back of the crowd.

Two men had been talking about something witnessed the day before. Rahma related, "One of them is an assistant to a local doctor who was sent to decide if the Báb was sane enough to be put to death or not. He said there were three doctors—two of them Persian and one English."

"Oh, that must be Dr. Cormick. We ran into each other a few times last winter."

"Wonderful. Then you can introduce us."

"To find out what happened, yes?"

"Yes. Shall we go?"

<hr />

They found Dr. Cormick's home empty and spent a couple of hours at a local café, passing the time and talking in low voices about the trial that had just transpired. Then they went back to Dr. Cormick's home just as the good doctor was returning from somewhere. The physician was unsurprised to find men at his doorstep. Much of his business either came to him or came to get him for someone else. He was a little surprised to learn why they were on his doorstep, however. Few people came seeking news.

He was quite sorry to have to disappoint them. In his very clear Persian he said, "It is very sad, but I cannot oblige you. There are rules of conduct for doctors. We are not allowed to discuss our patients without their permission. Thus I can only relate to you the public portions of my meetings with the Báb, and none of the medical treatments. You understand?"

Rahma blurted out, "He needed medical treatment?"

Kapriel admonished, "Rahma, he just said he can't discuss that." Turning his attention to the physician he said, "Thank you. We would appreciate whatever information you are morally able to give us."

Dr. Cormick looked from one to the other of his visitors curiously. He opened the door and invited them in.

They set themselves down in the doctor's front room. It had been arranged for the public since many of his patients came to him. He described his first encounter with the Báb the previous day. [5] "Nothing of any importance transpired in this interview, as the Báb was aware of my having been sent with two Persian doctors to see whether he was of sane mind or merely a madman, to decide the question whether to put him to death or not. With this knowledge he was loth to answer any questions put to him. To all enquiries he merely regarded us with a mild look, chanting in a low melodious voice some hymns, I suppose. Two other Siyyids, his intimate friends, were also present . . . besides a couple of government officials. He only once deigned to answer me, on my saying that I was not a Musulman and was willing to know something about his religion, as I might perhaps be inclined to adopt it. He regarded me very intently on my saying this, and replied that he had no doubt of all Europeans coming over to his religion. Our report to the Sháh . . . was of a nature to spare his life . . . On our report he merely got the bastinado . . ."

Kapriel asked, "And judging by the timing of your arrival here and some other factors, were you called to treat Him after the bastinado? That will seem like private information, but everyone will know that much soon, as well as what the exact punishment was."

The doctor nodded, telling them that eleven strokes had been applied to the Báb's feet, and one stroke, whether intentional or not, had gone astray and hit His face.

Kapriel conjectured, "And so he asked for you, who had at least shown kindness and interest, rather than the Persian doctors."

Dr. Cormick nodded agreement. Then, looking at Kapriel, he changed the subject. perhaps because he realized Kapriel's ancestry. He had heard nothing of Bábí doctrine from the Báb directly, although he had an idea that it contained some approach to Christianity. "He was seen by some Armenian carpenters, who were sent to make some repairs in his prison, reading the Bible, and he took no pains to conceal it, but on the contrary told them of it. Most assuredly the Musulman fanaticism does not exist in his religion, as applied to Christians, nor is there that restraint of females that now exists."

A few minutes of interesting chat later, a knock on the door announced a new patient. The friends thanked him profusely for his time, heading back into the street to go about their business.

Several days later, they discussed the repercussions of the trial: the believers were just as strong in their faith, with a few converts having declared themselves after hearing the words of the trial. The enemies of the Báb were even more intent on His demise and the destruction of His Cause. The undecided people were leaning away, assuming that a Messenger of God who could be given the bastinado was no Messenger at all, despite the history of all religions. Rumors were rife with wildly different accounts of the trial. From accuracy to a complete trouncing of the Báb or His accusers, the stories clashed to produce nothing more than frustration.

By that time, the Báb was on His way back to Chihriq, escorted into the hands of the same guards as before.

Kapriel and Rahma had a decision to make: what would they do now?

15

Tabríz to Tihrán, Late Summer, 1848

It was only a few more days until a new direction made itself apparent. Kapriel and Rahma were meeting with a few Bábís in one of their larger homes. There were only a few believers present because here, as in Zanján, they were now being watched, and they met at night to enjoy the cool air after the heat of high summer days.

First the uncle of young Muhammad-i-Zunúzí—the distraught youngster imprisoned in his own home—informed them of the complete change in the youth. He had a dream after the Báb left Tabríz.[1] In that dream, the Báb assured him he would be able to sacrifice himself to the Cause, joining in the martyrdom of the Báb. Since then he had been completely calm; there was no more weeping, no desperate heartache. His uncle said, "In fact, he has been filled with joy, completely transformed. He is doing all he can to help his family every minute of wakefulness. Oh, and the Báb gave him a new name. He is now Anís."

Rahma asked, "Does anyone hear of news from afar? It has been a while since we have heard from any Letters of the Living."

One local man told them, "Many Letters of the Living have been out east, in Sháh-Rud, with others who were invited by Mírzá Husayn 'Alí. It sounded as though some sort of a conference was to happen."

Kapriel queried, "When was this? And where is Sháh-Rud?"

The same man answered, "The invitations went out last spring. They were confidential, of course, or thousands of us would have gone and frightened the government with our numbers. By now they should be on their way back, so it seems safe to tell you.

"And Sháh-Rud is about as far east of Tihrán as Zanján is to the northwest. It is a caravan city, the last stop before the long desert crossing to Mashhad."

Kapriel theorized, "Then if they are likely to be moving west toward us, we could go east to find them. Perhaps meet up in Tihrán?"

Rahma's right hand went to rubbing his chest, causing Kapriel, with difficulty, to restrain himself from rolling his eyes. The farmer asked, "What about the Báb? What will happen now?"

One of the others consoled him, "He is safe, for now. The crown prince would not even allow a second trial and punishment, let alone execution. He is in God's hands. He knows His fate and can face it willingly. All we believers can do is carry forth His Message, live according to that high standard He set, and for some, hope to set down our lives for His Cause."

Rahma nodded slowly, still rubbing. He turned to Kapriel and agreed, "Tihrán, then. Let us see what we can learn there."

Kapriel smiled, "Yes, and maybe spend the winter there. I hear it is warmer than Tabríz."

The next morning they gave their regrets to their employers—Rahma to the farmer for whom he worked, and Kapriel using a tack to hold up a page with "Gone Traveling" in three languages at his spot in the bazaar. By noon they were on the road again, setting a quick pace to reach Mílán by nightfall. Seasoned travelers by this time, they knew what to expect and how fast a pace to set.

They caught up with a caravan in Mílán and headed out with it the next morning. Over the three weeks it took to reach Tihrán, they both made a couple of friends among fellow travelers. Kapriel found the head drover to be a reasonable and honest man. When he learned the mule train would turn south for Shíráz after a few days in Tihrán, Kapriel put together another package for his family and paid the drover to deliver it.

He had never heard back from his relatives, but he supposed any return letters had been lost with all his moving around. Perhaps in Tihrán he could find someone who would hold letters for him.

——◆——

Tihrán, the current capital of Persia, was enormous. Kapriel's jaw fell as they topped the final rise and beheld the sprawl of that city. It spread across a wide valley at the foot of the Alburz mountains. They arrived in the evening, as the sun cast a golden light across the pale buildings. It was now mid-August, 1848.

The friends took a room at a caravanserai, as usual, but this time they had the bounty of the drovers to ask which caravanserai was operated best and most honestly. This was important in a city so large, with so many places to choose from.

The city itself was in better condition than most in Persia. It was, of course, relatively newer than the others. When the Qajars had taken over and made this their capital fifty years earlier, it had been a small town. The Qajar sháhs had grown the city around them, creating the need for growth by their very presence. How does one sell something to the sháh? By being nearby, naturally. Workers had streamed in as the new capital was being built, with the palace going up and monuments, administrative buildings, and new mosques being constructed to accommodate the regal families and growing masses. Then there were the embassies and their needs. All of this growth combined to create a wondrous conglomeration of people, cultures, and architecture.

The pair resumed their guise of Armenian merchant and body-guard/retainer the next day, touring the city at their leisure. Kapriel had to remain constantly vigilant over his own emotions once they entered the main bazaar. It was so exciting! The bazaar was huge, a small town in itself! There were goods from everywhere, even Europe and China. They even found a vendor with items from North America! He had a few weapons—one was something called a "Kentucky long rifle" that he said was used in the "Indian" wars (Kapriel wondered when America had gone to war with India)— books in English made on a printing press, and strange clothes made of a plant fiber called cotton (as opposed to their usual linens and silks). The vendor, an American with an accent heavy on 'r's, even had seeds of plants Kapriel had never heard of—*corn* and *tomato*, among others. Apparently those two, at least, were for food.

The booth had two large wood carvings, nearly full size, of men with medium brown skin and large noses. Each carved man was wearing an odd feather headdress that draped down on both sides nearly to the ground, and simple, painted-on clothing, with the hands making a space to hold rolls of tobacco called a "cigar." The carvings seemed childish to Kapriel, like caricature drawings. Surely no one really looked like that. The thought brought up more questions, but the vendor was too brash for Kapriel's liking, so they moved on.

Other booths in that area were also imports from distant lands. One had French items, including special thin cloth and strong perfume. Another had products from England, including the collected works of someone named "Shakespeare." That vendor explained Shakespeare wrote plays and was considered a great writer by Europeans, much like Hafiz in Persia. The friends smiled, trying not to laugh rudely at this foolishness.

Kapriel's head was soon spinning. One of their goals in visiting the bazaar had been to acquire new clothing because their old attire was getting a bit threadbare for public. Kapriel clung to that goal, narrowing his focus to block the wild possibilities and curious desires that assailed him in the foreign import area.

They made their way to the clothier street, and it was more than one street. They had both collected enough pay in their recent stay in Tabríz to afford two new whole outfits. Rahma stuck with simple attire, but Kapriel found a small section with Armenian clothiers, and he bought a light brocade abá (a jacket-like garment that hangs to the knees) and a heavier one for winter. Then they headed straight back to their room, agreeing to explore the bazaar a little at a time.

That evening they followed directions given to them by one of the Bábís in Tabríz to a believer's home in Tihrán. It was much safer than asking around the city for the nearest Bábí. They found the home in a less-prosperous part of the city, with the houses just a bit smaller than in their home neighborhood in Shíráz.

A man answered the door and accepted the letter of introduction a Tabríz Bábí had sent with Rahma. They were welcomed with great cheer and ushered through the house into the garden. Introductions were made, their host being Muhammad Reza,* a tall man—though not as tall as Rahma—of slight build with a surprisingly short beard, perhaps thirty-five years of age. A green turban, designating him as a siyyid, sat on a shelf near the door. His eyes were a clear grey, full of mirth, at having these two unusual friends in his home. When he heard their question about the events to the east, he called for a boy of about ten, who came running from a back room, and sent the child off to bring another person.

The three of them exchanged news, with Kapriel relating his firsthand view of the attempted trial and Rahma speaking of the months in Máků. Muhammad Reza told them of the news in Tihrán, that the city's Bábís were privileged to have Táhirih in the house of Mírzá Husayn 'Alí for the better part of a year.

Rahma wondered, "Who is Táhirih?"

---

* Fictional character.

Reza bowed, hand on chest, to apologize. "I'm sorry, I forgot already. As you may have heard, a conference of some of the Báb's followers took place recently. At the conference, many disciples were given new names, but we will speak of that later. Táhirih (the Pure) was Qurratu'l-'Ayn before the conference."

"She was here?" Rahma exclaimed.

"Yes, Mírzá Husayn 'Alí arranged her escape and disappearance—oh, nearly a year ago. She and the rescuer sent by our beloved nobleman rode like the wind, covering the distance between Qazvín and Tihrán in one night. She lived in Mírzá Husayn 'Alí's Tihrán mansion until late last spring, when they left for Sháh-Rud and Badasht."

Kapriel asked, "Was she kept hidden? The Bábís of Qazvín did not tell us this when we passed through in spring."

"She was kept safe, not hidden. The family of Mírzá Husayn 'Alí is wealthy and powerful. They move in the highest levels of the government. It would risk the wrath of the Sháh himself to do violence to his noblemen and their families.

"No, Táhirih was not hidden. She gave lectures in her host's home, speaking to seekers from behind a curtain. She often had little 'Abbás, Mírzá Husayn 'Alí's oldest son, in her lap, but we heard little from him. He is so well-behaved, and only four years old. She also often played with Bahíyyih, the two-year-old daughter, as she sparred one-handed—one might say—with the wayward who tried to best her in contests of doctrine and meaning.

There was an odd knock at the door. "Ah, that will be my son with another guest."

The door opened to reveal the same ten-year-old with a man of much greater age. Kapriel estimated him to be in his fifties, his weathered skin belying the black hair dye so very much in fashion. He was introduced as Mullá Hasan Husayn of Semnán,* a participant in the conference at Badasht.

---

* Also fictional.

Kapriel had to know, "I thought they went to Sháh-Rud. Where is Badasht?"

"Yes, they did—please call me Hasan—and it is just a short ride east of Sháh-Rud." The man's kind eyes softened the gentle reprimand for Kapriel's jumping in too quickly. "Reza's boy said you wish to hear about the conference. Shall we start at the beginning?"

A girl of about twelve entered from the kitchen carrying a tea tray. Reza thanked his daughter, setting the tray on the floor between them and pouring the tea himself. He served Hasan first, then filled two cups and offered them to Kapriel and Rahma at the same time. Those who wanted sugar put a piece the size of a fingertip between their back teeth and let the very hot tea flow over it.

Mullá Hasan took a slurp. "Ah, thank you Reza. And please thank your daughter for me. She is doing well in taking over her mother's work."

Reza smiled, "She will be glad to hear that." He looked at his other guests and simply said, "Cholera took my wife last year."

They both gave condolences and waited, though perhaps not patiently inside, yet maintaining an outward calm.

Mullá Hasan spoke mere moments before Kapriel would have exploded with questions.

"Last spring, certain Bábís received an invitation from Mírzá Husayn 'Alí to meet in Sháh-Rud at the beginning of summer. We met there, arriving at different times, from cities in several directions. When Mírzá Husayn 'Alí directed us to, we began our trek to Badasht, all drinking in the beauty of the area as we shared rides and walking, communing with each other without regard for anything other than our goal of serving the Cause of the Báb.

"Mírzá Husayn 'Alí arranged to rent three conjoined gardens, a stream of mountain snowmelt running through them, in the little village of Badasht. The village itself is very small, not worthy of notice to travelers en route to Mashhad. Tents were set up, with one large tent in each garden for three leaders of the Cause: Qurratu'l-'Ayn, Muhammad-'Alí, and Mírzá Husayn 'Alí."

Kapriel didn't quite know how to politely interrupt this venerable figure, so he raised a hand.

It worked. "Yes, Kapriel?"

"Sorry, but would that be the same Siyyid Muhammad-'Alí who went with the Báb on pilgrimage and was sorely tormented when he returned to Shíráz?"

"Yes it would."

The friends nodded to each other.

"He was the last to arrive. There were eighty-one of us gathered in those gardens. It was a glorious time, the like of which surely only a few in history have ever experienced. Each of us was given a new name. Qurratu'l-'Ayn became Táhirih, Muhammad 'Alí became Quddús (Most Holy One), and so on. Mírzá Husayn 'Alí gave himself the name Bahá (Splendor), though we called him Jináb-i-Bahá (Honorable Splendor). And before you ask, yes, I also have a new name, but am not yet ready to share it with the world."

Kapriel closed his just-opened mouth, setting his hand back in his lap.

"Several other Letters of the Living were present, almost half their number. Four were notably absent: Mullá Husayn, who was being held in custody of Prince Hamzih at Mashhad; Mullá 'Alí of Bastám who is somewhere in Iráq; Siyyid Yahyá of Dáráb could not make it; and Mullá Muhammad-'Alí of Zanján, given the name Hujjat years ago, who is still under arrest in the governor's home here in Tihrán.

"We arranged our small tents around the three larger ones, helping each other throughout the days. Every day, Jináb-i-Bahá would reveal a tablet that would be chanted for all of us. Every day, veils fell away as the old laws were ended and new laws took their place. Each day, we were carried closer to the truth. Never again would we be able to rely on those doctrines in which we were raised.

"During these days, a rift was developing between Quddús and Táhirih. Quddús wanted to keep as much as possible to the old ways, while Táhirih voiced her preference to throw the old ways out entirely, clinging only to the new laws announced in the Bayán. It was difficult for us. After all, Quddús's name means *Most Holy.* One who is most holy cannot be in error. He advocated a traditional approach that we knew well. It was comfortable for us. But Táhirih, the Pure One—so revered for her knowledge and chastity that none would even risk a glance at her shadow—surely *she* could not be mistaken!

"One day Jináb-i-Bahá claimed to feel ill, keeping himself to his bed. Quddús was the first to visit, rushing to his side and seating himself at Jináb-i-Bahá's right hand." Turning to Kapriel, Mullá Hasan said, "This, of course, has great meaning in Islám, but I will not bore you with the details." He returned to his tale.

"Others who asked about his condition were admitted, one by one, until we stood shoulder to shoulder around the edge of the tent, surrounding the bed. Suddenly Muhammad Hasan, acting for the conference as Táhirih's door guard, entered with a message for Quddús. She urgently invited him to her garden.

"Well, none of us was surprised when he refused. He said, 'I have severed myself entirely from her. I refuse to meet her.' This sent the messenger back immediately to convey the response.

"However, the messenger quickly returned, reiterating the invitation. He said, 'She insists on your visit. If you persist in your refusal, she herself will come to you.'

"Quddús did not need to speak a word to show his refusal. The messenger laid his unsheathed sword at the feet of Quddús, then said he refused to return to Táhirih without Quddús, and that the illustrious Quddús could accompany him or cut off his head using the sword just laid there.

"Quddús not only still refused, but said, 'I am willing to comply with the alternative you have put before me.'

"The poor man sat on his heels and put his head forward to receive the fatal blow as Quddús picked up the sword.

"The curtain at the door flew back and Táhirih appeared in the tent, her face uncovered for the first time among us.

A gasp escaped from Rahma as Kapriel's eyebrows nearly met his hairline.

"Yes, you can well imagine the turmoil we all felt. There is a sacred tradition in Islám regarding the unveiling of Fátimih, whom we regarded Táhirih as the incarnation of, on Judgment Day. Well, some looked away in agony, others felt there must be punishment for the abrogation of such a fundamental law of chastity, still others were bewildered at the thought that this may, indeed, be the Judgment Day.

"She silently crossed the carpets in front of us to sit at Quddús's right hand. She was supremely serene, in contrast to the men around her. One man was so disturbed he pulled out a blade and slashed his own throat, then ran from the tent. A few ran after him, either to help him or to save themselves.

"Quddús, with the sword he was about to use to sever the messenger's head still in his upraised hand, seemed ready to use it on Táhirih.

"Still calm and confident, with perhaps a gleam of triumph in her eyes, she rose in great dignity, addressing the majority still in the tent. She spoke of the need for change, to let go the old and accept the new religion wholly. The words were vague to most of us, who were still in a confused whirl. However, she ended her speech with a quote from the Qur'án: 'Verily, amid gardens and rivers shall the pious dwell in the seat of truth, in the presence of the potent king.' There she made a quick little glance to her left, which could have been meant either for Jináb-i-Bahá or Quddús. She continued, saying, 'I am the Word which the Qá'ím is to utter, the word which shall put to flight the chiefs and nobles of the earth!'

"She then actually rebuked Quddús for what she termed his failure to do what was 'essential for the welfare of the Faith' in Khurásán.

"Quddús did not see how she had any authority over him, and said so.

"Then, to our further amazement, she invited us to celebrate this great occasion. Jináb-i-Bahá called for the recitation of the Súrih of

Resurrection, which begins, 'When the inevitable day of judgment shall suddenly come, no soul shall charge the prediction of its coming with falsehood: it will abase some, and exalt others. When the earth shall be shaken with a violent shock, and the mountains shall be dashed in pieces, and shall become as dust scattered abroad . . .' and on, to the end which says, 'Therein they shall hear no idle talk, no cause of sin, only the saying "Peace, Peace."'

"That was the end of the action, though the repercussions continued for days. Those who had fled were invited to return. The one who injured himself was treated and returned to health. But now it was obvious to all. This new faith was not a reform of Islám but a break from it—a whole new religion that would arise from the ashes of the old. Some were unable to quickly let go of the past and argued against Táhirih, taking their complaints to Jináb-i-Bahá or Quddús.

"Most of us were able to turn from the old ways, but we had no idea what to do instead. We had been set adrift, cut off from our anchors.

"Finally, after some further days, Jináb-i-Bahá brought Táhirih and Quddús together in view of all and brought about their reconciliation. At last, we had our direction. We did not have to choose one or the other, but instead we acknowledged our common foundation and moved ahead to a new revelation.

"We had been occupying Badasht for twenty-two days when it was time to leave at high summer (15 July). All of the tents were packed, our belongings stowed on horses and mules, the gardens cleaned up. We left for several directions—some traveled east to join Mullá Husayn near Mashhad, and some rode west toward Tihrán or north through the Alburz to take a cooler, more beautiful route through Mázindarán along the Caspian Sea. This last route was taken by Jináb-i-Bahá and the majority of the attendees.

"My chosen route was to return here, and here I am."

Mullá Hasan smiled at them, then winked as he asked, "Do you have any questions?"

———

It was a late night for the four of them, the children had taken themselves to bed hours ago. Before the farmer and scribe left, they were told how and where to contact other Bábís, plus they were graciously given help in finding work.

Much of the food for Tihrán was brought in from other provinces, but there was work for Rahma picking fruit for the harvest season. Kapriel was given the name of an actual shop of scribes who copied books and wrote letters for customers. The friends were quite happy to again have positive cash flow.

Only a week after their arrival, they were enclosed in another meeting with Tihrání Bábís (10 August), now with many believers in a large home. There were two tracks of urgent discussion. The first topic concerned the group of Badasht attendees who had gone north to Mázindarán. The second concerned the raising of the Black Standards.

When the second matter was mentioned, most of the group gasped, their eyes suddenly alight. Kapriel had no idea of why.

Telling of the first item, however, had already started. The Badasht attendees had joyfully proceeded homeward, with the majority going north and west toward Mázindarán, chanting and singing odes composed by Táhirih regarding the new faith.[2] A few of the adherents, not sure just how free women should be in their new status as unveiled equals, caused offense in the small town of Níyálá where the large group had stopped for the night. At dawn the next morning, the group was awoken by a rain of rocks, propelled by the townspeople, scattering the believers and driving them away. They ran for their lives (all except Táhirih and one man protecting her), leaving their belongings behind. The abandoned property was promptly pillaged. Jináb-i-Bahá returned to the town to effect the return of some of their belongings.

Damage had been done, and the previously happy group of travelers had been dispersed in several directions. Jináb-i-Bahá sent Quddús ahead to Quddús's home town of Bárfurúsh* for safety, and for the same reason sent Táhirih with a protector to Jináb-i-Bahá's own mansion in the district of Núr. Jináb-i-Bahá then continued on their course north and west into Mázindarán with a few remaining companions.

Kapriel's fellow attendees in the Tihrán meeting were anxiously awaiting the second topic. Fortunately, not all of them understood the significance of the news, helping to cover Kapriel's confusion since he had never heard of this Black Standard before.

Mullá Hasan was there and graciously informed them all on the topic. "The expectation of the Black Standards comes from something Muhammad, peace be upon Him, said long ago: 'Should your eyes behold the Black Standards proceeding from Khurásán, hasten ye towards them, even though you should have to crawl over the snow, inasmuch as they proclaim the advent of the promised Mihdí, the Viceregent of God.' No one had truly understood this tradition until now.[3]

"But just a few weeks ago (21 July), just after the Báb's trial and immediately following the attack on the Badasht gatherers, Mullá Husayn received a package sent weeks before. The package, hasted on its way from Chihriq, was delivered in Mashhad and contained one of the Báb's green turbans and a message to raise those long-awaited Standards. Mullá Husayn acquired a steed, gathered together the Bábís of Mashhad, sent word ahead to all districts, and proceeded east and north toward Mázindarán. He told them, 'This is the way to our Karbilá.'"

The Bábís suddenly took on a look of fervor, as though they might run from the room all the way to eastern Mázindarán to join up. Kapriel quickly reviewed his paltry education in Muslim

---

* Now called *Bábol.*

history. Ah! He remembered. Imám Husayn, grandson of Muham-mad, met his demise in a protracted battle at Karbilá. And those under the Black Standards would be led by Mullá Husayn! The scribe was nearly overcome with . . . he couldn't put a name to it, something like destiny, doom, and glory all mixed up together. Throw in the terror resulting from a glance at Rahma and that about summed it up.

Rahma was aglow with zeal. The feverish excitement he had shown years ago in Shíráz, which had carried them thousands of miles across Persia to follow the Báb, was about to take them to Mázindarán.

16

Mázindarán, Fall 1848

Kapriel refused to leave for Mázindarán immediately. He gave Rahma several reasons, including the need to have enough money to get there, and the fact that others would be joining from much further away, meaning they had a few weeks in which to work.

Rahma was doing his utmost not to become frustrated in his need to leave *now*! He decided to put his excess energy into earning income, harvesting like a man possessed. He usually picked a bit more than the average, but now he went after every fruit in rapid succession, doubling his previous haul and thus doubling his wages. The extra income meant only a few days were necessary to earn enough for basic supplies.

During those few days they both heard wild rumors about the sháh. There were always rumors, but even with the large number of people whispering, the range of the suspicions all centered on his health. He was dying; no, he had only a light cold. He had been cursed by a witch. That evil minister Áqásí had put a djinn on him. He could not eat, he could not drink, he could not stop vomiting. He had sprained a wrist beating a subordinate. On and on the rumors went, with increasing vigor.

They were soon ready to go. Once again they said their good-byes, claimed their beasts of burden, packed, and set out, just three weeks before the autumnal equinox (31 August).

This time they headed east out of Tihrán, then angled north-east around Damavand Mountain, up the dry southern slopes of the Alburz mountain range, the grass there dead and brown in the late-summer heat. They climbed higher and higher, up a tight, zig-zagging valley to the pass. The slopes to either side were steep, climbing to the great height of the peaks.

It was a busy travel time. The friends had company on the road. Caravans were nearing the end of their annual circuit, most of them intending to go south or go home for the winter after this late run.

Two days after their departure, at the very top of the pass, Kapriel quickly steered his horse to one side and stopped, staring, his lower jaw somewhat slack. Rahma pulled up beside him.

Kapriel exclaimed, "Look! Do you see?!"

Rahma nodded, saying only, "Yes."

"It's . . . green!"

Except *green* was so inadequate for what he saw. He turned in his saddle, popping several places in his back and neck. Yes, there behind them were the browns and tans of semi-arid steppes, the deserts in the distance, the land he had known since birth.

He turned back toward the north and again saw green—bright green on the nearer slopes, deep dark green further out—fading to a hazy blue.

"Are those trees?" he asked himself out loud.

"Yes," a passing drover stopped a moment to enlighten the igno-rant Armenian. "The bright greens are fields and meadows, many of which will be flowering now. The dark greens are trees—forests that go on and on without a break. At the bottom are the swamps, which are usually not the best places to go, and finally—you can't see it through the haze, it's maybe thirty or forty miles away—is the Caspian Sea." He turned back to his chain of laden donkeys, on the verge of laughter at Kapriel's open astonishment.

Rahma urged them on, "Come, my friend. You will finally ride among the forests you have so long wished to see."

Kapriel hesitated a brief moment, then urged his horse forward. "But what is this haze the drover spoke of? Is it the blue . . . blur out there? What is it made of? Why can we not see much farther through it?"

He persisted with a few more questions, realized how silly it was to ask questions of air like a child, and then lapsed into a happy, curious silence. The answers were soon found.

The supremely dry air of the pass gained a bit more moisture as they descended. Then it acquired the scent of life, of plants, flowers, and animals living hidden in the vegetation. It smelled like early spring in Shíráz, here in late summer on the northern slopes of the Alburz mountains.

The humidity did not settle at a nice, comfortable level. It continued to thicken as they left the steeper slopes with meadows for flatter ground. Trees became more populous, from a smattering here and there to deep, impenetrable forests. They changed from evergreens on the higher slopes to leafy deciduous lower down. The branches arched over the trail, cutting off breezes until an opening here and there let a draft through. The atmosphere became so thick both friends began to feel they were drowning.* There was simply too much air, and it didn't move.

The travelers passed down the last gentle, tree-filled slopes to nearly flat land with few trees. The approach to Amul was quite warm—almost the same as Tihrán—but there were ponds, swamps, and lakes all around, thickening the air still further, adding fetid stenches of rotting vegetation around swamps. The air seemed to be its own decay-filled lake.

Kapriel had never been so wet. The mist seeped into his clothes, all the way to his skin. He was sweating freely, though he would have been quite comfortable at that temperature on the dry side of the

---

* The average humidity in that region is 82% for most of the year. From the Web site Weather2.

mountains. Trickles ran down his back, eased through his eyebrows into his eyes, and soaked the clothing intended for arid climes.

Rahma had an advantage in his simple farm clothes without the brocade overcoat, but a disadvantage in his size. There was so much more of him to cool.

Finally they arrived (roughly 4 September). A cotraveler with healthy animals went directly to a particular caravanserai, so the pair followed, hoping it meant better care for their tired beasts. They found a decently dry paddock and rooms reasonably flea-free.

Scribe and farmer drank a large portion of their safe water before setting out to listen to rumors in the evening. This proved to be another mistake. Few people were out after sunset unless they were smeared with some foul, awful-smelling goo. Any not so endowed were viciously attacked by swarms of mosquitos. The friends ran back to their room at the caravanserai chased by whining masses, to the amusement of the fragrantly anointed. Inside they were protected only by a curtain from the droves of pestilential insects. They set to work by lamplight, attempting to spread and close the curtain so that no space, no matter how small, was open to invaders.

They waited to midmorning before venturing out, both of them itchy all over. The first and most urgent priority was to find some of that stinking ointment. Asking around, they were quickly directed to the herbalist area of the market, with conflicting advice on from whom to purchase the ointment. The choice was made for them when a somewhat honestly sympathetic man stepped out from behind his table of wares to greet them.

"Ach, terrible, is it not? These voracious mosquitoes. And the discomfort they cause! You must be under great duress not to scratch. But it is true, do not scratch. That will only make it worse. Ah, like the large welt on your hand." He pointed to Rahma's left arm. There was, indeed, a very large welt on the back of that hand.

Kapriel glanced to the other herb vendors and noticed angry glowers at their competitor's win.

"First you will need this." He handed over the stinking ointment. "Do not put it on yet. You have horses? Take them with you
to the Caspian and walk right in. The salt water and minerals will
relieve the itching. Stay there. Soak as long as you can. Oh, you
have been swimming before?"

The friends looked at each other in confusion. Rahma answered,
"I have been to the bathhouse many times."

The salesman responded, "No, no, that is not the same. The
sea moves, and gets deeper than you are tall. Yes, even you. Hold
onto your horses as you go in to keep you from falling under. Many
people go to swim in the sea. It is good for the health, very good.

"When you cannot stand the water anymore dry off and before
the sun sets, put this on your exposed skin and anywhere your
clothing is one layer. They can bite right through a single shirt."

They made the purchase, thanking him for the advice, but before
they left he said, "Oh, you must not eat just before going into the
water. Eat, rest, then go swim. It is maybe eight miles to the sea. If
you still itch tomorrow come back for this sea-mineral rub."

The pair left most of their belongings in their room, taking
only saddles and bridles for the horses, leading the mule by her
halter. The beasts, too, had been attacked by the swarms, great
welts joining where they had scratched and rubbed on walls and
each other.

Is was a long, itchy ride across wet plains filled with rice paddies,
during which Kapriel felt more and more itchiness, with the begin-
nings of a headache and shivers. At the beach, they found others in
various states of undress soaking in the water and sunshine. A beach
for women was over in a protected area. The uncomfortable looks
Kapriel received let him know to stay clear of other swimmers.

The two men and three herbivores found an empty area,
removed most of their clothing and the saddles, and walked right
in as directed. The horses and mule hesitated, leaning back against
their bridles. Just as in Shíráz, when they were coaxed through a

doorway, the animals soon gave up. Once they were all in the water, the itches quickly subsided. The animals caught on, standing happily while the men used cupped hands to put the miracle water on the parts not under the surface.

Kapriel felt less itchy but also more feverish. Still, they soaked and soaked until the hoofed ones felt meal time was overdue. They headed back to land through the mushy footing. The friends staked the hungry animals in a nice patch of grass, then went back to sit in the blessed water, and stayed there long.

The sensation of moving water was surprising to Kapriel, even with his now-pounding headache. He had never been in a bathhouse since it was strictly prohibited. His baths had always been with a cloth and basin. The idea of sitting there, just at the point of floating, was amazing. He watched others down the beach flinging their arms and kicking legs to move about in deeper water, not the least afraid of drowning. He had heard people would float in water, but the experience was nothing like he had imagined. Some of the others floated quite well while others, like himself and Rahma, sank more.

Rahma had been in the water only minutes before starting to quietly chant the Bayán. He spent their time giving praise and thanks for the relief, and asking for direction to find the group under the Black Standards.

They decided to camp that evening, smearing each other with the ointment and trying not to retch or flee from themselves. Rahma noted the abundance of red spots on Kapriel's torso, where there should be none. They also treated the horses and mule. There were fewer mosquitoes that evening. Perhaps the ointment worked. Perhaps the sea breeze confused the flying vampires. Whatever the cause, all five were content.

The campfire reminded Kapriel of their adventure at the edge of Persepolis, back when they first left Shíráz. It seemed so long ago. They had learned and seen much since then.

—◦—

The next morning Kapriel felt awful. He was nauseous, with no desire whatsoever to get up.

Rahma checked on him just after sunrise, rekindling their fire and cooking some broth from the dried meat. "You, my friend, look to have a pox."

Even the word was terrifying. "Which pox? Are you sure it isn't the mosquitos?"

"You sleep with your arms close to your sides, but you have new red spots near your armpits. It is not mosquitos. But I don't think it is the small pox. That makes a different kind of spot. My mother took me to see someone with that affliction so I could tell the difference. Most people assume it is all the same, but she showed me. Small pox are mostly on the face, hands, and feet. It is horrible! Turns beautiful children into unrecognizable monsters. The scars on those who survive are terrible! This milder one is mostly on the face and torso. The bumps are a little different, also."

"But, Rahma, you mustn't get sick. You have to join—"

Rahma put up his hands to stop Kapriel. "It's alright. I had this as a child. When someone has had a certain pox they cannot get it again. I thought you would know this. You're the smart one."

"Smart doesn't mean all-knowing." He started to shiver, again.

Rahma took good care of him over the next week. There were many trips carrying Kapriel into the water to cool him during a fever, and wrapping him up under several layers when the chills came. There was no point in hoping for a doctor. Besides the long ride to a large town, no treatment was known for any of the poxes, except perhaps morphine for those with smallpox.

Fortunately Kapriel's pox was shorter-lived than smallpox, which could last for two weeks before the sores crusted over and began healing. The scribe had only to endure a week before the fevers and chills ended and the red spots scabbed.

During that time, Rahma had spoken to some other campers and learned how to fish, then clean and cook the catch. He told Kapriel he had tried to dry some on a bush, but nothing seemed to dry in all that wet air. It had just rotted. He had managed to dry some fish by the fire, though. It tasted smoky and was very helpful in Kapriel's recovery.

They stayed by the sea for two weeks before Kapriel felt strong enough for the ride back to Amul.

That morning was beautiful! Kapriel had never seen a sunrise over a flat plain. Colors reflected from each pond, lake, and swamp as they rode back to town. Around noon, Rahma noted the clouds moving in from the west. They appeared to rise quickly out of the obscuring humidity. The rest of the ride was spent in a miserable drizzle, soaking them even more thoroughly.

They were happy to find their belongings still in their room at the caravanserai. Kapriel gratefully paid the owner for the two weeks of rent, and then they both climbed into dry clothing. Rahma went out later with their bowls to find dinner and brought back an interesting meal of fish and herbs on rice. He heard only a few rumors in the short outing, about some army of Bábí heretics and fanatics coming toward them from the east.

The scribe and farmer awoke the next morning to semisunshine through even thicker air than two days ago. They set out, ointment packed away, for Bárfurúsh, the next city. It lay about about twenty miles to the east. The road was mushy, their steeds occasionally slipping on the soft footing. Well into the day they were still moving through patches of thick mist. They could hear noises out in the marshes and rice paddies but could rarely see anything that might generate such sounds.

They reached their destination before evening, heading straight for the caravanserai recommended by the owner of the place at which they had stayed in Amul. This one looked larger and even cleaner, and it was set atop a small rise. The owner here immediately cleaned the hooves of their mounts, absently commenting on the problem of hoof rot if the feet could not dry out.

Trusting that their steeds were yet again in competent hands, Kapriel and Rahma carried their belongings to the room they had rented. Again, only a curtain separated them from the world.

The pair had become quiet once they returned to Amul from the sea, and they remained quiet most of the way to Bárfurúsh. They both sensed something was coming. Perhaps it would be sad, perhaps beautiful, but their friendship might well suffer.

They walked to the market area for dinner and gazed at the flat, nearly featureless land around them. The locals likely saw many features and landmarks, but farmer and scribe saw simply wet places and less-wet places. The Alburz mountains were a day's ride to the south, lost in the mists. The nearer hills were low and unimpressive to the two who had grown up in the midst of mountains.

Kapriel had lost his enthusiasm for excessive greenery, but Rahma's desire to fling himself away in the path of the Báb's Cause had not diminished at all. He listened eagerly to conversations regarding the approaching Bábí hordes. Some people supported joining the new Cause, others were curious, and many were wary. The only real news had come to town while they were camping at the Caspian. Several weeks earlier Muhammad Sháh had died.

"He is dead?" questioned Rahma.

Kapriel said, "I guess that means the prince Násiri'd-Dín is now sháh, right?"

"I am sure there must be some ceremony, but yes, eventually. You know what else that means? Minister Áqásí will be gone. Maybe his replacement will be better."

"Let us hope."

A man nearby said, "The ministers appointed a new prime minister until they approve young Násiri'd-Dín Mírzá as sháh. It could be another month or two."

They heard one other rumor: There was a prisoner in Sárí, a religious fanatic who was native to Bárfurúsh and well-loved by most. Muhammad-'Alí, now known as Quddús, had been arrested as he neared his home after the conference at Badasht. The townspeople were not kept from him, and consternation among the authorities was rising after he converted over three hundred people in one week.

Neither Rahma nor Kapriel bothered looking for work just yet. If the Bábís under the Black Standards were truly approaching, then the friends would soon be leaving to meet them.

A few days into their sojourn in Bárfurúsh, they heard the call of the town crier going out around the city. The lead priest would be giving "a sermon of such momentous consequence . . . that no loyal adherent of Islám in [this] neighborhood [can] ignore it!" [1]

Rahma found a way to get deep within the mosque: Kapriel was too wise from experience to get close to an excited crowd of Muslims. And there was quite a crowd. It seemed the entire small city had come to heed the warning of the crier. Even so, the priest was so loud that even Kapriel, carefully tucked away in an alley nearby, could hear him.

The priest ascended the pulpit at the appointed time and showed his agitation with great drama. He flung "his turban to the ground," tore "open the neck of his shirt," and let loose his message in ringing anger: "Awake, for our enemies stand at our very doors, ready to wipe out all that we cherish as pure and holy in Islám! Should we fail to resist them, none will be left to survive their onslaught. He who is the leader of that band came alone, one day, and attended my classes. He utterly ignored me and treated me with marked disdain in the presence of my assembled disciples. As I refused to accord him the honours which he expected, he angrily arose and flung me his challenge. This man had the temerity, at a time when Muhammad Sháh was seated upon his throne and was at the height of his power, to assail me with so much bitterness. What excesses this stirrer-up of mischief, who is now advancing at the head of his savage band, will not commit now that the protecting hand of Muhammad Sháh has been suddenly withdrawn! It is the duty of all the inhabitants of Bárfurúsh, both young and old, both men and women, to arm themselves against these contemptible wreckers of Islám and by every means in their power to resist their onset. Tomorrow, at the hour of dawn let all of you arise and march out to exterminate their forces."

Scribe and barely-controlled farmer returned with alacrity to meet in their room, packed up, paid up, and left to find the 'savage band,' riding at a fast pace to the east away from Bárfurúsh. There was no need to speak until they were well out of the city, when Rahma finally slowed his mount and let loose. "Abomination! Lies! Deceit and jealousy! He is no mullá, he is a . . ."

Kapriel had a sudden inspiration to fill in where Rahma lost his words. "He is a wolf in sheep's clothing."

"Yes, my God, that is it!"

"Comes from the Bible." He was trying to keep his hair from standing on end again as he was making connections between biblical prophecy and current events, seeing things few others bothered to look for.

Just a few hours into their ride they heard an odd sound in the distance. Both perked up, turning their heads as the horses turned their ears to find the source of the melodious noise. There, in the distance, slowly resolving out of the humid air, was a large group, perhaps a few hundred people, walking and riding together. They could barely make out a man in black, wearing a green turban and holding up a pole with black flags at the top, at the front of the group.

There they were, the Black Standards, and Kapriel's heart went cold. The sound rapidly defined itself as chanting. The entire group was intoning verses together, sending mass notes of devotion out to the world.

Rahma stopped his horse and turned to Kapriel with urgent words. "My friend, I must speak with you now."

Kapriel knew this was it, the end of their travels together, but he waited for more.

"There are things I have not told you. I am very sorry for that. It was too selfish of me, but I could not let you go. Promise me you will see this through to the end."

"What do you mean, 'see this through'? See what through?"

"All of it. I will join them as we go to our deaths at the hands of the ignorant. I know this. The words of the Báb, the warnings, my own heart—all tell me this. But please, see this through to the end, to when they kill the Báb. He has said many times this will happen. Someone trustworthy must be there to tell the truth, to let the world know what is happening. Will you do this?"

Kapriel could not withstand the pleading in his companion's eyes, though he had no idea what the consequences might be. "All right, yes, I will do my utmost to witness and tell accurately the events to the death of the Báb."

The chanting slowly grew louder as the tiny army of Bábís walked closer.

"Thank you. You have always been a better friend than I deserved." Rahma dismounted, ignoring Kapriel's discomfort. Handing the reins of his horse to Kapriel he said, "Here. Everything I own is now yours. I go to my death with nothing but the words of God you have helped me to read. They are in my memory and my heart, as are you."

Kapriel had known this was coming, but could not prepare for the great sadness.

Rahma hesitated, looking at the ground, taking a very deep breath before he spoke. "Kapriel, I apologize. I am truly sorry I did not tell you this a long time ago. After the Báb has ascended, please, go back to Shíráz and marry Mina."

Kapriel was stunned beyond description, nearly dropping the reins. So many questions, thoughts, and emotions happened at once that he felt faint.

Rahma continued, looking up at his dear friend on the horse while Rahma stood on the ground. "She will not have married, unless truly forced to. She is in love with you. She always has been. That is why she challenged every possible husband our father brought home to meet her. She wants a husband who is both smart and willing to accept the ideas of others after a good argument. That has been you, since we were children."

This was too much at once for Kapriel. He had no words at all. He dismounted as tears began leaking, gave his large friend a strong hug with a few back thumps, and said only, "I forgive you. Good-bye, my dearest friend."

The chanting was loud enough to make hearing each other difficult.

Rahma, too, had tears falling over his grateful smile. "Oh, I almost forgot." He shouted over the many voices. He dug into his shirt and pulled out a money pouch. "This is the last of my money. Use it well."

"But won't you need—"

"I go to God free of all material things. Please, you will need the horse for Mina. Go now, before we both behave like children and give in to our sorrows. Go. We will meet again on the other side."

Rahma turned as Mullá Husayn and the Black Standards passed, joining the marching men as they welcomed him with embraces and cheers.

Kapriel temporarily set aside his personal maelstrom as he watched these devoted, gentle men go by, singing songs of praise to God. He noticed Rahma's intuition had been right. None of them carried a pack or bag, not even on horseback. They had only the clothes they wore and weapons, mostly swords and a few farm tools. He saw the turbans of siyyids, mullás, and shaykhs, black lambskin caps of merchants, and small turbans and simple caps of tradesmen and farmers. This small 'army' was gathering men of learning and scholarship, illiterate laborers, and savvy vendors who normally had little use for the weapons they wore. None were obvious soldiers, and all were on fire with passion for their faith.

The scribe suddenly remembered Rahma's club. He unpacked his father's sword instead, mounted, and rode up to the end of the column. He got the attention of one of the marchers and handed him the sword, shouting, "For Rahmat'u'lláh-i-Shírází! He just joined!"

Then pulling up, he watched them pass it forward as they continued their chant. The sword was not Rahma's, meaning his friend had no attachment to it. He hoped it would be accepted as a gift.

Eventually he dismounted, then looked all around the open fields to be sure he was both alone and safe, and gave in to his desolation for Rahma and joy for Mina.

Evening found Kapriel still there, emotionally dry and empty, not knowing what to do. It occurred to him that he was truly alone. He would now be making decisions and traveling without companionship. Survival instincts began to reassert themselves. He had to get off of the road to prevent chance encounters with criminals. Light from the set sun was fading quickly. He tied Rahma's mare to his gelding's saddle and the mule to the mare. He searched for a dry path away from the road, walking carefully lest he or his charges fall into a mire. Ten minutes of walking took him to a small copse at the edge of a rice paddy. There he tied the horses to a line for grazing and made himself a cold dinner of dried meat and even drier travel bread, washed down with the wine water and followed by a few dried apricots.

A damp night on a sleeping mat took him to a wet morning of heavy dew, chilling him deeply. 'That's fine,' he mused, 'it goes with my mood. Damp. Cold.' He was moving by need, with little open thought. A few niggling issues kept deep in his mind raced each other in circles. Breakfast helped clear his head a little, which led him to the resolution to see through his last promise to Rahma. He would find the marching Bábís and witness events.

Now with a goal in mind, he realized that in his fog of the evening before, he had not unsaddled his mounts. He apologized to all three animals, mounted up, and rode at a fast pace, pulling Rahma's horse and the mule behind.

Keeping that pace he soon heard the marchers, who must have stopped nearby for the night. He found a path off the road to go around them and towards Bárfurúsh, hoping to get far enough ahead to find a good observation spot.

About four miles short of the city, he heard another commotion. The city's people had done as they were bidden by the bitter mullá. The road was completely blocked by men with firearms and ammunition, and behind them, many more men with whatever weapons they could find or make. They all, to the last, looked angry and ready to kill.

Kapriel, as always wishing to avoid encounters with incited mobs, looked about, finding a small hillock on which he and his charges could perch out of the way of stray weapons fire. At least, he hoped it was out of the way.

None of the mob objected to his redirection of course, nor hailed him in any way. It seemed the clothing that marked him as a target in most of the nation would now prove to be his protection. Even if he were a fanatical Bábí, he would have left Christianity to become such, not Islám, and thus be a heretic under someone else's purview. Since he had not been part of Islám, Muslims could not persecute him for leaving that faith.

It was only perhaps half an hour's wait before the marchers appeared, with Mullá Husayn still in the lead.

The crowd of city people began to shout curses and insults, the rough noise of their voices growing.

The Bábís came near, some starting to reach for their weapons. Their hands were stopped by words from their leader. Most unfortunately, Kapriel could not hear them over the ugly roar of their opponents. Then six Bábís were thrown to the ground by bullets. Again hands went toward weapons and were stayed by Mullá Husayn. Another Bábí fell close to the beloved leader. He looked down at the fallen companion, then up to God, uttering words Kapriel assumed were a prayer. When the words stopped, Mullá Husayn unsheathed his sword and charged the man who had fired the last shot.

Terrified, the murderer ran and tried to hide behind a small tree, holding his musket up to shield himself.

Mullá Husayn hesitated not a moment, raised his sword, and in one stroke clove tree, musket, and man each into two pieces. He then set to the assembled mob, felling every opponent he encountered, untouched by the missiles flying around him. He carved a path all the way through the panicking mob, then rode for the city.

Behind him the Bábís, unable to see their intrepid leader, also set to the miscreants, surged through the attackers and marched to the city.

Kapriel mounted and urged his small train around the battle area, gaining the road further along, first at a canter, then a full gallop with clear road ahead. He wished he could be several places at once, and he wondered what Mullá Husayn was doing. Setting fire to the city? No, that would kill innocents. Murdering the inciting mullá, who had sent his people out but then stayed safe at home? Possibly, if he could find the coward.

Then Kapriel was suddenly tempted to turn around as he wondered if Rahma had been hit and lay dying. No, he had a promise to keep, no matter what.

When he was nearly caught up to the Bábís who were on foot, he slowed to avoid damaging anyone, carefully passing them on one side of the road. When he had passed them, he again urged his mount on to his best speed, not catching up to the mounted Bábís until he spotted them in the city at a standstill, chanting, "Yá Sáhibu's-Zamán" ("Oh, Lord of the Age!") over and over. In front of them was Mullá Husayn, uninjured and still mounted. Arrayed around them were frightened people who had not joined the front line of defense, crying for peace.

The mounted Bábís dismounted, walking over to Mullá Husayn to respectfully kiss his stirrups.

Kapriel sat in awe of the feats he had seen and the reverence of the disciples. Unsure of what would happen next, he tied the horses and mule to a nearby post, and to their great relief unsaddled them. In the unrest and chaos, none complained of his odd parking place. He was near the center of the city and was thus able to see and hear most of what happened.

That afternoon, the Bábí leader agreed to the peace the city folk pleaded for. Many had gathered, still fearing violence, listening for every detail of the agreement. They still listened as he said to them, "O followers of the Prophet of God, and shí'áhs of the imáms of His Faith! Why have you risen against us? Why deem the shedding of our blood an act meritorious in the sight of God? Did we ever repudiate the truth of your Faith? Is this the hospitality which the Apostle of God has enjoined His followers to accord to both the faithful and the infidel? What have we done to merit such condemnation on our part? Consider: I alone, with no other weapon than my sword, have been able to face the rain of bullets which the inhabitants of Bárfurúsh have poured upon me, and have emerged unscathed from the midst of the fire with which you have besieged me. Both my person and my horse have escaped unhurt from your overwhelming attack. Except for the slight scratch which I received on my face, you have been powerless to wound me. God had protected me and willed to establish in your eyes the ascendancy of His Faith."

He immediately rode to the Caravanserai of the Green Park where Kapriel, following the disciples and leading his hastily resaddled animals, found him welcoming his brethren inside.

When the Bábís had all been assembled in the caravanserai for several minutes, a few went back out through the gates. Kapriel, standing just outside the gate, heard them asking citizens the way to the city well and to bakeries, obviously in search of water and food. None would answer them. They soon returned empty-handed. After the last had returned, the gates were closed.

Kapriel found a place away from the gate and to one side of the park on which the caravanserai opened, which he suspected would soon be the scene of further attacks. He ensured that he could still see the gates and again snacked on dried rations and prepared water.

With the gates closed, the city zealots outside the caravanserai felt safe in approaching through the park, setting up minor battlements, bringing ammunition, and loading a few weapons. They were careful to keep the muzzles up in order to keep the ball and powder in.

The sun was setting when the gathered crowd set up a murmur. A young Bábí had climbed onto the caravanserai roof from the inside. He chanted the words, "Alláh-u-Akbar—" and fell off the roof dead, either from the bullet or the fall caused by it.

So much for peace, thought the scribe.

A few minutes had passed when another Bábí youth climbed up, also attempting to chant the Call to Prayer. He was able to get further but was also shot from the roof. A third man climbed up and was able to nearly finish the Call when he, too, fell dead.

The gates suddenly reopened, and Mullá Husayn, sword in hand and on his charger, fierce in his countenance, led the companions against their assailants. Those miscreants who had assembled in the grizzly, murderous crowd outside the caravanserai gates died quickly, except a few who managed to flee. The wrath of the Bábí leader was terrible.

The park was suddenly empty of enemies except for the dead, and the Bábís retreated inside the gates.

A pattern quickly developed, with the chief priest encouraging and inciting the populace, sending them out to attack those in the caravanserai, and the attackers being repulsed. It went on for nearly a week.

When the futility of the efforts became undeniable to even the most ardent opposition, a small group of well-dressed men approached the caravanserai gates. They could be seen by the light of their lanterns. Kapriel crossed the park to hear what was to transpire as the gates opened.

The men were on foot, beseeching humbly the mercy of Mullá Husayn for their city. One said, "God is our witness that we harbour no intention but that of establishing peace and reconciliation between us. Remain seated on your charger for a while, until we have explained our motive."

Mullá Husayn dismounted, inviting them into the caravanserai.

Kapriel had to get near to the open gates to hear more. One of the city noblemen was speaking and said, "We, unlike the people of this town, know how to receive the stranger in our midst." The nobleman then ordered tea to be served, causing Kapriel to give a snort of disdain.

He thought, *Do not let them have food or water, but now that the big men are here, let us all have tea.* Several of the noblemen's attendants went to fetch food and drink.

The lead nobleman continued, "The [head priest] was alone responsible for having kindled the fire of so much mischief. The people of Bárfurúsh should in no wise be implicated in the crime which he has committed. Let the past be now forgotten. We would suggest, in the interest of both parties, that you and your companions leave tomorrow for Amul. Bárfurúsh is in the throes of great excitement; we fear lest they may again be instigated to attack you."

Kapriel had difficulty hearing the response, catching just enough to hear Mullá Husayn agree to the plan, though not in ringing tones of trust and endorsement.

One nobleman said something about bringing his Qur'án, then two of the noblemen swore on it that they would treat the Bábís as guests that night. The next day they would order some man named Khusraw-i-Qádí-Kalá'í and "a hundred horsemen to ensure their safe passage through Shír-Gáh." One promised, "The malediction of God and His Prophets be upon us, both in this world and in the next, if we ever allow the slightest injury to be inflicted upon you and your party."

The attendants who had gone for victuals returned at that point, with more of the city notables following them. It was a large group of the city's highest ranks and Bábís of all ranks who dined together that night (10 October).

Kapriel wondered how many meals the Bábís had missed within the caravanserai. He slept in the park again, still in an obscure spot not easily seen from the gate. He felt surprisingly safe, knowing the next round of action would wait for dawn.

More than an hour after sunrise, a new man arrived with the two noblemen who had sworn the oath. The other nobleman who spoke the night before was not present.

Kapriel assumed the new man to be this Khusraw, who was to lead the escort. The scribe again walked up to the gate to hear whatever he could hear. When the escort leader was introduced to Mullá Husayn, the latter stated, "'If ye do well, it will redound to your own advantage; and if ye do evil, the evil will return upon you.'² If this man should treat us well, great shall be his reward; and if he act treacherously towards us, great shall be his punishment. To God would we commit our Cause, and to His will are we wholly resigned."

At the end of the ominous warning Mullá Husayn called out, "Mount your steeds, O heroes of God!"

Some of the escort led the way, riding at a walk through the city streets, and others followed at the back. Khusraw and Mullá Husayn stayed together in the middle, riding side by side, with a few of the escort positioned to the left and right of the long column of Bábís.

The escort led them on a different track than the one Kapriel and Rahma had taken from Amul, though Kapriel supposed this would lead them to the escort's destination of Shír-Gáh and on from there to over to Amul. This road led southwest, rather than due west where the friends had ridden.

Kapriel was following well behind, barely keeping the last escort in sight. This felt, and looked, so very much like another betrayal with the escort surrounding the Bábís. They had gone twelve or more miles, well into the afternoon, when he saw the forest in the distance and figured the forward riders were already in the wood. Suddenly the column stopped, and Kapriel heard sounds in the distance. Were they odd bird calls, or screams?

He continued forward to the point where he could vaguely make out the center of the long line, and he could see Mullá Husayn kneeling in a posture of prayer and Khusraw using threatening gestures. Suddenly, all along the line, the call "Oh Lord of the Age" went up, and the Bábís turned on their escort, slaughtering them to the last. No, not all of them had been killed—he could see Khusraw's attendant standing, attending the still-praying Mullá Husayn. That attendant fell at the feet of the Bábí leader.

Kapriel wondered if he had simply been struck down last as the least dangerous, but then Mullá Husayn handed him something. The attendant took it and, after a few moments listening to the Bábí leader, began walking back to the city. Kapriel dismounted to prevent frightening the man. As the attendant neared, Kapriel said, "Excuse me. Could you please tell me what just happened? It looked like the Bábís rose up and slaughtered their escort."

The man was nervous, shuffling his feet and fidgeting with his hands around an expensive prayer rug, gems glistening at the edges. "Yes, well, they did. But only after the escort attacked them. Khusraw was under orders to kill every last Bábí and take their belongings."

Disturbed, Kapriel asked, "By those who had sworn an oath on the Qur'án?"

"No, one of the other noblemen. Anyway, Khusraw picked the men of the escort, and each one was willing to kill on command. The goal was to get into the trees and attack, which they did. The men at the front killed some of the Bábís. We heard the screams. That Mullá Husayn," he spoke the name with fear, "asked me put out his prayer rug. This I did, just as Khusraw was demanding the mullá's sword and horse under threat of death. Suddenly Khusraw was dead, and so was his escort—all but me." He now looked near fainting.

"Thank you for your help." Kapriel sent him on his way, knowing moving away from the scene of such terrible events would help the man.

The Bábís appeared to be taking care of their own and preparing camp for the night.

Kapriel did the same with trepidation. He did not know of any special religious protection he was under, unlike the marching Bábís. They also had the advantage of large numbers, as they still numbered around three hundred men. And Kapriel was alone.

That fact hit him hard again as he set up a simple, cold camp. He had occasionally seen a head above the others during the march and wondered if it had been his large friend. Now he wondered which fire Rahma sat at with his true brethren, freed from material worries. The entire group bent to say prayers at dawn. The Bábís woke up, having slept on the ground during the whole night and, having no belongings to pack or supplies to consume, simply began saying prayers.

Kapriel was just close enough to hear Mullá Husayn briefly address them before they left. Once they had gathered he said, "We are approaching our Karbilá, our ultimate destination." He turned, starting to walk on foot down the path. A few followers thought to bring some things left behind by the dead escort. He told them to leave everything but their horses and swords. "It behooves you to arrive at that hallowed spot in a state of complete detachment, wholly sanctified from all that pertains to this world." Then they headed into the forest.

Kapriel followed again, a little closer to the Bábís now, with the dense wood surrounding them. They had not gone far—maybe one mile—when the entire group filed off to one side. There, in a wide clearing, was a small shrine, perhaps ten paces wide and twenty paces long. A local man, stunned at this appearance of so many, gaped at them, unmoving as the group filed past. Kapriel, still well behind the Bábís, approached him, inquiring, "Excuse me. What is this small building?"

The man answered, "That is a shrine. The tomb of Shaykh Tabarsí." Then he turned and fled.

17

The Shrine of Shaykh Tabarsí, October 1848 to May 1849

The Black Standards had settled at the shrine of Shaykh Tabarsí (12 October). Mullá Husayn immediately set the men to designing and building fortifications around an area enclosing the shrine. This was in a clearing in the surrounding forest, the trees not yet starting their fall change of colors.

Kapriel wished neither to distract Rahma—whom he saw on occasion helping to create tools from the wood around them—nor did he wish to be reminded of his aloneness near that close group of servants of the Almighty.

He followed small paths and found himself at a good-sized village near noon. He towed his three herbivores behind him through the gate in a small, somewhat symbolic wall. Perhaps they had less trouble with predators, human and animal, than on the south side of the Alburz. A local woman noticed him, calling in an old voice for a nearby child to get the head man.

Kapriel waited, just inside the gate, while the head man trundled out of his home and across the central square to the visitor. That man, Nazar Khán,* negotiated with the scribe for use of an empty home. Nazar wanted to know why Kapriel was there at all, rather

---

* Real, historical person.

than in a city where he could scribe. Kapriel told him, truthfully, "There are events happening in the area. I have promised a friend to learn of these events."

Nazar seemed to know what was being referred to and set to business. The villagers had no need of a scribe, but they could use both extra hands and extra beasts of burden for late harvests and for gathering wood to keep warm in winter, along with various other projects, and he would have Sundays off since he was a Christian. The headman directed him to an empty hut in return for his labor. Kapriel agreed they could use the horses and mule, with his rather protective supervision, in return for free hay.

The scribe happily set up his new home, cleaning out dried leaves and such, putting his bed mat in the driest corner, and arranging everything just so. He got a little help patching the thatch roof—a job with which he was quite unfamiliar—and replacing the disintegrating cloth "door." *That,* he thought, *will have to be replaced by something more sturdy before winter, if we're here that long.*

Near evening, a great tumult broke out. Kapriel ran outside to see horsemen with swords waving and women screaming. The women shouted that this was not Qádí-Kalá and that they had nothing to do with those people, continuing to scream for some minutes.

The leader of the assailants suddenly called his men to stop, to let him investigate the situation.

Kapriel approached at a walk. He heard someone tell the leader of the invaders that this hamlet was owned by Nazar Khán, not Khusraw who had led the traitorous escort, and that these horsemen had just killed Nazar Khán's mother.

Aghast, the man spoke loudly, "We did not intend to molest either the men or the women of this village. Our sole purpose was to curb the violence of the people of Qádí-Kalá, who were about to put us all to death."[1] He apologized for this tragic scene.

Kapriel surmised that these were Bábís who had been attacked while at work around the shrine, then ridden to repulse the attackers but had taken a wrong trail.

The headman emerged from his home grieving for his mother, but he listened to the words of the attackers, including their apologies. In spite of his sorrow he invited the lead swordsman, Mírzá Muhammad Taqí, to his home to explain. Taqí stayed all night, escorting Nazar to meet Mullá Husayn in the morning. The rest of the village had other work to do that day, which meant Kapriel was unable to follow.

The village headman returned later that morning and set everyone to preparing food for the Bábís, so impressed had he been with their story and their leader. He frequently lamented out loud his lack of sons to offer as a sacrifice to the Lord of the Age. He and Kapriel now had much to discuss as Kapriel related his adventures with Rahma, showing him the Bayán and other writings of the Báb that the headman could not read.

Kapriel's village home was close enough to the shrine that he went early every Sunday, and a few Fridays when the others gave him no tasks on their rest day. He stayed as long as he could before dusk turned to darkness, staying back in some obscuring foliage to observe the preparations of the new fort.

Frequently various villagers, repeatedly incited by the same chief priest of Bárfurúsh according to Nazar's sources, would attack the Bábís as they worked on constructing their fort. Each attack was repulsed with humiliating swiftness.

The fort was taking shape, and trade with friendly villages helped advance the project. They had made great progress in only a couple of weeks. A large, rounded enclosure, about eighty paces by sixty paces,[2] had been created by an earth-and-post wall most of the way around. Two long, slim buildings had gone up to nearly fill the remaining gap, leaving only a gate for access between them. The buildings even had two stories and tile roofs. Other work had been done to help sustain and keep safe the Bábís, but once the buildings were up, Kapriel could see nothing of the continued work inside. Surely they must have built some form of water catchment to reduce reliance on outside sources. He had seen an orange tree in there, but he did not know how they would feed over 300 men (he had carefully counted and ended up estimating the total number of the group) on a few oranges.

———•———

The fort around the shrine of Shaykh Tabarsí was almost complete when a surprise visitor arrived in Afrá, the village of Nazar Khán. Jináb-i-Bahá had come with provisions for the people in the fort.

Kapriel heard the buzz while he was out helping to harvest pomegranates. One of the village youth came running out to tell the harvesters the news, and they all returned to meet the nobleman of the nearby district of Núr.

Kapriel was especially interested to meet the man who had been contacted by Mullá Husayn when the Letters of the Living dispersed from Shíráz four and a half years earlier; who had taught, enlightened, and brought into the new faith thousands of believers; who had engineered the escape of Táhirih from Qazvín; and instigated and at least partly run the conference of Badasht.

Here he was, right in this village, Mírzá Husayn 'Alí, Jináb-i-Bahá, son of ministers to the sháhs, wealthy nobleman of Núr and Tihrán. And as Mullá Hasan had told them back in Tihrán, he was short—perhaps a head shorter than Kapriel, and definitely of less height than the Báb. This outward size in no way diminished his nobility. His bearing, his air of authority, the fine silk brocades he wore, all spoke of things beyond physical size.

The servants who had come with him were reverently deferential, not obsequious or frightened by their master.

A messenger was sent to the fort to inform Mullá Husayn of Jináb-i-Bahá's imminent arrival there.[3] The headman nodded to Kapriel to come along, since this was exactly the type of event the scribe was looking to record.

Soon they were off, walking in front of the animals that were carrying the provisions. When Jináb-i-Bahá arrived, Mullá Husayn—looking much as he had back in Shíráz—greeted him with a gentle hug and the greatest respect. All the companions stood as their leader gazed at the face of Jináb-i-Bahá with awe. The rest of the company seemed somewhat confused by such admiration on the part of Mullá Husayn, their glorious leader.

After a few minutes, Jináb-i-Bahá bade them all be seated, speaking to the group at large with words of spiritual import.

That afternoon the exalted guest inspected the fortifications, giving his approval. He gave one instruction to Mullá Husayn: "The one thing this fort and company require is the presence of Quddús. His association with this company would render it complete and perfect." Then he bade Mullá Husayn assign seven men to ride to Sárí and demand deliverance of Quddús from the man who was holding him prisoner. "The fear of God and the dread of His punishment will prompt him to surrender unhesitatingly his captive."

Then Jináb-i-Bahá gave them words of encouragement, directing them to abide by the Almighty, and added, "If it be His will We shall once again visit you at this same spot, and lend you Our assistance. You have been chosen of God to be the vanguard of His host and the establishers of His Faith. His host verily will conquer. Whatever may befall, victory is yours, a victory which is complete and certain." He commended them all to the care of God and left to return to the village with Nazar Khan.

Kapriel followed them, glad to be in the background where he could think quietly. As he had looked around the fort's interior, he had seen Rahma toward the back of the crowd, near a few head of cattle, and gave thanks that his friend was still alive. This nobleman from Núr, however, was a puzzle: one which Kapriel felt an urgent need to figure out.

That nobleman left for Tihrán the next morning, intending to go by his home in Núr on the way. There was no more possibility of investigating the esteemed personage at that time.

Nazar learned in the next few days—and passed along to Kapriel—of the successful release of Quddús the same night Jináb-i-Bahá had been there, and his welcome to the fort in the night by about a hundred Bábís with two candles each who had gone out into the forest to greet him and light his way through the darkness.

During the following weeks, as fall cooled the days and lengthened the nights, Kapriel found new events unfolding at the fort. A small open square, or Maydán, adjoined the fort and would often be occupied by Quddús, seated among his companions, chanting, writing prayers and poems of love for their Lord, which the companions would then recite. Those who knew the words of the Bayán or Qur'án would chant them for the company, and after abstruse passages were recited, he would explain the meanings completely.

These devotions took place every morning and evening, despite continued strikes of the enemy, frequent hails of bullets from riled locals, and attacks from all sides. No matter the circumstances, Quddús continued his daily devotions undistracted and unperturbed by events around him.

Kapriel did not see, from his hidden vantage, that Quddús was repressing any emotion. He simply did not get upset or fearful, ever.

Nazar Khán kept Kapriel apprised of whatever information he gleaned from his people's trips to Bárfurúsh and Amul. Kapriel kept him updated on observations of the fort.

The inciter of Bárfurúsh was urging the regional congregation to blockade the fort, to stop anyone from approaching and rendering aid or commerce which might assist the Bábís.

The residents of the fort had not taken in any more cohorts since the last one arrived the day after Quddús's release. Some had come to visit, to see the amazing fort put up so quickly. There were also passers-by who were curious as to the cause of such enthusiasm on the part of the Bábís. Questions were rife in the district, and the lead clergyman, the same who had begun the persecutions against

those under the Black Standards, took great offense to their seques-
tration in his district.

The populace was no longer allowed to even speak to the community inside the fort. Nazar Khán and a few others continued to
send provisions whatever way possible, but the Bábís were increasingly cut off from supplies and assistance. Inhabitants of several villages faithful to the clergy worked to cut off access, keeping back the
helpful and the curious. Yet Kapriel noticed that so far each crisis
had been followed by resounding victory. Surely help was coming.

Nazar Khán received word in late fall that the lead clergyman of
Bárfurúsh had sent a letter of complaint to the young sháh. Help in
eradicating the fort and its population had been asked for. Troubles
were multiplying.

Winter was only a month away, yet the daytime and nighttime
temperatures were still tolerable to one of southern blood. There
was more rain here, in soggy downpours that occasionally threatened home foundations. Kapriel began to think he would rot there,
in the rain and the humidity. They had as much rain in one month
as Shíráz received in half the rainy season.

It was during this approach to the winter solstice that the army
arrived. Kapriel was shocked when he saw them. The authorities
apparently felt it necessary to gather and send around twelve thousand men to extinguish some three hundred lives.[4] The letter to the
sháh must have been impressive, indeed!

Kapriel first saw the army not at the fort, but when it marched
into his town of Afrá, setting up an occupation and overwhelming
the town with their numbers. Attacks on the enclosed Bábís had
immediately begun. Every means was used to prevent provisions
from reaching the fort. Orders were given to shoot to kill anyone
leaving its gate.

The daily bread from various supportive villagers stopped, and the daily excursions of the Bábís in the fort to get water became impossible under the hail of gunfire. Barricades were being set up around the fort's only gate.

But the day of violence ended in a night of torrential downpour. The army's barricades were washed away, their ammunition was ruined, and the men in the fort were supplied with fresh water from the rain.

The very next night, still three weeks from the beginning of winter, a great snowfall accumulated, creating manifold increases in the difficulties of the army. The day after the snow, the soldiers still prepared for the next round of battle.

A day and a half after the snow, in the cold, mushy early morning, Kapriel placed himself further from the gate than his usual observation point. The army made it quite difficult to get close enough to watch events. Still, this new location was sufficient, and he would hopefully be able to avoid stray bullets.

The army was in place and ready two hours after sunset when Quddús, with Mullá Husayn and three companions, rode out of the gate, "followed by the entire company on foot behind them." When they cleared the gate, the entire group of companions called out, "O Lord of the Age!" with such fervor and confidence that the soldiers were terrified. Most of them fled into the forest, leaving fellow soldiers and belongings behind. Less than an hour was necessary to complete the rout, with the companions having brought a swift end to over 430 of their enemies including several officers and their general.

Kapriel watched all of the Bábís return to their fort, none having perished. They were assisting the only man who had been badly wounded.

This sent the scribe off on another round of musing about the contrasts between the two armies. The cohesion of the believers was obvious, as was their devotion to their leaders. The soldiers, on the other hand, were a loose conglomeration of men with no cohesive ideals and no devotion to any particular leader. In watching them over the next few days, he learned that many soldiers admired the Báb and saw no reason for killing His followers. They were trained, however, to follow orders; thus, if they were ordered to kill innocent men, they would do so.

The routed army took some days to reassemble. In that time, the men of the fort ventured out to dig a moat around their wall to slow attacks. This project took nearly three weeks to complete. There was no need to find water for it—ground water seeped right in. Kapriel found them at work on this project from his early arrival on his days off to late, late into the night.

There were no more visitors. Some local villages and towns had set up roadblocks and guard posts to ensure the isolation of the men in the fort. The few who tried to get close were turned back. The trickle of supplies had stopped completely.

Kapriel was spending his time at Afrá leading the horses and mule around in a tiny caravan while he and others gathered wood for the village. It was sweaty work even on cold days, keeping him wet. He noticed white, itchy patches developing on his skin, especially in areas that continually stayed damp. He went to Nazar Khán to ask about it. The headman immediately sent his son to a local healer for an herbal ointment, joking with Kapriel about southern skin not being able to take a little mist.

The scribe built a more solid door after that, cutting off the wind. Then his fires could not only warm him better, but more thoroughly dry his little hut and his skin, saving his books and paper from impending mold.

Word soon came to Afrá that another army approached, this one lead by a prince. The new army had camped at Shír-Gáh, then transferred headquarters nearby in the town of Vás-Kas.

Kapriel was happy to be at his observation post when a messenger arrived at the fort from the prince. He called out to those behind the gate, asking for Mullá Husayn by name. He said that he had been "commanded by the sháh to ascertain the purpose of his activities and to request that he be enlightened as to the object he had in view."

Mullá Husayn had responded, "Tell your master that we utterly disclaim any intention either of subverting the foundations of the monarchy or of usurping the authority of Násiri'd-Dín Sháh. Our Cause concerns the revelation of the promised Qá'im and is primarily associated with the interests of the ecclesiastical order of this country. We can set forth incontrovertible arguments and deduce infallible proofs in support of the truth of the Message we bear."

The conversation went on for a bit, greatly affecting the messenger. He finally asked, "What are we to do?"

Mullá Husayn replied, "Let the prince direct the 'ulamás of both Sárí and Bárfurúsh to betake themselves to this place, and ask us to demonstrate the validity of the Revelation proclaimed by the Báb. Let the Qur'án decide as to who speaks the truth. Let the prince himself judge our case and pronounce the verdict. Let him also decide as to how he should treat us if we fail to establish, by the aid of verses and traditions, the truth of this Cause."

That was rapidly agreed to, and the messenger promised it would take place in three days, coinciding with the winter solstice (21 December).

The day of that appointment arrived, not with clergy arriving for discussion and debate, but with regiment after regiment of cavalry and infantry prepared for a major assault on the little fort in numbers much greater than the twelve thousand of the first assault.

The town of Afrá could hardly keep from hearing so many troops moving so near their homes in the night. Kapriel was one of those who woke and ran to learn what they could. Shortly before dawn the amassed army, situated on a hill above the fort, was given the order to open fire. Thousands of propelled lead balls flew into and around the fort. The sound was thunderous! Barely above the gunfire could be heard a voice from the fort shouting, "Mount your steeds, O heroes of God!" The gates were thrown open and over two hundred of the companions rode out to battle at full speed.

Even with snow and mud churning and splashing under their horses' hooves and the thousands of soldiers arrayed against them, nothing could daunt the faith of the Bábís. They broke through the lines of the soldiers and headed directly for Vás-Kas, where the prince and his lieutenants oversaw the action.

Unable to follow on foot to see the events, Kapriel had to wait for late morning to get the rest of the news.

The army leadership had, again, been completely routed. The prince in charge had left his apartments through a window, barefoot, to escape the charge of Mullá Husayn. Two other princes had fought and been eliminated, along with many more men.

The prison of Vás-Kas, which held a number of Bábís captive, was opened and the prisoners released.

Another engagement happened at the outskirts of that town as the Bábís regrouped. They were suddenly attacked by a split detachment, with each half of the detachment coming at them from different directions. Mullá Husayn charged toward one group of attackers, while Quddús and the rest of his companions spurred their mounts toward the other. Mullá Husayn's opponents suddenly changed course, rushing toward the the rest of the detachment and trapping the main Bábí contingent in the middle. Firearms already prepared, both halves of the detachment shot into the group of Bábís.

Quddús was hit in the mouth, causing a significant wound. Mullá Husayn rushed to him, agonized over the injury. He borrowed Quddús's sword and, with one sword in each hand, leaped at the enemy. About a hundred of his companions followed, facing a far greater number of soldiers and cavalry. They fought with all the faith they possessed, and within thirty minutes had dispersed the entire army.

The calm after the army's retreat gave them time to collect their wounded and return to the fort.

It was hard to believe this retold account, but Kapriel was assured by his source that he had questioned the witness and was convinced of its accuracy.

Nazar Khán informed Kapriel of another setback for the Bábís some days later. Jináb-i-Bahá had been on the way to the fort with companions and provisions when the entire party was arrested and taken to Amul. The governor of that city had been assigned to assist the army of the prince, and he had assigned a kinsman to govern in his absence. Upon the arrival of the small Bábí party, the acting governor had sent for the clergy and leading siyyids to meet them.

They were accused of attempting to help the rebels in the fort at the shrine of Shaykh Tabarsí. One had in his possession a manuscript that was assumed to have been written by the Báb. Jináb-i-Bahá gave convincing testimony to the impromptu trial, but his words only inflamed the agitation of some. The siyyids demanded punishment for the presumed heresy. The acting governor agreed to the least possible action: They would all receive the bastinado and be held until the governor returned, when they could be sent to Tihrán.

Nazar Khán relayed that this punishment was not fully carried out. Somehow Jináb-i-Bahá had convinced the accusers that each of his companions was innocent, and he alone received the bastinado for all of them. They were conducted to the prison but soon were assisted by the acting governor to escape to the governor's home. They were being treated well and were safe from the besieging siyyids.

The situation at the fort continued to worsen over the next month as winter was nearing its midpoint, the rain and snow alternating through the wettest part of the season. Alone, Kapriel contemplated Christ's birth and daydreamed of his family—as well as of Mina, far away in a dry place. He did not complain. How could he, when Rahma and hundreds more were certainly starving in their fort?

The army regrouped, and several regiments of reinforcements arrived, creating the largest opposition yet. They built seven layers of barricades around the fort, displaying weaponry and numerical strength with growing confidence.

It was near midnight one night (2 February 1849) when everyone in the vicinity of the fort was again awoken by the reverberating cry of, "O Lord of the Age!"[5]

Kapriel and his observing companion again raced down welltrodden paths to see what they could see.

By the light of the stars, the onlookers could tell that the first barricade had already been broken, its defenders either dead or scattered. The second barricade was under attack by a man of ferocious energy, backed by over a hundred more. Then the third barricade broke. Bullets again rained down on the companions, felling very few in an astounding denial of the thousands of bullets descending on them. The fourth barricade was destroyed, then the fifth, sixth, and seventh. The horse of the lead rider from the fort became entangled in a tent outside the last barricade, stopping further progress. The rider suddenly dismounted and managed a few steps before falling. Two others grabbed him and carried him back to the mass of Bábís.

The attack proceeded until some unknown goals seemed to have been met, at which time the Bábís returned to their fort and closed the gate, taking their many wounded with them.

Most observers were rooted to the cold earth, awaiting dawn to see the final results of the resistance. Kapriel could not understand why villages, towns, cities, and armies kept attacking. The only village harmed by those under the Black Standards had been Afrá, and that was accidental. Afrá had become staunch supporters of the Bábís. He wondered about the man who had led the way through the barricades. Could that man, struck down near the end of the sortie, have been the indomitable Mullá Husayn?

Morning light revealed complete devastation on the field of battle. The army was gone, assumed to be regrouping elsewhere. The barricades were in shambles. The fort stood strong, its gate closed.

More weeks passed. The scattered armies, completely demoralized by the attack of so few in the night, had retreated in different directions under their original leaders. One segment had set up camp in a village two miles from the fort. The guard posts and road blocks stayed up. The Bábís starved.

Ten days before Naw Rúz of that year (11 March), the town of Afrá received word that the nearest army was on the move again. This group was under a leader who was reported to be more arrogant and overconfident than his peers in the other armies. Kapriel ran through the trees in the early morning light, barely arriving at his vantage point before the army. He saw a much smaller body than the previous force—only two regiments of cavalry and infantry.[6] They encompassed the fort and opened fire on the sentinels. How could they hope to defeat what the entire previous mass of military might could not stand against?

Minutes passed with the continual discharge and reloading of weapons. Suddenly the call of "O Lord of the Age" again rang through the area. The gate opened, and just nineteen mounted men raced out to meet the enemy. They charged the camp, stopping for nothing.

The small army, shocked and terrified by the uncompromising charge, fled all the way to Bárfurúsh in shame. Their leader "was so shaken with fear that he fell from his horse. Leaving, in his distress, one of his boots hanging from the stirrup, he ran away, half shod and bewildered . . ."

The nineteen horsemen returned, unhurt. They pulled extra horses from the enemy camp with them, perhaps for replacement mounts, perhaps to ease their starvation. Mullá Husayn was not among them.

Naw Rúz came, and Kapriel missed his friend terribly. He went to the fort by his secret paths, standing behind a few screening trees, where he could hear the songs of praise and joy being sung by the men inside. He fasted for the day, in recognition of the circumstances the inhabitants must be in.

He silently joined the songs Rahma had taught him, sending his companion hopes to have what he wished for most. Perhaps, now that spring had arrived, the siege would stop.

Nine days later (30 March) the latest army opened fire.[7] They had come in the greatest numbers yet—tens of thousands—to exterminate the diminishing number of defenders. The army had taken a few days to dig trenches and construct barricades around the fort. They built towers higher than the fort walls from which to shoot inside the protecting battlements.

And they had brought artillery.

Two cannons and two mortars were placed on an overlooking hilltop. They also had a new weapon, an explosive which could be thrown a good distance (700 meters) and ignite anything combustible it touched.

It seemed there was no course other than defeat for the heroes in the fort. Yet, surprising things were happening at night. The long nights gave the besieged time to build, increasing the height of the walls above that of the towers. Once the bombardment began, walls breached by cannon were rebuilt in darkness.

Kapriel stayed in his spot, sleeping on the ground through the incessant rain. Nazar Khán, wanting to know what was happening, sent a youth who had previously observed events with Kapriel. The boy brought provisions to share with the scribe, leaving Kapriel alone at their post in the evening and returning when possible in the morning.

Despite the cannon fire, mortar rounds, and blazing inferno of their tents and straw or grass barriers, and disregarding the continual rain of bullets, the Bábís intoned the Call to Prayer, recited verses, and chanted congregational hymns that could be heard by all, as would have been intoned in any peaceful mosque. Without this reminder of their existence, they would have seemed to have already expired.

One of the generals then had a tower built much closer to the fort, and able to hold a cannon. When finished, this cannon fired directly into the center of the fort.

Near evening, nineteen horsemen again galloped through the gate to the wild chant of "O Lord of the Age," rushing the offending tower and crashing it to the ground. They then took on barricade after barricade, demolishing several before being forced by darkness to return to the fort.

Kapriel could barely make out their returning number, but he counted nineteen still in the saddle and waving a sword, tugging more abandoned horses behind them.

There was peace for a few days, then an explosion inside the army camp, apparently in an ammunition tent, put an end to further attempts for a month. The affected divisions withdrew to await resupply.

The partial withdrawal of the army allowed civilian observers— including Kapriel—to take turns at a closer vantage point. Back in Afrá, the town learned of the extreme hunger of the Bábís through these observers. The besieged and increasingly thin men had been seen to emerge, a few at a time, to cut the grass outside the fort and take it back inside with them. That meant the grass inside the fort was gone, whether already eaten or trampled to nothing. They wondered if the grass was for the horses or the humans. All lamented the inability to get food to the Bábís.

Five weeks after Naw-Rúz the next round began with further artillery fire and still larger forces raining death inside the fort. At the same time an attack force of several regiments, with both cavalry and infantry, began a violent assault on the fort walls.

This time, thirty-six horsemen left the gate, and even from a distance observers could see their skeletal frames through rotting clothes. Yet they again raised the ominous call of "O Lord of the Age" and set about their task as if they had never missed a meal. Once again, the attackers were put to flight. This time five companions were carried, unmoving, back to the fort.

It was several peaceful days later when the youth who traded observing with Kapriel brought news back to Afrá. A messenger had arrived, walked to the gate, and asked for a specific person, purportedly a relative. The man he had asked for appeared above the wall, looking down at his kin.

The two had spoken for a few minutes, the words difficult to make out from so far away. He caught some of the exchange, about a son who needs his father, which was swiftly countered. Then there was something about an offer from the prince, setting free those who left without a fight.

The next day a few of the men left the fort—Kapriel later learned of the prince's assurances of safety—and were slaughtered on the spot.

No further violence took place for several more days. Spring had reached it midpoint when another messenger approached the gate (9 May, 1849). This man, calling himself an emissary of the prince, requested two representatives of the fort be appointed to "conduct confidential negotiations with them in the hope of arriving at a peaceful settlement . . ."[8]

Shortly two emaciated men did leave the fort, escorted into the army camp.

Observers were surprised when not much later the two men returned, seemingly unhurt. One carried a book in one hand.

Kapriel's curiosity was nearly overpowering. It peaked even higher a little later. Horsemen, pulling lines of saddled horses behind them, rode up to the gate. The Bábís emerged and several pulled themselves up in the saddles, the rest ready to walk. Kapriel quickly counted, coming up with about two hundred surviving defenders. Astonishing! About a third had been lost to battle, then. Despite their emaciation, it looked as though few or none had died of starvation. After six months in the fort, with five of those months cut off from supplies, the Bábís were still alive. They carried almost nothing, having brought little more than their now-ragged clothing and weapons when they joined.

But what could have induced them to leave? And why were they receiving assistance and not being cut down?

Soldiers directed them on a path to the main encampment. A Bábí who must have been Quddús was in the lead.

Once they were in the forest Kapriel's curiosity overcame his common sense. He rushed into the still-open gate, deciding Quddús's room would be on the second floor of one of the buildings to either side of the gate. He entered the one to his left, seeing only remnants of saddles and belt buckles in a corner. So, that is part of what they had eaten—anything made of leather. Upstairs was also barren. He ran to the other building and up the stairs. There, to one side, he saw a book. It was a Qur'án. He quickly opened it, checking inside the cover and beginning to turn pages.

There it was, on the first page of the first Súrih, written in the margin: "I swear by this most holy Book, by the righteousness of God who had revealed it, and the Mission of Him who was inspired with its verses, that I cherish no other purpose than to promote peace and friendliness between us. Come forth from your stronghold and rest assured that no hand will be stretched forth against you. You yourself and your companions, I solemnly declare, are under the sheltering protection of the Almighty, of Muhammad, His Prophet, and of Násiri'd-Dín Sháh, our sovereign. I pledge my honour that no man, either in this army or in this neighborhood, will ever attempt to assail you. The malediction of God, the omnipotent Avenger, rest upon me if in my heart I cherish any other desire than that which I have stated." It ended with the personal seal of the prince, Mihdí-Qulí Mírzá.

A horrible feeling of danger engulfed Kapriel—a heavy, cold weight on his back as if he were about to be stabbed. He turned suddenly, but no one was there.

The scribe left the fort cautiously, checking around every corner for soldiers. Regaining the woods, he ran to the village of Afrá, straight to the home of Nazar Khán.

When the headman heard the words written by the prince, he began wailing in grief. Soon the entire town was weeping. They spent the rest of the day and the entire night in prayer that the prince would keep his sacred oath.

Nazar sent a youth to the camp the next morning to inquire as to the needs of the army and to check on the fate of the Bábís. He did not return for most of the day. Cannon fire was again heard at the empty fort, the military apparently intent on destroying what the Bábís had built. Late in the afternoon, the youth returned, shaking and pale, clearly near collapse. The tale he told broke the heart of every man, woman, and older child in Afrá.

At first he could only give brief details. The Bábís had been separated into groups of about thirty for dinner. They were given meager food, most of them refusing to partake of the insult. This morning, one group was surrounded and taken captive, the intent being to sell them into slavery. Lies were told to other groups in the name of Quddús, hoping to lead the Bábís astray, but the Bábís recognized the lies and refused to be deceived. Then the slaughter began. The youth could not recount the varied and awful ways that the soldiers thought up to kill their victims, but he told them that through it all, the praise of God could be heard from the dying.[9]

After several minutes of raging grief, he recovered enough to say that a few of those held as captives—those of high rank or wealth—were being held for ransom, and Quddús was still being held by the prince.

Kapriel did the tally. With about thirty going into slavery, and perhaps twenty held for ransom, there was at least a chance of several surviving to tell the tale of what had happened inside the fort. He had a momentary flare of hope that Rahma may have been one of the survivors, but then realized the futility of it. His friend had wanted to be a martyr for the Cause from his first true listening to the sacred words of the Báb four and a half years ago. No, his friend's heartfelt desire had surely been fulfilled.

The town spent the night in mourning, taking turns in a vigil to ease the path of the heroes still left, and exalting those who had ascended in defense of their Lord.

Kapriel was able to get at least some sleep that night, falling exhausted on his mat. Alone with his thoughts in the morning, he found the one thing most prominent on his mind was relief. The men of the fort no longer suffered. Those to be sold as slaves would be fed, as would the captives held for ransom. They would not starve. The rest were with God.

Several more days of mourning passed, but life went on. The people of Afrá had to go back to work, planting, working the soil, building, loving, helping each other.

Five days after the slaughter, they heard word from Bárfurúsh that Quddús had been taken there, and after several days was turned over to a mob again incited to murder by the chief cleric and his cohorts. Another brilliant light had been put out.

Kapriel worked hard for the next week, putting all his energy into helping the town. The headman knew what this meant. On the following Sunday, which Kapriel had not taken off, Nazar tracked down their guest.

"My friend, I believe you intend to leave us soon. This is why you work yourself to nothing, yes?"

"My purpose for being here is done. You have all been so helpful, taking me in and helping in my task of observing the fort. Also, your village has very much benefited from the extra horses and mule, and they will be going with me. I wish to make up for that loss to your people."

"Do not trouble your heart over this. Our dealings with the various armies have brought a good income to us. I had already planned to buy more animals. We will miss you, though." Changing to a more positive tone, he asked, "Then, where will you go?"

"From what we have heard, the Báb is still in Chihriq. It would be good to be at least a bit closer. And drier."

The headman laughed.

"Also, I have almost no money left. I think, if the scribe shop in Tihrán will have me, I will stay there a while, perhaps through next winter if no news comes from the Báb. Then return to Tabríz."

"This sounds like a good plan. It is not good to prolong good-byes. You will leave tomorrow?"

18

Tihrán, May 1849 to April 1850

Kapriel did leave Afrá the next morning. He rode straight to Amul, waiting there at the caravanserai only long enough to join a group headed to Tihrán.

He spoke to no one beyond the basic pleasantries required by politeness in securing provisions and paying for himself and the horses to stay. His thoughts were unpleasant, brightened only by the distant hope of going home, and maybe finding Mina still single, perhaps willing to marry him. He was, at least, headed in the right direction.

He had seen the mysterious forests of the north, wreathed in mists and thick air, and would recount the tale to any who wished to hear it. He would not, however, return. Ever. The white patches of fungal infection were still visible. The horses had bumps of fungus called rain rot after every shower. At least their feet had stayed healthy.

It was a great relief to ride high in the mountain pass, above the tree line, where the air was again light and dry. And the view of the drab tan and grey desert south of the mountains, contrasted with the bright greens of mountain and field in spring, was wondrous!

He settled himself in a caravanserai on the outskirts of Tihrán and went straight to the scribe shop. Luck was with him, or Divine Providence, or something. The shop owner had a commission of several books in Armenian and needed help right away. The next stop was the main bazaar, where he went to the Armenian clothier, untempted by any sights or delights, and spent most of his scant reserve funds on new clothing.

Back at the caravanserai he warmed a bucket of water, washed thoroughly, put on the new clothes, and threw most of the old out.

Next he attacked the tack, making rags of his old undershirt and cleaning the mold and mildew from the saddles, bridles, and other gear, scrubbing rust from every bit of metal. Finally, he unpacked every bag but one, throwing out the stale or moldy rations and anything that had been purchased up north. The bags had also suffered from the dampness, but until he could buy replacements these would have to stay.

He also threw out all of his bedding, preferring the bare floor to any moldy reminder of the events over the past months. He slept on the bare, cold, concrete floor with a small fire in a pot next to him.

The next morning he awoke from bad dreams and set off to work. He bent great effort to his task, hoping to drown out distracting thoughts. The shop owner, Kambíz, was a gentle Muslim, and asked during a break if Kapriel was suffering from illness. "You look different from last summer. The happiness in you seems to have gone out."

Kapriel only smiled lightly and thanked him for his concern.

That evening he made contact with the Bábís. They had already heard most of the news, one of the captive men having been ransomed and rejoining them. They remembered Rahma and chanted a prayer for him, moving Kapriel to tears, again.

There was great comfort in that group, giving the scribe hope that maybe he would eventually heal.

He learned of other events happening around Persia. Hujjat, still a prisoner in Tihrán last summer, had learned of the young sháh plotting his destruction and had left in disguise. He returned to his home city of Zanján and was again leading his large congregation of Bábís there.

Táhirih had gone missing at some point after the Badasht conference. She was assumed to be safe in a wealthy family's home.[1]

Jináb-i-Bahá and his retinue had returned to his homes in Núr and Tihrán after he received the bastinado last fall in Amul.[2]

Around the country Bábís were increasingly persecuted and still increasing in number. They would hear of another murder, a mutilation, or a humiliation happening to Bábís in cities all over, even in Iráq.

There were no changes, as far as they knew, in the conditions under which the Báb was held. All agreed that if a change was coming it would originate in Tihrán, and they would know in time for some to travel swiftly and see the event.

Kapriel had a personal issue to ask for help with. What should he do with the horses and mule? He would need them at some point, but leaving them stuck in a paddock for months would do neither them nor his finances any good, and could cause them to transform into sore-plagued beasts of a different color.

Several local Bábís were farmers and could use an extra animal. As at Afrá, Kapriel ensured they would be treated well, not left in saddles or harnesses to get sores or be abused in any way.

A few days later the horses and mule went to a temporary home. This Bábí farmer had a large amount of land but little cash to buy horses or mules. He showed Kapriel the animals he already had, all of which were in excellent condition. The scribe gratefully handed over the reins, tack, and feed bags, thanking the man for taking all of them so he would not need to visit several farms whenever it was time to move on.

The farmer was, of course, grateful to be lent such healthy animals for free.

Now Kapriel's days could settle into a routine. Except for Fridays, when the shop was closed, and Sundays, to keep the appearance of being Christian, Kapriel worked diligently to complete whatever project was assigned him. Fridays he went to the Armenian quarter and scribed there. Sundays were spent in his room reading, usually, though sometimes he chose to explore the bazaar alone and occasionally attended services at the Armenian Apostolic Church in that city. On certain evenings he gathered with the Bábís for news and friendship.

Weeks passed, and the finances eased with solid income. The final moldy reminders of Mázindarán were replaced and thrown into a fire, except for one last, untouched bag. Letters were sent via Armenian merchants to his family in Shíráz and Julfa, though vague and lacking much content.

Summer began with blessed dry heat, just as Kapriel felt it should be. His skin healed, the white spots finally fading away. A trip to visit the horses and mule showed them to be healthy and without any sign of rain rot.

The months passed into fall with still no change in the Báb's captivity. The only news from Chihríq was that the Báb had stopped all writing and recording any more from His revelation on hearing the news of the atrocities in Mázindarán, and had not yet ended His grieving.

Summer became fall, still lusciously dry, there having been no rain since well before Kapriel's return in spring. The Armenian merchant who had taken letters to his family visited the shop with replies, surprising Kapriel and brightening his week.

He still saved every coin he earned, minus meals and room rent. If Mina was willing and able to marry he would need to resave all that he had spent in the last three years of travel. The scribe shop and work in the Armenian quarter paid better than in Shíráz, perhaps due to the greater demand. He was even able to help Kambíz with a Kurdish customer who needed a letter written in Arabic. This greatly impressed the shop owner, who gave Kapriel a little extra pay for that.

During the fall, on the one-year anniversary of Rahma joining the tiny army of the Black Standards, Kapriel at last took out his friend's pack and went through it, item by item, to see what might have been damaged in the northern air. It was still a difficult task, all these months after his Rahma's passing. There were a few mementos of Shíráz and his childhood. Some bags of food had to be discarded. The bulk of the contents were writings of the Báb, a few in Rahma's own atrocious writing, which caused Kapriel great joy. These bits of parchment and books had been all carefully wrapped in waxed paper and oilcloth, well preserved from the rot most things had succumbed to.

The salvageable items were carefully repacked and the bag set aside in one corner. Kapriel realized he had not looked at the inscription Rahma had written in the gift copy of the Bayán for nearly a full year. He took it out now, gratefully remembering the day Rahma had so bashfully given it to him. Now Kapriel could truly smile.

Fall rains came gently and dried quickly. Nights lengthened and days cooled as fall became winter. Word came that the Báb had again taken up His pen after six months of mourning.

The stirring of mischief present throughout Persia was again increasing. In Tihrán, there were suspicious words from pulpits and whispering behind hands. Homes were being watched more carefully and the Bábís of the capital city wondered if it would now be their turn for martyrdom.

Kapriel joined the local Armenians in the celebration of the birth of Christ that winter, happy to have a few hours in somewhat familiar surroundings. He often wondered if he should declare himself a Bábí and throw in his life with the others, but he had a promise to keep. That promise required that he stay safe, for now, and that he be able to move when necessary.

Shortly before midwinter Táhirih was found, as suspected, in a home where she had been taken care of in Núr. She was arrested and moved to the house of the mayor in Tihrán, where she was treated respectfully and was still able to teach the wealthy women of the city who came to visit.

The weather was warming when, about a month before Naw-Rúz and the vernal equinox, fourteen Bábís were suddenly arrested in the capital city (14 February 1850). Roughly thirty-six more were being sought, but some escaped and a few took temporary refuge in the sanctuary of a masjid. Others were out of town during the time of the arrests or were able to otherwise stay hidden.

Kapriel happened upon a local Bábí in the street. They walked and conversed together as business acquaintances might. In this manner, the scribe endeavored to keep up with events.

Those who were captured were some of the most prominent of the Tihrán believers, including the maternal uncle of the Báb who had raised that sacred child. They were imprisoned in the lower levels of the mayor's house, that same home where Táhirih remained captive on an upper floor.

The house was beset by large crowds demanding to know what was to be done with the pious and well-respected men being held. Some of them were among the most notable men in the city.[3] The wealthy among the citizens attempted to pay ransom for some of the men, frequently visiting the mayor himself. State officials from various regions attempted to intercede, pleading for restraint. The city had been plunged into turmoil.

The local believers quickly learned that it had been one of their own, a man suspected of duplicity, who had written the names of fifty Bábís down and given the list to the authorities.

Part of the clergy was, as several times before, demanding immediate execution of all the prisoners. They pressed their case continually, berating officials for lagging in their duties. The most vociferous in calling for extermination was the new prime minister, Mírzá Taqí Khán, who had been put in office after the death of Muhammad Sháh and the dismissal of his predecessor, Hájí Mírzá Áqásí.

Four weeks passed, during which most of the city appeared to have visited the mayor's home to push for or against the prisoners. Seven of the captured men were suddenly released, painfully telling their fellows of the tortures they had endured, and of the final threat of immediate execution that had overwhelmed their strength, causing them to recant their faith and be set free (15 March 1850).

Kapriel forced himself to hear their stories, but when they spoke, his mind was filled with the sounds of cannons and gunfire from the final month of battle in the forests of Mázindarán.

That very afternoon multitudes gathered for the public executions of the remaining seven captives. The first few, given a brief trial and final chance to recant, chose not to flee from God, Whom they would soon meet. Kapriel was nearby, on a side street where he could not accidentally see anything, but the noise of the crowds drove him near to fainting. He envisioned buildings exploding and skeletal men riding out to stop the executioners. He simply could not stay.

Later in the evening he chanced upon another believer, who quickly removed the Armenian from the street into a small, quiet alley.

"My God, man, what is wrong with you?"

But Kapriel had no words. He just stared at the man until he could finally admit his failure, complete and entire, to fulfill his promise to Rahma.

The man ordered Kapriel to follow him down the alley, guiding him to a place that was not watched. They entered the tiny room, which Kapriel found to be the storage room of a small shop. A cup of tea appeared in his hands, and the smiling face of the other man made a curious thought deep in his mind as the man sat on the floor opposite Kapriel.

"How long were you walking?" the man asked.

Kapriel shrugged, feeling safe in this dim, tiny room surrounded by trinkets and facing a calm person. "All afternoon. I couldn't stay." It was odd, like he was driving his body but not really in it.

"Stay where? With that mob of vultures at the executions? What sane man would want to stay there?"

Kapriel explained his promise to observe.

"So, you saw nothing. Good. Such things are ugly. Most historians do not observe directly. They interview, they research, and they write documents, but they are not able to be at every event."

The gentle man talked with Kapriel well into the night, bringing them a meal when they got hungry. The scribe finally came out of the place he had gone that day. He had thought himself healed last fall when he could go through Rahma's bag. Now that he was thinking, he remembered how he had been unable to face crowds since the day of his beating during the parade of Muharram in his childhood. He had absolutely avoided risk in frenzied gatherings from that time on. And today he had walked into that mob as if it was something he always could do.

Having much to think about, he finally asked whether the executions had been carried out.

"Yes, they were. And the men went to their martyrdom magnificently! Each of the seven refused to recant, ready to throw down his life for the Cause. The first, Siyyid 'Alí of Shíráz, uncle of the Báb, not only refused to recant, but asked to be the first beheaded by the executioner's sword, and seems to have converted the executioner in the process.

"The second, the famed Mírzá Qurbán-'Alí—dervish, teacher, holy man, loved and well-regarded by the denizens of this city—was interceded for by the mother of the sháh, a friend of the man. She believed a mistake had been made in his arrest, but he also refused to recant, calling on the executioner to hasten his journey to the next life.

"The third was Hájí Mullá Ismá'íl-i-Qumí, gleeful that his ardent desire for thirty years was finally to come to pass. While he was praying, he forgave the executioner and signaled him to do his work.

"Next was Siyyid Husayn-i-Turshízí, valiantly attempting to convert the masses up to his last moment. He was stabbed by the officer who held the death warrant.

"Fifth came Hájí Muhammad Taqíy-i-Kirmání. He saw the bodies of those gone before him demanded to be slain so that he could join his close friend.

"But before the heavy sword could fall, the sixth, Siyyid Murtadá, proceeded from the building, flung himself across his friend who was already on the chopping block, and demanded to be executed first. His words moved the crowd and distracted them.

"During the confusion the seventh man, Muhammad Husany-i-Marághi'í, came out, threw himself upon the previous two, and also demanded to be beheaded first. The audience was astounded at such behavior. Not knowing which to execute first, it was finally agreed to let them all go at the same time, with one massive stroke of the sword."

Kapriel thought a moment. "You seem to be fine with all this. Does it not disturb you?"

"Well, I think it depends on the point of view. The list handed over to the authorities had fifty names. Why were only those fourteen found and arrested? Do we dwell on misfortune or the joy of those who chose glory? Shall we beat ourselves in shame and anguish over the depravity of our fellow humans, or give thanks for the potent examples of virtue present in the martyrs? Such virtue could not be seen if it were not for the depravity, just as a candle requires darkness to show its purpose. Do you choose to look only at the darkness, at the blinding flame of the candle, or at the illumination around us that requires both darkness and candle?"

Still confused but willing to reflect on it, Kapriel thanked the man for saving him from the street, among other things. He headed back to the caravanserai for sleep.

The heads and bodies of the martyrs were left in the park next to the imperial palace, exposed and unguarded for the unbridled abuse of the riled citizens for three days. Indignities were heaped upon the corpses by those who spit, kicked, cursed, and dumped garbage on them, and other barbarous acts committed with no regard to restraint or civility. When the three days had passed and the ugly passions of the people were spent, the seven were buried.

Rumors grew yet again over the next couple of weeks. The prime minister was agitating for a final blow to the offending faith. Surely the rebellious movement would die if they cut off its head.

Kapriel had little access to the Bábís of the city now, but he could hear the stirrings in the streets. It was time to move to Tabríz.

19

Tabríz, April through July, 1850

The journey to Tabríz was quite pleasant. It was yet another spring, with flowers among the grass on southern slopes of the Alburz Mountains.

Kapriel had waited in Tihrán to join a caravan heading west. In Qazvín, where the people were so hostile to Bábís, he avoided the caravanserai where he had stayed with Rahma.

Zanján had even more Bábís, and a buzzing tension filled the city. He happened across one previous acquaintance who mentioned that over half of the city had now enlisted in the ranks of followers of the Báb. Hujjat was indeed back and exhorting the city to calm and peacefulness.

Arriving in Tabríz in mid-spring, Kapriel set up in a new place in the city's main bazaar. He did not wish to renew old acquaintances and answer awkward questions that would bring up thoughts of Rahma.

This city was, as the others, brimming with tension, which gave Kapriel a steady business. Many people were willing to pay for copies of treatises written by this religious authority or that venerated scholar on the truth or heresy of the young Bábí faith. He would frequently be paid to read such documents to the illiterate customers.

The location of Tabríz made it a perfect place for the blending of many tribal and national identities, languages, and accents.

Caravans streamed through the city from east and west, bringing Arabs, Turks, Kurds, Persians, Armenians, Azeris, and many others through the streets. After a few days, the scribe found a Kurd who was willing to help him refresh his Kurdish by spending a few meals giving him lessons to fill in a few gaps in his Kurdish vocabulary.

Word came of armed hostilities in Zanján within a few weeks. Kapriel found and interviewed someone who had just arrived from that city. He was told that the struggle had begun with a normal childhood quarrel between two boys, one of whom was the child of a Bábí.[1] The Bábí child had been unreasonably arrested, bringing about protests from the boy's family and his parents' friends. Hujjat had tried to negotiate a ransom, but misunderstandings and the rancor of the authorities had escalated to an attempt to arrest him (16 May, 1850). It was a short jump from the Bábís' armed defense of their beloved leader to violent conflict. Those who had gone to arrest Hujjat, humiliated at their inability to carry out the task, had attacked an unarmed Bábí whom they had happened across and had carried the injured man to the governor. Then all of them, including the governor, had set upon the man, murdering him.

This created quite a tumult in the population. A town crier was soon sent out to inform the citizens, "Whoever is willing to endanger his life, to forfeit his property, and expose his wife and children to misery and shame, should throw in his lot with Hujjat and his companions; and those desirous of ensuring the well-being and honour of themselves and their families, should withdraw from the neighbourhood in which those companions [reside] and seek the shelter of the sovereign's protections."

The city had suddenly split, with families forced to separate and friends and neighbors torn asunder. In a panic, many Muslims of the city abandoned their homes and attempted to find family members and property to escape the endangered neighborhoods. Calls were sent out to towns and villages around Zanján to raise a militia large enough to subjugate the "uprising" and put an end to Hujjat.

The Zanján man Kapriel had interviewed in Tabríz had been unable to subject his family to the turmoil of the coming struggle and had left with all that he and his family could carry.

The days passed with increasing excitement and anxiety as the news continued to worsen. The fighting in Zanján was now fully engaged, and combat progressed from house to house. Hujjat, it was reported, had not wished for innocents to be injured and so had taken three thousand Bábís with many of their families into a fortress in the city, acquiring all the supplies they could find.[2] It was, again, a matter of large armies and armaments against an isolated and poorly armed group.

Summer neared as more unhappy news came. A venerable and highly respected siyyid by the name of Yahya had been attacked in Yazd, a city east of Isfáhán. He had been a companion at Badasht, given the name Vahíd. After the attack, he left in order to protect the friends in Yazd, going to town after town to teach the message of the Báb on his way to his hometown of Nayríz, near Shíráz in the province of Fars.

Tabríz itself was at an emotional state near to boiling, for a band of the sháh's couriers had gone through the city with orders from the young sháh and his advisors. The orders stated that the Báb was to be brought to Tabríz for execution.

The arrival of summer came and passed in an atmosphere of increasing expectation and suspense. A week later, more belated news of Nayríz and Vahíd arrived. The lag due to travel time put the actual happening about four weeks before the arrival of the news. Vahíd and many fellow believers were besieged in a large fort a day's walk from his hometown.[3]

Kapriel did his best to prepare for the impending execution. He and Rahma had strongly suspected nearly six years ago that this would happen. He knew there would be huge crowds. He knew the people who had once greeted the Báb with echoing calls of "God is Most Great" would turn on Him, viewing His execution as a just punishment for a heretic leader, and as a legitimate entertainment.

The scribe tried every day for a week to picture himself calmly amidst the crowds hearing neither cannon fire nor screams, nor smelling the sulfurous smoke from the battles in Mázindarán. For Rahma, to fulfill this last promise, he would stay and see it through.

Two weeks into summer the Báb arrived (8 July). At first, He was taken to the governor's home, but outrage on the part of the clergy caused His move (with His companionate secretary, Siyyid Husayn) to the military barracks for incarceration. His green turban and sash, both symbols of His heritage as a descendant of Muhammad, had been removed.[4]

Even the Báb's simple walk from the house to the barracks had caused vast crowds to gather, the people vacillating between fear, indignation, and confusion. Were they truly going to kill a holy man, or a heretic? Were the people to be saved or condemned to eternal flames for supporting this execution? What to do, where to turn?

Kapriel forced his way through agitated masses to the less-crowded roof of a building situated on the barracks courtyard to gain a good vantage point. It was hot, with the sun pounding the rooftops. People were sweating profusely, the smell of their bodies becoming stronger by the moment. More people climbed up onto the roof, adding to the scents and taking up vital clear space.

Fear began to drill into the scribe's mind, but he took a deep breath and, rather than trying to become invisible, looked around. Amazingly, he found no one was interested in him at all. No one was shouting or cursing at him; in fact, no one had cast even a glance toward the Armenian. He remembered the city's nearness to his family's homeland and the large numbers of Armenians in the area. No wonder they were much less offended by his presence— they were used to his countrymen.

The courtyard was quite large and unadorned, as it was used primarily as a training ground for the military. It was surrounded by various buildings with walls that were broken only by a few alleys and doors. Columns partly protruding from the walls supported the barracks roof.

The escort made room through people filling the streets and straining to see the prisoners. The guards had their weapons out and cracked their whips to threaten those who did not move out of the way quickly enough. They were approaching the barracks through the masses of people in the courtyard when suddenly a young man thrust through the edge of the crowd to throw himself at the Báb's feet. Murmurs of astonishment arose all around, some from those close to Kapriel.

"Isn't that Muhammad 'Alí-i-Zunúzí, the one given the name *Anís* by the Báb?"

"Yes. Didn't he go crazy last year?"

"The year before, just before the trial of the Báb. But then he calmed down."

"Yes, he has been helping the poor and those in need ever since. A wonderful lad. Look, now they have arrested him, too!"

Two more men were able to throw themselves forward, adding to the number to be confined with the Báb and Siyyid Husayn.

The escort entered the barracks and shut the door. No more action was forthcoming at the moment. The crowds dwindled, heading off in a state of unrelenting anxiety. Soon he was alone on the roof.

Kapriel was not sure whose roof he was on, but he was determined to return there after buying some food and stay all night, if necessary. He found his preparations for the crowds and awareness of his own fears had greatly mitigated the terrifying sounds in his head.

He did end up sleeping on the cool roof that night, enjoying memories of past summer nights spent under the stars and relieved of worries that he might miss something while at the caravanserai. The roof he was on belonged to some business, rather than a home, so he was able to be alone for the night. He did not see or hear anyone on the adjacent roofs, something he pondered as he lay down to try to get some sleep. He reasoned that being there meant far more to him than to the townsfolk. Soon, his mental wandering faded and he slept.

Early the next morning, he heard movement in the courtyard below. Looking down from his perch, he saw some guards in escort formation crossing the courtyard to the barracks door and entering. Kapriel assumed they would be right out, but after a few minutes he became determined to find out what was happening. Running down the external steps (with no railing) he gained the courtyard and crossed it, ignoring the rare early-riser who had come for the day's events and wary in case guards might stop him.

The men at the door did signal Kapriel to stay back, but he told them he only wished to listen. Perhaps they also were trying to listen, since they used hand signals to tell him he could go to the open door, no further.

It was enough. He had arrived in time to hear the Báb's gentle voice speaking. "Not until I have said to him all those things that I wish to say can any earthly power silence Me. Though all the world be armed against Me, yet shall they be powerless to deter Me from fulfilling, to the last word, My intention."

There were no further voices, but footsteps echoed out to Kapriel. He stepped quickly back, taking up a somewhat relaxed posture against the wall a few feet to one side.

The escort, led by someone in a uniform of higher rank, led Siyyid Husayn away.

This was one of those times when Kapriel needed Rahma there, for he could only be in one place at a time. He stayed by the barracks and kept watch, seeing others slowly file in and around the courtyard.

Siyyid Husayn was brought back, and another companion was taken. Time passed and this was repeated. Eventually the Báb Himself was taken from the barracks.

Kapriel asked one of the guards at the door if he knew where they had gone.

He answered, "For trial, of course. If they do not deny their belief in this heretic, orders for execution will be written."

"And for the Báb?"

"Those orders were written a long time ago. They probably will not even speak to him."

A frisson went through the rapidly gathering crowd. The Báb was returning, and people were shouting that the final order had been signed.

Kapriel quickly crossed the courtyard through arriving crowds, made his way up the waiting steps, and returned to his perch on the swiftly-filling roof, just in time to see the Báb escorted into the courtyard and held to one side. Young Anís suddenly burst back out of the barracks begging to return to his Master. The youth was escorted over to someone who looked like he was in charge of the regiment of riflemen filing into the yard now. Words were exchanged between the guards and captain of the riflemen, and Anís was placed in the riflemen's custody.

The captain, somewhat surprisingly, bent his head to converse with the Báb.*

If only Kapriel could be there, too!

The captain nodded his head, spoke some words Kapriel could not hear and gestured to a column supporting the roof near the end of the barracks.

With the word of the final decree of execution came a flood of the city's inhabitants. Rooftops filled in all around. People nearly spilled over the low ridge around the roof edges. Those who could not fit on roofs jammed into the back edge of the courtyard, behind

---

* The captain was Sam Khán, leader of a Christian regiment from Urmíá. He was unsure of the appropriateness of his assignment and offered to the Báb to refuse carrying it out.

the regiment now arranging itself. Kapriel estimated around ten thousand spectators had come for the great event.

Two men were hammering a large spike high up into the column their captain had chosen. Their fellow riflemen were positioning themselves in three lines of two hundred and fifty men each, with the second line immediately behind the first and the third line behind the second. They were loading their long rifles with powder, wadding, and shot.

The Báb and Anís, still waiting to one side in the courtyard, had not yet been allowed back in the barracks with their companions.

The hands of the two were now being tied as the murmur of the crowd became even louder. They were guided over to the column with the new spike. Ropes were thrown over the spike and then tied to the ropes around their wrists. The captain's men pulled the other end of the ropes, hoisting the captives partway up the wall, their feet well clear of the ground. The free ends of the rope were then anchored securely.

Anís seemed to be asking for help with great urgency. One of the guards helped to swing him around in front of the Báb, with his head resting on the Báb's chest and his body between the bullets and his Lord. This immediately calmed the youth.

The entire city seemed to have come to view the execution, yet voices were dimming. The men under the prisoners had cleared out. It was time.

Kapriel saw the first rank go down on their heels, the second on one knee, and the third stay standing as they raised all seven hundred and fifty rifles to aim at the suspended men.

The scribe, determined not to close his eyes as tears fell, at least stuck his fingers in his ears.

The signal was given. A thunderous sound erupted as each rank of rifles emptied in succession. Echoes reverberated down the alleys. The smoke was thick and acrid, filling the courtyard and darkening the sky as it slowly floated up above the roofs.

Kapriel felt faint from despair, knowing that beautiful soul had passed on, and a brief echo of cannons sounded in his mind. It was time to go, but he had to have one last look to see the final results. He let his fingers fall from his ears and heard . . . chaos, confusion!

There were guards running about at the barracks wall. Looking toward the end of the barracks through the thinning smoke and darkness, Kapriel could see that there were no bodies on the ground. Anís stood there, unhurt, with the rope that had suspended him severed—no, more like shredded. The Báb was nowhere to be seen, though the second rope was also severed, pieces lying on the ground.

How could seven hundred and fifty riflemen miss?

People in the crowds were shouting, shocked, unbelieving. The noise of confusion continued to swell to near-deafening levels. Spectators on the ground were dashing about, searching here and there.

The captain appeared from inside the smoke, reorganized his men, and marched out. He was talking with the man in charge, apparently arguing as he left. It looked as if they were refusing to have further involvement. The farrásh-báshí, the attendant who had been organizing the execution, soon also left, refusing to become any further involved.

A rougher man in a different uniform stepped forward and spoke to the man in charge. Receiving a nod, he left. Exclamations were made that the man was a colonel in the military.

Many minutes passed in bewilderment before word came that the Báb was back in the barracks cell with Siyyid Husayn, finishing an earlier conversation.

Guards were holding up pieces of rope to the crowds, telling the people that there was no miracle, only bad aim. Some were relieved, but others saw it for the folly it was. Seven hundred and fifty bullets could not all miss, even if they had tried.

Morning was close to its end when another regiment arrived. It was led by the rough-looking colonel. The crowds had stayed, all waiting for the next act in this miraculous and macabre play.

The same arrangement was created, with the Báb and Anís suspended from the spike and the youth resting in front of the Báb. The regiment of body guards prepared their rifles. The vast numbers of people were quiet, wondering what would happen next. Into this hush the Báb spoke.

"Had you believed in Me, O wayward generation, every one of you would have followed the example of this youth, who stood in rank above most of you, and willingly would have sacrificed himself in My path. The day will come when you will have recognised Me; that day I shall have ceased to be with you."

The signal was given at noon, and the volleys hit their targets. This time the smoke was suddenly and completely blown away by a gale, throwing dust and debris into the air. The dust was instantly so thick as to turn the day to night. Briefly, enough clarity remained to show two bodies permanently mingled by the bullets, though their faces were nearly untouched. The Báb and Anís had finished their earthly days (on 9 July 1850).

Kapriel threw himself down on the roof, covering his face with his summer abá to keep some of the dust out of his lungs as he was pelted by debris. He stayed huddled there, unwilling to face a fall off of the stairs or off of the wall if he tried to leave. He heard screams from people in all directions—on the roofs, down in the courtyard, and in the streets. He imagined they cried out in fear, though some may have fallen in their haste to get out of the storm. He was left alone on the roof, reliving the worst parts of the past few years, and seeking hope. It was a long afternoon of grieving in the darkness.

The storm finally abated in the evening. Kapriel roused himself in the clearing air to see several guards picking up the mangled remains of the Báb and Anís. He quietly followed them out to the edge of the city where they threw the bodies into the surrounding moat. Ten men were there to guard the remains, keeping anyone from coming near.[5]

So, Kapriel sadly thought, *it is done.*

Epilogue

July through August, 1850

Kapriel walked slowly toward his room at the caravanserai, in serious need of clean water to drink and wash with. True night had closed in, allowing little to be seen in the narrow byways by the slight light of the moon and stars.

The populace was still in turmoil, though the streets were mostly clear. Occasionally, an individual or small group could be discerned running up an alley, as if they feared the falling of the sky. *And yet,* he mused further, *they just don't believe.*

"Get him!" an enraged voice shouted behind him.

Kapriel turned to see a man, sword raised, bearing down on him. He glimpsed others with the madman, hearing only, "No! Wait!" from another as he raised his arms to defend his head.

The sword had just hit his right hand when a companion of the madman stopped the swordstroke in its downward movement.

Kapriel yanked his injured hand away, numb with surprise.

"You must not!" another voice said. "Look at him! He is Armenian! If he is a heretic it is for his church to say!"

Kapriel realized his hand was not just bleeding, but spurting where his last two fingers used to be. He clutched his hand and ran to the only place he could think of: Dr. Cormick, the Englishman.

It was several long alleys away. He could feel himself beginning to lose clear thought as he neared the barely-remembered door. Falling at the threshold, he managed to knock by kicking the door. It took several fading minutes for the door to open and a lamp to appear. He heard the words, "Good God!" and that was all.

Kapriel's first clear thought occurred several days later. He awoke to find his hand wrapped in clean bandages and himself in bed, completely unclothed. Grateful for the light, covering sheet, he gazed around the room at the expensive rugs and chandelier of unlit candles. The light was coming from a window, a real stained-glass window. Part of the glass was clear, letting him see green out the other side.

This must be the back of the house, next to the garden, he decided. *But what house?*

He waited in silence for some time, until nature finally forced him to speak. "Hello? Excuse me." He paused. "Is anyone—"

Just then a woman bustled in. She wore an Armenian dress, though he supposed that could have been by choice rather than heritage. "Ah, you are awake. Good. I will get the doctor."

He waited just a moment longer before sitting up at the edge of the bed.

The doctor appeared and warned him, "Don't get up yet."

But it was too late. The room went into motion as if he were inside a child's spinning toy. He let the doctor guide his head back to the pillow and put his legs back up on the bed. The room quickly regained its normal immobility.

"Easy now. I'll get you a bed pan, but it will be some time yet before you can get up."

A few minutes later the doctor was spoon-feeding him broth. "You will have to drink all you can. You nearly bled out from your hand, you know, at the brink of death when you arrived."

Kapriel looked at his hand.

The doctor nodded, telling him, "The third and fourth fingers are gone. The third was still attached, but only by skin. If we had managed to save it, it would have been useless to you—just a chunk of unresponsive flesh."

Nervous for the answer he might receive, the scribe asked, "Will I be able to write?"

"You are a writer?"

"Scribe."

The doctor's expression fell a little, his eyes going to the injured hand. "We'll see. You should be able to. But, it will take work once the hand is healed to relearn balance and placement. You may need to create a spacer of wood, something to rest the second finger on as it would have rested on the lost fingers."

Kapriel began to feel an upwelling of despair and loss, but he remembered Rahma and all the others who had given up absolutely all to be called Bábís. What were two fingers and a bit of work?

Despair averted, he noticed the bags and tack at one side of the room. His eyebrows rose in surprise.

Dr. Cormick explained, "I sent a man to the caravanserais asking if an Armenian of average height were staying there. When he found the right one, he brought your possessions and paid for the care of your animals. You have three horses and two mules?"

"Eeehh, two horses and one mule."

"Figures. My man negotiated down from an entire herd. You have been conned even while asleep. I hope you don't mind that we paid out of your funds."

"No, that's fine. Thank you for . . . all of this."

The doctor turned curious, "Didn't we meet a couple of years ago?"

"Yes, we did."

"You were with that big Muslim. Odd friendship, hard to forget. Is he with you?"

"No. He died near the shrine of Shaykh Tabarsí."

Dr. Cormick gave his heartfelt condolences and left Kapriel to sleep.

—•—

Two more weeks were required to recuperate before the doctor would let Kapriel leave. He had seen his finger stumps, the skin sewn shut over the remnants. It was healing.

He paid the doctor more than asked for in appreciation for the fine care. After a stop at the bazaar for road food and then collecting the horses and mule, he packed up his and Rahma's belongings and joined a group heading east. It was difficult to manage the reins with two fingers, so he held them in his left hand. Dr. Cormick had ordered him to be very gentle on that right hand or he could undo the previous healing.

It was odd. He could still feel his fingers, occasionally dropping things his mind said were in his grasp. How interesting the mind could be.

The travelers stayed at the edge of Zanján, not wanting to accidentally become part of the siege still going on. In the evening, they heard a few thousand Bábí voices raised in unison, chanting five titles of God, nineteen times each: God the Great, God the Most Great, God the Most Beauteous, God the Most Glorious, God the Most Pure.[1] The sound was tremendous! People panicked, running about in consternation, sure the end of the world was at hand.

Kapriel was not concerned, though it did bring up disturbing memories. He had seen and heard similar calls before. As they rode through the city the next day, Kapriel could see that the damage from the siege was unmistakable.

Qazvín was also still unstable. Kapriel happened across a Bábí acquaintance who told him other news. The siege near Nayríz had ended just as the one in Mázindarán had. Oaths on the Qur'án were given, promising safety for the Bábís if they would surrender. Accepting the oaths and confused by the subterfuge and lies, the besieged were massacred.[2]

Kapriel stayed on the outskirts of Tihrán when passing that city, not wishing to enter the place of such barbarity as shown last spring.

He was with a caravan as they passed Qum and Káshán.

Isfáhán was one of the most beautiful sights he had ever seen, though not for its appearance. It had been four years, nearly to the week, since he and Rahma had ridden through this city on their path to follow the Báb.

He stayed with his Aunt Marem and Uncle Hovnan for several days. They did not ask him much, mostly letting him rest, but they sent a message with another caravan to inform Kapriel's parents of his arrival in Julfa. There was a haunted look about Kapriel that opened no doors for curiosity, though they were very curious. What had he seen and done to change him so? Where was his big friend?

Dr. Zadour checked his hand while he was in Julfa. He complemented the English doctor, advising Kapriel to begin strengthening his hand and relearning to write.

He left with the next caravan bound for Shíráz as summer was drawing to a close. During the ride he became nervous. What had happened since he had left? Aunt Marem had not heard any bad news from Kapriel's parents, but when had they last written? And then his heart jumped, wondering if Mina . . .

They stopped at the caravanserai on the north side of Shíráz, the same one where he had bought the horses. The ownership of the place had changed, but Kapriel still did not trust it well enough to leave his horses there, as he was not sure they would be the same ones the next day. He trundled along pulling the horses behind him, choosing to walk the streets he knew so well. He ambled past the Vakíl Bazaar and the neighboring mosque, south past the gardens, then east down tiny alleys to the edge of the Armenian quarter.

He passed the door to Rahma's family, leaving that for later. He noticed it had been replaced and the frame repaired, implying some nasty incident. And there it was, the door to his own home.

Home. There was so much meaning in that single word. This was part of what so many had given up for God.

He raised his hand to knock, but the door opened before his knuckles made contact. He had to pull his hand back quickly to avoid hitting the face that beamed out at him, in a nice dress with no other covering.

Mina!

She turned to the room behind her, saying, "Yes, it is Kapriel!"

Then she turned to him, grabbed his still-raised hand, and said, "Come, husband. We will take care of the horses in a moment."

Mute with bewilderment, he followed her into his home, greeted his parents with hugs and kisses, and turned to see another woman in the room. This last lady was dressed as a Muslim in chador and head scarf, but no veil. She was older and reminded him of someone.

"Kapriel," his father said, "This is Shahnáz Khanum, mother of Rahma and Mina.

The scribe managed a few words of greeting.

She asked hopefully, "Has my youngest son attained his goal?"

He answered, "Yes, Khanom, in Mázindarán."

She nodded sadly, but answered, "Well, he is happy now. And I have a new son." She beamed at Kapriel, again throwing him into confusion.

Mina explained their presence, "Last year a mob went looking for heretics to kill. They assumed since Rahma left at the same time as the Báb that he must have been a Bábí."

"A lot of people left then."

"Yes, but most took their family. And anyway, a mob is not reasonable, is it? They assumed that if Rahma were a Bábí, so were his family. They broke down our door. Father was dragged down the alley and murdered. Only mother and I were home, since my other brothers and sister had moved out with their new families years ago.

"They were coming back up the alley for us, but we went out the back and over the walls to your family's home. Your parents were very kind. They took us in, and we have been here ever since."

Kapriel again hugged his father and kissed his mother with gratitude.

Mina suddenly gave a small squeak. "Kapriel, your hand! What has happened?"

He smiled gently. "Please explain to me how we are already married, and I will tell you the very long story of what happened to my hand."

His father spoke up, "We arranged it." Not seeing comprehension in Kapriel's eyes, he continued, "The marriage. Your mother and I negotiated with Khanom Shahnáz and came to an agreement. Mina is a Bábí, so you can't be married in the Armenian church. Nor can the marriage be affirmed under Muslim law. We don't know the Bábí laws, so we declared you married almost a year ago."

Kapriel, astounded, slowly smiled. That smile deepened to a profound laugh at a situation so absurd yet logical. The laughter continued until he was out of breath, and at that point the three parents demanded that he and Mina go to their room and discuss while the "adults" took care of the horses and mule.

Back in his room, now somewhat redecorated with Mina's things, they sat, and Kapriel began to talk. His mother brought a wonderful, mother-made stew for them to share as they talked through the night. Kapriel related all the major events and characters. They spoke of the Báb's works, and the scribe was amazed that Mina knew some of them by heart.

"Rahma taught me to read. As he learned from you, he would teach me. And I taught myself to write from the letters in the books. I just copied them until they looked the same. Reading those sacred words and seeing the changes in Rahma, I, too, believed in the Báb."

Kapriel stared at her a moment, astonished at her wonderful audacity, then grabbed a lamp and went downstairs quietly with Mina following. He rummaged through one pack, finding his copy of the Bayán, then went back in their room and showed Mina the note from Rahma in the barely legible scrawl. She glowed with pride for her brother's accomplishment.

They spoke of the Báb's repeated references to "He Whom God will make Manifest," Who was due to become known soon after the Báb left.

Mina asked, "Do you know who that might be?"

"Not for sure, but there is a man, a nobleman from Núr, who has the most wondrous knowledge and understanding of things. He is selfless and yet authoritative, gentle but strong—"

"Then we must go."

". . . Go where?"

"To find him, of course. If the Báb said to seek Him, then that is what we will do."

Kapriel was nonplussed. "Right now?"

Mina smiled. "No, my husband. You must rest from your journeys, and we will work to make enough money to see us through. And then—"

"We go."

Chronology of Major Events

EVENT	DATE
Declaration of the Báb	22 May, 1844
The Báb leaves on pilgrimage.	2 or 3 October, 1844
The Báb returns. Persecution of Quddús and two others	23 June, 1845
The Báb leaves Shíráz.	23–24 September, 1846
The Báb arrives in Isfáhán	September–October, 1846
The Báb leaves Isfáhán.	Mid-March, 1847
The Báb stays twenty days in Kulayn.	29 March to 18 April, 1847
The Báb stays forty days in Tabríz.	Approx. mid-May to late June, 1847
The Báb's incarceration in Máku.	July, 1847 to 9 April, 1848
The Báb's incarceration in Chihriq	10 April, 1848 to June, 1850
Conference of Badasht.	26 June to 17 July, 1848
The Báb's trial in Tabríz.	Late July, 1848
The raising of the Black Standard.	July to September, 1848

Arrival of the Bábís at the Shrine
of Shaykh Tabarsí. . . . . 12 October, 1848

Death of Mullá Husayn . . . . 2 February, 1849

End of the siege at Tabarsí . . . . 10 May, 1849

Death of Quddús. . . . . 16 May, 1849

Arrest of Bábís in Tihrán . . . . 14 February, 1850

Execution of Seven Martyrs
of Tihrán . . . . 19 or 20 February, 1850

Dividing of Zanján, first martyrdom
at Zanján . . . . 16–19 May 1850

First Nayríz upheaval . . . . 27 May–21 June, 1850

End of siege near Nayríz . . . . 21 June 1850

Martyrdom of the Báb. . . . . 9 July 1850

End of siege at Zanján . . . . January, 1851

Notes

Prologue

1. The events described in this chapter are taken from Nabíl-i-Aʻzam, *The Dawn-Breakers: Nabíl's Narrative of the Early Days of the Baháʼí Revelation,* chapters 1–3.

1 / 22 May 1844

1. According to Encyclopædi Iránica, "Travelers who passed through it (notably Tavernier in the years 1632 and 1668, Chardin in 1669–72, Daulier Deslandes in 1664, and Kämpfer in 1683; their accounts are given with commentary by Afsar, pp. 120–69) reported that it was a city of gardens full of sweet myrtle and trees of various kinds (cypress, sycamore, oak, elms, pines, mastics, and maples) and orchards of fruits (oranges, lemons, pomegranates, grapes, apples, pears, apricots, plums, almonds, figs, dates, cherries, and peaches). In addition, Shíráz produced excellent wine (reputedly the best in Persia, Curzon II, p. 100), mosaic on wood (kātam-kāri), metalworks, and outstanding chain mails. The English East India Company set up a factory in Shíráz in 1621, and Dutch and French merchants frequented the town" (Encyclopædi Iránica, "Shiraz i. History to 1940").

2. Executions were quite bloody and usually well-attended as an entertainment. If the reader is sensitive to cruelty, do not read this note further. Lord Curzon wrote in his book Persia and the Persians, "Up till quite a recent period, well within the borders of the present reign, condemned criminals have been crucified, blown from guns, buried alive, impaled, shod like horses, torn asunder by being bound to the heads of two trees bent together and then allowed to

spring back to their natural position, converted into human torches, flayed while living" (Nabíl, *The Dawn-Breakers,* pp. xxviii–xxix).
3. Pourafzal, *Hafez: Teachings of the Philosopher of Love,* p. 4.

2 / Mid-June, 1844
1. Niewenhuizen, "A Journey of Chance," unpublished memoir.
2. Nabíl, *The Dawn-Breakers,* p. 69.
3. Ibid., pp. 69–70.
4. Ibid., pp. 72, 77, 80; Balyuzi, *The Báb: The Herald of Days,* p. 32.

4 / Late October, 1844
1. John 10:1–3, 10:9. "Verily, verily, I say unto you, He that entereth not by the door into the sheepfold, but climbeth up some other way, the same is a thief and a robber. But he that entereth in by the door is the shepherd of the sheep. To him the porter openeth; and the sheep hear his voice: and he calleth his own sheep by name, and leadeth them out . . . I am the door: by me if any man enter in, he shall be saved, and shall go in and out, and find pasture."
2. Wine is forbidden in the Qur'án, and promised as a reward in the next life. The Qur'án reads, "They will ask thee concerning wine and games of chance. Say: In both is great sin, and advantage also, to men; but their sin is greater than their advantage. They will ask thee also what they shall bestow in alms." The Qur'án, Sura 2 - The Cow. Also referred to in Sura 5 - The Table. And after ascension, "A picture of the Paradise which is promised to the Godfearing! Therein are rivers of water, which corrupt not: rivers of milk, whose taste changeth not: and rivers of wine, delicious to those who quaff it; . . ." The Qur'án (Rodwell tr), Sura 47 - Muhammad. Many assume this is spiritual wine, or closeness to God (Alláh) causing intoxication. Others prefer literal interpretation. According to Wikipedia's article on wine, "Iran had previously had a thriving wine industry that disappeared after the Islamic Revolution in 1979. In Greater Persia, mey (Persian wine) was a central theme of poetry for more than a thousand years, long before the advent of Islam. . . ." http://en.wikipedia.org/wiki/Wine.
3. These three quotations are from Pourafzal, Haleh, *Hafez: Teachings of the Philosopher of Love,* pp. 61, 82, 81.
4. Ibid., p. 198.
5. Ferdowsi, *Shah Namah,* p. 65.

5 / *Winter through June, 1845*

1. H. M. Balyuzi, *The Báb*, pp. 82–84.
2. The Surih of Joseph is a chapter of the Qur'án. The commentary was chanted and written in part to Mullá Husayn during the night of 22 May 1844, as part of the Báb's declaration to His first believer.
3. The Báb, *Selections from the Writings of the Báb*, 2:1:1.
4. Luke 11:4.
5. No exact date is given for these events, and different sources give varying dates. The author put it on a Friday to place the main character at home and the mass of the citizenry in mosques. In *The Báb*, pp. 76–77, H. M. Balyuzi quotes an article of the *London Times*, which gives an account dated June 23 of 1845. In that article, the beards were burned one day and the victims led through the streets the next, being turned out of the city immediately after. In *The Dawn-Breakers*, pp. 146–47, Nabíl gives no date but puts the burning and parading on the same day, with the expulsion "soon after."
6. 'Alí Qabl-i-Muhammad is a reference to the Báb. Baqíyyatu'lláh means "Remnant of God," referring to the next Manifestation of God. The quote is from Nabíl, *The Dawn-Breakers*, p. 144.
7. Sura 2 - The Heifer.
8. Ibid.
9. Ibid.
10. This episode is taken from Nabíl, *The Dawn-Breakers*, p. 147.

6 / *Late June, 1845, to September, 1846*

1. Nabíl, *The Dawn-Breakers*, pp. 147–48.
2. According to David Ruhe, *Robe of Light*, p. 105, they met in the last days of June, 1845. This is an amazing story of humility and kindness, told beautifully in the Nabíl, *The Dawn-Breakers*, pp. 148–50. Reading the original paragraphs is highly recommended. Most unfortunately, the complete details will not fit properly in this novel.
3. This episode is quoted and paraphrased from Nabíl, *The Dawn-Breakers*, pp. 150–51.
4. Qur'án 49:6.
5. Nabíl, *The Dawn-Breakers*, pp. 150–54.
6. The details of this event are slightly different between firsthand accounts given in Nabíl, *The Dawn-Breakers*, pp. 150–54, and Balyuzi, *The Báb*, pp. 96–98.

7. Balyuzi, *The Báb*, p. 89.
8. Ibid., pp. 90–91.
9. Nabíl, *The Dawn-Breakers*, p. 177.
10. Ibid., p. 197.
11. The account of the cholera epidemic is paraphrased, with quotes, from Nabíl, *The Dawn-Breakers*, pp. 195–98.

7 / Late September, 1846

1. Farah Nieuwenhuizen, "A Journey of Chance," unpublished memoirs.
2. Pourafzal, *Haféz: Teaching of the Philosopher of Love*, p. 29.

8 / Isfáhán, Fall 1846

1. Bishop, "Journeys in Persia and Kurdistan," pp. 172–73.
2. William R. Polk, "Understanding Iran," pp. 62–63.
3. William Floor, Encyclopædia Iránica, " Čápár" (Courier)
4. Nabíl, *The Dawn-Breakers*, p. 202.

9 / Julfa and Isfáhán, Winter 1846 to Spring 1847

1. Nabíl, *The Dawn-Breakers*, p. 209
2. Pourafzal, Haleh, Haféz: *Teachings of the Philosopher of Love*, p. 143.
3. 'Abdu'l-Bahá, *A Traveler's Narrative*, p. 11. The episode that follows is paraphrased from Nabíl, *The Dawn-Breakers*, pp. 209–14.

10 / Qum to Zanján, Spring 1847

1. The escort had also avoided Qum, taking the Báb around the city to a village on the north side called Qumrúd. This was the village of relatives of one of the groups' two leaders. See Nabíl, *The Dawn-Breakers*, p. 224.
2. Nabíl, *The Dawn-Breakers*, p. 224.
3. Ibid., p. 227.
4. This entire event is paraphrased with quotes from Nabíl, *The Dawn-Breakers*, p. 228.
5. Nabíl, *The Dawn-Breakers*, p. 230.

11 / Tabríz, Late April, 1847

1. The account given of this event is a fictional attempt at portrayal with only scant facts available. From Balyuzi, *The Báb*, pp. 124–26. The quote of the Báb is from Ruhe, *Robe of Light*, p. 76.

2. Balyuzi, *The Báb,* p. 126. The event is only slightly reworded from the account in Balyuzi's book.
3. Ibid.
4. Ibid., p. 127.
5. Nabíl, *The Dawn-Breakers,* p. 239.

12 / Mákú, Summer 1847 – Spring 1848
1. The altitude of the town is about 5,361 feet, slightly higher than that of Denver, Colorado.
2. Balyuzi, *The Báb,* pp. 129–30.
3. Nabíl, *The Dawn-Breakers,* p. 250.
4. He revealed two books named "Bayán" while in Mákú. One was in Persian, considered the more thorough and weighty of the two. The other, not a translation but a separate book, was in Arabic. Peter Smith, *A Concise Encyclopedia of the Bahá'í Faith,* p. 91.
5. According to Peter Smith's *A Concise Encyclopedia of the Bahá'í Faith,* p. 61, the Báb Himself "refers to having composed over 500,000 verses [by 1848—the equivalent of eighty books the size of the Qur'án], one fifth of which has been disseminated."
6. The grand vizier, Hájí Mírzá Áqásí, was once again unhinged by word of the Báb's influence over His jailers. Additionally, he was pressured by the Russian Minister in Tihrán. The Russians had seen religious upheaval recently and wanted no such events near their border. The Báb left Mákú on April 9, 1848. Balyuzi, *The Báb,* pp. 131–32.

13 / Chihriq to Qavín, Spring 1848
1. The Báb, *Selections from the Writings of the Báb,* 3:4:1.
2. Ibid., 3:21:1.
3. Nabíl, *The Dawn-Breakers,* p. 275.
4. This entire episode is paraphrased from Nabíl, *The Dawn-Breakers,* pp. 276–85.

14 / Tabríz, June through July, 1848
1. Description based on a letter written by a Dr. Cormick, included in note 1 on p. 320 of Nabíl, *The Dawn-Breakers.*
2. The following account is paraphrased and quoted from Nabíl, *The Dawn-Breakers,* pp. 309–11.
3. The following account is paraphrased with quotes from Nabíl, *The Dawn-Breakers,* pp. 315–19.

4. Qur'án 29:51. According to footnote 2 on p. 319 of Nabíl, *The Dawn-Breakers,* accounts differ on the exact content of the trial, but at some point the Báb tired of the meaningless questions and self-congratulatory accusations, and left.

5. The following is adapted from Nabíl, *The Dawn-Breakers,* p. 320, note 1, which is from a letter written by the doctor several decades later. All the words of the Dr. Cormick in this account are direct quotations from that letter.

15 / Tabríz to Tíhran, Late Summer, 1848

1. According to Nabíl, *The Dawn-Breakers,* p. 307, this dream and destiny were told only to one person and then kept a secret until after the martyrdom of the Báb.

2. Adapted from Ruhe, *Robe of Light,* pp. 91–92.

3. Adapted from Ruhe, *Robe of Light,* p. 100.

16 / Mázindarán, Fall 1848

1. The events in and near Bárfurúsh are paraphrased with quotations from Nabíl, *The Dawn-Breakers,* pp. 328–43.

2. Qur'án 17:7, quoted in Nabíl, *The Dawn-Breakers,* p. 341, footnote 1.

17 / The Shrine of Shaykh Tabarsí, October 1848 to May 1849

1. Quoted from Nabíl, *The Dawn-Breakers,* p. 346. Incident paraphrased from Nabíl, *The Dawn-Breakers,* pp. 346–47.

2. These measurements and description come from Nabíl, *The Dawn-Breakers,* p. 348.

3. Paraphrased from Nabíl, *The Dawn-Breakers,* pp. 349–50.

4. This account is paraphrased and quoted from Nabíl, *The Dawn-Breakers,* pp. 360–68.

5. This account is paraphrased from Nabíl, *The Dawn-Breakers,* pp. 379–82.

6. This account is paraphrased from Nabíl, *The Dawn-Breakers,* p. 386.

7. This account is paraphrased from Nabíl, *The Dawn-Breakers,* pp. 391–95.

8. This account is paraphrased from Nabíl, *The Dawn-Breakers,* pp. 391–95.

9. It is truly horrible. If you want to know, see Nabíl, *The Dawn-Breakers*, pp. 403–13. For a list of most of the men who died at or near the Shrine of Shaykh Tabarsí, see Nabíl, *The Dawn-Breakers*, pp. 414–27.

18 / Tihrán, May 1849 to April 1850
1. She was at the home of Jináb-i-Bahá in Nur. Nabíl, *The Dawn-Breakers*, p. 440.
2. Nabíl, *The Dawn-Breakers*, p. 376.
3. Episode paraphrased from Nabíl, *The Dawn-Breakers*, pp. 445–63.

19 / Tabríz, April through July, 1850
1. Paraphrased from Nabíl, *The Dawn-Breakers*, pp. 540–45.
2. Number of "companions" in fort given as 3,000. Nabíl, *The Dawn-Breakers*, p. 546.
3. They entered the fort around the first of June, 1850. Nabíl, *The Dawn-Breakers*, pp. 478–79.
4. Events paraphrased with quotations from Nabíl, *The Dawn-Breakers*, pp. 507–19.
5. The bodies disappeared a few nights later, taken into hiding by Bábís. Rumors were circulated of wild animals dragging them away or dogs chewing them up, but such rumors were beneficial to protecting the remains and were not refuted. Nabíl, *The Dawn-Breakers*, p. 519.

Epilogue
1. No date is given for this event in *The Dawn-Breakers*, only that it took place after the Bábís were surrounded in the fort and before they left the fort. It was probably a couple of months later than in the story. Nabíl, *The Dawn-Breakers*, p. 552.
2. The siege near Nayríz ended on 29 June, 1850. Nabíl, *The Dawn-Breakers*, p. 499.

Bibliography

Works of the Báb
Selections from the Writings of the Báb. Compiled by the Research
   Department of the Universal House of Justice. Translated
   by Habib Taherzadeh et al. Wilmette, IL: Bahá'í Publishing
   Trust, 2006.

Works of 'Abdu'l-Bahá
A Traveler's Narrative. Translated by E. G. Browne. Wilmette:
   Bahá'í Publishing Trust, 1980.

Other Sources
Balyuzi, H. M. *The Báb.* Oxford: George Ronald, 1973.
Benjamin, S. G. W. *Persia and the Persians.* Boston: Ticknor and
   Company, 1886.
Bishop, Isabella. *Journeys in Persia and Kurdistan.* New York: J. P.
   Putnam's Sons, 1891.
Dhilawala, Sakina. *Cultures of the World: Armenia.* New York:
   Marshall Cavendish Benchmark, 2009.
Nabíl-i-A'zam (Mullá Muhammad-i-Zarandí). *The Dawn-
   Breakers: Nabíl's Narrative of the Early Days of the Bahá'í
   Revelation.* Translated and edited by Shoghi Effendi.
   Wilmette: Bahá'í Publishing Trust, 1932.
Polk, William R. *Understanding Iran.* New York: Palgrave
   Macmillan, 2009.
Pourafzal, Haleh. *Haféz: Teachings of the Philosopher of Love.*
   Rochester, VT: Inner Traditions, 2004

Ruhe, David S. *Robe of Light.* Oxford: George Ronald, 1994.

Smith, Peter. *A Concise Encyclopedia of the Bahá'í Faith.* Oxford: Oneworld Publications, 2000.

Thackston, W. M. *An Introduction to Persian.* Revised Third Edition. Bethesda: Iranbooks, Inc., 1993.

Tusi, Ferdowsi, and Hakim Abol-Qasem. *The Shah Namah.* Translated by Helen Zimmern. Forgotten Books, 2008.

Map references

Ottoman Empire - http://www.naqshbandi.org/ottomans/maps/. Expansion and Decline of the Ottoman Empire.

Russian Empire - http://qed.princeton.edu/index.php/ User:Student/The_Territorial_Expansion_of_the_Russian_ Empire_1795-1914 Oxford Atlas of World History, Oxford University Press, 1999. General Editor Patrick K. O'Brien. (p. 180).

Persian Territories - http://3.bp.blogspot.com/-bNylMsZLOT0/ ToJKwpgMVjI/AAAAAAAABTs/S9kBU0lVecM/s1600/11-boundaries_of_iran_map.gif. Territorial Changes of Persia/ Iran in the 19th and the 20th Centuries.

Topography - http://commons.wikimedia.org/wiki/File:Iran_ Topography.png. Sadalmelik, Topographic map of Iran. 14 October 2007.

PUBLISHING

Wilmette, Illinois

Bahá'í Publishing and the Bahá'í Faith

Bahá'í Publishing produces books based on the teachings of the Bahá'í Faith. Founded over 160 years ago, the Bahá'í Faith has spread to some 235 nations and territories and is now accepted by more than five million people. The word "Bahá'í" means "follower of Bahá'u'lláh." Bahá'u'lláh, the founder of the Bahá'í Faith, asserted that He is the Messenger of God for all of humanity in this day. The cornerstone of His teachings is the establishment of the spiritual unity of humankind, which will be achieved by personal transformation and the application of clearly identified spiritual principles. Bahá'ís also believe that there is but one religion and that all the Messengers of God—among them Abraham, Zoroaster, Moses, Krishna, Buddha, Jesus, and Muḥammad—have progressively revealed its nature. Together, the world's great religions are expressions of a single, unfolding divine plan. Human beings, not God's Messengers, are the source of religious divisions, prejudices, and hatreds.

The Bahá'í Faith is not a sect or denomination of another religion, nor is it a cult or a social movement. Rather, it is a globally recognized independent world religion founded on new books of scripture revealed by Bahá'u'lláh.

Bahá'í Publishing is an imprint of the National Spiritual Assembly of
the Bahá'ís of the United States.
For more information about the Bahá'í Faith,
or to contact Bahá'ís near you,
visit http://www.bahai.us/
or call
1-800-22-UNITE

Other Books Available from Bahá'í Publishing

DARK SIDE OF THE MOOD
A JOURNEY THROUGH BIPOLAR DISORDER TO RECOVERY
Sheri Medford
$16.00 US / $18.00 CAN
Trade Paper
ISBN 978-1-61851-071-6

A stirring and courageous autobiographical account that reveals the internal reality of someone dealing with the effects and stigma of bipolar disorder.

Dark Side of the Mood illustrates how the support of a community, as well as daily meditation and reflection, can lead to a strengthening of self and faith. Author Sheri Medford takes us on a brave and powerful journey as she recounts, in a series of evocative vignettes, her experiences with bipolar disorder. Inviting the reader into her internal landscape, Medford looks beyond the physical needs to the deeper spiritual needs of someone encompassed by a chronic invisible disability in today's society. As her journey progresses, she comes to see her illness as a gift that leads her to her true self—her soul—which, she comes to understand, is not ill. It is hoped that those who suffer from bipolar disorder, or have loved ones struggling with it, will find Medford's journey to be helpful and inspiring.

DISCOVERING THE MOON
Jacqueline Mehrabi
Illustrated by Susan Reed
$12.00 US / $14.00 CAN
Trade Paper
ISBN 978-1-61851-072-3

Follow the story of a soon-to-be fifteen-year-old girl as she explores, through deep spiritual conversations with her loving family members, what it means to be in charge of her own spiritual destiny.

Discovering the Moon tells the story of a soon-to-be fifteen-year-old girl named Fern who lives on the remote Orkney Islands in northern Scotland. Fern's conversations with the members of her family soon open up a world of discovery regarding the importance of prayer. These conversations focus on discussing the Long Obligatory Prayer, one of three prayers that every Bahá'í over the age of fifteen is required to choose from and recite daily.

Author Jacqueline Mehrabi draws on her own experiences living in Scotland to create a lush, true-to-life setting for *Discovering the Moon.* In the Bahá'í Faith, the age of fifteen marks the end of childhood and the beginning of an individual's sole responsibility for the progress of his or her spiritual existence. Fern, by involving her family and friends in her exploration of deep spiritual themes, offers a great example of drawing on many generations and perspectives when working on self-discovery. *Discovering the Moon* asks deep questions and challenges readers, in a relatable and gentle way, to learn about the teachings and expectations of their own religious beliefs the same way that Fern does upon turning fifteen.

KYLE JEFFRIES, PILGRIM
Gail Radley
Illustrated by Taurus Burns
$11.00 US / $13.00 CAN
Trade Paper
ISBN 978-0-87743-712-3

A touching story for middle-grade readers about a young boy embarking on a Bahá'í pilgrimage with his family. Along the way, he learns much about his Faith and thinks deeply about his future.

Kyle Jeffries, Pilgrim is the tale of a little league baseball player who feels torn when he learns that his family's long-awaited pilgrimage to the Bahá'í World Center in Haifa, Israel, is coming up—it will mean his missing the All-Stars game. Although being in Israel is exciting, Kyle can't seem to stop thinking about everything that he's missing at home. To make matters worse, a lively smaller boy, Carlos, latches onto him almost as soon as the pilgrimage begins. The last thing Kyle wants to be is a babysitter!

But slowly the magic of the pilgrimage takes root in his heart. As Kyle and his family visit the Bahá'í holy sites around Haifa and 'Akká, Kyle learns what it really means to be a Bahá'í and how he can serve others by doing what he loves most.

GLEANINGS FROM THE WRITINGS OF BAHÁ'U'LLÁH
Bahá'u'lláh
$24.00 US / $26.00 CAN
Hardcover
ISBN 978-1-61851-073-0

Selections from the chief writings of Bahá'u'lláh, the founder of the Bahá'í Faith.

Gleanings from the Writings of Bahá'u'lláh is an extremely important compilation that sets out the teachings of the Bahá'í Faith on a myriad of subjects. Among the themes that fall within its compass are the greatness of the day in which we live, the spiritual requisites of peace and world order, the nature of God and His Prophets, the fulfillment of prophecy, the soul and its immortality, the renewal of civilization, the oneness of the Manifestations of God as agents of one civilizing process, the oneness of humanity, and the purpose of life, to name only a few.

To those who wish to acquire a deeper knowledge and understanding of the Bahá'í Faith, *Gleanings* is a priceless treasury. To the members of the Bahá'í Faith, it has been a familiar companion for many decades, bringing spiritual fulfillment to countless people throughout the world. This new and exquisite hardcover edition includes paragraph numbering for easy reference, as well as a revised and expanded glossary.